ECLIPSE

A Song Called Youth
BOOK ONE

JOHN SHIRLEY

DOVER PUBLICATIONS, INC.
MINEOLA, NEW YORK

Copyright

Copyright © 1999 by John Shirley
All rights reserved.

Bibliographical Note

This Dover edition, first published in 2017, is an unabridged republication of the revised 2012 edition of the work published by Babbage Press, Northridge, California, in 1999, which was a revised and updated edition of the work originally published in 1985.

International Standard Book Number

ISBN-13: 978-0-486-81789-7
ISBN-10: 0-486-81789-X

Manufactured in the United States by LSC Communications
81789X01   2017
www.doverpublications.com

*For my sons, Byron and Perry and Julian,
in the hope that I'm wrong about the world they will grow up in.*

◆

AN IMPORTANT NOTE FROM THE AUTHOR
This is not a post-holocaust novel.
Nor is this a novel about nuclear war.
It may well be that this is a pre-holocaust novel.

Prologue

There was a small bird made out of titanium and glass. It had mechanical wings, electronic guts, and its head was a camera. But it was shaped much like a thrush and was about the same size. Its wings whiffed like a hummingbird's as it flew through the damp, battered city... The city was Amsterdam.

In the winter of the year 2039, Amsterdam was occupied by the NATO forces which had, for the moment, succeeded in driving out the armies of Greater Russia, the shock troops of the neo-Com dictator, Koziski...

Global warming. Climate change. It had radically reduced the output of Russian agriculture—of the availability of fresh-grown food, and stock feed, in many places—and that meant food had become hard to get. The Russians were on the edge of starvation—some of them over the edge—when Koziski had decided that Russian armies would swarm into Eastern Europe, and keep on going, in order to corral food resources...

So far, it was a world war that hadn't gone nuclear.

On the belly of the bird were serial numbers. The bird was a surveillance device, registered with the United Nations Intelligence Regulation Agency. Anyone punching the right serial numbers into a computer modem'd to UNIRA, along with the proper clearance codes, would be informed that the bird was licensed to British Naval Intelligence, under the auspices of the North Atlantic Treaty Organization.

The battery-powered bird had been activated on a British aircraft carrier twenty miles off the crumbling coast of Holland, at the request of the officer in charge of Civilian Law Enforcement. CLE was working out of an apartment building in one of the drier suburbs of half-sunken Amsterdam. The deserted building had been occupied by NATO Forces' Dutch Command Unit as a temporary headquarters.

The CLE officer was an American from Buffalo, New York. His name was Yates. Captain Yates had a memo on his desk from the Second Alliance International Security Corporation (the SAISC, or SA for short) asserting that the SA's supply lines had been "repeatedly disrupted" by the "civilian gang calling itself the *New Resistance*." The SA memo pointed out that it had been authorized by The Hague—those members of the States-General whom NATO had been able to contact—and by the UN Security Council, to police Amsterdam and the surrounding areas. The Second Alliance would see to it that the civilian population remained orderly, as well as safe from looters and other lawbreakers. To do that (the SA response memo went on peevishly), the SA had to move into Amsterdam, and it could not move the rest of its men in unless there were supplies in Amsterdam to sustain them. "I hardly need point out," the memo continued, "that while the SAISC is a civilian private-police force, it must nevertheless work in close cooperation with the NATO military forces, and cooperation is a two-edged sword." Yates frowned, reading that part. Cooperation as a sword? "The terrorist gang known as the New Resistance," the memo shrilled, "is a danger to the NATO armies as much as the SA inasmuch as it commonly steals supplies from NATO forces and disseminates antimilitary tracts which irrationally lump NATO and the Russian forces together as if both were the aggressors in the area."

Yates had shrugged and sent the communiqué to the nearest NATO ship with surveillance equipment, the *Lady Di*.

And the bird had been set free.

But not free to fly about at random. It flew in a widening spiral pattern through the civilian areas, looking and listening for gatherings of "four or more civilians." There weren't many people left in Amsterdam, so the job wasn't as time-consuming as it might seem. When the bird found gatherings of four or more civilians (not very often) it attached itself to the outer wall of the building in which the gathering was taking place, and it laid an egg. The "egg" was actually a tiny hemisphere of nanomaterials that clung to brick or concrete or glass or plasteel and sent out minute sensors. The sensors picked up the heartbeats of people, and if there were enough heartbeats close together, it transmitted a signal. Under martial law it was illegal for more than three persons to gather together without supervision, except in designated areas. The designated areas were under even closer surveillance.

The commander of The Netherlands unit made the gathering-size rule as there had been some trouble with what he described as "low-grade terrorist conspiracies."

Yates, having dispatched the birds to watch for illegal meetings, dispatched another communiqué to the SAISC, telling them what he'd done. Soothing them.

The SA, receiving the message, communicated with their contacts in the USAF Jumpjet Reconnaissance Unit. SA sympathizers in Jumpjet Recon were given the frequency specifics of the transmitting "eggs," and were urgently requested "in the spirit of cooperation," to "triangulate these terrorist cabals and do what is necessary to put them out of business."

The bird flew from one block to another, mile after mile, occasionally attaching eggs. After the third time, it flew past a certain high-rise, where it startled a real bird, a crow, which had been restlessly circling the building.

The crow was shaken by this close encounter with a "UFO" and took itself to the nearest terrace railing to recuperate. It settled onto the railing, looked around, and saw with relief that the bird with the metal wings and a glass head had flown away.

But someone else was there, at the other end of the terrace.

Part One
SMOKE

1

"This city is dead." He said it out loud, to a crow. The big black crow was perched on the concrete railing that ran mostly intact around the rubbled terrace. They were thirty stories above the flooded street, where dusk darkened the floodwater to indigo.

The crow heard, tilted a glare at him. Smoke went on, "This city is dead, and I'm someone. I'm still someone. Being here hasn't helped." He spoke to the crow and to the clammy, acidic breeze—it smelled like a ruptured car battery—that lifted the edges of the rain-caked stack of printouts some looter had tossed onto the terrace. "I'm still Smoke, Jack Brendan Smoke, or Brendan Jack Smoke or Smoke Jack Brendan. Mix it up the way you want, it's still there. I thought it would leach off here, crow. Like . . . " He paused, not sure if he was speaking aloud or thinking it now, and wondering which it was. He shrugged and went on, "Like you have a pan of water, nothing else, just dead flat calm water, and you pour, say, a little ink into it, and the ink spreads out, gets all diluted, in a few days, you can't see it anymore. But it didn't work. The ink is still there. I'm still Smoke . . . I could leave Amsterdam, crow. I might not be Jack Smoke where there's enough people. Lost in a crowd. I could go to Paris. There're still a lot of people in Paris."

The crow's claws made a skittering sound as it shifted on its perch. Shifted a little closer to him.

It occurred to Smoke that the crow might not be real; might be a cybernetic fake. But he was past caring.

Smoke put his hands on the railing, felt the concrete's cold bite his palms. He looked at his hands. They seemed creatures apart from him: clawlike gray things, with horny, overgrown yellow nails. He looked that way, all of him: clawlike, gaunt, dark with grime, his layers of scavenged shirts and jackets and pants gone all raggedy edged and uniformly dirt-colored, so he looked like a crow himself, in molting. He had long, matted black hair and beard, and a bird's bright black eyes and an eagle-beak nose. He chuckled softly, thinking that perhaps the crow had mistaken him for one of its own . . .

"It'd be better to be a crow," Smoke said. He looked away from his hands, out over the railing at the city—the necropolis.

This section of Amsterdam was relatively intact, as if mummified, and that amplified the absence of human movement; as if someone had thrown a switch that simply turned off the people the way you'd switch off a hologram: click . . . zip, they're gone.

Smoke tried to visualize Amsterdam the way it had been just five years ago: The streets feverish with cars and buses, most of them self-driving and electric; traffic pulsing on the bridges of the "city of one thousand and one bridges"; flat barges gliding on the Amstel and on sedate, tree-shaded canals flowing slow and thick as green candle wax. It was a city built in rings of streets and canals, most of the architecture remaining as it had been, gabled and red-bricked, when it was built in the seventeenth century. The city had permitted only a few high-rises, in certain zones, like the shell Smoke and the crow perched in now. Now, and all was the same as five minutes ago except it was just a dilute ink-wash darker. There was no going back in time. There was only going forward, one second at a time, as things fell apart.

The clammy wind soughed like an ache through the concrete corridors; the flood made a hollow *whush* like the sea heard in a seashell.

The overcast sky was a lowering ceiling of smudged charcoal black on charcoal gray; the upper reaches of the high-rise faded into cloud, as if the building became less real as it went up and was entirely imaginary at its peak.

Smoke leaned over the balcony and looked down. The floodwaters filling the avenue were sinuous with current, moving, tugging the yellow blob of Smoke's rubber raft tied up at the second-story window ledge. The water was rising. Perhaps the Zaider Zee would return, to reclaim Holland.

"Oh, you could *say* the city was still alive," Smoke said to the crow. It must have been aloud, because the crow fluttered its wings in response. "Because there are still people in it, on the higher ground, squatting here and there. Maybe a few thousand, maybe a few hundred. That's life, but it's the life in a corpse—micro-organisms that live on after the host has died. Hair that grows though the skull is empty. And the SA will be here soon. So the corpse'll be maggoty. And, you could say, 'Maggots are alive.'"

The crow looked interested. "But still, Amsterdam is dead... New York is alive, Tokyo and Cairo are alive, very much alive. But this city..."

The crow made a caw that somehow sounded reproachful.

"What is it?" Smoke asked. "Is it that I talk to myself? Because talking to a bird, or anything that can't talk back, is really talking to myself? Is that it? I remember being twenty-five and feeling sorry for people who talked to themselves on the street. They were crazy. Or senile. And now I do it—I don't say anything that would compromise Steinfeld, though. So I guess I'm not so far gone. Well I did just say his name. So maybe I'm losing it. And I'm only thirty-five now. I look older, crow, but I'm not. At least, I *think* I'm thirty-five. And something."

The crow cawed again, and Smoke thought it sounded sympathetic.

"I talk to myself compulsively," Smoke said; "I think I once wrote a paper about the phenomenon... I tried to make myself stop, for the sake of dignity. But dignity"—he gestured toward the flooded streets—"is underwater, with Rembrandt's house. The water reaches into houses and floats the corpses out..."

Color caught his eye. A fantail of sunset red creeping across one of the southeast windows of the building across from him. Windows on the southeast side were often intact, because most of the tactical warheads had detonated in the northeastern part of the city. And the red glaze reminded him to check his radbadge. He fumbled in the folds of his shirts, the four shirts he wore one atop the next, and found the radiation indicator like a convention badge pinned to his rotting jogger's sweatshirt. Only a faint corner of the badge had gone red, which was all right.

"It's all right," he told the crow. "Voortoven says he wishes they'd dropped a Big One on Amsterdam. Instead of torturing us with this slow war. Reneging on their promise to get the third one over in a few minutes. You ever feel that way? Like you wish they'd just *gone for it?* You want some bread? I think it's safe. I stuck a radbadge—I got a sack of them from Steinfeld—I stuck a badge, in the—here it is—" Rummaging in a greasy knapsack. "Left it in overnight, not a smidge of red. So the bread's okay . . . Here." He found the stale bread in its plastic bag, carefully unwrapped it, cursed when a few crumbs dropped. He licked a finger, touched the crumbs, sucked them into his mouth, watching the crow. The crow observed him fixedly, hopping nearer on the concrete rail.

He broke off a corner of the bread and held it out to the crow.

The crow's utter lack of caution surprised him: it hopped up and plucked the bread from his fingers like a man accepting a stick of chewing gum. Casual, familiar.

Smoke watched, fascinated, as the crow placed the crust on the ledge, then held it down with a claw to keep the breeze from stealing it, and meticulously chipped the bread apart, throwing its head back to down the crusty stuff, till only crumbs were left, and the wind got them.

"I'm supposed to be recruiting," Smoke confided to the crow. "Steinfeld says there are likelies here. In one of the rises. Not in this one, though."

He looked out over the city, saw it bruised in sunset. There was another high-rise a block north. It looked as lifeless as this one. He felt an alien touch on the index finger of his right hand and thought, *A bombspider*, and twitched his hand away, revolted—

The crow flapped on his finger, clinging despite his sharp motion, looking at him crossly as it adjusted.

He gaped for a moment and then laughed. "You're trained! You belonged to someone!"

The crow twitched its wings in a way that was eerily like shrugging.

Experimentally, he put his hand to his right shoulder, and the crow fluttered onto a new perch there, settled down, perfectly at home, and all of a sudden Smoke felt just a little bit different. About everything.

2

SMOKE WALKED into their trap, waited till they'd closed the trap around him, and all the time politely pretended not to know it was happening. He pretended to be watching the L-5 Colony.

The artificial star glittered in the night sky like a fine timepiece, forty degrees from the horizon. He saw it for ten seconds through a break in the clouds, and then it was erased by mist. He wondered if the War had reached out to the Space Colony—halfway to the moon—and, if it had, if anyone was still alive there.

And then the crow tensed and made a rasping sound Smoke was to learn meant *Watch your ass!* . . . and the three men closed in on him from three directions. The crow fluttered; he whispered to it, and it quieted down, pleasing him with its responsiveness.

He was standing at a window, looking out at the gray stalagmite outline of the high-rise where he'd met the crow. "I was over in that 'rise," he told the men, "and I looked at this one and couldn't see a fire or anything moving."

He heard one of them cock a gun.

And then again, Smoke was not so different, even after feeling that things had shifted: he still found himself hoping that the man would use the gun.

But behind Smoke, a man with a leader's voice said, "Turn around."

Smoke turned slowly around and saw a compact young man in his early thirties—but, no. Wrong. Subtract the etchings of wartime stress and fatigue and hunger, and the man was perhaps mid-twenties. He was gaunt from hunger; his chin was just a shade too prominent, like the old drawings of the man-in-the-moon at quarter-phase, and his forehead was high; he had a straight nose; a wry, red-lipped mouth; and small, dark-lashed green eyes rimmed with sleeplessness. His hair was thatchy, oily because it was something he ignored. When it was clean, it was probably blond. He was not more than five-seven, and lean in a weathered brown flight jacket that looked like it had done its flying in bad weather; ancient, faded Levi's; motorcycle boots held together with duct tape.

He was carrying a . . . Smoke stared. "Where'd you get the old Weatherby?" he asked, interested. The boy was carrying a Weatherby Mark V hunting rifle. Gun must be thirty, forty years old, Smoke thought. Bolt action, .460 Magnum. Long, long rifle. Developed for big-game hunting. Anomalous thing to find here, Smoke thought.

The man with the green eyes chuckled and shook his head. His eyes didn't change expression when he laughed. They remained flat, hard, candid. "You're supposed to be scared," he said, "not asking where I got my gun."

"So he knows all about guns," one of the other men said. Moved to Smoke's right. He was a big-framed man who had the look of someone who'd been overweight, starved down to sagging folds. He wore a long black coat, open at the front. And to Smoke's left there was a twitch-eyed vulture of a man breathing noisily through his open mouth. He wore a raincoat and beneath that something so ragged it was unidentifiable. The starved bear carried a .22 rifle, and the vulture carried a sort of mace made from nails soldered to a long pipe. "If he knows about guns," the bear went on, "he ain't some wanderin' tramp."

"That logic is questionable," Smoke said. "A wandering tramp is someone who used to be someone *else*—and when he was the someone else he might have made guns his hobby. I am, in fact, a wandering tramp. That doesn't mean I don't have business. I have business. But I'm not an eye for the Armies. And I'm here unarmed."

"What's your 'business'?" the green-eyed one asked, jeering the word *business*.

Smoke was thinking that the starved bear should have the big Weatherby, and the green-eyed one should have the .22, because he was smaller, and because he was the leader, so he should have known better. But maybe the gun was the totem of power here. And the king should carry the scepter.

"Here's where I take a chance," Smoke said. "I'm going to refuse to tell you my business. Except to say it's no threat to you."

The starved bear took a step toward him, and Smoke closed his eyes and said, "I hope they don't hurt my crow."

Not sure if he'd said it out loud.

"Jenkins," the green-eyed one said, not very sharply. But that's all it took. The big guy stopped, and Smoke, even with his eyes shut, knew the starved bear was looking at the green-eyed one for his cue.

"Lez go through his stuff," the vulture said. "Might be food."

"Animals," Smoke said, opening his eyes. "One's a starved bear and one's a vulture, and you make me think of a coyote or a wolf." He looked at the leader. Again the guy made the smile that didn't travel to his eyes.

"You're just a roost for a crow," he said. "You got a name?"

"Smoke."

"I heard about you, something. Like you barter, black market or . . . " He shrugged. "What's to be so mysterious about?" Smoke didn't answer, so the guy went on, "What's your crow's name?"

"I haven't decided. We're of recent acquaintance. I'm wavering between naming him Edgar Allan Crow or Richard Pryor."

The green-eyed one lowered his rifle, maybe only because it was heavy. "Edgar Allan Crow is corny. What's 'Richard Pryor' mean?"

"He was my father's favorite comedian, and he was black. That's all I know about him."

"We could eat that bird," the vulture suggested. He looked at the green-eyed leader. "Let's eat the bird, Hard-Eyes. Fuck it, huh?"

Hard-Eyes. Quite a monicker.

Hard-Eyes said, "No. Crows are good luck where I come from."

◆

The clouds had congealed into rain and the rain had wormed and nosed and nudged its way into the high-rise's ten thousand hairline cracks, and it was seeping out of the cracks in the ceiling and dripping with a smell of dissolved minerals into a large bathtub—which someone had dragged from its original mooring just to catch the rain—and into a wooden box which itself was beginning to discolor and leak.

The crow was asleep on Smoke's shoulder.

"I wisht we could have a goddamn fire," Pelter was saying. Pelter was the vulture.

They were sitting on red plastic crates around a dead TV set. The TV screen had been painted with a symbol:

... in red paint. They weren't looking at the screen. But it was a kind of chilled hearth for them. They'd eaten a tin of sardines and a pound of cheese Steinfeld had given Smoke "to soften them up." Smoke had brought it out as soon as they'd arrived at the squat. "This's our squat," Hard-Eyes had said, just as if he'd wanted to displace the word *bivouac* in Smoke's mind, in case Smoke was working for the Armies after all.

There was a jumble of old furniture in the room, mysterious geometries in the half-darkness. They'd blacked out the window with three thicknesses of taped-on black plastic; the plastic's wrinkles made glowworms of the anemic yellow light from the two chemlanterns. Smoke said, "You're gonna need a new lump for your lanterns. That solid fuel seems like it's going to last forever, then all of a sudden you're in the dark."

"I don't like the way this guy talks," Pelter said. "He's gonna bring us bad luck."

Hard-Eyes ignored Pelter. He looked across the cone of lampglow at Smoke and said, "You're not talking just about lamp fuel."

Smoke shrugged. "It's all in the lanterns. Energy and attrition and entropy."

Hard-Eyes blinked, looking skeptical. Then his face cleared and he nodded. "And glass going black."

Jenkins and Pelter looked at one another, then at Hard-Eyes and Smoke and then at the floor.

"What's the TV fetish-sign about?" Smoke asked.

He nodded toward the red symbol on the screen. He'd seen it the first time in Martinique, ten years before. He'd seen it on pendants and on screensavers. No one had explained it, except to say, "It's good luck." Later, in Harlem, seeing dead TVs turned into household iconography, he'd figured it was big-city cargo cultism, in a way, and something more: an invocatory variation on the Gridfriend sign.

"You believe in Gridfriend?" Smoke asked.

Gridfriend, god of the global electronic Grid. The internet, the web, satellite communication, wifi, dark web, all of it. The Grid gives TV, and news, and private communication on the web—and creds, which translates into food and shelter. Pray to Gridfriend and maybe the power company's computers lose your bill, and you go an extra month before they turn off your lights; pray to Gridfriend and maybe Interbank makes an error in your favor, computes you five hundred dollars you shouldn't have. And then forgets about it. Pray to Gridfriend and the police computer loses your records. Or so you hope.

"That's not the Gridfriend totem," Hard-Eyes said. "It's Jenkins' thing. It's Jenkins' invocation to the Big Organizer, the god who manufactures patterns—and luck. Jenkins used to do a lot of meth."

"Big Organizer? Just another Gridfriend. You a believer in luck?"

"I make my own."

Smoke smiled at the movie-melodrama sound of "I make my own." It went with the monicker.

"That's why you're here, Hard-Eyes? In this fucking icebox?"

Jenkins snapped Smoke a look. "Hey, you got nothing better goin', Rags. You ain't even got lanterns. You shouldn't be talkin' about our lanterns, man."

The crow stirred on Smoke's shoulder, disturbed by Jenkins' tone. Smoke crooned to it. It tucked its head back under its wing.

He smiled. "Look at that. That's completion . . . This crow and I met today and we're fast friends already. Just like that. Makes me almost believe in reincarnation."

"We should eat 'im," Pelter said, wiping a trail of snot from his bony nose with a crusted sleeve. His eyes were red, swollen, and he coughed sometimes, and now and then his head dipped as if he might fall asleep sitting up. Smoke thought Pelter was sick and would die soon.

"The bird will more likely be pecking your dead eyes out," Smoke said, and then regretted it. He hadn't intended to say it aloud. But Pelter didn't hear. His head had drooped and he was breathing with a bubbling sound.

Jenkins was scowling. "You hear that, Hard-Eyes? His bird pecking Pelter's eyes?"

Hard-Eyes shrugged. "Smoke resents people talking about roasting his designer squab. Makes a man say bitter things."

Smoke laughed. Hard-Eyes made the short, snorting sound that passed for machismo laughter. But his eyes stayed hard.

As the rain made hollow *plips* in the tub of water.

◆

Jenkins and Pelter were asleep, stretched out on pallets of cardboard. Jenkins slept with his face in his curled arm—like the crow with its beak under a wing—his hands now and then clutching, closing on something he dreamt about; Pelter slept with his mouth open, his breath coming raggedly.

There was only one lantern still lit. As if Smoke had spoken an omen, the other one had used up its fuel and gone out, just like that.

"Not going to make it," Smoke muttered.

"The other lantern?" Hard-Eyes asked.

"Pelter. Maybe the lantern too."

"Pelter's been sick," Hard-Eyes said, nodding.

"Been with you long?"

Hard-Eyes shook his head. "Six, seven weeks. Jenkins has been with me longer. Jenkins, he's not dumb. Just a different focus. He's handy with chip-splicing, accessing, like that."

"Not much use for computer skills in Amsterdam just now." They both smiled wearily at that; it had been too obvious a thing to say and they both knew it.

"You still worried about me?" Smoke asked.

Hard-Eyes shook his head. He smiled flickeringly. "The crow vouched for you."

"I'm a little worried about *you*. You could almost be one of their background men. Looking for the underground. Or for anybody that smells like they wish the Armies would snuff each other and fuck off."

Hard-Eyes shrugged. "You want the story?"

Smoke nodded.

So Hard-Eyes told his story.

◆

I was in London, (Hard-Eyes said), and I was at a club called The Retro G. They were into cultural retrogressing. That month they had a ska motif, ska music. Two months before they'd had thrash. And before that it was hard core and before that worldbeat and before that angst rock, and before that it was dub and before that it was core-dub and before that, melt-pop, which is what was hot when the club opened. If the club were still there I guess they'd have worked back through the nineteen-nineties, eighties, seventies, sixties, back to rockabilly and bebop and blues. But it's not there now because that part of the town is rubble. Me, I'm from San Francisco, California. I was in Britain for a seminar on Social Democracy. Watered-down socialism. I was a grad student. Yeah, a student with a fucking satchel for carrying his books. Political science major. And deep into applying structuralism to problems of diplomacy. Jesus. And then politics got real for me. The truth behind politics. Aggression and acquisition . . . We were at the Retro G, dancing, and the DJ sliced in that meltpop tune, "Dancing with the Russian Brothers," not part of the ongoing retro motif, so it made you wonder, and then the DJ said it was dedicated to the Russian Brothers who'd just driven their tanks across the frontier into Poland. It shouldn't have been all that surprising; the Ukraine, Belarus, Kazakhstan—it'd all been reunited into Greater Russia not that long before, and did we really think they were going to quit there? But still, we thought he was kidding, until we heard someone else talking about a radio broadcast and we went outside to Dody's car. Dody—man, what an airhead. But she was worried about her business because she marketed designs from some Polish designer. And on Dody's car radio they said the Greater Russian army appeared out of nowhere, no one could understand how they got so many troops to the border without alerting NATO. It was a long time before word filtered back about the maxishuttle drops out of orbit. NATO saw the drops, but the Russians told them it was emergency medical supplies because of some outbreak, and then the fucking troops were in place . . . Okay, that's the version I heard. You hear different versions . . . Anyway, they took Warsaw, moved the Greater Russian Liberation Army's western front HQ in. And this girl Dody, all she could think about was her business going down the drain. I wanted to stuff her up the exhaust pipe of her Jaguar Gasless.

But after that, I was no better. All I could think about was covering my own ass, getting back to the States. Only, you couldn't get a flight out of London, they were all restricted for government use or booked solid. Everyone wanted the fuck out of Europe. You ever read about the Vietnam war? Right, well, you know how when the NVA moved in at the end, there was this rabid scramble to get out of Saigon on anything that moved, people running to cling to the runners of choppers . . . It was like that for a whole continent, in the big cities . . . I went to the airport and some guy was scalping the airline tickets, wanted twenty-five thousand quid each. People climbing over people to buy from the motherfucker . . . People clamoring at the embassy demanding help and getting thrown out and finally breaking windows, getting shot at . . . At the airport somebody once an hour tried to pull off a hijacking . . . it was worse at the docks. But I found a dude with a boat was on his way to Amsterdam, said he knew somebody had a private jet there, could get us both on, and for some reason I bought the story. I was panicked. Yeah, you laugh *now*. He got me to Amsterdam and took my money to "make the connection" for us, and then he never came back, of course. The money wasn't worth much, anyway. But I found him, eight months ago, and he had this Weatherby, he'd looted it from somebody's house. Never gave him a chance to use it on me. I used the twenty-two on him first... But wait, I left out a lot. Only, you were probably here for what I left out. NATO forces declare martial law in Holland, Russians move in, Russians get driven back. The riots. The public executions and the riots because of the public executions and then more executions. Me, I watched it all from up here. Tried to stay out of it.

But I'll tell you something funny. It was almost a relief to me. The whole thing. Even the war. It was like—before the war, nothing was real. I mean... people talked about things that happened in download movies and VR and online RPG, like they were anecdotes about people they actually knew and... It was like our lives before the war were just long, detailed movie lives or TV lives or VR lives... I can't explain. But I had this feeling that nothing was real and nothing mattered until the war.

Anyway, I was living with a Dutch girl, Luka. How I met her, she went out one day to try to buy some food, and there was a food riot and she was attacked because she had a bag of food—I'd been in line with her, and when the riot started I helped her get away from it and she was grateful, so she gave me a place to stay—well, okay, maybe it wasn't just gratitude, she was lonely—and it was pretty much an instant thing, like we'd always been shacked up; there were no further questions. She had hair that looked like... you ever see cornsilk? She was a big girl, but handsome, Amazon handsome. Always neating things up. Maternal, like your aunt, except in bed. She was... And then of course after the Russians blockaded the port and the siege started, the food riots spread from the market to the high-rises. The masses, you know, usually have the wrong idea about who's pulling what strings, and they thought the people in the 'rises were hoarding food, which was bullshit; Luka and I had to stand in the same ration lines as everyone else, but there's no reasoning with hungry people. And they came in and tore the place apart and...

... and they threw her out a fucking window. Out a window, and she fell forty stories down, and I opened up on them with my rifle. I was firing at a monster, this mass of arms and legs and screaming heads; it backed out and left some of its parts behind with my bullet-holes in them, and I looked with binoculars and saw they were just ordinary people. I had shot two old women, a fifteen-year-old boy, and a guy who looked a lot like my brother Barry except he had a mustache.

It was a shock. I'd, y'know, shot *individual people*. And everything was changed. The mob came back and some of them had guns now, so I went to the roof and hid in the little house for the elevator motor, and they didn't find me. And they left the place pretty much the way you see it. Then two weeks later the lines broke and the Russians moved in. Occupied the town. And it was just another army. A lot of people thought the Russians would be better than the NATO armies. But there was no food and more people starved ... You must have been here—No? How long have you been here? Oh, you were in a Camp then ... And then the Allies tried to retake Amsterdam with the tactical nukes and we couldn't believe it. Small warheads, short-term radiation. No big problem, right? Only kill a fourth of the town's population—you make an omelet you gotta break some eggs. At least a fourth of the town died. In a week. And then the earthworks were sabotaged, and some of the Dutch actually immolated themselves in the squares. The work of centuries to take Holland from the sea reduced to nothing in days, and they couldn't handle it. Some days I understand why they did it and some days I don't. People saw the old men set fire to themselves and most people took no notice. The gangs liked it, though, because it broke the monotony; they made a big production, big joke, of toasting ration bread on sticks over the coals of the guys who ...

I tried to get out of the city again and stole a boat, but NATO spotters caught me. Convinced I was on a mission for the Russians. They had Jenkins prisoner, too. That's where we met. But he had the brig's lock program dazzled, so he and I escaped, and there was no place to go but here, back here ... We've done okay. We got a way into the spotter camps, steal supplies now and then. We had to shoot some scavengers one day, but mostly we stay out of trouble, out of anything that looks like it might remotely be considered subversive, and they don't come looking for us. The Armies... we don't even talk them down. Either side. Because none of them give a fuck. NATO, the Russians, Americans, Brits, Czechs. Everybody calls them The Armies. Nobody cares *which* army. If you're army, you're The Man in the Helmet...

◆

Smoke didn't say anything for a long time. Not even to himself. He was too tired. He knew there was a lot more, but it was more he didn't have to ask about.

A little later Hard-Eyes mentioned family in the States. Mostly he tried not to think about them, because the scramble screen blocked transmissions—all the civvy frequencies anyway and lots of others—so there was no way to get news. Social networking was blocked. Fones blocked. Why torture yourself wondering... wondering what it was like in the States now.

◆

From an end-of-term report by thirteen-year-old Gary Krueger, of Cincinnati, Ohio, entitled "The Cause of the War." Gary's report grade was B+.

> Different people have different ideas about why the Third World War started. I asked my C-driver Seeker to look in the Internet to see if there was a list of reasons. It found thirty-three reasons which don't agree with each other, and they come from seventeen different groups of people.
>
> The most commonly given reason is the one given by registered members of the Republican Party. They say that Greater Russia has been building up its strength in secret for years. They were making it look like less than it was, with underground training places. Then they saw that the North Atlantic Treaty Organization was not maintaining its strength

in Europe and was letting the United States carry the burden, so they saw they had a chance to take advantage of this weakness. Also they say that there were crop failures and industrial problems and all that corruption and mobster activity and other problems in Russia and the Warsaw Pact countries were rebelling and wanted to be independent. So Koziski of Greater Russia, after the coup in 2031, he thought that a war would distract people from these problems and bring the old Warsaw Pact countries back together because they would unite against an enemy. Also the Russians were running out of power supplies and wanted to capture coal and oil and atomic energy plants and microwave receiving stations that get orbital power. They also wanted to embarrass the Americans like they did after the "Bay of Pigs fight," [sic] which was something that happened to the USA in the twentieth century that made the USA let the Soviet Union get concessions, even though this Greater Russian government is a different government than the USSR government.

The Democratic Party people mostly say that the US government pushed the Russian government into starting a war by installing the Milstar 7 and Milstar 8 military satellite systems in orbit. The Russians' satellites weren't as good and they were paranoid that we could use our system to shoot down their missiles and so we could invade them or attack them and they wouldn't be able to defend themselves. So they wanted to take new territory over in Europe to capture Europe ground-based missiles and to create a "buffer zone" to stop invasion, and also, the Democrats agree on this part, they wanted to unite their people against an enemy and make them forget their problems.

The third group of people say that it is because of an "international conspiracy of Jews and Muslims to destroy the United States" that made the Russians do it. I think this a dumb idea because Jews and Muslims don't work together and how could the Jewish people control the Russians when the Russians are persecuting them all the time?

I think the war was caused by all the reasons said by the first two groups.

◆

A note to Gary Krueger from the teacher: *This is a good report, but I think you use too much Internet material, too much online searching. Too many students do that! That's letting the computer do your work for you. If you do it that way, you won't remember what you learn. Also, be careful when you make sentences not to run them together with so many and's. You are making run-on sentences.*

◆

The following is a poem written by a student in Gary Krueger's World Affairs class, Barbara Wycowski, twelve years old:

ON A DAY PRETTY SOON

Joe Smith didn't finish eating his apple
Jane Jones didn't finish reading her book
Bob Farmer didn't finish playing his video game
Ann Franklin didn't finish posting on Facebook
Jim Banks didn't finish wrapping his present
Mary didn't finish writing her letter
Dan didn't finish singing his song
Barbara didn't finish writing her poem
Because the hydrogen bombs exploded and
everyone died and the whole world was finished and it
was the end of everything completely and absolutely.

◆

The following is from a report from Barbara Wycowski for her World Affairs class entitled "Why There Hasn't Been Nuclear War So Far":

. . . In 2030 the USA and Greater Russia signed a treaty called the Conventional War Limitations Treaty in which they agreed that if they had an armed conflict they would limit the use of nuclear weapons to small tactical warheads. The use of those kind would be controlled by an upper limit of how many can be used. A lot of people said that agreeing to make a war in any way was immoral, but this agreement so far has prevented the world war from being a nuclear holocaust. But I think it is only a matter of time and pretty soon it will escalate into a world war, and then we'll all get killed, so I don't know why I'm writing this, except so I can stay in school to make my Mom happy until we're dead . . .

◆

A photocopy of Barbara's poem and essay was sent by her teacher to her school guidance counselor. On it the teacher wrote, *"I am very worried about Barbara and a lot of other students who seem to have despaired of ever growing up. There is also another group of students who seem to be reacting to the danger of a wide nuclear war by sliding into a jingoism which I also find disturbing . . ."*

◆

They were lying in the dark, each wrapped in his black-market US Army blanket. The cardboard pallet under Smoke's blanket was cold, slightly moist, enough to give him chills.

Smoke said, softly, "Hard-Eyes."

"Yeah."

Sure, the guy was awake. No way he trusted Smoke yet. Lying there with his old-before-their-time eyes wide open and smoldering in the darkness.

"Hard-Eyes, there are some who are worse than others. Some Armies."

"That right?"

"Yeah, The Second Alliance."

"You call that an army? More like multinational MPs."

"Uh-uh. SA's run by the Second Circle. You know what that is?"

"I saw the NR leaflets. Say they're fascists. Maybe, but no one takes them seriously. Just another gang."

"That's what a fascist army is, a big *gang*. The SA's the Second Circle's army. NATO's using them, but they're using NATO . . . You heard about the new war front?"

"No." The cardboard rasped on the concrete floor—the looters had torn up the carpet—as he got up on an elbow. Hard-Eyes asked, "You been outside?" An edge of accusation. A traveler from outside the city was expected to share news, and rumors—which were indistinguishable. Survival protocol.

"Haven't been outside Amsterdam except once this year," Smoke said. "I've been mostly over by where the port used to be. Last time I was outside I got indentured into the NATO logistics line. Supposed to've been a 'civilian freight porter' with a salary."

Hard-Eyes snorted.

"But you know," Smoke said, "we ate once a day. Guaranteed."

"That's all right. Not bad. And you were behind the fighting."

"Except some of the camp got a dose of forty-four."

"Neurotoxin forty-four? I think that's what's wrong with Pelter. Got a dose of forty-four. He was raving, on and off, when we first found him. It shot his immune system to hell."

"You took in a sick guy? You don't seem like Red Cross volunteers..."

Two-second hesitation. Then Hard-Eyes said, "Jenkins knew him. Jenkins is a little limp-dicked in some ways. And it was like taking in a sick cat, nurse the cat to health and in gratitude the little fucker gives you ringworm or something... You said 'we' a while ago. About coming into town with someone."

"I came in with..." He almost said the name. "A guy who still has connections with the Allies. But they don't run him."

"As far as you know."

"As far as I know," Smoke agreed.

They were quiet for a couple of minutes, because of a spasm of coughing from Pelter. He wheezed for a while and then it subsided. His lungs rattled when he inhaled.

Smoke shivered and pulled his grimy army blanket more closely around his shoulders.

"So how's the front moving?" came Hard-Eyes, suddenly, a sharp question out of the darkness.

"It's moving completely out of Western Europe."

Silence, except for the dull patter of raindrops in the tub.

"Did you hear me?" Smoke asked.

"I heard some horseshit."

"The guy I mentioned, he got it straight from the Allied commander's radio code officer. NATO's leaving a skeleton force in Amsterdam, Paris, Dresden... They've pushed the Russians back, and the story is the Russians are regrouping to hold the line along their traditional borders and around what used to be Warsaw Pact countries. Concentrating on a naval push. The Russians are losing the land battle and winning the sea battle, so who knows how it'll equalize..."

"The Russian naval push. Finally. Those outdated nuclear subs. With the nasty missiles..." Sounding almost convinced. "Could be rumor number ten thousand five hundred and two." In wartime Europe, contradictory rumors came and went like autumn leaves in a hurricane.

"You know it's not. It feels right."

"And you think the SA will step into the vacuum left by the Russians and NATO."

"You really believe NATO can police the back-territory? That much land? Who's left to do it? Who'd do it here? Paris is hanging together on a smaller police force than New York's got in Central Park. They can hang together because of the military presence. The military moves out and the place is down the drain. And they're moving out, mostly. So the Second Alliance is hired to move in to police things. The UN Security Council sponsored the SA in this."

"The SA..." Hard-Eyes was quiet for a moment, then, all in a rush: "NATO couldn't be that... I mean, just to turn it over to them. NATO'd try to set up provisional governments modeled on the ones that fell."

"That's what they're calling it: transitional period to get them into the provisional government stage. 'Until autonomy is practical.' In the meantime the SA is providing the men to keep order, supposedly..."

"No, dude. Everybody knows about the SA. NATO wouldn't give it *them*..."

"Are you serious? Are you that naïve?"

Silence. Then, "I guess mostly it's people in the underGrid that know... but NATO couldn't be that stupid."

"NATO is mostly shot to hell except for Scandinavia, Spain, what's left of Britain, the States. And who pulls the strings in the States? SA sympathizers."

After a moment Hard-Eyes said, "No, come on. Okay, maybe it's true. Then what? Is the blockade still up?"

"No, but the SA will be empowered to 'enact migratory containment.'"

"Where'd you get that phrase?"

"Steinfeld has a printout—" *Let him think it's a slip. Oh, no, I said the name.*

"Steinfeld. You're with Steinfeld."

The rasp of cardboard as Hard-Eyes sat up.

Smoke said, "I'm just a recruiter." *Too hasty.* "I'm not initiated NR."

"Shit: I've got a New Resistance operative in my squat. The NATO MPs will be dropping in, and we'll all go to the work camps."

"Nobody's made me as NR. I'm freelance. I've known Steinfeld for a while, we were indentured together. He used Mossad connections, got us out. Some others. But I didn't follow him like a puppy, just for that. I'm freelance, Hard-Eyes, for real. I wasn't supposed to bring you along at this stage. But what the hell, come on, come with me. At first light, I'll take you to meet Steinfeld. The man can do one thing for you, in exchange for a little work: he can get you out of Amsterdam. To Paris."

"One crater to another. Foxhole to foxhole. Big deal."

"Now *that* is real, bona fide horseshit, the certified stuff. You know it's better there. Maybe it won't be better for long. But you won't have to stay there long."

Hard-Eyes didn't reply to that. His silence said, *That's hype, and it's all been hype.*

The crow was nestled on the back of Smoke's neck now. It made a small, warm place there with its body. A circle of warmth and mindless friendship three inches across. Thinking contentedly, *They might just kill me in my sleep. It's fifty/fifty.* Thinking that, Smoke focused on the three-inch circle and fell into it, and it was a gateway.

◆

Smoke sat up and looked through the half-light at Pelter, and knew instantly that he was dead. The crow was gone. Something went cold in Smoke then.

You pathetic asshole, he told himself. You're like a man in prison making a pet of a cockroach.

Jenkins and Hard-Eyes were gone, and Smoke didn't care. Except, he thought, *Those pricks have eaten the bird.*

But he heard a rustling behind him and turned to see Richard Pryor's tailfeathers emerging from his canvas pouch. It had its head in a bag of bread.

Smoke tried not to feel too happy about it, but it was useless. He felt good.

A little dull-blue light shafted glumly from a hole in the ceiling. Probably from a window in the room above. Smoke looked around and saw that Hard-Eyes and Jenkins had taken all their stuff. Were definitely and completely gone. Truth was, he didn't care much. Except he'd liked Hard-Eyes, and he knew Hard-Eyes had the necessary restlessness that Steinfeld looked for.

But fuck it. At least the crow had signed up. "Richard!" Smoke shouted.

The crow fluttered again and backed comically out of the pouch, looked at him with not a trace of remorse. The look said, *Stop yelling, asshole.*

Smoke reached past the crow, into the pouch. The crow hopped onto his wrist.

"Who trained you, huh?"

The crow made a door-creaking sound in its throat.

Smoke fed it the last of his cheese and said, "Looks like I blew the recruiting. They're gone. Their gear is gone, so they aren't coming back. Let's go back to Steinfeld and ask if we can go with him to Paris."

◆

But in the raft, when he let the currents whirl him through the echoing, swishing canyons of brick and concrete, under cover of the morning fog, he glimpsed another boat behind, and the silvery jut of the Weatherby, and knew then that Hard-Eyes was following him. Simply checking him out. And maybe Smoke would have his recruiting fee after all.

3

It was utterly artificial, and it was the most natural thing in the world. And the world wasn't a planet anymore.

The world, now, for the Colonists, was an inter-relationship. The world was the inter-relationship between the Colony proper and its tethered satellites; between the Colony and the tethered satellites and the free-orbiting satellites, the moonbase, and various control stations on the planet Earth. Relating by lasered messages, microwaved data input, radio waves, fusion-powered ships. Each unit of information and material relation struggling to assert itself, driven by the will of the builders, despite the flux and surge of solar radiation, cosmic rays. And in fantastic defiance of the flotsam of space: meteors and asteroids.

Their world was a web of data and materialized information, and at the center of the web: FirStep. Or just, *The Colony*. An artificial world, turned outside-in. Artificial, but in his dedication speech, five years before at the official opening of the still-uncompleted Colony, Dr. Benjamin Brian Rimpler asserted that something created of human artifice is more fully natural than a biologically conventional living organism; the Colony, Rimpler said, was a compounding of nature; a splendid elaboration of nature, as an anthill, together with its ants, is a natural growth demonstrating even more principles of nature than a leaf of grass.

Claire was trying to get the general idea—human artifice as a product of nature—across to her first-grade class, and some of them understood, and others were indifferent, and still others rejected the idea out of some undefined resentment against comparing human colonies to insect colonies.

Claire stood on a grassy knoll sculpted to look as if it had come there by geological chance, and around her sat twelve children. Six boys and six girls, as per demographic control.

From the outside, the six-mile-long Colony looked like a cylinder that had swallowed something big and was digesting it boa-style. The bulge at its middle was a Bernal sphere, itself a mile and a half in diameter. The concave interior of the sphere was to have been the main inhabitable area of the Colony. It was Pellucidar. It was Mu, sunken Atlantis, the Hollow Earth. The landscape stretched away to an inside-out horizon, curving up when it should have curved down. The lengthwise axis of the Colony was pointed toward the sun, and sunlight, filtered and reflecting from enormous mirrors, glowed from circular windows at the sunward end of the oblate spheroid and was reflected by other mirrors at the farther end. It was given an auroral tint, at times, by the envelope of heavy gases artificially maintained around the Colony by the Lode-Ice Station. Almost before they'd begun to build the Colony, UNIC—the United Nations Industrial Council—had sent a series of teams into the asteroid belt where high-orbit satellite-mounted telescopes had found huge lumps of frozen gases; the "lodes" looked like great agates, but were in fact more like interstellar icebergs. A series of mining teams in UNIC-owned spacecraft had used channeled-force nuclear blasts to drive a Wagnerian procession of ten-mile-thick lumps of frozen gas back to a synchronous orbit with the slowly growing shell of the Colony. Then they built plants on the frozen asteroids, airtight factories dug into the crystalline surface, which broke the ice down into gas and, after seeding it for heightened energy absorption, routed it via electromagnetic fields into a protective envelope around the Colony: its sole purpose was filtering—it filtered the solar wind and cut back on cosmic rays, making it possible for people to live on the Colony without resorting to strangling thicknesses of heavy insulating materials. From space a comet's tail of gases slowly burning off from the Lode-Ice Station streamed in a spectacular iridescence around the space station, making it look like some celestial tropical fish about to flicker into the deeps.

The Colony rotated once every five minutes, creating a subtle centrifugal artificial gravity. Here on the hill the gravity was slightly less than on the shore of the lake, thirty yards below them.

Overhead, filigreed clouds blurred the land . . . the land that was also overhead.

Toward the sunny end, the arbitrary south, the difference in atmospheric drag between the inner and outer layers of contained air created a hurricane's-eye effect; cloud spirals formed and pulled apart there. You could get dizzy looking into it; you could imagine you were falling—falling up. Look "east" or "west" and you saw the curving vista of brown-and-green landscaping, like a tidal wave of land curling back on itself, a wave never breaking; the landscape was checkered at asymmetrical intervals by the Colony's central housing developments.

Claire and her class sat in a cleared area just above the cactus garden, between the eccentric shapes of gray-green euphorbias and lime-green succulents. The children wore their school jumpsuits, but in the tradition of the Technics Section, the outfits were patched and pinned with ribbons and their parents' work-section badges and viddyprogram logos. The logo patch fad came across like gang colors, a resemblance which made Claire nervous. The most popular patch advertised Grommet the Gremlin. Grommet was a cartoon monster, a *cute* monster, for God's sake, who giggled moronically as he pulled out the wires sustaining your life-support systems if you didn't feed him access credit for sweet-rations. He was a feral, free-floating giga-pet. His bug-eyed face leered idiotically from patches on the shoulders of eleven of the twelve children.

Claire Rimpler wore a white technicki jumpsuit, a kind of bluff social camouflage. But she was Admin, was teaching the technicki children as a volunteer—really as part of her father's program to better relations between Admin and technicki—and had been doing it for two weeks, and for all fourteen days she'd regretted it.

Claire was twenty-one, but looked sixteen when she was smiling. She was small, with a rose-tipped pallor, soft-looking auburn hair clipped short like an EVA worker's; her lips were a shade too large for her doll-like face. Her expressive eyes were brown-black. Her eyebrows were a trifle too thick to be feminine. But the whole, as an ensemble, was far more attractive than she knew... Her petiteness and girlish features deceived people into expecting docility. "The truth is, Claire's pure Admin," her brother Terry had said of her. "Gives orders as naturally as a technicki gives back-talk." Her father had lectured Terry about making "classist" remarks about technickis.

No, she'd never been docile. But there were times she'd been passive, introspective, before her brother's death—before Terry had been snuffed into a statistic, in the Third EVA Disaster. Her brother had been supervising a technicki hull-team in the construction of section D, the Earth-end of the cylinder, two years before. An EVA pod had come too close to a tethered satellite. One of the pod's landing struts had snapped the comsat's tether, so the satellite tumbled into the extra-vehicular team on D-sec, striking two, who spun to hit two more, a weightless domino effect that in turn spun thirty-one men off into space, most of them with ruptured suits. Only one of them was recovered alive. Six bodies were never recovered at all. In the wake of the disaster—and with the ongoing problem of the Colony's costs outweighing its financial benefits—public pressure on UNIC had almost cut off funding. Claire's father tried to resign as Colony Committee Chairman and Design Supervisor. New funding had come from select UNIC members, certain big corporate investors, like the Second Alliance. The SA... Rimpler had been persuaded to return to work...

But her dad was never the same. He wouldn't look out the ports, into space. Maybe he was afraid he'd see Terry floating out there. Floating up to the glass. Staring accusingly.

And Claire was different after that. The occasional moods of passivity vanished forever. She blamed Admin laxity for Terry's death. Which meant she had to become Admin, to set things right. And she was Admin now. Almost completely.

◆

Claire had explained to the children why the land overhead wasn't going to fall on them, and how if they walked in a straight line to arbitrary east they'd eventually come back to the spot they'd left, arriving from the west, all in the same day if one walked fast enough. The children were patient through all this, except, of course, for Anthony, who ostentatiously smoked a syntharette through it all, expecting her to rebuke him for inhaling nicotine vapor, frustrated when she pointedly would not play that game.

They ate a lunch of pressed fruit, from produce grown in the Colony's agripods, and soybutter 'n' jelly sandwiches. And when they'd finished, Claire said, "We're going to have to go back soon. So if anybody has any more questions . . . ?"

Chloe raised one of her small black hands and asked, "Whunna finzuhruzat?" She pointed to the arbitrary north, the inner part of the sphere away from the sun. The land here, between the meager areas of finished developments, looked calico, brown and yellow in patches, with outcroppings of raw blue metal.

"First of all," Claire reminded her, "ask the question in Standard English. Technickinglish isn't what you're here to learn."

Chloe sighed and said, laboriously, "When . . . they are—"

"When are they."

The little girl made a moue of frustration and went on, "When *are they* going to . . . finish the . . . rest . . . of zuh—no—*of that?*"

"Good! To answer your question, the Colony is about two-thirds finished. Maybe five years more and it'll be done."

"But who's going to live in the new part when it's finished?" Anthony asked abruptly, showing off his command of Standard English.

She'd been expecting the question. And she could feel their attention had shifted, suddenly, from whispered jokes, giggling, teasing, complaining—shifted to her. Now, now they were listening.

Maybe we shouldn't bring them on these excursions till we can move them out of the dorms, she thought. Maybe it only makes them feel frustrated.

"Everyone will be able to live there," Claire said. "Everyone! Not all at once. There will be lots drawn to see who's first."

"Who's going to program the lottery computer?" Anthony asked, and she wondered if he was really that precocious or if someone had coached him.

"The computer will be an Admin unit," she admitted, "but it will be fair. Everyone will have a chance."

"But—"

"Now," she interrupted, blithely as she could, standing, "let's go to the arcade!"

"I don't wanna go there," Anthony said, crossing his legs.

Claire jammed a thumbnail in her mouth, began to chew—then remembered the children were watching and quickly pulled it away, using another finger of that hand to point at Anthony. "Tony, don't play that game with me. You love the arcade. You spend hours there. You complained when you had to come out here; you said it gave you headaches. Don't give me that evac about not wanting to—"

"I like it here, and I want to stay."

"Anthony, has someone been—" And then she broke off, seeing the men from TechniWave coming, and she understood it all.

There were three of them. One with the cam-transmitter. Beside him was a guy with his look so burnished he must be the anchorman. And a third guy, an X-factor, might be the one who'd planned this.

The cameraman wore a backpack-fed shouldercam/directional mike and a headset; the cam was mounted on his shoulder like a second, robotic head.

She recognized the reporter, now—Asheem Spengle. He wore the fashionable triple-Mohawk in the technicki colors—white, silver, and gold—and also a white I'm-just-one-of-the-people jumpsuit. He was regular-featured, glib, a human cipher. The third man wore a flatsuit: a suit in which the jacket and vest and tie were false, just lapels and a tie-knot and vest-front sewn onto a one-piece outfit. He was sharp-eyed, coning his lips to seem perpetually thoughtful.

Anthony jumped up excitedly, seeing them. "Misser Barkin!" he began. "I—"

The man in the flatsuit shook his head at Anthony but smiled, showing an overbite.

Anthony caught the cue and shut up. The reporter and the cameraman stopped just a few yards from Claire and the class; the reporter stepped in front of the camera, facing it, his back to Claire, and nodded. The cameraman was already focused, waiting. He hit a switch on his belt. A green light flashed on at the side of the little camera, and Spengle said, *"Routen Admin Park talkwid Adminteach Claire Rimplerner stoods—"* And went on.

Stunned, mentally treading water, Claire listened, translating for herself. *We're out in Admin Park talking with administrative teacher Claire Rimpler and her students and trying to get her reaction on a disturbance that was reported to be taking place here—*

Claire thought, Should I just walk away from it? That might make us look pretty bad. And I'm responsible for the kids. And then they'd just quote Anthony. Or whoever'd coached him.

But then Spengle turned to her and asked her a question.

The camera was on her. His question had been recorded, Claire's reply would be recorded, a recording to be edited for a TechniWave transmission to the whole technicki pop of the Colony.

Translated from technicki:

CLAIRE: If you want to talk to me, I have to know if this is live or recorded.

SPENGLE: We're recording, Ms. Rimpler.

CLAIRE: I had two years of communications, and I know that machine: it can transmit. If you'll do this live so I can say my piece without editing, I'll submit to an interview. Otherwise I can't be sure of getting a fair opportunity to reply.

SPENGLE: I can't guarantee—

CLAIRE: Then I can't answer questions. It's not fair.

Spengle conferred with the flatsuiter.

Claire used the delay to call Admin on her fone. She explained the situation to Judy Avickian in Central Telecast. "Just watch the broadcast, Judy. Ring me if it's not coming through live."

"You got it."

Claire replaced the fone in her pack and turned to Spengle.

Spengle said, "Ms. Rimpler, we'll have link-up in a minute or two. In the meantime—"

He looked at the gawking assemblage of children. "I heard someone up here has refused to go back to the dorms."

"Anthony!" they chorused. "Z' Anthony!"

Claire said, "That's something you must already know, Spengle, since your people—"

Anthony interrupted her by stepping up to Spengle, half turning so the camera could pick him up clearly. He'd been drilled well.

A finger-sized directional mike on the bottom of the camera swiveled back and forth between Spengle and Anthony as they spoke.

"We've got live," the cameraman said, pressing the earplug of his headset.

Spengle nodded, repeated his earlier spiel, and bent to interview Anthony. From technicki:

"Your name is Anthony Fiorello?"

"That's right."

"You're one of the children refusing to go back to the dorms?"

"There's only one refusing!" Claire broke in. Spengle ignored her. And probably it didn't pick up on the mike.

"Why is that, Anthony?"

"It's crowded there and it smells bad and I'm just as good as Admin people, so how come I can't live in the Central with the parks where it's nice like the Admins?" Just a touch mechanical, hinting at rote.

"Anthony—how many people live in Colony? Do you know?"

"Sure, we learned that. About ten thousand people."

"And how many live in Central in the nice dorms, or in the Open out of all that?"

"One thousand."

"Does anything else bother you about all this, Anthony?"

"Well, I came out here and it looks so empty! There's some houses down there, but they're a long way away! There's room here for technics and maintens!"

Claire was fed up. "You want to interview me, it's got to be now. I'm due back at Admin," she called out. "Come on, kids!" She turned to the others. "Get your things together; we're going to have to go soon." Some of them stirred, others stood unmoving, gaping at the cameraman, mesmerized by the technological totem on his shoulder. The reporters, she realized, had usurped her authority over the children. And that was a bad omen.

"Ms. Rimpler," Spengle said, "has just said she *hasn't got time* to talk with us." Heavy sarcastic emphasis on *hasn't got time*. "So we'll have to go back to you, Ben, at TechniWave Central—"

"It isn't true!" Claire shouted, rushing up to the camera. "That's not what I said!—" And then she stopped talking, just stopped, feeling foolish, realizing the light was out on the camera, that it was no longer transmitting and hadn't been for a while.

And Spengle had turned his back to her, was walking away in close, soft conversation with the flatsuiter...

Half an hour later Claire stood alone on the platform of the park railstop, watching the car that had come along the axis rail-line to take the children back to the dorms; watching it recede as it carried the children to the north end of the Colony, the dorms and the uncompleted area, while she waited for the train that would take her to the arbitrary south. Hating the glaring symbolism of the moment, she chewed a thumbnail, thinking that once the camera was gone, Anthony had lost interest in boycotting the dorms. He was first on the train, eager for the arcades.

She'd crossed to the southward station and stood looking toward the huge retina-like windows above Admin central. A ring of verdant green encircled the windows. Within the ring, mist curled in gentle spirals, refracting the light in muted rainbows. It was quiet in the parkland; there was a gentle, manufactured breeze smelling of growing things—and only faintly of air filterant—and for a moment the place looked like the paradise it had been designed to be. But then the vent-breeze shifted and she caught the soiled-socks odor of the dorms' overworked air recycler. And the paradise was gone. Paradise has always been fragile.

◆

"Japanese tourists," Samson Molt said, "never change. The Japanese keep their traditions. Their tea rituals. Their sushi schools and their chopsticks and that Japanese packaging. And the way they act in foreign places is always the same. Since I was a boy, they never changed. They're faddish in some ways—but really, they never change. Could almost be the same tour group I saw in New York as a lad."

Samson Molt and Joe Bonham were lounging at an "outdoor table" at the south end of the arcade. The six clubs, two digital arcades, a handful of boutiques, and two cafés were "the Strip," which was the closest thing the Colony had to authorized nightlife. Molt and Bonham preferred the unauthorized nightlife. But that didn't start for hours yet, end of the third shift, when the maximum number of B-section workers would be freed up to spend cred.

The tourists were eight nearly identical (to Molt's eyes) Japanese with the faddish forehead-strapped cameras, each camera with its remote focuser that snapped down over the right eye, transforming the socket into something reptilian. They wore onepiece Japanese Action Suits, JAS for short, in tastefully splashy pastels, soft material. They chattered and pointed, winking to make the headband cams take pictures. Each stop along the arcade was an orgy of you-take-my-picture-and-I'll-take-yours, posing in front of everything, so that half of what they were photographing was blocked by their bodies.

Molt wondered which ones were industrial spies. The Japanese were said to be planning their own space colony.

Their guide was a tall, demure black woman making a valiant effort to look interested as she droned, "... the Colony took twenty-four years to achieve basic livability for non-astronaut personnel..." drone "... begun in secret early in this century... Richard Branson was an..." drone "... now owned by UNIC, the United Nations Industrial Council, five major international corporations who pooled their resources for matching funds from the UN..." drone "... The Colony manufactures goods which can only be made in zero or light gravity, as well as operating the first of a chain of interplanetary solar power stations which soak up solar energy and transform it to microwaves transmitted to receptors in the Gobi and Mojave deserts . . . " drone "Although UNIC is still operating in the red, it expects to break even next year and to begin a profit-making phase in the following year . . . We begin our tour at the arcade because it links Tourist Arrival with Colony Open, the parkland area which as you will see in just a moment verges on the paradisial in its . . . " Drone.

The tourists clicked and snapped and chattered on, and the Strip was itself again, shorn of the kitschy glamor of their enthusiasm. Like most of the Colony corridor areas, the Strip seemed more worn, more used, more frayed and grimy than things on Earth, though it had been built only a few years before. Which surprised visitors. They expected the pristine polish of a top-tech chips clinic. But the Colony was almost a closed system. And replacing anything, repainting anything, was more costly here . . .

And now the Strip was like a third-generation hand-me-down toy in a grubby nursery, its colors faded or smeared with the grease of too much touching; like a seaside amusement park long since gone to seed.

Across from the French-style Café Crème was the white seashell-shaped metal awning of the Captain Halfgee club. Soft, moving lights glowed behind the mermaids painted on its plastex windows; two customers came out, still dripping chlorinated water, towels draped over their shoulders, carrying drinks in plastic cups.

The "street" of white synthetics was nine yards wide, and dingy; the ceiling, three yards overhead—unusually high for a Colony corridor—was blue, fluffy clouds painted on at intervals. The clouds looked as if they ought to be laundered with bleach.

Molt's gaze wandered down the street, where the crowd thickened at the one Admin-sanctioned casino. He considered going up for blackjack. But no one in the casino was permitted to lose more than ten newbux in cred, nor win more than twenty, and there was no way, in Molt's view, you could work up a good gambler's sweat when the stakes were so low.

The other clubs and cafés were articulated in bright, brassy, circus-rococo colors, neon-trimmed and flashing, but it was all Admin operated; and to Molt it looked like a miniature setup for children, like the department store "Santa Claus Lane" of his boyhood.

"See the fucking elves making toys," he muttered. Even the Strip's pornography parlor was watered-down, the porn softcore and revoltingly well photographed. Tasteful. Not much fun at all.

He lit a syntharette, not because he wanted one, but because this was one of the few areas in the Colony where the nico-vapor was permitted. And because there was nothing else to do. Just nothing else to fucking *do*.

Molt was a heavy man with a brickish complexion and sharp blue eyes and a tousle of rusty hair. He leaned both elbows on the plastic table, his cup of three percent beer between his hands. He wore genuine faded Levi's, and a real-wool knit pullover, dull yellow, holes at the elbows and shoulder seams. Bonham—a sad-eyed man with thinning brown hair, a long nose—wore a gray pilot's uniform without insignia, two-piece, the short jacket taut across his wide, flat chest. He wasn't a pilot, which is why the uniform had no insignia. The uniform was supposed to help him pick up women. Like Molt, Bonham was a pilot's second, which officially made both men Technic Union. Both had two years of college and, socially, both looked down on technickis. But both men were Neo-Marxists and in the political abstract regarded the technickis as brethren workers.

Bonham had a way of fading in and out of conversations like a radio with a faulty frequency modulator. He could be dreamy and then diamond-hard analytical, by quick turns. He leaned back in his chair, one hand toying with an empty glass, his mind somewhere else.

"Bonham," Molt said, leaning forward, lowering his voice meaningfully. "Fuck these tourists. You want to go to that club they got in the Open?"

Bonham stared glassily at a smudged cloud on the ceiling.

"Joe, dammit!" Molt said sharply.

Bonham snapped his eyes down from the cloud. "Yeah, I heard you. Japanese tourists. Pain in the ass."

"I asked, You wanna go to the club in the Open?"

"The Tavern on the Green? Out in the Admin's Open? You know what that place costs? Three bux for a cup of tea."

"Yeah? It's just—I never been there. But now that you mention it—I can't feature those prices. Forget it."

"Of course, the cost is one way they keep it exclusive, keep the technics and the maintens out. I say we spend the money and make ourselves seen there. A Statement, man."

"Isn't worth the price."

"It would be for the principle of the thing."

"I can't afford the principles. And I'm on probation. If you get drunk, start making speeches, you'll get us into shit with Security." He shook his head dolefully. "Hey, Joe—those new Security bulls they got are *mean*. Fuck it, let's wait for the Afters. You can get something that'll get you drunk, lose some real money, get yourself sick like a man ought to be able to."

Bonham nodded. "Something in that."

The talk and the place were ordinary, and that felt all right: they were between duty-pulls, they had a week, and they could amble through everything and the week wouldn't have to go as fast as usual, if they were careful.

But everything was going to change in twenty minutes.

"You catch the news about the Admin bimbo?" Bonham asked.

"One bimbo at a time. I'm gonna go see—"

"Kelly? She costs more than she's worth, Molt."

"She digs me."

"Whores pretend, Molt, that's all. They're consummate actresses, for one role and one only. And don't try to tell me you made her cum—"

They went on like that for a while, neither man attending the conversation with his whole mind. And in fifteen minutes everything was going to change.

"So what'd you see onna news?" Molt asked, at last.

"Rimpler's daughter. Cute little thing but super-chilled, I heard. She was taking some kubs out into the Open and one of 'em refused to come back, made a great speech how they were being cheated of their fair share of Open. Spengle made her look like—"

"Yeah. Yeah, I did hear about that. Somebody had a handset on the shuttle and—yeah, the technickis on the shuttle were glued on that one, man."

"Smart move, whoever set that up," Bonham mused. "There's a protest tomorrow. You wanna come along?"

"Maybe. But . . . *you* know, Christ . . . " The two men exchanged commiserating looks and sighed. They'd be surrounded by technics yammering technicki at the demonstration. But they had principles to live up to. Molt shrugged. "Where's it going to be?"

"Corridor D-five."

"Yeah, okay. What the hell." He looked at his watch. "Let's go to Bitchie's, it's probably open for—"

"Is that all you ever think about? Listen, you hear about the SWS readings for the dorm sections?"

"The what? Oh. No. What about it?"

SWS: Solar Wind Shield. The atmospheric envelope generated at the Ice-Lode Station. There were persistent rumors that the Admin crews didn't keep the shield's regularity field in place over the Colony's technicki section; that they were indifferent to cancer risks for technickis.

"The reading was negligible, that's what. About as much field as my mother has testicles."

"The field has to be uniform for the Colony to go on working at all."

They argued Colony politics for the next ten minutes. Molt was the voice of moderation. Social Democrat to Bonham's Post-Trotskyite. At least, that's the way Molt was until he got angry, scented violence. But just now, he was quiet as a bomb before it explodes.

In five minutes everything was going to change.

The waitress, Carla, wandered by the tables, picking up glasses, yawning. She was a horsey bleached blonde with a Reservationist's tattoo half showing through her body stocking. Molt and Bonham exchanged banter with her for four minutes.

In one minute, everything would be different.

Carla went inside to bring out two more weak beers. She came out a minute later, without the beer, her hand clapped over her mouth.

"What's the matter?" Bonham asked. "What's the story, Carla?" Molt asked. Their questions jumbled together.

She looked at them, her bloodshot blue eyes stricken, her face paler than usual. She mumbled something through her hand.

Scared by inference, Molt irritably pulled her hand from her mouth and said, "Dammit, Carla, transmit!"

"The Russians. I heard it on the vid just now."

"The Russians what?" Molt asked, thinking, Oh, shit, maybe they finally launched the big ones.

"They blockaded the Colony. Activated their laser platforms, the battle stations . . . Got ships hanging out there . . . *They won't let our shuttles through. We're cut off.*"

Bonham was scared and looked it. But the fear melted away in Molt, and he realized he'd been waiting for this. He'd been holding something back for a long time. This meant he could let it all out. He could kill a few assholes.

Because everything was different. Now.

4

THE RAINSTORM had blown onward. The sky had cleared, except for a soft breakage of clouds, light blue against the dark blue twilight.

Smoke was at the window, looking out at the sky, squinting as he tried to see some detail of the Colony; but it was just a pale glimmer, a fragment of Bethlehem's marker, forty degrees above the horizon. "They made that thing up there out of asteroids and pieces of the moon." He spoke to Richard Pryor and the crow tilted its head as if listening, and Smoke was grateful. Talking to yourself didn't look quite so undignified when you had something, someone, to pretend you were talking to.

Dignity. A haggard, grimy, stooped, gaunt, bearded man. His gray-shot black beard matted, his eyes too intense, his hands always faintly shaking and dirty as rat's claws. And we're talking about dignity?

But dignity was everything to Smoke.

Hard-Eyes and Jenkins were behind Smoke, their backs to him, talking to Steinfeld and Voortoven and Willow. Yukio was there, too, but he wasn't talking. Smoke knew Yukio was listening, though.

Smoke listened to bits and pieces as Hard-Eyes and Steinfeld interrogated one another. Smoke tuned in and out.

He kept his eyes on the man-spark hanging in the blue-black sky.

(Just below the window ledge, on the outside, gleaming with rainwater, was the egg, the metal bird had attached the day before. It was sending a signal that meant *They're in the room now*...)

Smoke looked at the sky, and, now and then, he listened.

"Let's talk basics," Hard-Eyes was saying. "We're talking no salary, not even after the revolution, supposing that ever happens."

"No salary: correct. But I didn't say anything about a revolution. We're not revolutionaries. We're international partisans. We want to re-establish the republics that existed before the war. Elimination of the jurisdiction of the Second Alliance is obviously a prerequisite."

"'Elimination,'" Jenkins said. "Has a nice clean sound to it." There was no subtlety to Jenkins' sarcasm, "How big you say the SA weighed in at?"

Steinfeld hesitated. Smoke couldn't see him, but he knew the man and his mannerisms. He could imagine stocky, tired-eyed Steinfeld with his long, iron-gray hair neatly parted in the middle, caught up in the back with a twist of wire. With his black beard, the white streak down the middle so neat-edged it could almost have been dyed there. The short, blunt fingers raised, fanned out just above the top of the scarred desk, the deltas of fine lines at his eyes deepening as he concentrated on his reply. His ineffaceable sense of mission never faltering no matter how much he backed and filled and weaved and bobbed in his dealings. *Whop*—the hands coming down flat on the desk as Steinfeld spoke: "Half-million, it's said. And growing."

"Half-million. They have a half-million men in Europe." Jenkins said it with stagey disbelief.

Steinfeld went on to answer the unasked question hanging in the air. "And all told, if we count splinter groups, factions, the NR could muster four, five thousand. But on this front of the resistance, we're not going after them head-on. We sabotage, we guerrilla their flanks, we chew a lot of little wounds in them till they weaken from bleeding."

"Go back to the part about 'this front,'" Hard-Eyes said. "What's the other front?"

"Negotiating for help. From the Japanese. And others. We're working on it."

"What about the States?" Jenkins asked.

"You must be bloody joking," Willow said. Willow—in olive-drab fatigues, tennis shoes rotting apart, stolen AK-49 assault rifle across his lap. Broomstick skinny, thatch of colorless hair, a beard that belonged on some aging Chinese emperor, bad teeth; spoke in a monotone, the British mumble. "Fucking Yanks wanking off the fucking Nazis." He pronounced it *Nazzies*. "They like the fascist takeover becorz they figure it's either that or commies. And they got big promises for big business deals from the fascists."

"All this . . . " Steinfeld tilting his head back, making the beard jut at the ceiling. So Smoke pictured it (all the time watching the indistinguishable movement of the Colony). "All this . . . supposition. But I do think they have come to *some* accommodation."

"Mark me," Willow said, "they plan to divide fucking Western Europe up betwixt the blewdy power brokers."

"I'm still thinking about 'no salary,'" Hard-Eyes said flatly.

"What do you believe in?" Voortoven asked. He was a broadchested, muscular man, always clean. Curly brown hair.

"What?" Hard-Eyes was a little startled.

"Do you believe in anything at all? You just want money to bribe your way back to the States? You going to play the drifter who does not get involved? Or you are, maybe, a mercenary?"

"We're not above using mercenaries," Steinfeld said, a fraction hastily. "'Mercenary' is no insult."

Voortoven snorted.

Steinfeld went on, "We can't pay money, but we can pay in goods and, eventually, in transportation."

"I want to know what he believes in," Voortoven said.

Forty-five seconds of silence as they waited for Hard-Eyes to declare himself.

Hard-Eyes said, finally, "When I find it, I'll know it."

"To know what we are takes time," Steinfeld said. Steinfeld was Israeli. Long history of involvement in radical movements, Democratic Socialist, but never stained Marxist. It was assumed he had a family in Israel. He'd never mentioned them, but there were pictures in his wallet no one had seen up close. And it was assumed he was run by the Mossad—which might be a wrong assumption.

Hard-Eyes had heard that one, too. "You might be anyone," he said, looking at Steinfeld. "I could get killed and never know who I'd been working for. Dying for."

A full seventy seconds of silence this time. And then Jenkins said, "You say we could trade some mercenary work for *transportation*. We work for you awhile and then..."

Smoke stopped listening. He focused on the Colony and said, "Richard, you know how many tons that thing is, up there? More than the membranes of thinking can carry."

The crow fluttered and dug at its breast for a louse.

"You're not impressed? Crows take bright things into their nests, Richard. The Colony construct is both a nest and a bright thing. You know how many tons that nest is, Richard?"

The crow shook itself.

"I don't either. Hundreds of thousands. Millions. At least it'd weigh that on Earth. They're supposed to be making it bigger and bigger. There are no crows there..."

Looking at the Colony, a city tossed into the sky, Smoke felt a sucking vertigo. He looked away from it, down to the Earth. He and the crow gazed out at the wrecked harbor, beyond to the Ijsselmeer, and Smoke had a strange sense of being *in place*, wedged somewhere outside the flow of time.

The harbor's flooding had submerged the docks and boardwalks; it had thrown boathouses up past the sidewalks, half crushed them against the swamped bases of the buildings; it had wedged boats into alleys and had made trucks and cars the new housing development of octopi and sea anemones. There was a whirlpool marked by twisting fluorescent foam where the outflowing currents from the rivered streets met the tidal push of the sea. The harbor's sea vista was hobbled by half-sunk ships, boats, tankers jutting like tombstones. There, and there, well apart, were two dull red throbs, where campfires illuminated stanchions and deck fittings on the upthrusting superstructures of two foundered ships; a couple of squatters there, perhaps three more over there, feeling relatively secure on the wrecks with expanses of cold seawater between them and everything else; more security than in the city, where scavengers roamed the rooftops or sculled the narrow, flooded streets in boats.

Smoke's eyes were drawn by movement; the high movement of electric light. One of the Armies' aircraft. There—over the collapsed roof of the warehouse. A USAF jumpjet. Recon patrol, maybe; hovering, and bobbing up and down the way a jet shouldn't be able to, moving almost like a kite. Casimir force combined with standard thrust, tiltable jets. Now and then it darted a searchbeam into windows.

Ought to close this one before it notices us, Smoke thought.

But then the jumpjet veered off, due east. Gone.

Drone of voices behind him. But he was turned outward, to the mortuary peace of the harbor.

A movement of cold air—too slow to be a breeze, more of an oozing than a blowing, numbing Smoke's nose and cheeks, making his ears sting. It was scented with the brine and the clean rot of the ocean—strange there could be a clean rot but in the absence of men it was so—and a trace of oil, and woodsmoke.

A fog was curling in, sending wraith outriders, and tentatively entwining rusty hulls, the wooden snags of pylons, battleship superstructures, and sailing-yacht yardarms. Under the wrecks, the sea drew all light into itself. And yet there was movement there; Smoke thought he saw the ghostly figures of men and women running in slow motion through streets where flame unfurled... and this phantasm passed, replaced by the marching of a great army, an army of men in mirrored helmets, their faces hidden in circles of opacity—

Someone was speaking to him. Had been speaking to him for a while. He knew it, just that suddenly. "Smoke! Open your ears!" It was Steinfeld.

"Maybe 'e' deaf," Willow suggested sincerely, "from the shells. I lost some of me 'earing when they was shellin.'"

Smoke turned, and Richard Pryor flapped against the sudden motion. "I was thinking, is all," Smoke said.

"You were daydreaming," Steinfeld said. "Best not to show a light."

Smoke closed the blacked-out windows, locked them in place at the bottom.

"And come over here, Smoke. You can hold on to your independence, if you want to keep up the pretense, but I want you to contribute to this."

Smoke nodded, feeling claustrophobic, cheeks and nose tingling in the warmth of the sun-charged heater glowing cherries of red light to his left. The room was rectangular, high-ceilinged—once someone's bedroom. Now the main furnishings were a blond-wood desk, one leg missing, that corner supported by stacked bricks, a few cracked wooden chairs, and a wooden crate. There were two pools of light, at each end of the room—a reddish pool from the heater and a yellow one from Steinfeld's lantern, on a dented cabinet behind his desk. Hard-Eyes and Jenkins leaned against the wall to the right of the desk. They stood there, Smoke guessed, to be near the door and so no one could get behind them. And for the first time he wondered if he'd made a mistake bringing Hard-Eyes here. Hard-Eyes was almost unreadable. The nickel-plated hunting rifle glinted like a frozen lightning bolt in his hands. Jenkins, rifle in hand, bulked beside him, the thundercloud.

Maybe, Smoke thought, these men want to kill us all, and turn us in for bounty. Or maybe they're planning to locate Steinfeld's black-market stuff. Kill us in our sleep, take the stuff.

Smoke wondered, but all he said was, "I saw a jumpjet. USAF, I think. Headed off east."

Steinfeld frowned. Then he shrugged. "Can't go running off every time the fox comes sniffing around, or it'll catch us out of the henhouse . . . " He smiled. "I heard that one from an American soldier from Oklahoma."

Smoke moved to stand against the wall, across from Hard-Eyes.

"You've got an in at both the camps, Smoke," Steinfeld was saying.

"The Russians treat me best," Smoke said, mostly to the crow. The crow made a ratcheting sound. "It was a surprise to me, too."

"You hear a lot about the SA. Let's collate what we've got, for Hard-Eyes and Jenkins. The SAISC was founded by a man named

Predinger. An extremely conservative American millionaire. Far right as you can get without being locked up in an asylum. He founded it sometime in 1984, fittingly.

"Initially, the Second Alliance was to be a sort of, um, global security outfit to be used by any international corporation or conglomerate who needed it—something like Xe or Halliburton Security but bigger and with more . . . agenda." Steinfeld shrugged and went on: "It soon became obvious that the SA was in fact an 'antiterrorist' intelligence outfit. Privately owned, to be sure. This was, of course, at a time when terrorists were beginning to make concerted bombing strikes and kidnappings against big business, especially if it was rooted in the United States or in the allied nations . . . " Steinfeld paused to sip from a cold cup of ersatz coffee. He grimaced and went on. "Not surprisingly, the Alliance concentrated on leftist underground political groups, and ignored the rightist variety. It placed a great many people under surveillance, anyone it suspected might have connections with Marxists and hard-core Jewish-rights activists. The SA ignored the anti-Israeli terrorists unless they were clearly anti-American Communists. After a period of surveillance they would take the 'suspects' in for 'questioning'—something they'd do quite without legal authorization, but sometimes with sanction from the local authorities. About two-thirds of the 'suspects' were people with left-leaning tendencies but no actual connection with terrorists. Their inquisitors were always masked. Sometimes the suspects came out of it alive and only bruised, sometimes they disappeared entirely. But—the governments of the countries where the SA operated covered for them. The SA would claim it had fired some people who were 'overzealous.' The furor would die down and the SA would go back to its old activities . . . Radical activism continued to escalate, and in response the SA took to assassinating radical leaders it believed were aligned with activists. Most of the time it was assassinating the moderates who kept the extremists in check. It may have done this knowingly—knowing that when extremists filled the void, the frightened world would tend to tolerate—would *welcome*—the SA's activities. It would grow in respectability and therefore in contacts; with contacts came power and influence. And, of course, all of this was augmented by Predinger's judicious use of cold cash. Campaign contributions, soft money party donations, and some outright payoffs. Bribery was part of the SA's ordinary, day-to-day operation. Once they almost went too far, even for their allies. Their Buenos Aires chief learned that two identified men on their kill list were in attendance at a leftist political rally in a Buenos Aires union hall. The SA simply blew up the hall. Two hundred people were killed. It was never proved against Predinger's people. There is some evidence that the CIA and Argentina's own secret police may have been of covert assistance—"

Hard-Eyes broke in, "This sounds like a lot of propaganda. Left-wing conspiracy-theory stuff. The SA is right-wing, sure—too far right to be running things. But you make it sound like . . . " He shook his head. "You say there is some evidence, and then you don't cite it. Same kinda talk from the Lyndon Larouche Memorial Society. Only, they talk the same way about leftist people."

"In fact, the Larouche Society is one of the SA's cover organizations—"

Hard-Eyes shook his head, chuckling. "Sure. Just like they claim the world is controlled by a secret conspiracy of the British Secret Service in league with Jewish bankers, right?"

Steinfeld smiled. "Coming from the States as you do, I can see how all this would seem like just so much more fringe political background noise . . . But the SA is what I say it is, and here in Amsterdam you will shortly be able to see the SA in operation . . . They're moving in, setting up here. Wait, and you'll see it confirmed. And remember: I'm not a leftist. Here we're in favor of restoring only what existed before the war. Yes, the bad with the good. We are not revolutionaries. We are resistance—to what is shaping up to be a neo-fascist takeover. Spearheaded by the SAISC."

"Why you going to so much trouble to convince us?" Jenkins asked.

"I need . . . " Steinfeld hesitated, looking for the right words. "There are men who are like seeding crystals. You drop them into the solution, and other crystals form around them. I need such men. To form the . . . the core of a much stronger resistance cell. And Smoke here"—Steinfeld gestured helplessly—"he has an uncanny sense for finding such people. He found Voortoven, and Yukio. And he has recommended you." Steinfeld shrugged.

"I'm not sure I should be flattered," Hard-Eyes said.

Steinfeld said, "Do you want to hear the rest of the... propaganda?"

"Go ahead."

◆

When a man tells another man a story, much of the story is untold. That is, it's not told out loud. The unspoken part is the freight of secondary meanings and resonances attached to the spoken thrust of the story. It's a part of the story already understood by the two men. Part of their mutual context.

What follows is what Steinfeld told Hard-Eyes. And here we speak aloud what wasn't spoken at all.

Smiling Rick Crandall. He was one of the youngest Fundamentalist ministers in the country. By the time he was twenty he had his own internationally syndicated program. He was exporting Christian Coalition beliefs and values to the rest of the world, and he was succeeding because he, and his associates, kept tying it in with wealth. Decline or not, America still had the rep for being the wealthiest country. And Crandall kept saying it was his religion and his way of life that made it that way. Predinger bought the station that ran Crandall's show, tripled the man's salary, and gave him a new assignment. He was to be a sort of SAISC goodwill ambassador to the governments of foreign nations, and to other groups who were not government but were sympathetic to the Second Alliance's aims. That was Crandall's job, ostensibly.

But the truth is, Crandall was a recruiter. He used his international fame, or simple bribery, to gain access to people high in governments, people on the fringe of governments, people in opposition to governments. And he recruited them into a new branch of the Alliance. This was called the AntiTerrorist Lobby. And it was a cover. It might have been more appropriately named SAISC Army Recruiting. Crandall was a recruiter for a new, multinational military and political machine. The men inducted into the machine used their influence to legislate a fund that would make their nation an official SA member. They would pay the SA to help them control their domestic terrorism—sometimes real terrorism, just as often it was mere dissent—and they agreed to contribute resources and manpower for the control of *international terrorism* . . .

Each "member nation" provided men—reassigned from the military—for indoctrination in the SA's Worldview Camps. The first and imperative goal of the operators of the Worldview Camps was to instill an absolute and undying loyalty to the SA in all "processees." The processees were taught—brainwashed—to regard the SA as their true father and mother, their sovereign nation, and, most importantly, their link to God Himself. There was to be no possibility of sending men out for Alliance "actions" who were not genuinely loyal to Alliance aims. The Second Alliance had a public credo and a private credo. The private credo was the core of its real identity. It comes in onion-layers. Those who were first-layer processees in the Second Alliance heard a kind of standard Christian Born Again rhetoric. But in the second layer, the Initiates hear a kind of Identity Church theology preached. It is, in fact, a more refined version of the Christian revisionism taught by the Kingdom Message organizers who declared themselves to the public about 1983. That's about when they began to rob banks and armored cars to finance their acquisition of automatic weapons and the other toys of right-wing "survivalists." They called themselves "the Church of Jesus Christ Christian" or "The Covenant, the Sword, and the Arm of the Lord" or "the Aryan Nations" and they held that Jesus Christ was not a Jew, was in fact of Aryan descent; that Great Britain and the United States were the true promised land, the true Israel referred to in the Bible; that blacks and other minorities were mongrel peoples who had no souls and were of no greater spiritual worth than animals.

And they maintained that Hitler has been unfairly vilified by the Jews; that the Holocaust never happened. In 1985 there were about 2,500 people in such organizations in the United States—chiefly in Washington, Idaho, Oregon, and California. Many of them were recruited out of prisons, always hotbeds of racism . . . Supposedly there were "several hundred-thousand" sympathizers scattered across the country. Some of the more enterprising members of the Identity Church realized that they looked like country yokels, which kept people who were otherwise sympathetic from taking them more seriously. So they formed a secret society, called the Secret Aryan Fraternity. They linked up with more public groups, like the Georgia-based Council of Conservative Citizens. Groups like these were paranoiacally cautious about publicity, and security. And, very carefully, the SAF and friends began to integrate their people into urban and suburban middle-class society; into colleges and country clubs and lodges and offices. They began to support political candidates, or mount their own candidacies—without ever honestly declaring their actual political stand. They played moderate or simple conservative—when in reality they were beyond merely "conservative." They were social time-release capsules, moles, of sheer racial hatred. Predinger is believed by some to have been one of the SAF. It's never been proven. It may be just coincidence that the SAF and the SAISC share the same first two initials. But it *has* been determined that Crandall's father was a member of The Covenant, the Sword, and the Arm of the Lord . . . Summary: The SA's general theological creed, its public creed, is ordinary Christian fundamentalism, with no overt racist tinge. Its Initiates are privy to the Identity Church's Jesus-as-Aryan hardcore-racist variation. Initiates administer the general membership. The Initiates in turn are governed by the Second Circle.

The Second Circle, the inner ruling council of the SA, is reported to have a more intellectualized racist vision that doesn't insist on a belief in Jesus' Aryan heritage. Jesus, for the Second Circle, is simply an arbitrary symbol chosen to represent genetic purity. The DNA molecule itself, twisted into a circle, is the Lord's halo . . .

Politically, the SA's private credo was, simply and bluntly: fascism.

And we are not talking fascist here as a left-wing dilettante calls a war-hawk "a fascist," as an insulting term, a mere pejorative. We are talking about definitive fascism. Predinger and Crandall were both, privately, admirers of classic fascist and racist demagogues, including Mussolini and Hitler himself. They were anti-Semitic and anti-black...

◆

"Anti-black?" Hard-Eyes interrupted. "You said they recruited partly from third-world countries."

Dreamily, almost offhandedly, Smoke said, "Actually, they deceived certain black African military dictatorships into providing money and other forms of support. But they kept them in the dark about the real SA political goals. And they didn't recruit soldiers from black countries."

Jenkins looked at Smoke in amazement, hearing Smoke's pedantic side emerge. A scholar hidden in rags and grime.

"The third-world recruits—" Steinfeld began. Then he broke off, listening. Looking at the ceiling.

They all heard it. The rumble and drone of a jumpjet nearby. The Armies—searching for the NR, maybe...

Smoke felt a thrill of fear and thought, *I'm scared of dying. How long has it been since I felt that way? What's happening to me?*

The sound of the jumpjet, the rumble, the drone...died away.

Steinfeld looked at his hands. He took a deep breath, and went on. "The third world recruits were obtained mostly from rightwing dictators in Central and South America. And then certain factions of Indians, anti-Semitic Pakistanis, Eastern Europeans—there are a good many Nazi Serbs around... But the real core of the SA, its initiate administration, were American rightwing extremists—including sympathizers in the CIA—British, Dutch, and a great many Afrikaners. There are thousands of them... They're a separate division of the Alliance, elite troops. The division has a German name which translates as 'Men Chosen to Die First.' The SA's administration is uniformly white. Bravado, you see. Fanaticism. White South Africans from the elite are in charge of the lesser divisions. And the lesser divisions are made up of Spaniards, Italians, Guatemalans, anti-Communist Cuban nationalists..."

"Perhaps this is the wedge," Yukio said. Said it succinctly and at just the right moment, a fine and definitive brushstroke. So like him, Smoke thought.

Voortoven nodded and said, "We have men within the—"

Steinfeld cut him off with a glare—Hard-Eyes and Jenkins weren't yet trusted.

Hard-Eyes and Jenkins glanced at one another.

Suddenly everyone in the room knew that if Steinfeld decided he could not trust Hard-Eyes and Jenkins, he would have them killed. And this would not have been the case before Voortoven had said, in that particular context, *We have men within*...

Men in place, moles in the Second Alliance, who hope to drive a wedge between the "colored" divisions and their white administrators. It wasn't necessary to say it aloud now.

Steinfeld looked at Hard-Eyes a touch apologetically.

Smoke could see Hard-Eyes' knuckles whitening on the big rifle.

Jenkins had picked up on the tension. He watched Hard-Eyes for a cue.

Voortoven and Willow and Yukio looked to Steinfeld.

Smoke prepared to throw himself aside. His preparation showed only in his reaching, almost languidly, to lay a hand on the crow, so it wouldn't fly away if he had to throw himself down when the shooting started.

Steinfeld opted to go on as if nothing had happened. Continuing the lecture was a way to reassure them. A way to say, *Wait and see.*

"Predinger is said to have died recently, though there are conflicting rumors about that. At any rate, Crandall and his sister have been elevated to supreme command of the SA—"

"*His sister?*" Hard-Eyes' surprise drew tension out of the air. There was soft laughter from Voortoven and Willow.

"His sister," Smoke confirmed. "Ellen Mae Crandall. Apparently she's been a driving organizational force. She did all the dickering when he was first syndicated."

Steinfeld nodded. "They come from a strict Southern Baptist family. Crandall's the spiritual leader of the SA, but for the most part he no longer makes public appearances as a minister—outside the SA. Crandall is the SA's Commander in Chief, though his main military strategist is a man named Watson. A former colonel who worked for the neo-racist underground trying to undermine post-Mandela South Africa... The SAISC had its first field-military testing in rural parts of South Africa. They didn't prove out, there, but they learned from it. They've proven themselves militarily putting down insurrections in Pakistan, Ethiopia, Guatemala..."

Hard-Eyes showed a touch of impatience, interrupting, "And NATO plans to turn most of Western Europe over to these people? This... this cover organization for neo-Nazis? Just like that?"

"They're calling the SA a 'non-Allied security force.' They're maintaining that—and some of them believe it—they're simply hiring a large international security corporation to keep the peace until full political order is restored. They're desperate for order... which is roughly why the National Socialists were able to come to power in Germany in the 1930s. People were desperate for stability. Hitler promised everyone economic growth. He promised an end to the political chaos of the Weimar Republic. He promised to reunite Germany."

"Oh, you can't really believe it's... like that."

"Not entirely. It's a little cleverer than that. The men in European and American government—especially the Americans and the British—who support 'the SA arrangement,' are part of the new crop of anti-Semites and racists. It's been a growing resurgence for decades. Apologists for fascism like the French New Right, the British National Front. In America, the Council of Conservative Citizens and the US Labor Party... the Unification Church... others. The SA has been using its media contacts—bought with Predinger's money—for eight years to create an impression of a Jewish conspiracy on which to blame the world's misfortunes... And they blame domestic crime on immigrants..."

Hard-Eyes nodded slowly. "I saw some of that on American TV... None of it real obvious stuff, but... almost subliminal sometimes."

Willow said, "Bloody SA's 'police force' is in Italy, Germany, Britain, Belgium, Spain. France soon enough. And 'ere, mate. 'Ere."

"And you think," Hard-Eyes said, looking at Steinfeld closely, "that they and the NATO people who put them in place are setting up some kind of coup?"

Steinfeld nodded. "A military coup for the whole of Western Europe."

There was silence, except for the creak of bodies shifting on chairs. Then, Jenkins asked, "Just how closely in Hitler's footsteps you think these people are gonna follow?"

Steinfeld took a deep breath. "Where they are in place, they have already isolated Jews and blacks and Muslims into barricaded sections of the towns. Crandall is said to hate Muslims even more than Jews..."

Hard-Eyes snorted and shook his head. "If it's true... what do you think you're going to do about it?"

Steinfeld shrugged. "You know already. A guerrilla war. You want to know more about our strategy?"

Hard-Eyes nodded.

Steinfeld shook his head. "No."

And once again, the men in the room looked to their respective masters for their cues.

That's when a man Smoke didn't know came in. He was a slender black man who wore horn-rim glasses on his nose and field glasses around his neck. There was a submachine gun on a strap over his shoulder. He turned to Steinfeld and then realized that what he had to announce should be said to everyone. He looked around at them and then said carefully, "Jorge got it on the radio. The Russians have blockaded the Colony. The space Colony. Orbital battle stations have gone on full alert."

And once more, every man thought the same thing, so that no one actually said it: *Maybe it's finally coming.*

There was always a feeling that any plans you made, any hopes you drummed up, were empty. Hollow. Like plucking fruit and cutting it open to find it dried out inside. Because it was assumed that, sooner or later, the conventional war would heat up into a nuclear war. And maybe that wouldn't be the end of the world. But it would be close enough.

Steinfeld was the first to shake off the paralysis of despair. "Another escalation." He shrugged. "But it's just taking the conventional war to a new battlefield."

Jenkins shook his head. "What's the point? What's the point of fighting for what's going to be radioactive ashes in a few months?"

Hard-Eyes said, "Maybe it's—"

He broke off, staring at the window. They all heard it. A jumpjet. Close this time. *Close.* The Armies.

Shouts from down the hall, and the roof. Steinfeld's sentries shouting warnings. The jumpjet had come suddenly. That was the jumpjet specialty: One moment the sky was clear; the next a jet was ten feet overhead, hovering on vertical retros.

The room shivered with the jumpjet's whine and grumble. Hard-Eyes moved toward the door.

The black sentry panicked, went to the window, put his hand on the latch—

Steinfeld stood, turning to shout at him, "No!" But it was lost in the roar of the jumpjet . . .

As the sentry flung the windows open.

The room's lamplight caught the pilot's eye.

Reflexively, Smoke—and Hard-Eyes—paused at the door looked past the sentry and out the window. Everyone in the room was frozen with looking.

The Harrier jumpjet was a swept-wing fighter jet designed in the early 1980s, this particularly adroit model mass-produced only in the early twenty-first century. The two oversized jets on the underside of its wings, computer-controlled for precision, were swiveled to point down, forward, backward, to the sides, so the jet could go virtually any direction; refined computer control and Casimir force generators added extra maneuverability and lift.

It hovered like a helicopter, thirty feet beyond the window, tilted back a little so you could just make out the USAF insignia on the underwings. They could feel the monstrous *engineering* of it, the precisely machined *bulk* of it, its engine heat reaching them, the chemical smell of its burning fuel choking the room.

But looking at it, in that compressed moment, Hard-Eyes thought of it as a plasteel dragon. In Smoke's mind, an insect. Dragonfly, to combine the two, a dragonfly from a Japanese horror movie. Sixty feet long, hovering, trembling as if with metallic rage, tilted up a little as if about to strike. Limned in starlight, glowing nacreously from the cockpit glass, the driver's head was an insignificant arc of darkness within the lozenge of the crystal. Perhaps this was one of those computer-reflexed planes that brought the pilot along mostly for the ride, and just in case. And perhaps the plane made the decision and not the pilot.

The decision to fire. The 60-mm cannon emerged from the socket on the underside of the plane, swiveling to point squarely through the window—the plane pulling back so as not to get caught in the backblast.

In the room, the paralysis passed. Steinfeld scooped up the papers from the desk, and with the expertise of long practice swept them into a vinyl briefcase, vaulted over the desk, and was out the door. Willow and Voortoven were close behind, Jenkins crowding after. Hard-Eyes hesitated, shouting something to Smoke, and Smoke turned, seeing Hard-Eyes raise the Weatherby—

Smoke thinking, the madman's going to shoot at that thing!

The Weatherby boomed. No ordinary rifle. Big motherfucker of a rifle. The so-called bulletproof glass on the jumpjet's cockpit starring, the arc of helmet jerking.

The plane wobbling. Steadying, the 60-mm guns returning to their target. All of this, from Steinfeld's grabbing papers to the gunshot, taking five seconds.

The crow flapped up, cawing, from Smoke's shoulder. He grabbed at it, lost sight of it. Saw instead the sentry still in the open window staring in horror at the plane. The plane pilotless but operating itself cybernetically now. Hard-Eyes trying to pull Smoke back out through the door.

Smoke thinking, *We're not going to make it.*

He never actually heard the blast.

As the 60-mm cannon fired. It was as if the noise was too profound for his auditory nerves, registering as a squeal like guitar feedback and an ugly metallic ringing. Then heat from a sheet of fire expanded to fill the room; a spatter of warm wetness: blood from the sentry as he was blown apart. All this just the background sensation. The primary sensation was the hardening of the air itself around the blast center. The soft damp air had become a slab of chilled steel that slammed him back into the wall. It *SLAMMED!* him. He could feel his body imprinting its shape in the plaster; feel things straining inside him, buckling—and then giving under the strain, bones creaking and then cracking, all time sadistically slowed so he could savor the hideously lucid sensation of his right arm popping from its socket and his pelvis cracking . . . breastbone cracking . . . cracking . . .

A white-hot freight train of pain roaring down on him.

And—

◆

He woke, thinking, *Where's my crow?*

He tried to say it, and a steel hammer struck a gong in him and he reverberated with pain. He tried to see, but his eyes were covered by a swarm of black bees.

"Give him more morphine," said a dream-voice. Steinfeld's voice.

Smoke never felt the needle. But its load drew a blanket of translucent numbness over the breakage in him; the pain still glowed, beneath, but muted like coals in a fog.

He opened his eyes: it was like lifting a window that had been painted shut; like it strained his back to open his eyes.

Saw through a feverish mist—a corner of a basement room; part of Yukio walking past; heard Hard-Eyes' voice.

" . . . we want a guarantee of passage out of France whenever we choose to take it."

"If you'll take my word as a guarantee. That's all I've got to offer." Steinfeld's voice. "But you're not fooling anybody. You could have split off from us when we ran, and we wouldn't have stopped you. You shot at the jumpjet to give Smoke time to get out. Who're you kidding? You'd have been safer away from us and you knew it! But you stuck with us."

Hard-Eyes is NR now, Smoke thought. I'm probably internally hemorrhaged, probably die, no doctors, no surgeons. The black bees swarmed over his head again. Stinging. The last thing he thought was, Where's my bird?

5

BENJAMIN BRIAN Rimpler, PH.D., the sixty-two-year-old Chairman of the FirStep Project, L-5 Colony One, was on his knees, on the white real wool rug in the bedroom of his plush quarters, worshiping a black rubber goddess.

Her name was Hermione, Herm to her friends, Mistress Hermione to Rimpler, when they were role playing. He paid her two hundred newbux an hour to give him relief.

She was well-padded, a tanned Amazon with dyed-coppery hair and white lipstick, white eye-shadow, which contrasted with the head-to-toe skin-tight black-rubber mistress's costume, breast tips and crotch of the outfit cut away to expose opulent rouged nipples—one of them flawed with a curling black hair—and her labia, also rouged.

Her breasts, each separately encased in its own form-fitting sheath of rubber, quivered with her slightest motion, and fairly rollicked with the stroke of the car-radio antenna—fitted with a black plastic handle—that she gripped in her studded right hand. The studs on the back of her hand were implanted into the skin in a connect-the-dots skull. Rimpler loved those little cartoon touches. Hermione was a better actress than the other girls from Bitchie's. But her Queens accent somehow undercut the required imperiousness when she gave him orders.

But when she hit him, Queens reediness didn't matter. The flash of pain sizzled away the illusion's seams. She hit him again, hard. Rimpler made an inarticulate whimper this time, and, feeling nausea building behind the flash, he muttered, "Wait." She was a pro, and she held off. Because there was no question about who was in charge here, really.

Rimpler. Smallish, pallid, blue-veined, bald—shaved bald—just a shade paunchy, his eyes squeezed shut now.

Unlike most of the Colony quarters, Rimpler's Admin Central flat had more than two rooms. It had three, counting the bathroom. He had, too, the condo in the Open. But he didn't use it anymore.

Here he'd dialed the bedroom walls to lozenge-shape. He'd switched off the images of Big Sur which usually glowed from the walls, and he'd dialed the light low, adding a sensuous dollop of red tinge. Penderecki's *The Passion According to Saint Luke* moaned from hidden speakers. "Okay, go ahead..."

Hermione looked at her watch and grimaced. When was the old bugger going to get it over with? He was mewling at her crotch, nosing at it like a pathetic blind puppy as she swacked his knobbed back, spat on his egg-head, told him he was cockroach dung—and he was still only half-tumescent!

"You haven't got your mind on your work, you little SHIT!" she hissed, raising welts between his shoulder blades.

Rimpler muttered apologies. Hermione was right. His mind wasn't on the game.

His mind was free-associating wildly, and parts of it seemed to break off from the main mass of his thinking and form venomous TV-eyed organs of pure self-consciousness; treacherous mental excrescencies that watched him, reported on him to some other sneering, sardonic part of his mind.

And the flashes of pain, instead of blinding his mind as they should have, instead of taking him out of himself, this time acted as eidetic drive-in movie screens, looming swatches of luminous white on which the derisive part of his mind projected images...

And he saw the thing he had built. He saw it on the screen of flash-pain. He saw the Colony. FirStep, ponderously rotating, a sort of technological totem-pole shape; in silhouette from just the right angle it was an Easter Island figure against the backdrop of space—space, the black and infinitely empty. Space, the brilliantly lit and overflowing with energy. Space, where the spectrum is unleashed.

And he seemed to see the thousands of tons of FirStep in blueprint, its world-class road map of wiring, its clusters of millions of computer chips, a thousand brains for its thousand segments, the people aswarm in it like *E. coli* in the belly of some enormous organism, independent of the organism but interrelated. And he saw its life-support systems, air and water filtration, the dozens of failsafes for airtight integrity against the ever-present gnawing of the vacuum of space, the reaches of insulation and the envelope of the atmospheric filter against the solar wind.

He visualized it in an infrared scan, with its areas of red and yellow for heat energy, its bluer areas where it radiated less heat, its solar-power panels shining with absorbed energy...

And he saw the thing in its skeletal stage, slowly coming together, something that had taken twenty years, now forming before his eyes in fast action, growing module by module like a coral reef, the construction pods darting fishlike around it. Growing from section A, a lonely outcropping in an endless sea, to an atoll to an island... A, B, C, D, and now E. Years of work materializing in technological crystallization.

And he had designed it, had overseen its construction, had made it grow around him.

Around him! He knew in that terribly clear, terribly ugly instant that it was only a hermit crab's shell. Something he had pulled over himself, taken refuge in to hide his nakedness. The Colony was simply armor for Benjamin Brian Rimpler.

Oh yes: he'd been fascinated with satellites as a boy; with the sky's ponderous celestial majesty; had nurtured a megalomaniacal adolescent fantasy of hoisting his own personal star into the sky. And later, horrified by the planet's swarming malaise, its feverish self-gouging environmental suicide, he'd wanted to create an alternative world, a self-contained, intelligently controlled ecosystem where man—and nature—would be given a second chance. An answer to the population explosion, because it would be the first of many such alternative worlds...

Anyway, that's what he told himself. And that's what he told the media. The Colony would employ and house the poor. And in fact the bulk of its settlers were low-income technicki workers. So it looked good. It looked unselfish.

But he saw it, now. The Colony was a monumental act of selfishness. And his obsessive drive to get it built had killed his son.

Here, in the 2/3-grav section, in the exclusive optimum-lifestyle quarters, he had wrapped its vast tonnage about himself in layers of elaboration that seemed, now, only the intricacy of neurosis. Each life-support system, each failsafe and airlock seemed a form of his pathetic anality.

He sat back on his haunches, looked at Hermione, and perceived that he'd allowed a sort of parasite to crawl into his shell with him.

"Get out," he said.

"What? Why, you little worm—"

"No, I mean it. I'm not trying to intensify the game. Get out."

"Hey, don't blame me because you can't get it up. A man gets old and not even the best pro can help. If you'd take some—"

"Get out."

She stepped back, lowering her whip, yawing between two poles, the overawed employee and the professional dominatrix.

"What? The price is still—"

"I paid you in advance. Get out."

Hermione perceived that her license was revoked. She backed away, then turned, without so much as muttering, went to the bed to get her jumpsuit. She'd picked up on his urgency. There wasn't even time to change out of the rubber. The little prick! (And she did mean little!) But he was the most powerful man on the Colony, except for maybe Praeger. Rimpler could have her jettisoned if he wanted. She went quietly, thinking, I'm in Admin section; I could stop at a credfone and call Praeger. He's into submissives; but what the hell, I can switch...

Rimpler watched her go, and one of the fragment outriders of his personality, the autoerotic, infantile part, looked after her with regret and whined to the rest of him. Mentally he slapped it and told it to shut up.

There was to be no more oblivion for him from that direction. It wasn't working anymore. Maybe drugs. Booze. Maybe—

He saw himself in an evac chute. *The gates open, the air sucks out, he's ejected naked into void—*

He recoiled, actually curled up and clutched at himself at the thought.

Terry was—

Recoiled again from that one, too, and tried to think instead about a stiff drink, something to eat...

He sat on his haunches, naked, parts of him smeared with Vaseline, his face still damp with her pheromone perfume, his back throbbing with welts, and fought an urge to run to the nearest airlock and jet himself naked into space—

That'd be real freedom, for a moment.

"Dad?"

His gut constricted. A muscle in his back jumped. Fear washed through him, acrid and cold. *Claire.* Claire's voice. He was more afraid of Claire, at this moment, than he'd been of his own ice-queen mother. He was afraid of his own daughter.

If she should see Hermione...

But her voice came from the grid in the front door. Hermione was going out by the service corridor. Claire wouldn't see her.

He shouted, "Claire—I'll be right out! I'm in the shower." Then he pressed the door button and said, "seven-three," into the grid. The door analyzed his voiceprint, confirmed it, and opened the front door for her. But left the door to his bedroom locked.

"I'll be right out," he shouted through the door to the living room. He went to the bathroom, let the ultrasound shower cleanse him, shivered with the tingling of it, felt a vague pleasure knowing that a composition by Stravinsky was worked into the sound waves; he couldn't hear the composition at that frequency, but he could feel it.

Still, he wished he could have water. The technickis would get word of it, though, if he had a water system installed. One of them would have to install it, after all. Their commentators would editorialize about wasteful luxuries among Admin elitists. *Admin washunmunener filzerbush,* they'd say. Admin washes in money and our air filter's broken.

Praeger, damn him, had had a water shower installed. The technickis had heard about it, every last one of them, an hour later.

Praeger, president of UNIC's on-Colony board. The sick feeling in Rimpler's gut returned when he thought of Praeger.

He stepped out of the shower, and it sank back into the tiled wall. He went to the mirror, punched 8 on the numbered row of buttons beneath the glass; the mirror reversed itself, showing him its shelved backside. He found the anesthetic spray and coated the welts on his back with it. Again with some regret. Then he dressed in Japanese house pajamas, airy blue silk, and found Claire in the living room. His stomach tightened as she said, "Hi, Dad," with a friendly enough smile, nothing censorious in her eyes.

"How you doing, babe?" he said, bending to kiss her on the forehead. He hadn't seen her for almost two weeks.

"Dad—I'm okay, but—"

He sat down across from her, thinking, *She seems coiled up.*

She wore a light, soft gray suit with a triple-flap skirt; her lips were pursed, her cheeks hollowed.

"You're going to give me more details about the wonderful viddy interview you did—" He laughed breezily. "Forget it! It was a put-up job and by now everyone's realized it."

"Dad..."

And then he saw the tension in her posture and the knuckles white on her knees. He thought, Shit, it's Praeger again.

"Dad, when you asked for a four-day in-house vacation—"

"You think it was bad timing? Right after your screw-up with the little technicki kid? I told you—"

"Dad! ... No. But—I only just found out that you had a no-calls up. I mean, no one could figure out why you weren't making a statement..."

"Well—sure. How could I have a vacation, a retreat, if everyone's calling me with the Colony's problems? There's a dozen people happy to—"

"Dad..."

This time her voice actually broke. He stared. He hadn't seen her show her humanity like that in years; not since Terry died.

"For God's sake, Claire, out with it."

"Dad, when you sealed the place off, you left it open for LSSE. Right?" There was accusation wrapped in the sarcastic twist she gave to "Right?"

He laughed nervously. "Well, of course!"

LSSE: Life-Support Emergency. There *hadn't* been an LSSE. Impossible.

"Dad—there *was* an LSSE. I mean—this is the sort of thing that keeps happening with you." She was in her bitchily maternal mode now. "Things are flying to hell around you and—Dad, there was a Bright Red. Full alert. *And Praeger gave orders that you were not to be told.* I mean, I don't *know* that for sure but... he must have."

He felt himself sinking. "What was it?" His voice a crust.

"Dad—"

"Will you stop saying that and just *tell me!*" His fear of her vanished. He was standing now, arms straight at his sides.

"The Russians have blockaded us. *We're in the war.* The last supply ship was boarded. Captured! There hasn't been another. No ships outgoing. They're even jamming communications. We get through now and then—"

"Why didn't you come to me before? I mean—how long has it been?"

"Three days. Dad, I couldn't get through to see you till today. And you had your screen down. The riots—we couldn't get through because of the riots."

"Riots."

"A man named Bonham has been asking for a general strike. There are four of these organizers really pushing it—a man named Joseph Bonham, a man named Samson Molt—"

"Oh, don't tell me their names, tell Security, I'm not the local thought police. Shit." He found he was staring at his decanters on the table. Wanting a drink and not having the courage even to reach across the table. Afraid the Colony was so fragile it would shiver apart if he moved. His shell, his armor. His insulation from Earth.

"These people are saying that now that we're cut off from Earth the techni-class has got to demand rights or they'll be completely powerless when it comes to martial law."

"There's something to that." He laughed bitterly. Now his hands moved of their own volition—squirting gin into a glass. He swallowed it and shuddered. "Praeger'll want—martial law, want to completely subjugate the technickis because of the state of emergency."

"You *agree* with these people?" More reproach than surprise.

He shrugged, took another drink. Laughed. "Riots!" Shaking his head in wonder. "I designed this thing . . . " He gestured vaguely at the walls, meaning the Colony itself. "And still it's three days before I know we're blockaded. And having riots."

"Dad—Praeger didn't want you to know."

They looked at one another, and the implication hung in the air between them. She gave it verbal shape. "I think there's going to be a coup. I think UNIC wants to take the colony over completely."

6

FIRSTEP FLOATED in the sea of space, a city afloat in the void.

And Freezone floated in the Atlantic Ocean, a city afloat in the wash of international cultural confluence.

Freezone was anchored about a hundred miles north of Sidi Ifni, a drowsy city on the coast of Morocco in a warm, gentle current, and in a sector of the sea only rarely troubled by large storms. What storms arose here spent their fury on the maze of concrete wave-baffles Freezone Admin had spent years building up around the artificial island.

Originally, Freezone had been just another offshore drilling project. The massive oil deposit a quarter-mile below the artificial island was still less than a quarter tapped out. The drilling platform was owned in common by the Moroccan government and a Texas-based petroleum and electronics products company. TexMo. The company that bought Disneyland and Disneyworld and Disneyworld II—all three of which had closed in the wake of the CSD: the Computer Storage Depression. Also called the Dissolve Depression.

A group of Arab terrorists—at least, the US State Department claimed that's who did it—had arranged a well-placed electromagnetic pulse from a hydrogen bomb hidden aboard a routine orbital shuttle. The shuttle was vaporized in the blast, as well as two satellites, one of them manned; but when the CSD hit, no one took time to mourn the dead.

The orbital bomb had almost triggered Armageddon: three Cruise missiles had to be aborted, and fortunately two more were shot down by the Russians before the terrorist cell took credit for the upper atmospheric blast. Most of the bomb's blast had been directed upward; what came downward, though, was the side effect of its blast: the EMP. An electromagnetic pulse that—just as had been predicted since the 1970s—traveled through thousands of miles of wires and circuitry on the continent below the H-blast. The Defense Department was shielded; the banking system, for the most part, was not. The pulse wiped out ninety-three percent of the newly formed American Banking Credit Adjustment Bureau. ABCAB had handled seventy-six percent of the nation's buying and credit transferal. Most of what was bought, was bought through ABCAB or ABCAB related companies... until the EMP wiped out ABCAB's memory storage, the pulse overburdening the circuits, melting them, and literally frying the data storage chips. And thereby kicking the crutches out from under the American economy. Millions of bank accounts were "suspended" until records could be restored—causing a run on remaining banks. The insurance companies and the Federal guarantee programs were overwhelmed. They just couldn't cover the loss.

The States had already been in trouble. The nation had lost its economic initiative in the early twenty-first century: its undereducated, badly trained workers, the outsourcing of jobs and manufacturing made US industry unable to compete with the Chinese and South American manufacturing booms. The EMP credit dissolve kicked the nation over the rim of recession and into the pit of depression—and made the rest of the world laugh. The Arab terrorist cell responsible—hard-core Islamic Fundamentalists—had been composed of seven men. Seven men who crippled a nation.

But America still had its enormous military spread, its electronics and medical innovators. And the war economy kept it humming, like a man with cancer taking amphetamines for a last burst of strength, while the endless malls and housing projects—built cheaply and in need of constant upkeep—got shabbier, uglier, trashier by the day. And more dangerous.

The States just weren't safe enough for the rich anymore. The resorts, the amusement parks, the exclusive affluent neighborhoods, places like Central Park West—all crumbled under the attrition of perennial strikes and persistent terrorist attacks. The swelling mass of the poor resented the recreations of the rich.

While the middle-class buffer was shrinking to insignificance there were still enclaves in the States where you could get lost in the media churn, hypnotized by the flashcards of desire into an iPad-trance fantasy of the American Dream as ten thousand companies vied for your attention, nagging you to buy and keep buying. Places that were walled city-states of middle-class illusions—like the place Hard-Eyes had come from.

But the affluent could feel the crumbling of their kingdom. They didn't feel safe in the States. They needed someplace outside, somewhere controlled. Europe was out now; Central and South America, too risky. The Pacific theater was another war zone.

So that's where Freezone came in.

A Texas entrepreneur—who hadn't had his money in ABCAB—saw the possibilities in the community that had grown up around the enormous complex of offshore drilling platforms. A paste-jewel necklace of brothels and arcades and cabarets had crystallized on derelict ships permanently anchored around the platforms. Hundreds of hookers and casino dealers worked the international melange of men who worked the oil rigs.

The entrepreneur made a deal with the Moroccan government, bought the rusting hulks and shanty nightclubs. And then he fired everyone.

The Texan owned a plastics company . . . the company had developed light, super-tough plastic that the entrepreneur used in the rafts on which the new floating city was built. The community was now seventeen square miles of urban raft protected with one of the meanest security forces in the world. Freezone dealt in pleasant distractions for the rich in the exclusive section and—in the second-string places around the edge—for technickis from the drill rigs. And the second-string places sheltered a few thousand semi-illicit hangers-on, and a few hundred performers.

Like Rickenharp.

◆

Rick Rickenharp stood against the south wall of the Semiconductor, letting the club's glare and blare wash over him, and mentally writing a song. The song went something like, "Glaring blare, lightning stare/ Nostalgia for the electric chair."

Then he thought, Fucking drivel.

All the while he was doing his best to look cool but vulnerable, hoping one of the girls flashing through the crowd would remember having seen him in the band the night before, would try to chat him up, play groupie. But they were mostly into wifi dancers.

And *no fucking way* Rickenharp was going to wire into minimono.

Rickenharp was a rock classicist; he was retro. He wore a black leather motorcycle jacket that was some seventy-some years old, said to have been worn by John Cale when he was still in the Velvet Underground. The seams were beginning to pop for the third time; three studs were missing from the chrome trimming. The elbows and collar edges were worn through the black dye to the brown animal the leather had come from. But the leather was second skin to Rickenharp. He wore nothing under it. His bony, hairless chest showed translucent-bluewhite between the broken zippers. He wore blue jeans that were only ten years old but looked older than the coat; he wore genuine Harley Davidson boots. Earrings clustered up and down his long, slightly too prominent ears, and his rusty brown hair looked like a cannon-shell explosion.

And he wore dark glasses.

And he did all this because it was gratingly unfashionable.

His band hassled him about it. They wanted their lead-git and frontman minimono.

"If we're gonna go minimono, we oughta just sell the fucking guitars and go wires," Rickenharp had told them.

And the drummer had been stupid and tactless enough to say, "Well, fuck, man, maybe we *should* go to wires."

Rickenharp had said, "Maybe we should get a fucking drum machine, too, you fucking Neanderthal!" and kicked the drum seat over, sending Murch into the cymbals with a fine crashing, so that Rickenharp added, "you should get that good a sound outta those cymbals on stage. Now we know how to do it."

Murch had started to throw his sticks at him, but then he'd remembered how you had to have them lathed up special because they didn't make them anymore, so he'd said, "Suck my ass, big shot" and got up and walked out, not the first time. But that was the first time it meant anything, and only some heavy ambassadorial action on the part of Ponce had kept Murch from leaving the band.

The call from their agent had set the whole thing off. That's what it really was. Agency was streamlining its clientele. The band was out. The last two download albums hadn't sold, and in fact the engineers claimed that live drums didn't digitize well onto the miniaturized soundcaps that passed for CDs now. Rickenharp's holovid and the videos weren't getting much airplay.

Anyway, Vid-Co was probably going out of business. Another business sucked into the black hole of the depression. "So it ain't our fault the stuff's not selling," Rickenharp said. "We got fans but we can't get the distribution to reach 'em."

Mose had said, "Bullshit, we're out of the Grid, and you know it. All that was carrying us was the nostalgia wave anyway. You can't get more'n two bits out of a revival, man."

Julio the bassist had said something in technicki which Rickenharp hadn't bothered to translate because it was probably stupid and when Rickenharp had ignored him he'd gotten pissed and it was his turn to walk out. Fucking touchy technickis anyway.

And now the band was in abeyance. Their train was stopped between the stations. They had one gig, just one: opening for a wifi act. And Rickenharp didn't want to do it. But they had a contract and there were a lot of rock nostalgia freaks on Freezone, so maybe that was their audience anyway and he owed it to them. Blow the goddamn wires off the stage.

He looked around the Semiconductor and wished the Retro-Club was still open. There'd been a strong retro presence at the RC, even some rockabillies, and some of the rockabillies actually knew what rockabilly sounded like. The Semiconductor was a minimono scene.

The minimono crowd wore their hair long, fanned out between the shoulders and narrowing to a point at the crown of the head, and straight, absolutely straight, stiff, so from the back each head had a black or gray or red or white teepee-shape. Those, in monochrome, were the only acceptable colors. Flat tones and no streaks. Their clothes were stylistic extensions of their hairstyles. Minimono was a reaction to Flare—and to the chaos of the war, and the war economy, and the amorphous shifting of the Grid. The Flare style was going, dying.

Rickenharp had always been contemptuous of the trendy Flares, but he preferred them to minimono. Flare had energy, anyway.

A flare was expected to wear his hair up, as far over the top of his head as possible, and that promontory was supposed to *express*. The more colors the better. In that scene, you weren't an individual unless you had an expressive flare. Screwshapes, hooks, aureola shapes, layered multicolor snarls. Fortunes were made in flare hair-shaping shops, and lost when it began to go out of fashion. But it had lasted longer than most fashions; it had endless variation and the appeal of its energy to sustain it. A lot of people copped out of the necessity of inventing individual expression by adopting a politically standard flare. Shape your hair like the insignia for your favorite downtrodden third world country (back when they were downtrodden, before the new marketing axis). Flares were so much trouble most people took to having flare wigs. And their drugs were styled to fit the fashion. Excitative neurotransmitters; drugs that made you seem to glow. The wealthier flares had nimbus belts, creating artificial auroras. The hipper flares considered this to be tastelessly narcissistic, which was a joke to nonflares, since all flares were floridly vain.

Rickenharp had never colored or shaped his hair, except to encourage its punk spikiness.

But Rickenharp wasn't a punkrocker. He identified with prepunk, late 1950s, mid-1960s, early 1970s. Rickenharp was a proud anachronism. He was simply a hard-core rocker, as out of place in the Semiconductor as bebop would have been in the 1980s dance clubs.

Rickenharp looked around at the flat-back, flat-gray, monochrome tunics and jumpsuits, the black wristfones, the cookie-cutter sameness of JAS's; at the uniform tans and ubiquitous FirStep Colony-shaped earrings (only one, always in the left ear). The high-tech-fetishist minimonos were said to aspire toward a place in the Colony the way Rastas had dreamed of a return to Ethiopia. Rickenharp thought it was funny that the Russians had blockaded the Colony. Funny to see the normally dronelike, antiflamboyant minimonos quietly simmering on ampheticool, standing in tense groups, hissing about the Russian blockade of FirStep, in why-doesn't-someone-do-something outrage.

The stultifying regularity of their canned music banged from the walls and pulsed from the floor. Lean against the wall and you felt a drill-bit vibration of it in your spine.

There were a few hardy, defiant flares here, and flares were Rickenharp's best hope for getting laid. They tended to respect old rock.

The music ceased; a voice boomed, "Joel NewHope!" and spots hit the stage. The first wifi act had come on. Rickenharp glanced at his watch. It was ten. He was due to open for the headline act at 11:30. Rickenharp pictured the club emptying as he hit the stage. He wasn't long for this club.

NewHope hit the stage. He was anorexic and surgically sexless: radical minimono. A fact advertised by his nudity: he wore only gray and black spray-on sheathing, his dick in a drag queen's tuck. How did the guy piss? Rickenharp wondered. Maybe it was out of that faint crease at his crotch. A dancing mannequin. His sexuality was clipped to the back of his head: a single chrome electrode that activated the pleasure center of the brain during the weekly legally controlled catharsis. But he was so skinny—hey, who knows, maybe he went to a black-market cerebrostim to interface with the pulser. Though minimonos were supposed to be into stringent law and order.

The neural transmitters jacked into NewHope's arms and legs and torso transmitted to pickups on the stage floor. The long, funereal wails pealing from hidden speakers were triggered by the muscular contractions of his arms and legs and torso. He wasn't bad, for a minimono, Rickenharp thought. You can make out the melody, the tune shaped by his dancing, and it had a shade more complexity than the M'n'Ms usually had . . . The M'n'M crowd moved into their geometrical dance configurations, somewhere between disco dancing and square dance, Busby Berkley kaleidoscopings worked out according to formulas you were simply expected to know, if you had the nerve to participate. Try to dance freestyle in their interlocking choreography, and sheer social rejection, on the wings of body language, would hit you like an arctic wind.

Sometimes Rickenharp did an acid dance in the midst of the minimono configuration, just for the hell of it, just to revel in their rejection. But his band had made him stop that. Don't alienate the audience at our only gig, man. Probably our *last* fucking gig . . .

The wiredancer rippled out bagpipelike riffs over the digitalized rhythm section. The walls came alive.

A good rock club—in 1965 or 1975 or 1985 or 1995 or 2012 or 2039 should be narrow, dark, close, claustrophobic. The walls should be either starkly monochrome—all black or mirrored, say—or deliberately garish. Camp, layered with whatever was the contemporary avant-garde or gaudy graffiti.

The Semiconductor showed both sides. It started out butch, its walls glassy black; during the concert it went in gaudy drag as the sound-sensitive walls reacted to the music with color streaking, wavelengthing in oscilloscope patterns, shades of blue-white for high end, red and purple for bass and percussion, reacting vividly, hypnotically to each note. The minimonos disliked reactive walls. They called it kitschy.

The dance spazzed the stage, and Rickenharp grudgingly watched, trying to be fair to it. Thinking, It's another kind of rock 'n' roll, is all. Like a Christian watching a Buddhist ceremony, telling himself, "Oh, well, it's all manifestations of the One God in the end." Rickenharp thinking: But real rock is better. *Real rock is coming back,* he'd tell almost anyone who'd listen. Almost no one would.

A chaotichick came in, and he watched her, feeling less alone. Chaotics were much closer to real rockers. She was a skinhead, with the sides of her head painted. The Gridfriend insignia was tattooed on her right shoulder. She wore a skirt made of at least two hundred rags of synthetic material sewn to her leather belt—a sort of grass skirt of bright rags. The nipples of her bare breasts were pierced with thin screws. The minimonos looked at her in disgust; they were prudish, and calling attention to one's breasts was decidedly gauche with the M'n'Ms. She smiled sunnily back at them. Her handsome Semitic features were slashed randomly with paint. Her makeup looked like a spinpainting. Her teeth were filed.

Rickenharp swallowed hard, looking at her. Damn. She was *his type*.

Only . . . she wore a blue-mesc sniffer. The sniffer's inverted question mark ran from its hook at her right ear to just under her right nostril. Now and then she tilted her head to it, and sniffed a little blue powder.

Rickenharp had to look away. Silently cursing.

He'd just written a song called "Stay Clean."

Blue mesc. Or syncoke. Or heroin. Or amphetamorphine. Or XTZ. But mostly he went for blue mesc. And blue mesc was addictive.

Blue mesc, also called boss blue. It offered some of the effects of mescaline and cocaine together, framed in the gelatinous sweetness of methaqualone. Only . . . stop taking it after a period of steady use and the world drained of meaning for you. There was no actual withdrawal sickness. There was only a deeply resonant depression, a sense of worthlessness that seemed to settle like dust and maggot dung into each individual cell of the user's body.

Some people called blue mesc "the suicide ticket." It could make you feel like a coal miner when the mineshaft caved in, only you were buried in yourself.

Rickenharp had squandered the money from his only major microdisc hit on boss blue and synthmorph. He'd just barely made it clean. And lately, at least before the band squabbles, he'd begun feeling like life was worth living again.

Watching the girl with the sniffer walk past, watching her use, Rickenharp felt stricken, lost, as if he'd seen something to remind him of a lost lover. An ex-user's syndrome. Pain from guilt of having jilted your drug.

And he could imagine the sweet burn of the stuff in his nostrils, the backward-sweet pharmaceutical taste of it in the back of his palate; the rush; the autoerotic feedback loop of blue mesc. Imagining it, he had a shadow of the sensation, a tantalizing ghost of the rush. In memory he could taste it, smell it, feel it . . . Seeing her *use* brought back a hundred iridescent memories and with them came an almost irrepressible longing. (While some small voice in the back of his head tried to get his attention, tried to warn him, *Hey, remember the shit makes you want to kill yourself when you run out; remember it makes you stupidly overconfident and boorish; remember it eats your internal organs* . . . a small, dwindling voice . . .)

The girl was looking at him. There was a flicker of invitation in her eyes.

He wavered.

The small voice got louder.

Rickenharp, if you go to her, go with her, you'll end up using.

He turned away with an anguished internal wrenching. Stumbled through the wash of sounds and lights and monochrome people to the dressing room; to guitar and earphones and the safer sonic world.

◆

"You gave him to me," Steinfeld said, leaning close to Purchase so he could be heard over the noise of the bar. "And I give him back. And I think we'll both keep him."

Purchase smiled and nodded. "Stisky's a find. A piece of luck."

Purchase was a big, sloppy-bodied man, his hair thin and his face wide. You could hear him breathe, even when he was at rest. But he laughed easily, and he didn't miss much. The two men liked one another, though they were NR for different reasons. Steinfeld had shaped the NR in the image of his own idealism. It was an extension of his convictions—some would say, his almost perverse obsession.

Purchase worked for Witcher, Steinfeld's chief source of funding. But no, Steinfeld reflected, as they slid into a booth in the Freezone cocktail bar, Purchase worked for himself. That should have made him suspect. Only, it didn't. Steinfeld trusted him more than he trusted some of the NR's political zealots.

"Any problem with the blockades?" Purchase asked, toying with his gold choker.

Steinfeld's brow furrowed. "Yes and no. I got through—but it was close this time. No one actually fired on us. But they would have if they'd picked up on us sooner. Sometimes I feel like asking Witcher's pilots not to tell me if we're tracked. I'd rather not know if I'm about to be shot out of the air . . . "

"You bring anyone else through?"

"A few people. We can't get more than a handful out at any one time . . . and it's a risk with just the handful. I won't be taking many more of these trips . . . " He grimaced and changed the subject. "That's a silk suit, isn't it? It's a little hard to tell in these lights, but I think it's *blue*?"

"It is. Dark blue silk." Purchase signaled for a drink. When the puffy-eyed waitress arrived, yawning, rubbing her temples, he said, "I want something big and glittery in an enormous glass. You choose. Something sweet. Sweet as whoever it was kept you up so late last night."

She almost smiled. "Something with a plastic mermaid? A little paper umbrella?"

"Both the umbrella and the mermaid are absolute necessities."

"I'll have a scotch, please," Steinfeld said. "On the rocks." They watched her walk away. She was wearing a gown that picked up wifi signals at random as the signals passed through the room and reproduced Web imagery down the svelte length of her. Collaged faces, mostly fashion models and breakfast-cereal-kids, rippled across her ass and the back of her thighs.

The bar was at the edge of a disco. Minimono droned and thudded on the dance floor. Lights whirled like UFOs landing in an old movie Steinfeld had seen as a boy.

They had to lean over the transparent plastic table to talk, but they'd picked the booth to discourage bugging.

The lights tinted Purchase's face, changing his color as if some expressionist painter were experimenting with his portrait. He was pinkish red dappled with blue when he asked, "How'd Stisky take to training?"

"A fish to water. The more rigorous the better. Well, he was a priest, once, after all... Does he have a name yet?"

"John Swenson. The cover had a good foundation: there was a John Swenson born the same year as Stisky. Died five years later. Looked a lot like Stisky did as a kid. His death went unregistered in his hometown—died in a boating accident with his parents on vacation, they all drowned. Death registered in Florida but never entered in computer records. We've put all the rest together. Worked up a set of false memories for mem-plantation... I think we've got some likelies, to take the implants..."

The expression on Steinfeld's face made Purchase say, "You've got qualms about mem-plants?"

"This business of toying with people's memories—I don't care which side it is doing it—no, I don't like it. It's—" He shook his head.

"Too close to interfering with the soul?"

Steinfeld said, "I am not sure I believe in the soul. But yes, it's too close—to interfering with the soul."

"We're up against it. Outnumbered. We've got to use all the tools at hand. If it's any comfort, we don't implant our own people. We should, but we don't. Just the enemy."

Steinfeld shrugged. "So be it. How high can you place him?"

Purchase fidgeted, looking unsure of himself. The waitress came back with their drinks. Purchase's was some sort of phantasmagorical daiquiri. A cartoon character flew across the waitress's stomach (What was his name? Something the Gremlin) to be replaced instantly by a hydrogen-cell vehicle crashing head-on into another, both bursting into flames. "Cars are crashing in your stomach," Purchase told her.

"That explains my heartburn," she said, snicking Purchase's Worldtalk expense account credit card through the credunit on her hip. She gave the card back and walked away, Marilyn Monroe waving at them from the small of her back. Monroe's breasts superimposed for one delectable instant on the waitress's buttocks.

"People are *wearing* the Grid now," Steinfeld said.

"Just pray to Gridfriend they don't make wallpaper like that. Come to think of it, they probably are making it..."

Steinfeld smiled; the smile was barely visible through his beard. He wore a cheap black-and-white flatsuit, a bit tacky here, but passable.

Purchase said, "I think... *think*, mind you... I can place Stisky—or Swenson, now, if you like—I think I can place Swenson in the Second Circle itself, after a short, ah, probationary period. Within a few weeks."

Steinfeld looked sharply at Purchase. "It took us three years to get Devereaux into the Second Circle. And that was fast advancement. He was in the lower echelons, as you call it, two years and then—"

"I know all that. But..." Purchase leaned nearer. "But I've gotten to know Crandall's sister. We modeled her transactional script patterns. She has an affair every two years—almost to the day! Usually something torrid. Then Rick gets rid of them or she loses interest. We believe that her next one will be somewhat more serious. And it's due in a week—and that's when I'll introduce her to Swenson. She has a growing need for long-term emotional security. We studied her preference profile: Swenson would be her archetype, which is why we picked him. She meets Swenson, Swenson romances her—and we both agree he's got the talent for that—and she will bring him with her. And of course he's done very well in their lower echelons."

"You're very certain of that."

"I'd swear to it: bet a cool million on it."

Steinfeld nodded. "A million. Well—you've just invoked the deity that means the most to you. I'm impressed. All right. If it gets that far... Devereaux might..."

Purchase shook his head. "You don't really think Devereaux is going to come through, do you? Do you know who's the new SA

Security chief? Old Sackville-West. Devereaux's the nervous type. Old Sacks will smell that."

"Then he may smell our Swenson."

"I think not. Swenson has the talent. And he'll have Ellen Mae's support. Trust me."

They took a moment to work on their drinks. Steinfeld looked down, through the table, and through the floor. The floor was transparent; the disco jutted from the side of a highmall rising two hundred stories over the main Freezone helicopter port; far below—and *directly* below—radio-controlled copters rose and landed, dragonfly bright in the ocean-burnished sunlight.

Steinfeld shivered with vertigo. He shifted his gaze to the expanse of cobalt sea. "Funny how from up here, the waves look regular, perfect and orderly. Down close they're all chaotic."

Purchase looked up from his drink. Without quite taking the straw from his mouth he said, "That supposed to be a parable of some kind?"

"No. But I guess it could be: from up here we're taking too much for granted." The waitress walked by, her dress flashing with forty TV channels at once. It made Steinfeld's skin crawl. "How much of that programming"—he nodded toward the televisioned dress—"is Worldtalk's doing?"

"Not a great deal in slices of time. But lots of it in small, regular pulses . . . Worldtalk'll be active on the SA account this week. Naturally Crandall wants me to shepherd it. And I'll have to do a good job of it. You know that."

"For a while. But try not to promote them *brilliantly*. Okay?"

Worldtalk. The globe-straddling agency for public relations and advertising. Purchase was a Chinese-boxes man, working from the inside box out: his own man and yet Witcher's man; Witcher's man and yet Steinfeld's; Steinfeld's and yet the SA's. The SA's and yet Worldtalk's. Steinfeld believed the sequence moved in that order of importance. He had to believe it, because he needed Purchase. There were too few like him.

There was Devereaux, of course. Who just might be a waste.

"You can pick up . . . Swenson, in an hour, at . . . " He took a plastic-tagged hotel keycard from his pocket and gave it to Purchase, who pocketed the key casually but quickly. "He'll be there. Report on placing him to Ben-Simon at the Israeli Embassy. He's still with me. And to Witcher. Let us know if he gets close to them . . . to her."

"You sound as if you doubt Devereaux's going to come through, yourself." (The light shifting, Purchase's face green, then blue.)

"Just thinking in contingencies."

"If Devereaux doesn't come through, we'll have to roll up his backup team, fast."

"They'll have to cope with it themselves. I'm leaving in a few hours. They'll do fine. They're . . . basic. But good."

He looked out over the sea, thinking, *If Devereaux doesn't come through . . .*

◆

There were eight people in the room, and, each in their own way, they were all killers. No: seven were killers. One was a man who had come here hoping to *become* a killer; to kill one of the other seven people within the hour, in this undersea conference room beneath Freezone.

Freezone's enormous octagonal raft was pocketed with air and layers of flotation synthetics. Most of the buildings in the exclusive Freezone Central complex—walled off from the rest of Freezone to guarantee safety for its inhabitants and visitors—extended like enormous undersea stalactites beneath the "flotation support structure" for greater stability and less vulnerability to winds.

In one of those buildings, the inverted wedge of the Fuji Hilton, Richard Crandall and Ellen Mae Crandall presided over the meeting . . .

The room was dimmed for the briefing screen. Five men and the woman sat at the table. There were two Security men standing behind Crandall at the head of the table. All were bathed in the sickly electronic-blue light from the screen that filled the upper half of the wall to the right of the door.

On three sides, it was a standard convention meeting room, a forty-by-fifty-foot "planning center." The walls were the usual imitation woodgrain, the table matching. The chairs were confoam swivels; soft track lighting overhead was muted now. A bank of remote controls for the screen and room service was inset at one end of the oblong table.

Behind Crandall, the fourth wall was a window of thick plate glass, looking out on the underside of the floating city. The dull blue vista was lit brokenly by flat white rectangles of light staggered along the down-juts of other buildings; the buildings looked like reflections in a pond, upside down. But look closer and you could see men in them: right-side-up men in upside-down buildings. Now and then some glossy, striped, gape-mouthed thing would swim up near the windows, attracted by the lights; jellyfish billowed up, pumping like disembodied heart valves.

Devereaux sat at the table, looking out into the undersea, carefully keeping up his mask of absentmindedness, carefully thinking only about jellyfish. Not permitting himself to think about the act he was about to perform. It was not yet time to think about it.

Best not to think about it at all. Best to let it happen the way an alarm clock goes off.

A voice droned through the air-conditioned room from the bluewhite screen, accompanying the charts and figures appearing and disappearing there. "Alliance registration in Brussels," the voice said, "rose forty-three percent in the last sixty days. Alliance coordinator for Brussels credits this abrupt rise to the anti-Russian/anti-American information campaign. Antipathy to the 'foreign warmakers' has drawn increasing numbers of Belgians into the Alliance, their registration always hinging on the Alliance's guarantee of eventual ejection of all foreigners. Coordinator Casterman expects very little abreaction from Belgian inductees during the Final Phase, anticipating that thorough Camp indoctrination will obviate any significant resentment when, in the words of the resistance leader Chartres, 'the country is taken over by foreigners who promised to protect us from foreigners.'"

Crandall stabbed a button. The narrative froze. He dialed the lights up and turned to Sackville-West, head of Internal Security, asking sharply, "Who wrote that report?" Crandall's faint Southern accent was almost undetectable. He was slender, almost gaunt, his black eyes a little sunken. His wide, flexible mouth could flare into a smile like a dove flushed from cover; could just as easily clamp down into a frown firm enough to use as a metal-shop vise. His hair was receding, and he compensated with long sideburns. A strong nose, craggy cheekbones—a face almost like a beardless Lincoln. He wore a suit and tie, brown leather and cream-colored silk. His sister, to his left, looked unpleasantly like him, to Devereaux's eye. Even without sideburns. Her face was a little softer, her lips redder—but like him. Maybe it was the expression.

"That report . . . " Sackville-West muttered, clearing his throat several times as he looked through his pocket filer. "Ah, that report was written by . . . ah . . . " Sackville-West was a pinkfaced Britisher with three chins and a comma of hair on his forehead. He was always sweating, even in an air-conditioned room. "Swenson wrote the report," Sackville-West said at last, looking up from his console.

Casually, Devereaux raised a hand to his cheek and pressed the stud under the skin, just below his right cheekbone. His Mossad-issue right eye increased its impressions-per-second ratio by five hundred percent. He rubbed at his left eye, as if it were tired, closing it so only the right took impressions. Details normally lost to the human eye showed up in his prosthetic perception: a flicker of fear in Sackville-West, the expression flashing through the face so rapidly Devereaux would have been unable to see it without the implant.

All it told Devereaux was that Sackville-West was physically intimidated by Crandall. Nothing new there.

Sackville-West was repeating, "John Swenson. SA Number 34428, inducted February of—"

"I don't like him quoting Chartres," Crandall interrupted.

"I can see that, Rick." Sackville-West responded, nodding effusively. Calling him Rick but in a tone that meant *Yes, sir*. "But—I think it was just his sense of humor. It says here his sense of irony is strong. I'd evaluate the remark as a kind of smug solidarity with us: mocking the resistance."

"I'm not so sure of that," Crandall said. "Have him observed."

"Quite right, Rick—I've already punched out an order to that effect." He tapped in something more on the pocket filer; its tiny keys were almost too small for his pudgy fingers.

Most of Devereaux's attention went to watching Ellen Mae with his fast-action eye. And something flickered across her face—zip, and it was gone. But Devereaux had seen: anxiety. Concern. For—

For Swenson. So they'd already managed to interest her in Swenson...

She glanced at Devereaux, and away. He thought: Mustn't draw attention to myself, rubbing my eye so much.

He opened the left eye and, as if scratching his cheek, switched off the overdrive in the prosthetic one.

Devereaux turned to watch Crandall, who had gone on to comment on the Belgian brief. " . . . I do think, however, that the new disinfo campaign is working very well, and we should continue through the same means—making sure it's as anti-American as anti-Russian. Our friends at NATO"—he smiled, and that was a cue for a companionable chuckle around the table, which dutifully came— "would hardly approve of such indiscrimination, if it came out."

Devereaux smiled and nodded as he was expected to. He glanced at the Security men behind Crandall, essentially mere bodyguards . . . and wondered if they *were* bodyguards. The damn eye-blanking helmets made them maddeningly inscrutable. He thought he felt them watching him.

Don't get nervous, he told himself. Don't think about the job at all. You'll do it when the time comes.

But Crandall was eminently paranoid; his Security knew it, and knew they were expected to be suspicious of everyone. Even now they stood behind him, between him and the window, because Crandall had instantly mistrusted the window when he'd come into the room.

"I just don't like it, my friends," he'd say. "Anybody could frogman right up to the window, fire a subaqueous rocket through it..."

But they were behind schedule, and he'd grudgingly agreed to the room with the glass wall.

Crandall switched the report back on. It droned out troop movement figures, confirming the Russian pullback, reporting the taking of crucial sectors. When it began on Paris, Devereaux felt the pressure rising in him again.

He wondered if the detection-shielding on the gun in his briefcase had been adequate. But they'd have arrested him by now if it hadn't been. He wondered, too, if he could shoot the Security men before Crandall, and still be assured of getting Crandall himself. No. He'd have to get Crandall first. Which meant Security would get him. And Devereaux would die.

He remembered a few lines from Rimbaud.

> *Mon âme eternelle,*
> *Observe ton voeu,*
> *Malgré la nuit seule...*
>
> My eternal soul,
> Redeem your promise,
> In spite of the night alone...

It was a silent prayer of Devereaux's own, as Crandall stood to offer a prayer for the meeting.

The olive-drab simuleather briefcase was on the tabletop beside Devereaux's notetaker. Devereaux laid his hand on the table beside the briefcase.

It was almost time.

Crandall's prayers took about three minutes. Every head in the room was lowered for the prayer, even the guards. Even Devereaux's. But his finger closed on the latch at the corner of the briefcase. The latch that would release the gun into his hand.

Another thirty seconds, he told himself, as Crandall intoned in polished rhythms, "We're asking your help, Lord, in this your battle, in this struggle to free the earth from the bonds of inbred social sin; from the sickness of miscegeny..."

Devereaux had twenty seconds. In those twenty seconds he found himself wondering, remembering—

Stop thinking about it, he told himself. Steinfeld told you, again and again, *When the moment comes, act, don't think. Act, don't think.*

But he saw himself at the New Right meeting, in Nice, raising objections, eliciting odd looks from the other members, realizing that he didn't belong there anymore. Saw himself approached afterward by one of Steinfeld's men. Bashung. Bashung had heard him voice a few cautious misgivings about the proposal to demand that the government oust all recent immigrants from France. Bashung had watched Devereaux through a perceptual prosthetic, identical to the one he now carried in place of his right eye. Had seen the flash of confusion and worry and sorrow and anger the others had missed.

It hadn't taken long to recruit him. They revealed a great many things about Crandall that were usually kept suppressed. They took Devereaux along when they went to record statements by two widows whose husbands had been assassinated by the SA. Bashung and Steinfeld had played video of Crandall's early meetings with his coordinators, at which he made a series of insane statements in tones so calm and measured as to make the hair stand up on the back of Devereaux's neck. Devereaux had entered the New Right chiefly out of his hatred for the Russians. But when you grasped what Crandall's full intentions were...

Crandall made the Russians look like playful imps.

Crandall was the one long awaited, long feared. The one they'd all known would come again.

And Devereaux had been recruited and trained to throw himself deeply into bogus support for the SA, to join the SA's ranks, to ascend to this very room, where he was adviser on the French SA takeover.

Devereaux seemed to hear the words of the boy poet again, the debaucher Rimbaud. *Mon âme eternelle*... My eternal soul...

"And we thank you, Lord," Crandall was saying, "for advancing our struggle. We ask that you take charge now of our eternal souls..."

Redeem your promise...

"In the name of Jesus the Redeemer..."

In spite of the night alone...

"...we stand against the armies of darkness. Praise God, and Amen."

What was the last line of the stanza? There was another line Devereaux had forgotten. It was...

Ah, yes. He remembered, now, as he pressed the switch that ejected the cool grip of the gun into his palm, as the others intoned *Amen.*

He spoke the last two lines aloud as he stood and turned and raised the gun to fire at Crandall. "*Malgré la nuit seule, et le jour en Feu.*"

In spite of the night alone, and the day on fire.

He fired the gun, the Teflon-coated slugs ripping through Crandall's bulletproof vest, but the Security men were already firing back. They *had* been watching him. He tried to track the gun muzzle to Ellen Mae, but the automatic pistols in the hands of the big men had punched holes in him, and he felt a terrible hollowness beneath his feet, as if someone had pulled out the center of the Earth, left it without a core, and it cracked open and he fell into the emptiness and died with a sickening pang of knowing that he hadn't hit Crandall squarely, the bastard would live, the bastard would live...

7

Rickenharp was listening to a collector's item Velvet Underground tape, from 1968. It was capped into his Earmite. The song was "White Light/White Heat." The guitarists were doing things that would make Baron Frankenstein say, "There are some things man was not meant to know." He screwed the Earmite a little deeper so that the vibrations would shiver the bone around his ear, give him chills, chills that lapped through him in harmony with the guitar chords. He'd picked a visorclip to go with the music: a muted documentary on expressionist painters. Listening to the Velvets and looking at Edvard Munch. Man!

And then Julio dug a finger into his shoulder.

"Happiness is fleeting," Rickenharp muttered, as he flipped the visorclip back. Some visors came with camera eye and fieldstim. The fieldstim you wore snugged to the skin, as if it were a sheer corset. The camera picked up an image of the street you were walking down and routed it to the fieldstim, which tickled your back in the pattern of whatever the camera saw. Some part of your mind assembled a rough image of the street out of that. Developed for blind people in the 1980s. Now used by viddy addicts who walked or drove the streets wearing visors, watching TV, reflexively navigating by using the fieldstim, their eyes blocked off by the screen but never quite bumping into anyone. But Rickenharp didn't use a fieldstim.

So he had to look at Julio with his own eyes. "What do YOU want?"

"N'ten," Julio said. Julio the technicki bassist. They went on in ten minutes.

Mose, Ponce, Julio, Murch. Rhythm guitar backup vocals. Keyboards. Bass. Drums.

Rickenharp nodded and reached up to flip the visor back in place, but Ponce flicked the switch on the visor's headset. The visor image shrank like a landscape vanishing down a tunnel behind a train, and Rickenharp felt like his stomach was shrinking inside him at the same rate. He knew what was coming down. "Okay," he said, turning to look at them. "*What?*"

They were in the dressing room. The walls were black with graffiti. All rock club dressing rooms will always be black with graffiti; flayed with it, scourged with it. Like the flat declaration THE PARASITES RULE, the cheerful petulance of symbiosis THE SCREAMIN' GEEZERS GOT FUCKING BORED HERE, the oblique existentialism of THE ALKOLOID BROTHERS LOVE YOU ALL BUT THINK YOU WOULD BE BETTER OFF DEAD, and the enigmatic ones like SYNC 66 CLICKS NOW. It looked like the patterning of badly wrinkled wallpaper. It was in layers; it was a palimpsest. Hallucinatory stylization as if tracing the electron firings of the visual cortex.

The walls, in the few places they were visible under the graffiti, were a gray-painted pressboard. There was just enough room for Rickenharp's band, sitting around on broken-backed kitchen chairs and one desk chair with three legs. Crowded between the chairs were instruments in their cases. The edges of the cases were false leather peeling away. Half the snaps broken.

Rickenharp looked at the band, looked clockwise one face to the next, taking a poll from their expressions: Mose on his left, a bruised look to his eyes; his hair a triple-Mohawk, the center spine red, the outer two white and blue; a smoky crystal ring on his left index finger that matched—he knew it matched—his smoky crystal amber eyes. Rickenharp and Mose had been close. Each looked at the other a little accusingly. There was a lover's sulkiness between them, though they'd never been lovers. Mose was hurt because Rickenharp didn't want to make the transition: Rickenharp was putting his own taste in music before the survival of the band. Rickenharp was hurt because Mose wanted to go minimono wifi act, a betrayal of the spiritual ethos of the band; and because Mose was willing to sacrifice Rickenharp. Replace him with a wire dancer. They both knew it, though it had never been said. Most of what passed between them was semiotically transmitted with the studied indirection of the terminally cool.

Tonight, Mose looked like serious bad news. His head was tilted as if his neck were broken, his eyes lusterless.

Ponce had gone minimono, at least in his look, and they'd had a ferocious fight over that. Ponce was slender—like everyone in the band—and fox-faced, and now he was sprayed battleship gray from head to toe, including hair and skin. In the smoky atmosphere of the clubs he sometimes vanished completely.

He wore silver contact lenses. Flat-out glum, he stared at a ten-slivered funhouse reflection in his mirrored fingernails.

Julio, yeah, he liked to give Rickenharp shit, and he wanted the change-up. Sure, he was loyal to Rickenharp, up to a point. But he was also a conformist. He'd argue for Rickenharp maybe, but he'd go with the consensus. Julio had lush curly black Puerto Rican hair piled prowlike over his head. He had a woman's profile and a woman's long-lashed eyes. He had a silver-stud earring, and wore classic retro-rock black leather like Rickenharp. He twisted the skull-ring on his thumb, returning a scowl for its grin, staring at it as if deeply worried that one of its ruby-red glass eyes was about to come out.

Murch was a thick slug of a guy with a glass crew cut. He was a mediocre drummer, but he was a drummer, with a trap set and everything, a species of musician almost extinct. "Murch's rare as a dodo," Rickenharp said once, "and that's not all he's got in common with a dodo." Murch wore horn-rimmed dark glasses, and he was holding a bottle of Jack Daniels on his knee. The Jack Daniels was a part of his outfit. It went with his cowboy boots, or so he thought.

Murch was looking at Rickenharp in open contempt. He didn't have the brains to dissemble.

"Fuck you, Murch," Rickenharp said.

"Whuh? I didn't say nothing."

"You don't have to. I can smell your thoughts. Enough to gag a faggot maggot." Rickenharp stood and looked at the others. "I know what's on your mind. Give me this: one last good gig. After that you can have it how you want."

Tension lifted its wings and flew away.

Another bird settled over the room. Rickenharp saw it in his mind's eye: a thunderbird. Half made of an Indian teepee painting of a thunderbird, and half of chrome T-Bird car parts. When it spread its wings the pinfeathers glistened like polished bumpers. There were two headlights on its chest, and when the band picked up their instruments to go out to the stage, the headlights switched on.

Rickenharp carried his Stratocaster in its black case. The case was bandaged with duct tape and peeling with faded stickers. But the Strat was spotless. It was transparent. Its lines curved hot like a sports car.

They walked down a white plastibrick corridor toward the stage. The corridor narrowed after the first turn, so they had to walk sideways, holding the instruments out in front of them. Space was precious on Freezone.

The stagehand saw Murch go out first, and he signaled the DJ, who cut the canned music and announced the band through the PA. Old-fashioned, like Rickenharp requested: "Please welcome . . . *Rickenharp.*"

There was no answering roar from the crowd. There were a few catcalls and a smattering of applause.

Good, you bitch, fight me, Rickenharp thought, waiting for the band to take up their positions. He'd go on stage last, after they'd set up the spot for him. Always.

Rickenharp squinted from the wings to see past the glare of lights into the dark snakepit of the audience. Only about half minimono now. That was good, that gave him a chance to put this one over.

The band took its place, pressed their automatic tuners, fiddled with dials.

Rickenharp was pleasantly surprised to see that the stage was lit with soft red floods, which is what he'd requested. Maybe the lighting director was one of his fans. Maybe the band wouldn't fuck this one up. Maybe everything would fall into place. Maybe the lock on the cage door would tumble into the right combination, the cage door would open, the T-Bird would fly.

He could hear some of the audience whispering about Murch. Most of them had never seen a live drummer before, except for salsa. Rickenharp caught a scrap of technicki: "*Whuzziemackzut?*" What's he making with that, meaning: What are those things he's adjusting? The drums.

Rickenharp took the Strat out of its case and strapped it on. He adjusted the strap, pressed the tuner. When he walked onto the stage, the amp's reception field would trigger, transmit the Strat's signals to the stack of Marshalls behind the drummer. A shame, in a way, about miniaturization of electronics: the amps were small, though just as loud as twentieth century amps and speakers. But they looked less imposing. The audience was muttering about the Marshalls, too. Most of them hadn't seen old-fashioned amps. "What's those for?" Murch looked at Rickenharp. Rickenharp nodded.

Murch thudded 4/4, alone for a moment. Then the bass took it up, laid down a sonic strata that was kind of off-center strutting. And the keyboards laid down sheets of infinity.

Now he could walk on stage. It was like there'd been an abyss between Rickenharp and the stage, and the bass and drum and keyboards working together made a bridge to cross the abyss. He walked over the bridge and into the warmth of the floods. He could feel the heat of the lights on his skin. It was like stepping from an air-conditioned room into the tropics. The music suffered deliciously in a tropical lushness. The pure white spotlight caught and held him, focusing on his guitar, as per his directions, and he thought, Good, the lighting guy really is with me.

He felt as if he could feel what the guitar felt. The guitar ached to be touched.

◆

Claire sat on the couch in her apartment, half the size of her father's, and waited, with quiet dread, for the InterColony news show to come on.

The main room of her apartment was now dialed to living room; the furniture changed shape for bedroom when she told it to. The walls around the screen were translucent, impregnated with a rain forest's greens and scarlets. The image shifted to a rain squall, and the enormous tropical leaves bounced in the rainwater, ran with crystal beads. A hidden aerator issued the scents of a jungle in the rain. She could almost feel the rainwater.

The all-media screen—a glaring anomaly in the projection of the jungle—showed a documentary about the European Congress of the New Right. The sound was turned off, but there were subtitles as the French *Front National* leader made a series of—she thought—wildly inflammatory statements with the calm of a TV chef explaining a recipe. The intense, pallid little man was saying "... the inevitability of conflict between cultures with fundamentally different roots can no longer be glossed over. The good intentions of those trying to reconcile Islamic Fundamentalists with Europeans only serve to prolong the pain of social redress. For, I assure you, social redress is necessary. Immigrants from cultures foreign to our own have muddied our cultural waters. It is foolish to assume we will ever occupy the same territory harmoniously. It is naive, unrealistic. This naïveté costs us time, money, yes, human lives. The truth must be faced: some races will always be unable to reconcile! The answer is simple: expulsion. It is out of our hands as to whether we are forced to resort to violence in the execution of our solution to the immigrant problem. Cultural vitality and racial purity are synonymous—"

She turned away, sickened. She sensed some obscure connection between the European situation and the Colony.

She made herself a cocktail spiked with an antidepressant neurohormonal transmitter and sipped it, quickly feeling better—artificially—as she waited for the news.

There it was. She dialed up the sound.

"... Technicki radical leaders Molt and Bonham agreed today in principle to a meeting with Director Rimpler but said they could not schedule the meeting without a close look at security precautions for both sides."

She shook her head sadly, muttering, "They think we're going to arrest them at a meeting. The depth of mistrust . . . " She took another sip of the medicinal-tasting cocktail, thinking, Everything's worse than I thought it was . . .

The news ran highlights from the last talk between Technicki Union leaders and Admin. There was the flatsuiter, Barkin, speaking in his nasal tone about " . . . a conflict of interest in the Colony's housing directors . . . Admin is being puppeted by UNIC to run things according to UNIC's priorities, and its priority is profit, always. Admin maintains that the technicki housing project for the Open would be much costlier than was originally believed, and that's why it was put off—but they haven't put off developing Admin housing. We have completely lost sight of the fact that the UN's matching-funds program for the Colony was offered because Professor Rimpler promised a home to Earth's disadvantaged— the disadvantaged get here and find themselves in overcrowded, badly filtrated dorms—a drearier home than the one they left behind . . . "

Claire nodded, ever so slightly. There was something to it.

And since then the Russians had blockaded the Colony, cutting off shipments of food and other necessities from Earth. They weren't starving yet, but the warehoused supplies were running low. The technickis were reacting to the increased rationing. Admin was rationed, too, but the technickis were skeptical—and maybe they were right, Claire thought. Were Praeger and the UNIC people really eating less?

InterColony was showing a clip of the Colony riots now. One of the Radics, a guy named Molt, with a pipe wrench in his hand leading a charge down Corridor D. Forty technicki men and women followed behind him—including preteen boys carrying what looked like Molotov cocktails. The faces in the crowd looked almost delirious with release. The image was shot from above and to the side; she guessed it was one of the surveillance cameras. Molt was shouting something through bared teeth. He saw the camera, mounted near the ceiling, and turned toward it, ran at the viewer, threw the wrench. The wrench struck the camera lens—

The image went black.

◆

Without consciously knowing it, Rickenharp was moving to the music. Not too much. Not in the pushy, look-at-me way that some performers had. The way they had of trying to *force* enthusiasm from the audience, every move looking artificial.

No, Rickenharp was a natural. The music flowed through him physically, unimpeded by anxieties or ego knots. His ego was there: it was the fuel for his personal Olympics torch. But it was also as immaculate as a pontiff's robes.

The band sensed it: Rickenharp was in rare form tonight. Maybe it was because he was freed. The tensions were gone because he knew this was the end of the line: the band had received its death sentence: Now, Rickenharp was as unafraid as a true suicide. He had the courage of despair.

The band sensed it and let it happen. The chemistry was there, this time, when Ponce and Mose came into the verse section. Mose with a sinuous riffing picked low, almost on the chrome-plate that clamped the strings; Ponce with a magnificently redundant theme washed through the brass mode of the synthesizer. The whole band felt the chemistry like a pleasing electric shock, the pleasurable shock of individual egos becoming a group ego.

The audience was listening, but they were also resisting. They didn't want to like it. Still, the place was crowded—because of the club's rep, not because of Rickenharp—and all those packed-in bodies make a kind of sensitive atmospheric exo-skeleton, and he knew that made them vulnerable. He knew what to touch.

Feeling the Good Thing begin to happen, Rickenharp looked confident but not quite arrogant—he was too arrogant to show arrogance.

The audience looked at Rickenharp as a man will look at a smug adversary just before a hand-to-hand fight and wonder, "Why's he so smug, what does he know?"

He knew about timing. And he knew there were feelings even the most aloof among them couldn't control, once those feelings were released: and he knew how to release them.

Rickenharp hit a chord. He let it shimmer through the room and he looked out at them. He made eye contact.

He liked seeing the defiant stares, because that was going to make his victory more complete.

Because he *knew*. He'd played five gigs with the band in the last two weeks, and for all five gigs the atmosphere had been strained, the electricity hadn't been there; like a Jacob's ladder where the two poles aren't properly lined up for the sparks to jump.

And like sexual energy, it had built up in them, dammed behind their private resentments; and now it was pouring through the dam, and the band shook with the release of it as Rickenharp thundered into his progression and began to sing...

Strumming over the vocals, he sang,

> *You want easy overnight action*
> *want it casually*
> *A neat little chain reaction*
> *and a little sympathy*
> *You say it's just consolation*
> *In the end it's a compensation*
> *for insecurity*
> *That way there's no surprises*
> *That way no one gets hurt*
> *No moral question tries us*
> *No blood on satin shirts*
>
> *But for me, yeah for me*
> *PAIN IS EVERYTHING!*
> *Pain is all there is*

> *Babe take some of mine*
> *or lick some of his*
> *PAIN IS EVERYTHING!*
> *Pain is all there is*
> *Babe take some of mine...*

◆

From "An Interview with Rickenharp: The Boy Methuselah," in *Guitar Player Magazine*, May 2037:

> GPM: You keep talking about group dynamics, but I have a feeling you don't mean dynamics in the usual musical sense.
>
> RICKENHARP: The right way to create a band is for the members to simply find one another, the way lovers do. In bars or wherever. The members of the band are like five chemicals that come together with a specific chemical reaction. If the chemistry is right the audience becomes involved in this, this kind of—well, a social chemical reaction.
>
> GPM: Could it be that all this is just your psychology? I mean, your emotional need for a really organically whole group?
>
> RICKENHARP (after a long pause): It's true I need something like that. I need to belong. I mean—okay, I'm a "nonconformist," but still, on some level I got a need to belong. Maybe rock bands are a surrogate family—the family unit is shot to hell, so . . . the band is family for people. I'd do anything to keep it together. I need these guys. I'd be like a kid whose mom and dad and brothers and sisters were killed if I lost this band.

◆

And he sang,

> *PAIN IS EVERYTHING!*
> *Pain is all there is*
> *Babe take some of mine*
> *Suck some of his*
> *Yeah, said PAIN IS EVERYTHING—*

Singing it insolently, half shouting, half warbling at the end of each note, with that fuck-you tone, performing that magic act: shouting a melody. He could see doors opening in their faces, even the minimonos, even the neutrals, all the flares, the rebs, the chaotics, the preps, the retros. Forgetting their subcultural classifications in the unification of the music. He was basted in sweat under the lights, he was squeezing sounds with his fingers and it was as if he could feel the sounds taking shape in his hands the way a sculptor feels clay under his fingers, and it was like there was no gap between his hearing the sound in his head and its coming out of the speakers. His brain, his body, his fingers had closed the gap, was one supercooled circuit breaker fused shut.

Some part of him was looking through the crowd for the chaotichick he'd spotted earlier. He was faintly disappointed when he didn't see her. He told himself, *You ought to be happy, you had a narrow escape, she would've got you back into boss blue.*

But when he saw her press to the front and nod at him ever so slightly in that smug insider's way, he was simply glad, and he wondered what his subconscious was planning for him . . . All those thoughts were flickers. Most of the time his conscious mind was completely focused on the sound, and the business of acting out the sound for the audience. He was playing out of sorrow, the sorrow of loss. His family was going to die, and he played tunes that touched the chord of loss, in everyone . . .

And the band was supernaturally tight. The gestalt was there, uniting them, and he thought: The band feels good, but it's not going to help when the gig's over.

It was like a divorced couple having a good time in bed but knowing that wouldn't make the marriage right again; the good time was a function of having given up.

But in the meantime there were fireworks.

By the last tune in the set the electricity was so thick in the club that—as Mose had said once, with a rocker's melodrama—"If you could cut it, it would bleed." The dope and smashweed and tobacco smoke moiling the air seemed to conspire with the stage lights to create an atmosphere of magical apartness. With each song-keyed shift in the light, red to blue to white to sulfurous yellow, a corresponding emotional wavelength rippled through the room. The energy built, and Rickenharp discharged it, his Strat the lightning rod.

And then the set ended.

Rickenharp bashed out the last five notes alone, nailing a climax onto the air. Then he walked offstage, hardly hearing the roar from the crowd. He found himself half running down the white, grimy plastibrick corridor, and then he was in the dressing room and didn't remember coming there. The graffiti seemed to writhe on the walls as if he'd taken a psychedelic. Everything felt more real than usual. His ears were ringing like Quasimodo's belfry.

He heard footsteps and turned, working up what he was going to say to the band. But it was the chaotichick and someone else, and then a third dude coming in after the someone else.

The someone else was a skinny guy with brown hair that was naturally messy, not messy as part of one of the cultural subcurrents. His mouth hung a little ajar, and one of his incisors was decayed black. His nose was windburned and the back of his bony hands were gnarled with veins. The third dude was Japanese; small, brown-eyed, nondescript, his expression was mild, just a shade more friendly than neutral. The skinny Caucasian guy wore an army jacket sans insignia, shiny jeans, and rotting tennis shoes. His hands were nervous, like there was something he was used to holding in them that wasn't there now. An instrument? Maybe.

The Japanese guy wore a Japanese Action Suit—surprise, surprise—sky-blue and neat as a pin. There was a lump on his hip—something he could reach by putting his right arm across his body and through the open zipper down the front of the suit—and Rickenharp was pretty sure it was a gun.

There was one thing all three of them had in common: they looked half-starved.

Rickenharp shivered—his gloss of sweat cooling on him, but he forced himself to say, "Whusappnin'?" It was wooden in his mouth.

He was looking past them, waiting for the band.

"Band's in the wings," the chaotichick said. "The bass player said to tell you... well it was *Telm zassouter.*"

Rickenharp had to smile at her mock of Julio's technicki. Tell him, get his ass out here.

Then some of the druggy feeling washed away and he heard the shouts from the audience and he realized they wanted an encore.

"Jeez, an encore," he said without thinking. "Been so fucking long."

"'Ey mate," the skinny guy said, pronouncing mate like *mite*. Brit or Aussie. "I saw you at Stone'enge five years ago when you 'ad yer second 'it."

Rickenharp winced a little when the guy said *your second hit*, inadvertently underlining the fact that Rickenharp had had only two, and everyone knew he wasn't likely to have any more.

"I'm Carmen," the chaotichick said. "This is Willow and Yukio." Yukio was standing sideways from the others, and something about the way he did it told Rickenharp he was watching down the corridor without seeming to.

Carmen saw Rickenharp looking at Yukio and said, "Cops are coming down."

"Why?" Rickenharp asked. "The club's licensed."

"Not for you or the club. For us."

He looked at her and said, "Hey, I don't need to get busted..." He picked up his guitar and went into the hall. "I got to do my encore before they lose interest."

She followed along, into the hall and the echo of the encore stomps, and asked, "Can we hang out in the dressing room for a while?"

"Yeah, but it ain't sacrosanct. You come back here, the cops can, too." They were in the wings now. Rickenharp signaled to Murch and the band started playing.

Standing beside him, she said, "These aren't exactly cops. They probably don't know these kind of places, they'd look for us in the crowd, not the dressing room."

"You're an optimist. I'll tell the bouncer to stand here, and if he sees anyone else start to come back, he'll tell 'em it's empty back here 'cause he just checked. Might work, might not."

"Thanks." She went back to the dressing room. He spoke to the bouncer and went on stage. Feeling drained, the guitar heavy on him. But he picked up on the energy level in the room and it carried him through two encores. He left them wanting more—and, sticky with sweat, walked back to his dressing room.

They were still there. Carmen, Yukio, Willow.

"Is there a stage door?" Yukio asked. "Into alley?"

Rickenharp nodded. "Wait in the hall; I'll come out and show you in a minute."

Yukio nodded, and they went into the hall. The band came in, filed past Carmen and Yukio and the Brit without much noticing them, assuming they were backstage hangout flotsam, except Murch stared at Carmen's tits and swaggered a bit, twirling his drumsticks.

The band sat around laughing in the dressing room, slapping palms, lighting several kinds of smokes. They didn't offer Rickenharp any; they knew he didn't use it.

Rickenharp was packing his guitar away, when Mose said, "You blew good."

"You mean he gave you a good head?" Murch said, and Julio snickered.

"Yeah," Ponce said, "the guy gives a good head, good collarbone, good kidneys—"

"Good kidneys? Rick sucks on your kidneys? I think I'm gonna puke."

And the usual puerile band banter because they were still high from a good set and putting off what they knew had to come, till Rickenharp said, "What you want to talk about, Mose?"

Mose looked at him, and the others shut up.

"I know there's something on your mind," Rickenharp said softly. "Something you haven't come out with yet."

Mose said, "Well, it's like—there's an agent Ponce knows, and this guy could take us on. He's a technicki agent and we'd be taking on a technicki circuit, but we'd work our way back from there, that's a good base. But this guy says we have to get a wire act in."

"You guys been busy," Rickenharp said, shutting the guitar case.

Mose shrugged, "Hey, we ain't been doing it behind your back; we didn't hear from the guy till yesterday night. We didn't have a real chance to talk to you till now, so, uh, we have the same personnel but we change costumes, change the band's name, write new tunes."

"We'd lose it," Rickenharp said. Feeling caved-in. "We'd lose the thing we got, doing that shit, because it's all superimposed."

"Rickenharp—rock 'n' roll is not a fucking religion," Mose said.

"No, it's not a religion, it's a way of life. Now, here's *my* proposal: we write new songs in the same style as always. We did good tonight. It could be the beginning of a turnaround for us. We stay here, build on the base audience we established tonight."

It was like throwing coins into the Grand Canyon. You couldn't even hear them hit bottom.

The band just looked back at him.

"Okay," Rickenharp said. "Okay. We've been through this ten fucking times. Okay. That's all." He'd had an exit speech worked out for this moment, but it caught in his throat. He turned to Murch and said, "You think they're going to keep you on, they tell you that? Bullshit! They'll be doing it without a drummer, man. You better learn to program computers, fast." Then he looked at Mose. "Fuck you, Mose." He said it quietly.

He turned to Julio, who was looking at the far wall as if to decipher some particularly cryptic piece of graffiti. "Julio, you can have my amp, I'll be traveling light."

He turned and, carrying his guitar, walked out, leaving silence behind him.

He nodded at Yukio and his friends and they followed him to the stage door. At the door, Carmen said, "Any chance you could help us find a little cover?"

Rickenharp needed company, bad. He nodded and said, "Yeah, if you'll gimme a hit of that blue boss."

She said, "Sure." And they went into the alley.

◆

FirStep. The Colony.

They all had to sit on the floor in Bitchie's because there weren't enough chairs. And Molt didn't want some of them on chairs and some on the floor. He wanted them all on the same level, where he could make easy eye contact.

There were twenty-two of them, eighteen men and four women, sitting in a circle on the mattress-covered floor. They were technickis just off the shift, or waiting to go on shift. The little room was fuggy with their smell; the air cycler in this part of the space colony was overtaxed. Had been wafting them green air lately anyway.

Wilson was going on, and on, his technickese slurring the sentences together so the monologue sounded like one big sentence, even translated: "... so the thing to do is to push for confrontation and then stop short of the actual confrontation and hold the confrontation out as a threat to make them deal with us because if we really push it and get down to fighting with them we're going to lose but even though they know they're going to win they still don't want the confrontation because it's going to endanger the Colony's air-tigh integ and it'll cost them a few men and it'll be expensive to repair everything that gets busted so I think we oughta ... "

On and on. Molt had had enough. Wilson was short, thick-bodied, his blond hair had been flared into a corona-shape, was losing its shape like a dying dandelion; he had small, squinty blue eyes and a bulbous nose, little red mouth always going, probably got an in with the pharmacy techs for uppers. Wearing his greasy air-systems mechanic's overalls. Wilson wanted badly to be a radic leader. Molt and Bonham and Barkin were the acknowledged leaders, and Wilson muttered about it because Molt and Bonham weren't real technickis, spoke it with the accent of someone raised in Standard English. Molt's opinion was: Wilson was a grasping scheming runt. Molt had tried to keep Wilson out of this meeting, but the little prick had wormed in, nudged his friends about till they got Barkin to invite him. Little prick'd sell out his granny, Molt thought.

Molt broke in on him with, "You had it a minute ago, Wilson, when you said they're scared of confrontation even though they'd win it. But you didn't carry it far enough." Though of course Molt said it in technicki. "They're scared enough of it, what we got to do is, hit 'em harder, go for it—we got more power than they want to admit because they're scared we'll—"

Bonham broke in, "There's something else we could do."

Molt glared at Bonham. He didn't like being interrupted. And he was beginning to mistrust Bonham, too. All their chumminess had evaporated when they got to be rivals in the new party. Bonham, sitting beside Wilson, shifted, wincing, to keep his long legs from going to sleep, ran his fingers through his hair with that goddamn Che Guevara look on his face, going on, "We could put up a barricade. Several. Take control of the heart of technickitown. That's a confrontation, but then again it isn't. I mean, a *big* barricade, maybe block off Corridor D completely."

"They'd be on us before we got it half done," Barkin said. No flatsuit today, Molt noticed. The fucking hypocrite wearing mech's overalls, like he ever ventured into the repair hangars. He was squatting in a way that kept him from coming into direct contact with the greasy mattress, except for the bottom of his feet. Doesn't want to get dried cum and sweat from Bitchie's customers on his legs. Nice clean mech overalls, probably bought 'em at a costume shop. Christ.

Bonham shook his head. "We stage a diversion, smoke bombs, whatever, up at the main crossover. We have forklifts, everything else we need, get most of it in place in no time."

"You defend a barricade in Corridor D," Molt said, "you got to use guns and you got to shoot to kill. Because they won't stand for a barricade, they'll rush it right off."

Wilson shook his head like a terrier with earmites. "No, hey, I think Bonham's right we'd just fire warning shots, capture some territory, they wouldn't want to move in right away because it'd force confrontation and they don't want that, leastways not yet . . . "

"I'm not so sure they don't want that," Barkin said, but no one was listening, except Molt. They were all jabbering at once now, hot on the idea of a barricade. And then a whistle came through the intercom, signal that the admin bulls were coming down the corridor, were going to raid Bitchie's, so the radics started moving out according to the drill, going out into the little service hallway and through the kitchen; the bulls would find the place empty . . .

But how did they know about the meeting?

8

IT HURT with every breath. But after a while that particular pain was part of the rhythm of being alive, was almost reassuring, and Smoke ceased to take much notice of it. The monotony, and the bedlam noises and smells of the place—that's what was hard to take. He tried to keep himself amused by guessing where he was, what was going on. But the body cast (and damn its itching!) kept him from looking around much. And there was no one who spoke English near him, at first. After a couple of days, he worked out that he was in Belgium, southeast of Brussels, in some kind of military hospital.

After they'd put on the body cast he'd spoken to the doctor only once. "You are lucky," the doctor said, in a heavy Belge accent. "We find no brain damage. Zare ess some internal bleeding and we stop it. You have fracture breastbone, fracture arm, fracture collarbone. Slight concussion. Burns—second degree, not zo bad. You are lucky alzo zince we have..." And then he said something in Belgian.

"What's that?" Smoke asked.

"A machine puts a current in zuh broken places of the bone, helps to heal faster. Good-bye." There was finality in that good-bye, and Smoke never saw him again except out of the corner of his eye as he ghosted around the beds of other patients in the big hospital dorm room.

"He is a bastard of a Belge," said the man next to him. A Frenchman. That was all Smoke could tell about him, because his casts made it impossible to turn and look that far to the side. "The Belge are imbeciles, all Belge," the Frenchman said. "And this electricity cure, this will kill you *bientôt*."

It hurt Smoke too much to talk, at that point, so he didn't reply, and that was their entire conversation. Two days later the Frenchman died.

Sometimes Smoke played with the pain. It came in waves, and when the waves were in a peak, the pain was something palpable. He had always had what he thought of as his inner hand. It was the area low in his chest where he felt the center of his sensations. The place that glows for gratifications and aches for emotional hurt. Sometimes he felt he could shape the locus of sensation there into a kind of ectoplasmic hand—he knew it wasn't ectoplasm, but he pictured it that way—and he could imagine reaching with that hand into other parts of his body, to test them. Reach into the left leg and it will tingle with sensitivity. If it was in pain, he could reach in and touch the pain. Now when the waves of pain came strongest, he reached out his inside hand and caught the waves of pain in the hand and parted them, split them up, or squeezed them like something gelatinous between fingers of internal self-sensation; and this "contact" produced, in his mind's eye, a kind of rainbow-on-oil shimmer he watched with childlike fascination. In this way the pain became objectified into visual terms, and was rendered neutral, defused. The pain became almost painless.

But sometimes the misery of the ward overwhelmed him. The sick were in cots and their cots were everywhere; there were, lately, men laid out on the floor. The place stank, of course, and sometimes the smell was given the extra pungency of humiliation when much of the stink came from himself—the overworked nurses were slow about his bedpans. And the noise of the place diminished at night, but it never ceased. There was moaning and, always, bitching in four or five languages. There were men babbling obscenities, an unceasing bubbling over of mental ugliness, and that was perhaps the worst. He was perversely grateful for the occasional *CRUMP* and quaking of the shellings—or were they bombs?—in the countryside around the hospital. They made it possible to visualize a world outside the infinitely monotonous grind of life in the hospital.

For a time some of the patients were refugees, adding the sirening of wailing children to the dissonant symphony of complaints bouncing from the ceiling. But there was a rule about the hospital being used only for NATO soldiers—Smoke heard a British Red Cross nurse complain about it—and the refugees were moved out to a camp where, it was said, death was certain for the very ill. There wasn't enough food to go around in the refugee camps. In keeping with triage, critically ill refugees simply were not fed.

Smoke had seen the Dutch refugee camps. Had heard the stories... Stories of a hundred thousand, two hundred thousand—an ever-swelling multitude of the displaced and homeless tramping the roads outside the European cities. At first they'd fled the war in cars—but the highways had become impassable with rubble and craters, and anyway fuel was hard to get. Now they walked, or pulled carts—often whole families pulling a cart made of a small stripped-down fiberglass car, propane or electric engines removed. Legions of people yoked to automotive shapes, as if enslaved to serve cars... Part of a dust cloud in summer, slogging through icy mud in the winter; learning about trenchfoot and scurvy, cholera and hepatitis, gangrene and lice. Some formed tribes for self-protection. The tribes were usually ethnocentric, which festered racial awareness. People who, before the war, had been indifferent to their neighbor's race, were reviling the "scheming Jews hoarding food" or the "thieving Arabs, steal your last crust if you're not watching with a gun in your hand!" By some unspoken consensus, the roads were usually a neutral place, where the tribes merged into one mass of tramping, weeping, cursing, death-eyed misery. Thousands more took to sea in improvised boats and those who didn't founder and drown sometimes found refuge in the Middle East, in Israel and Egypt; a few thousand were admitted to Scotland; thousands more to Canada and the USA. But the anti-immigrant feeling was strong in North America, now, with the global warming crisis and the propaganda, and the quota was quickly filled. The flow of refugees to America became a trickle and then stopped with the near-cessation of civilian air and sea traffic over the Atlantic.

Most of the refugees were trapped in Europe. And most had been cosmopolitan urbanites, whose major baseline concerns before the war had been the acquisition of new technology, or car repair, or money for the August holidays. And now their worries were food, water, weapons, shelter, warmth, medicine. The refugee camps provided enough food to prolong the suffering, but not enough to generate the energy to find a way out of the suffering. The camps were called "the shitpits" by the English speakers. Camp shelters were made from waterproofed cardboard, which turned out to be waterproof for only three or four rainfalls. At first the refugee camps were clean, and run like military bases, dreary but livable. But as the war dragged on the volunteers fell sick, or lost heart; the military could no longer spare men to help out; the Russians blockaded emergency-civilian supplies, believing they might also be supply ships for NATO. The Second Alliance was involved in shipping relief supplies, and Steinfeld claimed they diverted much of it for their own use. The camps swelled and rotted, teeming with people the way cysts teem with bacteria. Riots against the camp administration flared—and quickly died out. They accomplished nothing. But inter-tribal melees followed by guerrilla warfare became a fact of life, as one refugee racial group attacked another for food and medical supplies. And here and there were the advance agents of the Second Alliance, quietly distributing small amounts of food, and great bags of promises. Recruiting those the SA saw as having "special potential." These would disappear from the refugee camps, would turn up later in the Second Alliance, unswervingly loyal to the organization that had brought them out of starvation and squalor and hopelessness, shown them purpose and order and a reinforcement of their most cherished prejudices...

Smoke wondered for a while if he would be taken to one of the refugee camps, since he was no NATO soldier. But an orderly wheeling him for the bone-healing treatment, referred to him as "the American soldier." Perhaps he would be taken from the hospital when they discovered the mistake. Or perhaps Steinfeld had arranged this "mistake." Why? It must have cost him several favors. Why had Steinfeld done so much for him? Steinfeld was not an altruist by reflex. Steinfeld was a man obsessed.

Working on the fringes of the New Resistance operation, Smoke had picked up pieces of Steinfeld's history, had fitted them together. Smoke was sometimes privy to intelligence about the NR which didn't reach its rank and file. He had learned that Steinfeld had once been a field operative for the Mossad: Israeli intelligence.

Steinfeld had operated a listening post and then had been promoted to field officer, running agents. As Mossad field officer Steinfeld had run-ins with agents of the Second Alliance as they went about their recruiting. He became interested in them and gathered evidence that their ranks were riddled with active anti-Semites, including men who, decades before, had sheltered the doddering, wheelchair-bound Nazi war criminals from war crimes investigators. Steinfeld became a bit shrill in trumpeting the dangers of the Second Alliance to the Mossad. He was believed to have lost his objectivity. This, combined with his known sympathy for the Palestinians, cost him his post. He was pressured into resigning. He set up his own network, "going indie," at first cadging funds here and there from sympathizers—some said even from Palestinians. Now, an American businessman named Quincy Witcher paid Steinfeld's bills. And no one was quite sure why.

Steinfeld had his sympathizers in the Mossad; occasionally one of these gave him intelligence, or a little extra credit-grease, or food, or weapons. The Mossad brass pretended not to know about this, because Steinfeld was still useful to them. But he was also on their yellow list: the list of those who would be assassinated, should the correct juxtaposition of circumstances arise; should Steinfeld be viewed as dangerous. There were those who would have relegated Steinfeld to the red list: assassinate ASAP. *Suppose he was captured?* they argued. *He has seen us on the inside; there is much he knows.* Still, over tea in commissaries and wine in the better restaurants in Tel Aviv, it was decided that Steinfeld would not be shot or blown up or poisoned, at least not right away. Not by the Mossad. After all, he was doing work that was useful to the Mossad, but which they could truly disavow.

Lying rigid in his plaster carapace like a paralyzed lobster, staring at the same grime spots on the yellowing ceiling week after week,

Smoke thought about Steinfeld a great deal. So it was somehow not a great surprise when Steinfeld came to see him. It was as if Smoke had conjured him.

Steinfeld was wearing a blue nylon windbreaker. It rode up a little on his big belly. The New Resistance was based in Paris now, which was relatively comfortable compared to Amsterdam.

"Looks like there's more to eat in Paris," Smoke rasped when Steinfeld sat carefully on an unsoiled corner of Smoke's bed.

Steinfeld smiled and nodded. He looked at the IV stand, then at the lesions on Smoke's forearm. "You don't look so bad," he said. "Except for this arm. What's this?"

"It became infected," Smoke said. "The IV needle. They put it in the wrong place a few times, missed the vein. What's worse is when they forget to change the bottle. The damn thing empties and turns vampire, sucks blood out of me. The blood runs up the tube. Hurts like the devil."

Steinfeld said, "They have too much to do."

"I know. I don't complain—anyway, they ignore complaints."

"But once," Steinfeld said, looking at him, "you tried to tell them you are not a soldier, that you should not be here. So I heard."

"They don't listen no matter what you say."

"If they had, you'd probably be dead by now. Do you still have a death wish, Smoke?" Steinfeld asked.

Smoke said nothing.

"I think you do. That's the only problem with it."

"With what?"

Steinfeld said, "With the fact that you owe me now, Smoke."

Smoke said, with a faint smile, "I see."

Steinfeld nodded.

"You have plans for me," Smoke said.

Now it was Steinfeld's turn to say nothing.

"It itches in this cast," Smoke said. It was good to have someone to complain to.

"Yes. And the food here is . . . ?"

"Execrable," Smoke said.

"Go on," Steinfeld said.

"They rarely change the sheets," Smoke said with alacrity, "and they rarely turn me. I get bedsores, which they sometimes allow to become infected. Then they give me a general antibiotic, and the sores ease, and then they forget to turn me and the sores come back. And so forth. The crying of the others is an assault on sanity."

"I would say that it is better to be in such a place than dead in a shell of a building in Amsterdam—given that you won't be here forever. But we come again to the problem of your death wish."

"Are the others alive? Hard-Eyes and the others?"

"So far as I know. I've been away from Paris for a while."

There was something more that Smoke wanted to ask, but he felt foolish. And in this place there was little dignity; what one could scrape up, one hoarded.

He didn't have to ask it, as it happened: Steinfeld guessed what was in Smoke's mind. "The crow lived, and came along to the boat. I have it in my flat, in Paris. Someone's taking care of it."

Smoke felt an absurdly profound relief.

Steinfeld stood up. He took a chocolate bar and a vitaminpak from his pocket and put them in Smoke's usable hand.

"They're giving me a treatment with electric currents to heal the bones," Smoke said to keep Steinfeld there just a little longer. "A Frenchman told me it would hurt me, but I think it's helping. The pain is much less. It's just a few weeks since they started doing it."

Steinfeld nodded. "It works. We'll come to get you when they decide the casts can come off."

He turned to go. Smoke said quickly, desperately, "Tell me something. Anything. I need something to think about. You have plans for me. Tell me about it. Something."

"There isn't much I can say here."

"Then only what you *can* say."

Steinfeld nodded at the IV bottle. "I'll see to it they refill that thing."

"Tell them to take it away. I don't need it. Tell me something, Steinfeld."

Steinfeld took a deep breath, tugged at his beard, blew the breath out again. He looked at Smoke. "I know who you are. I found out the day before the jumpjet hit us. For a while I too thought Smoke was a nickname."

"Wait—" Smoke felt he was going to choke.

But Steinfeld bulled grimly on. "You don't want me to talk about it. You've become expert in not thinking about it, and you don't want me to undermine that expertise. Tough. You wanted something to think about. So think about this: you're Jack Brendan Smoke. You're American. You were in Amsterdam when the war broke out, to see a psychiatrist at the Leydon clinic. Before that, you won the United Nations Literary Committee prize for your *Search for a Contemporary Reality*. You were the spokesman for all the people who felt lost in the accelerated rate of change. You wrote a second series of essays in which you said, generally, that there were people manipulating the Grid for political ends, and you named Worldtalk. You predicted a return of fascism and you quoted something you'd heard about the Second Circle, the secret inner circle of the Second Alliance. The ones who make the SA's long-term goals . . . That essay was never published. Evidently someone at your publishing company was SA. Some men came to the clinic in ski masks. You were taken in the night and they—"

"Please . . . " A great weight on his chest made it hard to breathe. "Steinfeld . . . "

"They tortured you. They gave you a drug that made you feel that you were choking . . . "

He stopped, seeing Smoke was gagging. He waited. After a minute the spasm passed.

Smoke lay staring at the ceiling, breathing shallowly.

"I'm going to go on, Smoke," Steinfeld said.

Smoke just lay there.

Steinfeld said, "They wanted to know who you got the information from. About the Second Circle. You didn't tell them. They tortured you in many ways. In many imaginative ways. And then the choking drug, again. They tried to move you to another place, where they had access to extraction. You escaped, en route, and went back to the hospital, where you broke down completely. You were sent in secret to another clinic. The men would have found the clinic anyway, eventually, would have come for you again—if not for the war. That was the day the Russian tanks crossed into Germany. And a little while later the Russians were moving in on Amsterdam, and they shelled the city. Your clinic was shelled. Almost everyone killed..."

"I was in my safe, locked room," Smoke said, taking it up in a small voice. "But then the wall was blown in. I went to get someone to put the wall back. They were all dead. Except Dr. Van Henk. I saw him—his face was bloody. The sight of him bloody like that frightened me. I don't know why it affected me so strongly—I ran from him, we lost sight of each other in all the burning. Was it Van Henk who—?"

"Yes. I had this from Van Henk. He's still alive. So far as I know."

"I was the only patient not killed. Wherever I went there were only the dead. I wandered out of there. Sometimes the choking, from the drug—it would start again. It seemed to come back, maliciously, after me. The choking and the dead everywhere... For a long time I couldn't remember who I was. When I could remember—I wanted to forget again. Wanted to be someone else..." His voice was cracked glass.

Steinfeld said, "Sometimes your face looked familiar to me. But under all that grime... and the way a man gets wasted..." He shrugged. "So you wanted me to tell you something. There's this: you were a great writer. A great speaker, great humanist. The torture didn't break you—but then again it did. Even so, Smoke: you could help us. In the States the only ones who believe that the fascists are coming again are the ones trying to help them. As for the others—" He shook his head sadly. "Worldtalk pushes their buttons. But if people keep speaking up in the underGrid... You *could* help us! People remember you."

Smoke said, "I *can't*."

"Sometimes I see a man who's broken, or bent by torture, and I know he'll never change. Never heal. When I saw you with that crow," he smiled ruefully, "I knew you would heal. That meant the other possibilities I saw in you could become real. Now you have something to think about."

Steinfeld nodded, once, to say good-bye and went away. Leaving Smoke to just lie there, staring at the ceiling.

◆

Hard-Eyes and Jenkins were walking through the Parc Monceau. It was the flaccid end of late afternoon; the trees stood leafless and stark as nude crones. The forest looked dead, and misty wet, all grays and blue shadows and browns leached of life. But the smell of moldering leaves was good. Hard-Eyes inhaled it in hungry breaths and the cold air bit at his sore nostrils; pins and needles danced in his cheeks.

The HK-21 assault rifle in his hands was cold as a stone crucifix and felt nearly as heavy. He was tired; he was hungry. One meal a day was not enough.

"Steinfeld promised us more to eat," Jenkins complained.

Hard-Eyes had been thinking the same thing, but he said, "We're lucky to get what they give us. You get a look at that refugee camp outside town?"

Jenkins grunted. "You got a point." His hands were red from cold on the blue steel and plastic stock of his assault rifle. They'd traded in the Weatherby and the .22 for more practical weapons.

Hard-Eyes glanced over his shoulder, wondering why the instructors were hanging back so far. And then he stopped.

He couldn't see them at all now.

"They're fucking with us, Jenkins," Hard-Eyes said.

Jenkins stopped and they watched the trail behind them, expecting to see their guerrilla-warfare instructors strolling around the bend, through the attenuated bristle of bluish underbrush. Nothing.

There were no bird sounds. There had been, a few minutes before.

Hard-Eyes swallowed.

"Those guys don't like us," Jenkins said, his voice hushed. "What'd they say about 'robber packs'?"

"Said we hadda be careful because the noise of the gunfire might attract robber packs. Guys that live on the other side of the park, in the shack slum over there."

"Shit!—you think they set us up?"

"Steinfeld wouldn't risk men like that."

"But I'm telling you *these guys don't like us*. They've decided that Americans suck. They think we're CIA or some shit. And Steinfeld ain't around."

"They don't like us but they wouldn't—" He broke off, staring through the mist. There were men coming out of the woods.

The trees to the right of the trail were not thickly dispersed. The well-spaced trunks came together in the compression of distance, becoming a corrugated wall of gray about fifty yards away. From here it looked like a solid wall of trees. So when the men came out of that solid-seeming wall it looked as if they were squeezed out, like man-shaped drops of liquid. They looked as gray as the tree trunks, except there were smears of orange-pink for faces and pencil-thin strokes of blue-black and brown in their hands. Rifles.

Hard-Eyes counted eight and after that stopped counting. And looked for a place to run to. To his left was a broad, cracked parking lot. The French government scarcely existed now, and the skeleton of it that remained had no resources for park maintenance, so the parking lot was choked with blown branches and leaves; here and there were the rusty humps of stripped and abandoned cars. But the cars were too far away to be used for cover. He and Jenkins would be shot in the back if they ran across the parking lot.

The trail up ahead looked safer, but the instructors had told them, "When pressed, ask yourself if this is a situation when we must disperse—or regroup? The answer depends on the nature of the enemy and their position with relation to your own unit's command."

If Hard-Eyes ran ahead, the enemy would become a wedge between Hard-Eyes' unit and the unit's command, the instructors. The command would be threatened, hemmed in by the enemy and when possible he was to regroup to protect command.

So Hard-Eyes said, "Back down the trail."

Jenkins said, "Shit, man—"

"Come on!"

The pack was close enough so that Hard-Eyes could make out the features in the orange-pink smudges. He turned and ran.

Hard-Eyes thought, This isn't the enemy, this is a bunch of half-starved Parisians hoping we'll be carrying something valuable or edible.

And he thought, The instructors have set us up so the robber pack becomes "the enemy." Like this is a war game where the other side doesn't know it's playing a game.

And then he thought, The fucking instructors are hoping we'll get our asses blown away. Or maybe we'll burn down a few of these problem thugs for them.

. . . As he heard the first popping sounds, and the echoes like a sheet of aluminum shaken to simulate thunder. A piece of turf threw itself in the air near his feet. Irrationally, he leapt back, as if the bit of jumping ground itself were the threat.

Hard-Eyes ran on, Jenkins a little behind and falling farther behind. The trees danced crazily past; the sky made a jerky windshield wiper movement. He ran past a tree and it spat bark at him; a piece of yellow wood-flesh showed where the bullet had scored away bark.

He heard Jenkins returning fire behind him, a thudding rattle, probably no hope of hitting anyone, trying to suppress them.

Thirty feet ahead the trail sank into thickets of blue bushes. There was not much cover at the opening of the trail between the bushes. If the pack got directly behind them, they would simply stop and shoot down the line of the trail, and cut them down.

If they reached that first bend, cutting left into the bushes, they might make it.

But just then Jenkins stumbled and gave a strangely high-pitched cry as he went down, skidding over the iron-hard, iron-cold earth, his rifle clattering. Hard-Eyes wanted to run on, part of his mind already making up excuses.

But he stopped. Huffing and cursing, he turned, going upstream against his own impulse to *get the fuck out*, fighting the current in himself. He heard a scornful humming, and he knew that a bullet had missed his head by an inch or two. Jenkins was getting to his knees, puffing. How could they miss him? He was such a big target! Hard-Eyes bent and tried to help him up, but Jenkins shook his arm off—both of them annoyed—and said, "Just cover me," as he reached for his rifle.

Hard-Eyes turned and opened up without aiming, the automatic rifle jumping in his hand; he felt like a fool when he saw that he'd shot six holes in the bole of a tree between him and the pack. Then he saw one of them coming at him from the right. The man paused about forty feet away and raised the rifle to his shoulder, aiming, like a man shooting at rabbits. He had a big nose, weak chin, gaunt cheeks. He wore a tagged brown cap. He fired. The bullet cut the air overhead. The man struggled to reload his rifle . . .

Hard-Eyes swiveled the HK-21 and fired another burst from the hip. He had ludicrous mental images of himself as a boy taking turns with his big brother cutting the lawn because when you started the lawn-mower it made a noise like the assault rifle. He saw himself spraying a water hose at his brother—shooting an automatic weapon sometimes felt like shooting a high-pressure water hose at someone; when you were close enough to the enemy with no time to aim, you pointed the hose, raking back and forth, and hoped for the best. The man in the brown cap spun half around and staggered, dropped his rifle, but didn't fall. He looked confused, then he turned and ran, holding his side. Wounded. Others were coming on through the trees, spread out. Hard-Eyes emptied the magazine at them, firing in little bursts. They dodged behind trees for cover—and then Hard-Eyes realized that Jenkins was up and running for the brush.

Hard-Eyes ran after him. Someone on his left shot at him. He felt a tightening sensation at the left side of his head: entirely psychosomatic; that was the place he imagined the bullets would hit him. Anticipating the sickening crack of a bullet impacting. Jenkins was about ten feet ahead, running with a wallowing motion, with poor coordination, looking as if he'd like to throw the encumbering rifle away.

And then the brush was sweeping past and Hard-Eyes felt a surge of relief as he turned the bend in the trail. For the moment he was out of their line of sight. Up ahead the trail stretched straight for a ways. That would be a good place to get shot in the back.

"Jenkins!" he hissed. "Hey—go find the instructors, I'm gonna be here in the brush on the left side, left side going this way, don't shoot in it when you come back even if you hear gunfire in it 'cause that'll be me!" He couldn't be sure Jenkins heard, but Hard-Eyes thought he saw him bob his head in response.

Hard-Eyes angled left, then pressed close to the brush, turned to move back up, parallel to the trail. The brush here hooked in a question-mark shape, roughly, and he was moving up the stem of the question mark toward the inside of its hook. The pack was on the other side of the hook. He was breathing hard as much from fear as exertion, his breath smoking out white in front of him, and he thought, What if they see my breath steam above the brush; they'll know my position...

He heard a babble of voices in French. He pressed into the wall of brush at the hook of the question mark, biting his lip to keep from yelling when a twig stung his right eye, other tiny jags raking his cheek and neck and hands.

He turned sideways to elbow deeper into the brush, thinking, Maybe this is stupid, maybe the brush will just hold me in place and I won't be able to run, and they'll see me in here and shoot into it till they get me.

He scrunched down, so that the thicker part of the brush was over him, and he felt better about it, because he could move here, the branches making arches over him. He heard voices and footsteps. He began to worm between the thick, horny stems of the bushes toward the bottleneck in the trail, dragging the rifle in his right hand, trying to keep dirt out of it. Pulling himself along on his elbows. The cold ground sent an ache up through his elbow bone. His cheek itched fiercely where the twigs had lashed him. His eye burned where it'd been scratched. It hurt when he blinked.

He could see the trail through the screen of brush now. He brought the rifle up and wedged it into firing position against his shoulder, about thirty degrees out of alignment with his body, his elbows planted, the breech propped in his hands, and sighted at the trail. And then he heard the French voices again and knew they were arguing. Some wanted to go down the trail into the brush. Others thought it might be too dangerous. Then three of them trotted down the trail, in a formation neat as bowling pins. He angled the rifle up a little more and then thought, Shit, I didn't put another clip in it! Idiot!

He laid the gun down, quietly, carefully, as they drew abreast of him. The front man was just fourteen feet away, ten feet beyond the screen of brush. Hard-Eyes reached behind him, fished in his pack. The angle was awkward. He ground his teeth in frustration. The man was walking past. Still fishing in the pack, Hard-Eyes felt something metallic cold under his fingers. He drew it out and looked at it. A full clip. He ejected the other clip and slapped the full one in—and heard a shot. Someone was bending to look in the brush. A rifle barked and a piece of twig lopped neatly in two, fell delicately across his rifle barrel.

Hard-Eyes sighted on the guy crouching in the trail. He took a deep breath, let it out, and when it had gone out of him and his body was still before the next breath, he squeezed the trigger—and at the same time the other man fired. Something sizzled past Hard-Eyes' right cheek. The man who'd shot at him did a little dance of frustration, dancing backward—no, that's not what he was doing, he was staggering back as Hard-Eyes' assault rifle stitched three rounds into his chest. Hard-Eyes expected to see bloodied holes but the places the bullets struck looked like black dots. The guy fell. Hard-Eyes kept firing, raking, centering the sights on the silhouettes of two other running men...

The rifle kicking his shoulder, acrid blue smoke clinging to the arching brush just overhead. A twig smoldering from muzzle flash. His ears aching with the detonations, the vibrations.

The men had stopped running. Were all, like him, on the ground; but they were on their backs. One of them making a mewling sound and a pedaling motion with his feet. Another turning to vomit blood. Hand clawing the ground. Twitching. Then not moving at all.

Hard-Eyes waited, but no one else came down the trail. After a while, when his hands were going stiff with cold, his elbows aching, his cheek throbbing, he heard Jenkins shout something. And then French voices behind him, and he knew one as the petulant voice of one of his instructors.

There was another sound: *wham wham wham wham wham wham*. After a moment he realized it was the sound of his heart pounding. He was amazed that he could hear it so clearly.

He wormed up, thrust head and shoulders out of the brush just enough to look down the trail both ways. He saw no one either way, except the dead. The three men he'd shot were all dead now. They weren't silhouettes anymore. But he couldn't help noticing that one of them was just a boy. Maybe fifteen. A boy with a rifle gripped in his white hands.

He stood up and brushed thorns and dried leaves off himself, feeling dizzy but energized.

Thinking, with more wonder than regret: They were just hungry. That's really all it was.

His instructors came around the bend in the trail, their rifles raised.

"Hold your fire!" Hard-Eyes yelled. Or tried to. The words came out mush because his mouth was numb from cold. His right ear felt cold too. Funny: just the right one.

They slowed, looking at him. They were frowning. He knew they'd have some complaint about how he'd done it. Jenkins was right: They didn't like Americans. But Hard-Eyes knew he'd mostly done it right.

Jenkins came lumbering along. He stared at Hard-Eyes open-mouthed.

"Your ear," he said. "You lost an ear."

◆

Molt was walking down the corridor, thinking he'd got off at the wrong level. It felt like Level 02. He felt heavier here than he should.

The corridor was deserted, which he thought was strange, too. It should be work time in this section. Wilson had said they'd meet on Level 00. He was sure of that. He was sure he'd pressed 00. But he saw a coordination indicator, Level 03, Corridor C13—no indicator for function.

He was in a part of the Colony he'd never been in before. The walls were the same kind of utilitarian studded gray metal you found down in Recycling or around a power station.

I pressed 00, he thought. I'm sure I did.

He turned to go back to the elevator. A section of the ceiling four inches wide slid down to become a wall, in front of him, ceiling down to floor. *Zi-ip*: that fast. It was a transparent wall, plastic but thick, and he knew he'd never be able to break it. He stared, feeling a panic of the sort he hadn't felt since having his first really bad childhood nightmares. He touched the wall to be sure it was real.

He looked around, gut clenching with a growing suspicion.

He'd pressed 00, but the elevator had taken him to 03. The bastards could control the elevators independently. Of course. They had brought him here.

He looked down the hall. There were other sections of the ceiling that looked as if they could slide down. He was sure he hadn't seen a ceiling like that at launch level or at the dorms. But he had seen them somewhere. Around Admin—when you went to Admin to get your pay chit stamped you saw ceilings with those sections in them, and you wondered what they were . . .

He backed away from the transparent wall, turned, and ran. He got forty feet. Ten feet ahead of him another section of wall slid down. He was boxed in.

He slowed, the run becoming a trot and then a walk. He walked up to the wall and pressed his forehead against it, looking down the stretch of empty corridor on the other side. He was breathing hard, clouding the transparent plastic. He slammed his fist against the wall—three times, almost fracturing the bones of his hand. He knew he couldn't break the wall. He hit it to let them know how he felt. Because he knew they were watching him.

He looked at the metal corridor walls between the transparent barriers, wondering . . . what next? Poison gas maybe? Or maybe he'd be ejected into space. No. The liberal wimps in Admin—at least on the Rimpler side of the board—didn't have the honesty to do it that way.

There was a door in one of the walls. It was opening.

Slowly, sliding back into the wall. It whirred faintly.

Molt thought, I'm expected to walk through there. Fuck that.

He moved to where he could look through the door without standing too near it. Through the doorway he saw an almost bare room. There was a rectangular panel in the wall that would be the cot, when it was pulled out. There was a toilet, a sink, a shower stall. Air-conditioning vents—not big enough to crawl through. That was all. A detention cell.

He sat down with his back to the wall across from the door. He wasn't going to give them the satisfaction of seeing him walk in here. Not right away.

He wondered, idly, why they'd done it this way. If they'd tracked him, why hadn't they sent the bulls in to arrest him?

Because the sneaky bastards knew if they'd sent the bulls in, it would have been a political act. It would have martyred him. They had to do it so no one would see. This way they could spread rumors he'd deserted to the other side or gone into hiding. Make him look like a coward.

Wilson. That skeevy runt must have sold him out.

He looked around, wondering where the cameras were. He looked at the ceiling and nodded to himself. Somewhere in the ceiling, one of those panels is two-way.

He stood up and dropped his pants . . .

◆

In the Admin conference room, they sat around a table shaped like a backward S and watched Molt on the screen. Molt dropped his pants, took hold of his dick, waved it at them, pointed at it with his other hand, and mouthed, clearly, *Suck this, you motherfuckers.*

Claire winced and looked away.

The curves of the S-table were softly contoured. Praeger sat inside the curve across and to the left from Claire. Her father sat in the form-fitting chair across from her. Ganzio, the Brazilian UNIC rep, sat to her immediate left, scowling. He'd been here for an inspection visit—and had been stranded when the Russians had blockaded the Colony. He wanted to go home.

Judith Van Kips, the Afrikaner rep, sat to Ganzio's left. To Van Kips' left sat Messer-Krellman, officially the union rep appointed by UNIC—puppeted by UNIC. Across from Messer-Krellman was Scanlon, the Colony Security chief.

The room was lit with soft, shadowless indirection. On Claire's far right, at one end of the cornerless, roughly rectangular room was the screen, and on the screen was Molt. On Claire's left, opposite the screen, was a bronze sculpture of a flock of birds taking flight from a pond.

Claire glanced at Molt, saw he was doing something even more obscene now, and fastened her eyes on the sculpture—with almost equal distaste. The sculpture seemed as false, as abstract and convenient, as UNIC's protestations of classless fairness. Everyone will have a chance here, Admin had been saying over InterColony channel. Everyone will have an opportunity to move into the Open when the time comes. When the blockade is lifted, we'll discuss pay raises and greater recreational credits. But in the meantime...

In the meantime they discussed security measures.

"Isolating this man isn't going to isolate the rebellion," Claire said. "The rebellion is widely supported. And it'll continue to be supported in the Colony—as long as we're hypocritical. We complain of not having money to improve their housing, but we sink four million newbux into expanding the security system—well before the rebellion began. And two million more into Admin housing improvements—"

Scanlon said, "Looks like we improved security not a moment too soon. The riots..."

"The riots don't *have to be*," Claire said wearily. "There would be no riots if the technickis were given what they were promised in the Articles. The technickis are convinced we've betrayed their trust."

"Are they really convinced?" Praeger asked. "I think not." Praeger was half-bald, and his pinkish head always made Claire think of a pencil eraser rounded by use. His eyes were weak, and he had some kind of phobia of implantation eye operations, so he wore thick, rimless glasses. His lips were bloodless, the same color as the skin of his face. He was thick-bodied, an athletic man—something you wouldn't think he'd be, looking at his head—and muscular under the gray three-piece suit. "They're reacting to stimuli, according to their social programming. They could just as easily react another way—with other stimuli. And if we're wise, we'll provide that."

"And let them know only what we want them to know," Rimpler said suddenly, startling them with his humorous tone. "And if they find out about the rest—tell them it's a communications problem." The "communications problem" was a reference to Praeger's failing to inform Rimpler of the emergency while he was on vacation. Praeger had claimed he'd given the order to a subordinate, who'd failed to implement it by simple oversight. In due course Praeger had produced a subordinate who claimed to be responsible for the error. The man had been put on pay suspension, and probably been well paid off. "Just a little commun-i-ca-shuns prob-lemmmm," Rimpler said, dreamily singsong. Making Claire think of the dormouse at the mad tea party. And making her think, What's happening to him?

Van Kips sighed. "I really think there's no point in dragging that one over the coals again, Doctor." Pursing her lips—the severest expression she allowed herself. Or, perhaps, that Praeger allowed her. Supposedly, she worshiped Praeger. She was an implausibly beautiful woman. Shaped to some artist's conception. Metal-flake blue eyes; a model's narrow, doe-elegant face. Her long, perfectly straight flaxen hair was parted in the middle, to fall over her shoulders with impossible artfulness. She wore a dove-gray suit and white silk blouse; the suit clung to her tall, willowy body when she moved. But now she sat rigidly upright, her hands folded in her lap. Moving only her eyes when she looked at someone.

"At this point," Praeger said, "it's meaningless to try to pin down the cause of the riots. First, we must quell the riots, the vandalism, the strikes. If we come out now and say, Yes, you're right, we've been remiss—well, that would encourage them in the idea that violence is the way to get through to us. The violence must cease before we concede anything."

"I sure have to agree with that, Bill," Scanlon said, in his faint Southern accent. He was a big, boyish-looking man, with tired eyes and a lot of seams in his wide, friendly face. Friendly face, and he'll have a jolly twinkle in his eye, Claire thought, when he gets around to ordering my arrest. "If we give in now we'll have to give in every time they threaten us. Things'll just get worse—for them and for us, too." He shifted in his seat and waited for a response, smiling like an angel. Claire remembered having heard he was some kind of born-again Christian.

"For them and for us, too?" Claire said. "That 'them and us' mentality is one of our problems. I move we release the prisoners Security took during the riots, on their own recognizance. Just to ease the tension a bit. Then we try to set up another meeting with the Radics—and we allow them to send a technicki representative to the meetings. Those aren't such great concessions."

"Jack here," Praeger said, nodding toward Messer-Krellman, "represents them. He's the union rep, is he not?" Messer-Krellman was a ferret-faced man with a bored expression and a habit of sighing after each statement.

"Yes, I seem to recall that's my function," he said sarcastically and sighed, looking with mild reproach at Claire.

Claire shook her head. "It should be a *technicki* rep! Born and bred a technicki! Someone who speaks technicki because he was raised in it. Jack has simply lost their confidence. It wouldn't be a concession to—"

"It would," Praeger said. "Because it's on their list of demands. Along with the release of so-called political prisoners. His demands." Nodding now at the screen. At Molt.

"Look at him," Judith Van Kips muttered, shaking her head. "This is one of the technicki leaders. You'd want someone like this at our meetings? *Here?*"

"He's not a technicki, actually," Claire said. "Not precisely... We'd pick someone more, um—"

"Look at him," Van Kips repeated, hissing it.

On the screen, Molt was pivoting in a circle, wagging his dick at each point of the compass.

Judith Van Kips made a noise of revulsion. "The man is evidently on drugs."

Rimpler shook his head. "I think not." He chuckled. "Molt knows we're watching, but he doesn't know where we are, so he's saying fuck you in every direction, just to make sure we get the message."

"You seem to approve, Doctor," Ganzio commented. He was a slim, dark man with a mustache so neat-edged it looked stenciled, and small, forever-shifting black eyes. He wore a gold-colored suit, which everyone privately thought vulgar.

"Oh, no, no," Rimpler said airily. "But one has to admire his nerve."

Molt was making an even ruder gesture now, and Praeger stabbed a finger at the tabletop's terminal. The image on the screen reticulated, folded into itself, was replaced with a view of the Strip. There was a crowd around the café, listening to someone standing on a table speak. Praeger punched for a close-up on the speaker. The image zoomed in. It was Bonham. They didn't have the audio on, but the crowd looked mesmerized by the speech. "Now, there's a fellow with talent," Praeger said. "Suppose he was speaking for *our* benefit. And suppose we controlled the technicki TV channel. If we provided the right stimuli, the technickis would drop their inane, self-indulgent rebellion of their own initiative. Willingly."

Claire felt a chill. She looked to her father, wishing he'd take some active part in supporting their side of things. He was looking wistfully at the refreshment panels in the wall across from him, probably wanting to dial up a cocktail.

Maybe it had been a mistake to insist he come to the meeting at all, Claire thought. He had changed, in the last few years. In the beginning, her father had considered the Colony an extension of himself, and, if anything, he'd been a micromanager, too fervently responsible for its development and maintenance. And then Mother had left him, refusing to make the move to the Colony. He'd considered it a personal betrayal. Claire had been almost relieved by the divorce, really—she'd never felt close to her mother. The woman was cold, self-involved... As if to compensate for his wife's betrayal of his dream—she had called the Colony "a vanity unprecedented in the history of mankind" and "a monument to the misbegotten"—Rimpler was more control-compulsive than ever.

But with Terry's death, he began to change. At first he became, by turns, defensive, sullen, inward. That stage had also been marked by feverish overwork.

And then he'd collapsed, in Admin Central Command, after spending twenty straight hours overseeing the installation of the new computer system—and dealing with all the problems that arose while the old system was down. Then came another stage, a sort of manic-depressive period. Claire suspected he was using his pass to the pharmaceuticals storerooms too liberally. He'd begun using intermediaries to hire girls out of Bitchie's and the other technicki Afters. And he became increasingly abstracted at work—as if he was thinking only of getting home, to another sexual psychodrama...

Still—he'd done what was expected of him, as an administrator—until the riots, and the news that he'd debauched right through a Colony life-support emergency. He reacted as if the Colony itself had rejected him. And he buckled under the psychological disorientation brought on by the sudden loss of control. Became childlike, prone to tantrums. Now, too often, she found herself forced into the role of chiding mother. He seemed to enjoy seeing her in that role—and at the same time he was afraid of her. More than once she'd found herself sick inside with self-disgust when she'd realized he'd drawn her into some almost incestuous dominatrix-style role-playing. She'd refused to play along—and he withdrew even more into drugs, drink, the search for oblivion—and when the real world intruded on his quest for oblivion, he responded by jeering at the thing he'd devoted most of his life to building...

What was it Praeger had said?

... *provided the right stimuli the technickis would drop their inane, self-indulgent rebellion of their own initiative. Willingly.*

Claire took a deep breath and turned to Praeger. "You feel they can be swayed with a broader media campaign. It won't work. Not with the blockade building up the pressure, making everyone a little more afraid every day ... "

Praeger said, "Media campaign?" He seemed abstracted. He smiled faintly. "Not precisely. Nothing so transparent . . . I think we've lost sight of the problem at this meeting. The problem is sabotage! The problem is a life-support risk! *This is a life-threatening emergency,* Claire! For their sakes as well as—well, for everyone's sakes, we have to take the reins in our hands. All of the reins."

Claire looked at the screen. "They're not so stupid as to damage the life supports. They don't want to eat vacuum any more than we do."

"When people get excited," Praeger said calmly, "they tend to forget common-sense considerations. The thing could get out of control—farther out of control than any one of them would like. An individual technicki is logical—a mob of technickis is not."

"And you propose to defuse them by taking control of their media? That'll only infuriate them!"

"You misunderstand me. I mean—we'll control it indirectly. They won't know we're doing it, if we do it right."

"But that's ... " She was at a loss for words. She looked again to her father. But he was standing up.

"Well, it's been delightful," Rimpler said. Smiling vacantly. He walked to the door, without saying anything more; without even looking around. Leaving her alone with them.

Claire grated, "Dad! Dammit—take some responsibility!"

He paused at the door, turned to her the look of a bad little boy caught doing what he shouldn't.

She looked away. Scornfully: "Oh, forget it. Go on."

He shrugged, turned, and opened the door. She thought, Maybe he manipulated me. Knew I couldn't handle that little-kid shit. Knew that'd force me to let him go ...

Scanlon was looking thoughtfully after Rimpler. Something icy-cold about the expression on Scanlon's face frightened Claire.

Rimpler closed the door behind him—effectively closing the door on his leadership in Colony Admin.

Praeger was gazing at the screen. "This man Bonham could be very useful to us," he said.

Messer-Krellman said, "I believe Claire made a motion a little while ago. Does anyone second it? Should we vote on it?" He liked the formalities. And he knew how the vote would turn out.

"Don't bother," Claire said. "I suggest we table any further action till 0900 tomorrow. We all need to think about this. Just keep in mind: the situation is explosive, with the blockade of the Colony. They know the Colony is blockaded, they know resources will run low. They're going to be more insistent than ever—you won't be able to manipulate them." She got up and followed her father out the door.

She paused for a moment before going out, and looked over her shoulder.

Van Kips and Praeger were looking at the screen. Praeger said something to Van Kips. She nodded.

Feeling helpless, Claire left the room.

9

RICKENHARP PUT on his dark glasses, because of the way the Walk tugged at him.

The Walk wound through the interlinked Freezone outfloats for a half-mile, looping up and back, a hairpin canyon of arcades crusted with neon and glowflake, holos and screens. It was involuted, intensified by layering and a blaze of colored light.

Stoned, very stoned: Rickenharp and Carmen walked together through the sticky-warm night, almost in step. Yukio walked behind, Willow ahead, and Rickenharp felt like part of a jungle patrol formation. And he had another feeling: that they were being followed, or watched. Maybe it was suggestion, from seeing Yukio and Willow glance over their shoulders now and then...

Rickenharp felt a ripple of kinetic force under his feet, an arc of wallow moving in languid whiplash through the flexible streetstuff, telling him that the breakers were up today, the baffles around the artificial island feeling the strain.

The arcades ran three levels above the narrow street; each level had its own sidewalk balcony; people stood at the railing to look down at the segmented snake of street traffic. The stack of arcades funneled a rich wash of scents to Rickenharp: the frenchfry toastiness of the fast food; the sweet harshness of smashweed smoke, gyno-smoke, tobacco smoke—the cloy of perfumes; the mixed odors of fish-ka-bob stands, urine, rancid beer, popcorn, sea air; and the faint ozone smell of the small, eerily quiet electric cars jockeying on the street. His first time here, Rickenharp had thought the place smelled wrong for a red light cluster. "It's wimpy," he'd said. Then he'd realized he was missing the bass-bottom of carbon monoxides. There were no combustion cars on Freezone. Some parts of America still permitted pollutive, resource-greedy gasoline cars, and Rickenharp, being a retro, had preferred those places.

The sounds splashed over Rickenharp in a warm wave of cultural fecundity; pop tunes from thudders and wrist-boxes swelled in volume as they passed, the guys exuding the music insignificant in comparison to the noise they carried, the skanky tripping of protosalsa or the calculatedly redundant pulse of minimono.

Rickenharp and Carmen walked beneath a fiberglass arch—so covered with graffiti its original commemorative meaning was lost—and ambled down the milky walkway under the second-story arcade boardwalk. The multinational crowd thickened as they approached the heart of the Walk. The soft lights glowing upward from beneath the polystyrene walkway gave the crowd a 1940s-horror-movie look; even through the dark glasses the place tugged at Rickenharp with a thousand subliminal come-hithers.

Rickenharp was still riding the blue mesc surf, but the wave was beginning to break; he could feel it crumbling under him. He looked at Carmen. She glanced back at him, and they understood one another. She looked around, then nodded toward the darkened doorway of a defunct movie theater, a trash-cluttered recess twenty feet off the street. They went into the doorway; Yukio and Willow stood with their backs to the door, blocking the view from the street, so that Rickenharp and Carmen could each do a double hit of blue mesc. There was a kind of little-kid pleasure in stepping into seclusion to do drugs, a rush of outlaw in-crowd romance to it. On the second sniff the graffiti on the padlocked, fiberglass doors seemed to writhe with significance. "I'm running low," Carmen said, checking her mesc bottle.

"Running low on drugs? Whoever heard of *that* happening?" Rickenharp said and they both burst in peals of laughter. His mind was racing now, and he felt himself click into the boss blue verbal mode. "You see that graffiti? *You're gonna die young because the ITE took the second half of your life.* You know what that is? I didn't know what ITE was till yesterday. I used to see those things and wonder and then somebody said—"

"Immortality something or other," she said, licking blue mesc off her sniffer.

"Immortality Treatment Elite. Supposedly some people keeping an immortality treatment to themselves because the government doesn't want the public to live too long and overpopulate the place. Another bullshit conspiracy theory."

"You don't believe in conspiracies?"

"I don't know—some. Nothing that far-fetched. But—I think people are being manipulated all the time. Even here ... this place tugs at you, you know. Like—"

Willow said, "Right, we'll 'ave our sociology class later children, you gotter? Where's this place with the bloke can get us off the fooking island?"

"Yeah, okay, come on," Rickenharp said, leading them back into the flow of the crowd—but seamlessly picking up his blue mesc rap. "I mean, this place is a Times Square, right? You ever read the old novels about that place? That was the archetype. Or some places in Bangkok. I mean, these places are carefully arranged. Maybe subconsciously. But arranged as carefully as Japanese florals, only with the inverse esthetic. Sure, every whining, self-righteous tightassed evangelist who ever preached the diabolic seductiveness of places like this was right—in a way—was fully justified 'cause, yeah, the places titillate and they seduce and they vampirize people. Yeah, they're Venus's-flytraps. Architectural Svengalis. Yes to all the clichés about the bad part of town. All the reverend preachers— Reverend who, Reverend—what's his name?—Rick Crandall ... "

She looked sharply at him. He wondered why but the mesc swept him on.

"All the preachers are right, but the reason they're right is why they're wrong, too. Everything here is trying to sell you something. Lots of lights and whirligig suction to seduce you into throwing your energy into it—in the form of money. People mostly come here to buy or to be titillated up to the verge of buying. The tension between wanting to buy and the resistance to buying can give you a charge. That's what I get into: I let it tickle my glands, but I hold back from paying into it. You know? Just constant titillation but no orgasm, because you waste your money or you get a social disease or mugged or sold bad drugs or something... I mean, anything sold here is pointless bullshit. But it's harder for me to resist tonight..." *Because I'm stoned.* "Makes you susceptible. Receptive to subliminals worked into the design of the signs, that gaudy kinetics, those fucking on/off bulbs—makes you flash on the old computer-thinking models, binomial thinking, on-off, on-off, blink blink—all those neon tubes, pulling you like the hypnotist's spiral pendant in the old movies... And the kinds of colors they use, the energy of the signs, the rate of pulse, the rate of on/offing in the bulbs, all of it's engineered according to principles of psychology the people who make them don't even know they're using, colors that hint about, you know, glandular discharges and tingly chemical flows to the pleasure center... like obscenities you pay for in the painted mouth of a whore... like video games... I mean—"

"I know what you mean," she said, in desperation buying a waxpaper cup of beer. "You must be thirsty after that monologue. Here." She shoved the foaming cup under his nose.

"Talking too much. Sorry." He drank off half the beer in three gulps, took a breath, finished it, and it was paradise for a moment. A wave of quietude soothed him—and then evaporated mesc burned through again. Yeah, he was wired.

"I don't mind listening to you talk," she said, "except you might say too much, and I'm not sure if we're being scanned."

Rickenharp nodded sheepishly, and they walked on. He crushed the cup in his hand, began methodically to shred it as they went.

Rickenharp luxuriated in the colors of the place, colors that mixed and washed over the crowd, making the stream of hats and heads into a living swatch of iridescent gingham; shining the cars into multicolored lumps of mobile ice.

You take the word *lurid*, Rickenharp thought, and you put it raw in a vat filled with the juice of the word *appeal*. You leave it and let the acids of appeal leach the colors out of *lurid*, so that you get a kind of gasoline rainbow on the surface of the vat. You extract the petrorainbow on the surface of the vat with cheesecloth and strain it into a glass tube, dilute heavily with oil of cartoon innocence and extract of pure subjectivity. Now run a current through the glass tube and all the other tubes of the neon signs interlacing Freezone's Walk.

The Walk, stretching ahead of them, was itself almost a tube of colored lights, converging in a kaleidoscope; the concave fronts of the buildings to either side were flashing with a dozen varieties of signs. The sensual flow of neon data in primary colors was broken at cunningly irregular intervals by stark trademark signs: SYNTHLIFE SYSTEMS and MICROSOFT-APPLE and NIKE and COCA-COLA and WARNER AMEX and NASA CHEMCO and BRAZILIAN EXPORTS INTL and EXXON ELECTRICS and NESSIO. In all of that only one hint of the war: two unlit signs, FABRIZZIO and ALLINNE—an Italian and a French company, killed by the Russian blockades. The signs were unlit, dead.

They passed a TV-shirt shop; tourists walked out with their shirts flashing video imagery, fiberoptics woven into the shirtfront playing the moving sequence of your choice.

Sidewalk hawkers of every race sold beta candy spiked with endorphins; sold shellfish from Freezone's own beds, tempura'd and skewered; sold holocube pornography key rings; sold instapix of you and your wife, oh that's your boyfriend . . . Despite the nearness of Africa, black Africans were few here: Freezone Admin considered them a security risk and few on the contiguous coast could afford the trip. The tourists were mostly Japanese, Canadian, Brazilians— riding the crest of the Brazilian boom—South Koreans, Chinese, Arabs, Israelis, and a smattering of Americans; damned few Americans anymore, with the depression. Screens scanned them, one of them caught Rickenharp with a facial recognition program and on it a sexy animated Asian woman cooed, *"Rick Rickenharp— try Wilcox Subsensors and walk in a glow of excitement . . . "*

As they got deeper into the Walk the atmosphere became even more hot-house. It was a multicolored steam bath. The air was sultry, the various smokes of the place warping the neon glow, filtering and smearing the colors of signs and TV shirts and DayGlo jewelry. High up, between the not-quite-fitted jigsaw parts of signs and lights, were blue-black slices of night sky. At street level the jumble was given shape and borders by the doors opening on either side: by people using the doors to check out malls and stimsmoke parlors and memento shops and cubey theaters and, especially, tingler galleries. Dealers drifted up like reef fish, nibbling and moving on, pausing to offer, "DH, gotcher good Dee Ech": Direct Hookup, illegal cerebral pleasure center stimulation. And drugs: synth-cocaine and smokeable herbs; stims, and downs. About half of the dealers were burn artists, selling baking soda or pseudostims. The dealers tended to hang on to Rickenharp and Carmen because they looked like users, and Carmen was wearing a sniffer. Blue mesc and sniffers were illegal, but so were lots of things the Freezone cops ignored. You could wear a sniffer, carry the stuff, but the understanding was, you don't use it openly, you step into someplace discreet.

And whores of both sexes cruised the street, flagrantly soliciting. Freezone Admin was supposed to regulate all prostitution, but black-market pros were tolerated as long as somebody paid off the beat security and as long as they didn't get too numerous.

The crowd streaming past was a perpetually unfolding revelation of human variety. It unfolded again and a specialty pimp appeared, pushing a man and woman ahead of him; they had to hobble because they were straitjacket-packaged in black-rubber bondage gear. Their faces were ciphers in blank black-rubber masks; aluminum racks held their mouths wide-open, intended to be inviting, but to Rickenharp whispered to Carmen, "Victims of a mad orthodontist!" and she laughed.

Studded down the streets were Freezone security guards in bulletproofed uniforms that made Rickenharp think of baseball umpires, faces caged in helmets. Their guns were locked by combination into their holsters; they were trained to open the four-digit combination in one second.

Mostly they stood around, gossiped on their helmet radios. Now two of them hassled a sidewalk three-card-monte artist—a withered little black guy who couldn't afford the baksheesh—pushing him back and forth between them, bantering one another through helmet amplifiers, their voices booming over the discothud from the speakers on the download shops:

"WHAT THE FUCK YOU DOING ON MY BEAT SCUMBAG. HEY BILL YOU KNOW WHAT THIS GUY'S DOING ON MY BEAT."

"FUCK NO I DUNNO WHAT'S HE DOING ON YOUR BEAT."

"HE'S MAKING ME SICK WITH THIS RIP-OFF MONTE BULLSHIT IS WHAT HE'S DOING."

One of them hit the guy too hard with the waldo-enhanced arm of his riot suit and the monte dealer spun to the ground like a top running out of momentum, out cold.

"LOITERING ON THE ZONE'S WALKS, YOU SEE THAT BILL."

"I SEE AND IT MAKES ME SICK JIM."

The bulls dragged the little guy by the ankle to a lozenge-shaped kiosk in the street and pushed him into a man-capsule. They sealed the capsule, scribbled out a report, pasted it onto the capsule's hard plastic hull. Then they shoved the man-capsule into the kiosk's chute. The capsule was sucked by mail-tube principle to Freezone Lockup.

"Looks like they're using some kind of garbage disposal to get rid of people here," Carmen said when they were past the cops.

Rickenharp looked at her. "You weren't nervous walking by the cops. So it's not them we're avoiding, huh?"

"Nope."

"You wanna tell me who it is we're supposed to be avoiding?"

"Uh-uh, I do not."

"How do you know these out-of-town cops you're worried about haven't gone to the locals and recruited some help?"

"Yukio says they won't, they don't want anybody to scan what they're doing here because the Freezone admin don't like 'em."

Rickenharp guessed: the *who* they were avoiding was the Second Alliance. Freezone's chairman was Jewish. The Second Alliance could *meet* in Freezone—the idea was, the place was open to anyone for meetings, or recreation; anyone, even people the Freezone boss would like to see gassed—but the SA couldn't *operate* here, except covertly.

The fucking SA bulls! Shit! . . . The blue mesc worked with his paranoia. Adrenaline spurted, making his heart bang. He began to feel claustrophobic in the crowd; began to see patterns in the movement around him, patterns charged with meaning superimposed by his own fear-galvanized mind. Patterns that taunted him with, *The SA's close behind.* He felt a stomach-churning combination of horror and elation.

All night he'd worked hard at suppressing thoughts of the band. And of his failure to make the band work. *He'd lost the band.* And it was almost impossible to make anyone understand why that was, to him, like a man losing his wife and children. And there was the career. All those years of pushing for that band, struggling to program a place for it in the Grid. Shot to hell now, his identity along with it. He knew, somehow, that it would be futile to try to put together another band. The Grid just didn't want him; and he didn't want the fucking Grid. And the elation was this: that ugly pit of displacement inside him closed up, was just gone, when he thought about the SA bulls. The bulls threatened his life, and the threat caught him up in something that made it possible to forget about the band. *He'd found a way out.*

But the horror was there, too. If he got caught up in this . . . if the SA bulls got hold of him . . .

Fuck it. What else did he have?

He grinned at Carmen, and she looked blankly back at him, wondering what the grin meant.

So now what? he asked himself. *Get to the OmeGaity. Find Frankie.* Frankie was the doorway.

But it was taking so long to get there. Thinking. The drug's fucking with your sense of duration. Heightened perception makes it seem to take longer.

The crowd seemed to get thicker, the air hotter, the music louder, the lights brighter. It was getting to Rickenharp. He began to lose the ability to make the distinction between things in his mind and things around him. He began to see himself as an enzyme molecule floating in some macrocosmic bloodstream—the sort of things that always OD'd him when he did an energizing drug in a sensory-overflow environment.

What am I?

Sizzling orange-neon arrows on the marquee overhead seemed to crawl off the marquee, slither down the wall, down into the sidewalk, snaking to twine around his ankles, to try to tug him into a tingler emporium. He stopped and stared. The emporium's display holos writhed with fleshy intertwinings; breasts and buttocks jutted out at him, and he responded against his will, like all the clichés, getting hard in his pants: visual stimuli; monkey see, monkey respond. He thought: *Bell rings and dog salivates.*

He looked over his shoulder. Who was that guy with the sunglasses back there? Why was he wearing sunglasses at night? Maybe he's SA—

Noooo, man. *I'm* wearing sunglasses at night. Means nothing.

He tried to shrug off the paranoia, but somehow it was twined into the undercurrent of sexual excitement. Every time he saw a whore or a pornographic video sign, the paranoia hooked into him as a kind of scorpion stinger on the tail of his adolescent surge of arousal. And he could feel his nerve ends begin to extrude from his skin. After having been clean so long, his blue-mesc tolerance was low.

Who am I? Am I the crowd?

He saw Carmen look at something in the street, then whisper urgently to Yukio.

"What's the matter?" Rickenharp asked.

She whispered, "You see that silver thing? Kind of a silvery fluttering? There—over the cab . . . Just look, I don't wanna point."

He looked into the street. A cab was pulling up at the curb. Its electric motor whined as it nosed through a heap of refuse. Its windows were dialed to mercuric opacity. Above and a little behind it a chrome bird hovered, its wings a hummingbird blur. It was about thrush-sized, and it had a camera-lens instead of a head. "I see it. Hard to say whose it is."

"I think it's run from inside that cab. That's like them. They'll send it after us from there. Come on." She ducked into a tingler gallery; Willow and Yukio and Rickenharp followed her. They had to buy a swipe card to get in. A bald, jowly old dude at the counter took the cards, swiped them without looking, his eyes locked on a wrist-TV screen. On his wrist a miniature newscaster was saying in a small tinny voice, "... attempted assassination of SA director Crandall today..." Something mumbled, distorted. "... Crandall is in serious condition and heavily guarded at Freezone Medicenter..."

The turnstile spun for them and they went into the gallery. Rickenharp heard Willow mutter to Yukio, "The bastard's still alive."

Rickenharp put two and two together.

The tingler gallery was predominantly fleshtone, every available vertical surface taken up by emulsified nude humanity. As you passed from one photo or holo to the next, you saw the people in them were inverted or splayed or toyed with, turned in a thousand variations on coupling, as if a child had been playing with unclothed dolls and left them scattered. A sodden red light hummed in each booth: the light snagged you, a wavelength calculated to produce sexual curiosity. In each "privacy booth" was a screen and a tingler. An oxygen mask that dropped from a ceiling trap pumped out a combination of amyl nitrite and pheromones. The tingler looked like a twentieth-century vacuum cleaner hose with an oversized salt-shaker top on one end: You watched the pictures, listened to the sounds, and ran the tingler over your erogenous zones; the tingler stimulated the appropriate nerve ends with a subcutaneously penetrative electric field, very precisely attenuated. You could pick out the guys in the health-club showers who'd used a tingler too long: use it more than the "recommended thirty-five-minute limit" and it made your skin look sunburned. One time Rickenharp's drummer had asked him if he had any lotion: "I got 'tingler dick,' man."

"To phrase it in the classic manner," Yukio said abruptly, "is there another way out of here?"

Rickenharp nodded. "Yeah... Uh—somewhere."

Willow was staring at a teaser blurb under a still-image of two men, a woman and a goat. He took a step closer, squinting at the goat. "You looking for a family resemblance, Willow?" Rickenharp said.

"Shut your 'ole, ya retro greaser."

The booth sensed his nearness: the images on the sample placard began to move, bending, licking, penetrating, reshaping themselves with a weirdly formalized awkwardness; the booth's light increased its red glow, puffed out a tease of pheromone and amyl nitrite, trying to seduce him.

"Well, where *is* the other door?" Carmen hissed.

"Huh?" Rickenharp looked at her. "Oh! I'm sorry, I'm so—uh I'm not sure." He glanced over his shoulder, lowered his voice. "The bird didn't follow us in."

Yukio murmured, "The electric fields on the tinglers confuse the bird's guidance system. But we must keep a step ahead."

Rickenharp looked around—but he was still stoned: the maze of black booths and fleshtones seemed to twist back on itself, to turn ponderously, as if going down some cubistic drain...

"I will find the other door," Yukio said. Rickenharp followed him gratefully. He wanted out.

They hurried through the narrow hall between tingler booths. The customers moved pensively—or strolled with excessive nonchalance—from one booth to another, reading the blurbs, scanning the imagery, sorting through fetishistic indexings for their personal libido codes, not looking at one another except peripherally, carefully avoiding the margins of personal-space.

Chuffing, sighing music played from somewhere; the red lights were like the glow of blood in a hand held over a bright light. But the place was rigorously Calvinistic in its obstacle course of tacit regulations. And here and there, at the turns in the hot, narrow passageways between rows of booths, bored security guards rocked on their heels and told the browsers, *No loitering please, you can purchase more time at the front desk.*

Rickenharp flashed that the place wanted to drain his sexuality, as if the vacuum-cleaner hoses in the booths were going to vacuum his orgone energy, leave him chilled as a gelding.

Get the fuck out of here.

Then he saw EXIT, and they rushed for it, through it.

They were in an alley. They looked up, around, half expecting to see the metal bird. No bird. Only the gray intersection of styroconcrete planes, stunningly monochrome after the hungry chromatics of the tingler gallery.

They walked out to the end of the alley, stood for a moment watching the crowd. It was like standing on the bank of a torrent. Then they stepped into it, Rickenharp, blue mesc'd, fantasizing that he was getting wet with the liquefied flesh of the rush of humanity as he steered by sheer instinct to his original objective: the OmeGaity.

They pushed through the peeling black chessboard doors into the dark mustiness of the OmeGaity's entrance hall, and Rickenharp gave Carmen his coat to hide her bare breasts. "Men only, in here," he said, "but if you don't shove your femaleness into their line of sight, they might let us slide."

Carmen pulled the jacket on, zipped it up—very carefully—and Rickenharp gave her his dark glasses.

Rickenharp banged on the window of the screening kiosk beside the locked door that led into the cruising rooms. Beyond the glass, someone looked up from a fat-screen TV. "Hey, Carter," Rickenharp said.

"Hey." Carter grinned at him. Carter was, by his own admission, "a trendy faggot." He was flexicoated battleship gray with white trim, a minimono style. But the real M'n'Ms would have spurned him for wearing a luminous earring—it blinked through a series of words in tiny green letters—*Fuck . . . you . . . if . . . you . . . don't . . . like . . . it . . . Fuck . . . you . . . if*—and they'd have considered that unforgivably "Griddy." And anyway Carter's wide, froggish face didn't fit the svelte minimono look. He looked at Carmen. "No girls, Harpie."

"Drag queen," Rickenharp said. He slipped a folded twenty newbux note through the slot in the window. "Okay?"

"Okay, but she takes her chances in there," Carter said, shrugging. He tucked the twenty in his charcoal bikini briefs.

"Sure."

"You hear about Geary?"

"Nope."

"Snuffed hisself with China White 'cause he got green pissed."

"Oh, shit." Rickenharp's skin crawled. His paranoia flared up again, and to soothe it he said, "Well, I'm not gonna be licking anybody's anything. I'm looking for Frankie."

"That asshole. He's there, holding court or something. But you still got to pay admission, honey."

"Sure," Rickenharp said.

He took another twenty newbux out of his pocket, but Carmen put a hand on his arm and said, "We'll cover this one." She slapped a twenty down.

Carter took it, chuckling. "Man, that queen got some real nice larynx work." Knowing damn well she was a girl. "Hey, Rick, you still playing at the—"

"I blew the gig off," Rickenharp cut in, trying to head off the pain. The boss blue had peaked and left him feeling like he was made out of cardboard inside, like any pressure might make him buckle. His muscles twitched now and then, fretful as restive children scuffing feet. He was crashing. He needed another hit. When you were up, he thought, things showed you their frontsides, their upsides; when you peaked, things showed you their hideous insides. When you were down, things showed you their backsides, their downsides. File it away for lyrics.

Carter pressed the buzzer that unlocked the door. It razzed them as they walked through.

Inside it was dim, hot, humid.

"I think your blue was cut with coke or meth or something," Rickenharp told Carmen as they walked past the dented lockers. "Cause I'm crashing harder than I should be."

"Yeah, probably... What'd he mean 'he got green pissed'?"

"Positive test for AIDS-three. The HIV that kills you in three weeks. You drop this testing pill in your urine and if the urine turns green you got AIDS. There's no cure for the new HIV yet, won't be in three weeks, so the guy..." He shrugged.

"What the 'ell is this place?" Willow asked.

In a low voice Rickenharp told him, "It's a kind of bathless gay baths, man. Cruising places for 'mos. But about a lotta the people are straights who ran out of bux at the casinos, use it for a cheap place to sleep, you know?"

"Yeah? And 'ow come you know all about it, 'ey?"

Rickenharp smirked. "You saying I'm gay? The horror, the horror."

Someone in a darkened alcove to one side laughed at that.

Willow was arguing with Yukio in an undertone. "Oi don't like it, that's all, fucking faggots got a million fucking diseases. Some side o' beef with a tan going to wank on me leg."

"We just walk through, we don't touch," Yukio said. "Rickenharp knows what to do."

Rickenharp thought, *Hope so.*

Maybe Frankie could get them safely off Freezone, maybe not.

The walls were black pressboard. It was a maze like a tingler gallery but in the negative. There was a more ordinary red light; there was the peculiar scent that lots of skin on skin generates and the accretion of various smokes, aftershaves, cheap soap, and an ingrained stink of sweat and semen gone rancid. The walls stopped at ten feet up and the shadows gathered the ceiling into themselves, far overhead. It was a converted warehouse space, with a strange vibe of stratification: claustrophobia layered under agoraphobia. They passed mossy dark cruising warrens. Faces blurred by anonymity turned to monitor them as they passed, expressions cool as video cameras.

They strolled through the game room with its stained pool tables and stammering holo-games, its prized-open vending machines. Peeling from the walls between the machines were posters of men—caricatures with oversized genitals and muscles that seemed themselves a kind of sexual organ, faces like California surfers.

Carmen bit her finger to keep from laughing at them, marveling at the idiosyncratic narcissism of the place.

They passed through a cruising room designed to look like a barn. Two men ministered to one another on a wooden bench inside a "horse stall" with wet fleshy noises. Willow and Yukio looked away. Carmen stared at the gay sex in fascination. Rickenharp walked past without reacting, led the way through other midnight nests of pawing men; past men sleeping on benches and couches, sleepily slapping unwanted hands away.

And found Frankie in the TV lounge.

The TV lounge was bright, well-lit, the walls cheerful yellow. The OmeGaity was cheap—there were no holo cubes. There were motel-standard living-room lamps on end tables; a couch; a regular color screen showing a rock video channel; and a bank of monitors on the wall. It was like emerging from the underworld. Frankie was sitting on the couch, waiting for customers.

Frankie dealt on a porta-terminal he'd plugged into a Grid-socket. The buyer gave him an account number or credit card; Frankie checked the account, transferred the funds into his own (registered as consultancy fees), and handed over the packets.

The walls of the lounge were inset with video monitors; one showed the orgy room, another a porn vid, another ran a Grid network satellite channel. On that one a newscaster was yammering about the attempted assassination, this time in technicki, and Rickenharp hoped Frankie wouldn't notice it and make the connection. Frankie the Mirror was into taking profit from whatever came along, and the SA paid for information.

Frankie sat on the torn blue vinyl couch, hunched over the pocket-sized terminal on the coffee table. Frankie's customer was a disco 'mo with a blue sharkfin flare, steroid muscles, and a white karate robe; the guy was standing to one side, staring at the little black canvas bag of blue packets on the coffee table as Frankie completed the transaction.

Frankie was black. His bald scalp had been painted with reflective chrome; his head was a mirror, reflecting the TV screens in fish-eye miniature. He wore a pinstriped three-piece gray suit. A real one, but rumpled and stained like he'd slept in it, maybe fucked in it. He was smoking a Nat Sherman cigarette, down to the gold filter. His synthcoke eyes were demonically red. He flashed a yellow grin at Rickenharp. He looked at Willow, Yukio, and Carmen, made a mocking scowl. "Fucking narcs—get more fancy with their setups every day. Now they got four agents in here, one of 'em looks like my man Rickenharp, other three look like refugees and a computer designer. But that Jap hasn't got a camera. Gives him away."

"What's this 'ere about—" Willow began.

Rickenharp made a dismissive gesture that said, *He isn't serious, dumbshit.* "I got two purchases to make," he announced and looked at Frankie's buyer. The buyer took his packet and melted back into the warrens.

"First off," Rickenharp said, taking his card from his wallet, "I need some blue blow, three grams."

"You got it, homeboy." Frankie ran a lightpen over the card, then punched a request for data on that account. The terminal asked for the private code number. Frankie handed the terminal to Rickenharp, who punched in his code, then erased it from visual. Then he punched to transfer funds to Frankie's account. Frankie took the terminal and double-checked the transfer. The terminal showed Rickenharp's adjusted balance and Frankie's gain.

"That's gonna eat up half your account, Harpie," Frankie said.

"I got some prospects."

"I heard you and Mose parted company."

"How'd you get that so fast?"

"Ponce was here buying."

"Yeah, well—now I've dumped the dead weight, my prospects are even better." But as he said it he felt dead weight in his gut.

"'S your bux, man." Frankie reached into the canvas carry-on, took out three pre-weighed bags of blue powder. He looked faintly amused. Rickenharp didn't like the look. It seemed to say, *I knew you'd come back, you sorry little wimp.*

"Fuck off, Frankie," Rickenharp said, taking the packets.

"What's this sudden squall of discontent, my child?"

"None of your business, you smug bastard."

Frankie's smugness tripled. He glanced speculatively at Carmen and Yukio and Willow. "There's something more, right?"

"Yeah. We got a problem. My friends here—they're getting off the raft. They need to slip out the back way so Tom and Huck don't see 'em."

"Mmm. What kind of net's out for them?"

"It's a private outfit. They'll be watching the copter port, everything legit . . . "

"We had another way off," Carmen said suddenly. "But it was blown—"

Yukio silenced her with a look. She shrugged.

"Verr-rry mysterious," Frankie said. "But there are safety limits to curiosity. Okay. Three grand gets you three berths on my next boat out. My boss's sending a team to pick up a shipment. I can probably get 'em on there. That's going *east*, though. You know? Not west or south or north. One direction and one only."

"That's what we need," Yukio said, nodding, smiling. Like he was talking to a travel agent. "East. Someplace Mediterranean."

"Malta," Frankie said. "Island of Malta. Best I can do." Yukio nodded. Willow shrugged. Carmen assented by her silence.

Rickenharp was sampling the goods. In the nose, to the brain, and right to work. Frankie watched him placidly. Frankie was a connoisseur of the changes drugs made in people. He watched the change of expression on Rickenharp's face. He watched Rickenharp's visible shift into ego drive.

"We're gonna need four berths, Frankie," Rickenharp said.

Frankie raised an eyebrow. "You better decide after that shit wears off."

"I decided before I took it," Rickenharp said, not sure if it was true.

Carmen was staring at him. He took her by the arm and said, "Talk to you a minute?" He led her out of the lounge, into the dark hallway. The skin of her arm was electrically sweet under his fingers.

He wanted more. But he dropped his hand from her and said, "Can you get the bux?"

She nodded. "I got a fake card, dips into—well, it'll get it for us. I mean, for me and Yukio and Willow. I'd have to get authorization to bring you. And I can't do that."

"Know what? I won't help you get out otherwise."

"You don't know—"

"Yeah, I do. I'm ready to go. I just go back and get my guitar."

"The guitar'll be a burden where we're going. We're going into occupied territory, to get where we want to be. You'd have to leave the guitar."

He almost wavered at that. "I'll check it into a locker. Pick it up someday. Thing is—if they watched us with that bird, they saw me with you. They'll assume I'm part of it. Look, I know what you're doing. The SA's looking for you. Right? So that means you're—"

"Okay, hold it, shit; keep your voice down. Look—I can see where maybe they marked you, so you got to get off the raft, too. Okay, you go with us to Malta. But then you—"

"I got to stay with you. The SA's everywhere. They marked me."

She took a deep breath and let it out in a soft whistle through her teeth. She stared at the floor. "You can't do it." She looked at him. "You're not the type. You're a fucking *artist*."

He laughed. "You say that like it's the lowest insult you can come up with. Look—I can do it. I'm going to do it. The band is dead. I need to . . . " He shrugged helplessly. Then he reached up and took her sunglasses off, looked at her shadowed eyes. "And when I get you alone I'm going to batter your cervix into jelly."

She punched him hard in the shoulder. It hurt. But she was smiling. "You think that kind of talk turns me on? Well, it does. But it's not going to get you into my pants. And as for going with us— What you think this is? You've seen too many movies."

"The SA's marked me, remember? What else can I do?"

"That's not a good enough reason to . . . to become part of this thing. You got to really believe in it, because *it's hard*. This is not a celebrity game show."

"Jesus. Give me a break. I know what I'm doing."

That was bullshit. He was trashed. He was blown. *My computer's experiencing a power surge. Motherboard fried. Hell, then burn out the rest.*

He was living a fantasy. But he wasn't going to admit it. He repeated, "I know what I'm doing."

She snorted. She stared at him. "Okay," she said.

And after that everything was different.

Part Two
KESSLER

10

His name was James Kessler, and he was walking east on Fourteenth Street, looking for something. He wasn't sure what he was looking for. He was walking through a misty November rain. The street was almost deserted. He was looking for something, something, the brutally colorless word *something* hung heavily in his mind like an empty frame.

What he thought he wanted was to get in, out of the weather. Walking in rain made him feel naked, somehow. And acid rain, he thought, could make you naked, if you wore the kind of syn-threads that reacted with the acids.

Up ahead the eternal neon butterfly of a Budweiser sign glowed sultry orange-red and blue; the same design since sometime in the twentieth century. He angled across the sidewalk, pitted concrete the color of dead skin, hurrying toward the sign, toward the haven of a bar. The rain was already beginning to sting. He closed his eyes against it, afraid it would burn his corneas.

He pushed through the smudge-bruised door into the bar. The bartender glanced up, nodded to himself, and reached under the counter for a towel; he passed the towel across to Kessler. The towel was treated with acid-absorbents; it helped immediately.

"Get any in your eyes?" the bartender asked with no real concern.

"No, I don't think so." He handed the towel back. "Thanks." The tired-faced men drinking at the bar hardly glanced at Kessler. He was unremarkable: round-faced, with short black hair streaked blue-white to denote his work in video editing; large friendly brown eyes, soft red mouth pinched now with worry; a standard printout grey-blue suit.

The bartender said something else, but it didn't register. Kessler was staring at the glowing green lozenge of a credit transferal kiosk in the back of the dim, old-fashioned bar. He crossed to it and stepped in; the door hissed shut behind him. The small screen on the front of the fone lit up, and its electronic letters asked him: D<small>O YOU WANT</small> C<small>ALL OR</small> E<small>NTRY</small>?

What did he want? Why had he come to the kiosk? He wasn't sure. But it felt right. A wave of reassurance had come over him . . . *Ask it what your balance is*, a soundless voice whispered to him. Again he felt a wave of reassurance. But he thought: Something's out of place . . .

He knew his mind as a man knows his cluttered desk; he knows when someone has moved something on his desk—or in his mind. And someone had.

He punched ENTRY and it asked him his account number and entry pin. He punched the digits in, then told it he wanted to see his bank balance. It told him to wait. Numbers appeared on the screen.

$NB 760,000.

He stared at it. He punched for error check and confirmation.

The bank's computer insisted that he had 760,000 newbux in his bank account.

There should be only 4,000.

Something was missing from his memory; something had been added to his bank account.

They tampered with me, he thought, and then they paid me for it.

He requested the name of the depositor. The screen told him: U<small>NRECORDED</small>.

Julie. Talk to Julie. There was just no one else he discussed his projects with till they were patented and on-line. No one. His wife had to know.

Julie. He could taste her name in his mouth. Her name tasted like bile.

Julie had been home only a few minutes, Kessler decided, as he closed the door behind him. Her coat was draped over the back of the couch, off-white on off-white. She liked things off-white or gray or powder blue, and that's how the place was decorated. Kessler liked rich, earthy colors, but she considered them vulgar, so that was that. She was bent down to the minifridge behind the breakfast bar. She stood up, a frosted bottle of Stolichnaya in her hand. "Hi, Jimmy."

She almost never called him Jimmy.

Julie came out with a vodka straight-up and a twist of lime for each of them. He'd learned to like vodka. She padded across the powder-blue rug in bare feet, small feet sexy in sheer hose; she was tall and slender and long-necked. Her hair was the yellow of split pine, cut short as a small boy's, and parted on the side. She was English and looked it; her eyes were immaculate blue crystals. She wore her silk-lined, coarse-fiber, off-white dress suit. She looked more natural in her suits than in anything else. She had "casuals" to wear at home, but somehow she never wore them. Maybe because that would be a concession to home life, would almost be a betrayal of the corporation family she belonged to. Like having children. What was it she said about having children? *If you don't mind, I'll continue to resist the programming of my biological computer. When DNA talks, I don't listen. I don't like being pushed into something by a molecule.*

He took off his coat, hung it up, and sat down beside her on the couch. The vodka, chilled with no ice, waited for him on the glass coffee table. He took a drink and said, "There's seven hundred and sixty thousand newbux in my bank account." He looked at her. "What did they take?"

Her eyes went a little glassy. "Seven hundred and sixty thousand? Computer error."

"You know it's not." He took another sip. The Stoli was syrupy thick from being kept in the freezer. "What did you tell Worldtalk?"

"Are you accusing me of something?" She said it with her icy Oxbridge incredulousness then, like, I can't believe anyone could be so painfully unsophisticated.

"I'm accusing Worldtalk. And . . . you're *theirs*. They do as they like with you, Julie. If Worldtalk says it's not *team-playing* to have kids, you don't have kids. If Worldtalk says listen for anything that might be useful, you listen. Even at home. You know, you wouldn't have had to quit your job—I can understand you wanting to have a career. We could have had the kid with a surrogate or an artificial womb. Gotten a nanny. They don't want employees, at Worldtalk, they want to *own you* . . . "

"It's childish to go over and over this. Worldtalk has nothing to do with my decision not to have children. I worked *eight years*—"

"I know it by rote: you worked eight years to be assistant second vice prez in the country's biggest PR and advertising outfit. You tell me *having children* is demeaning! Eight years licking Grimwald's boots—that's demeaning! Going to Worldtalk's Family Sessions for hours at a time—"

She stood up, arms rigid at her sides. "Well, why not! Corporation families *last*."

"A 'corporate family' isn't a real family. They're using you. Look what they got you to do! To *me!*"

"You got some seven hundred thousand newbux. That's more than you would ever have made on any of your harebrained schemes. If you worked for one of the big companies you'd be making decent money in the first place. You insist on being freelance, so you're left out in the cold, and you should be grateful for what they—" She snipped the sentence in two with a brisk sibilance and turned away.

"So we've dropped the pretenses now. You're saying I should be grateful for the money Worldtalk gave me. Julie—*what did they take from my memory?*"

"I don't *know!* You didn't tell me what you were working on and—anyway I don't believe they took anything. I—goddammit." She went to the bathroom to pointedly take her Restem, making a lot of noise opening the prescription bottle so he'd hear and know it was his fault she had to take a tranquilizer.

◆

Kessler was in a bar with his attorney, Bascomb. Herman Bascomb was drunk, and drugged. The disorder of his mind seemed splashed onto the room around him: the dancers, the lights, the holograms that made it look, in the smoky dimness, as if someone was there dancing beside you who wasn't. A touristy couple on the dance floor stopped and stared at another couple: horned, half-human, half-reptile, she with her tongue darting from between rouged lips; he with baroque fillips of fire flicking from his flattened nostrils. The touristy couple laughed off their embarrassment when the DJ turned off the holo and the demon couple vanished.

Bascomb chuckled and sucked some of his cocaine fizz through a straw that lit up with miniature advertisements when it was used, lettering flickering luminous green up and down its length. Bascomb was young, tanned, and preppie; he wore an iridescent Japanese Action Suit.

Sitting beside him, Kessler squirmed on his barstool and ordered another scotch. He wasn't comfortable with Bascomb like this. Kessler was used to seeing Bascomb in his office, a neat component of Featherstone, Pestlestein, and Bascomb, Attorneys at Law, friendly but not too friendly, intense but controlled.

My own fault, Kessler told himself; chase the guy down when he's off work, hassle his wife till she tells me where he hangs out, find out things I don't want to know. Like the fact that he's bisexual and flirting with the waiter.

The bar was circular, rotating slowly through the club, leaving the dance floor behind now to arrive at the cruising rooms. As they talked it turned slowly past flesh-pink holographic porn squirmings and edged into the soft music lounge. Each room had its own idiosyncratic darkness, shot through with the abstracted glamour of the candy-apple-red and hot-pink and electric-blue neon running up the corners to zigzag the ceiling like a time-lapse photo of nighttime traffic. The kitschy design was another annoyance for Kessler.

Bascomb turned on his stool to look at the porn and the live copulation; his mouth was open in a lax smile. Kessler looked over his shoulder. Again in the dimness the holos were nearly indistinguishable from the real article; a drunken swinger tried to fondle a woman with four breasts, only to walk through her, discovering her unreal. "Do we have to talk here?" Kessler asked, turning back to the bar.

Bascomb ignored the question and returned to an earlier one. "The bottom line, Jim, is that you are a nobody. Now, if you were, say, a Nobel Prize–winning professor at Stanford, we might be able to get you your day in court, we might get a grand jury to investigate the people at Worldtalk..." Bascomb was talking without looking away from the intermingling porn and people. "But as it is you're a mildly successful video editor who makes a hobby of working up a lot of rather ingenuous media theories. Every day some crank or someone looking for attention announces a Great Idea has been stolen from their brains, and ninety-nine percent of the time they turn out to be paranoids or liars or both. I'm not saying you're a paranoid or a liar. *I* believe you. I'm just saying I'm probably the only one who will."

"But I have the seven hundred sixty thousand NB...that shouldn't be there. That ought to be proof of something."

"Did you request the name of the depositor?"

"Unrecorded."

"Then how are you going to prove a connection?"

"I don't know. But I know an idea was stolen from me. I want it back, Bascomb. And I can't work it up again on my own from scratch—they took all my notes, files, recent research, everything that could lead me back to it."

"Sucks," Bascomb said sympathetically. They had rotated into the lounge; people on couches watched videos and conversed softly. Sometimes they were talking to holos; you knew when you were talking to a holo because they said outrageous things. They were programmed that way to ease the choking boredom of lounge-bar conversation. "I want it back, Bascomb," Kessler repeated, his knuckles white on the rim of the bar.

Bascomb shrugged and said, "You haven't been in this country long; maybe you don't know how it works. First off, you have to understand that..." He paused to sip from his cocaine fizz; he became more animated almost instantly, chattering on: "You have to understand that you can't get it back the way it was taken. Whoever it was probably came in while you were asleep. Which adds credence to your theory that Julie was involved. She waits up or pretends to sleep, lets them in, they gas you to keep you out, shoot you up with the receptivity drug. They've got microsurgicals in the big box they've brought with them, right? They look at the screen they've set up that translates your impulses into a code they can understand. They get some dream free-association maybe. But that tells them they're 'on-line' in your brain. Then they put a request to the brain, fed into it in the form of neurohormonal transmitter molecules they manufacture in their box—"

"How do you know so much about this?" Kessler asked, unable to keep the edge of suspicion out of his voice.

"We get a case like yours once or twice a year. I did a lot of research on it. The ACLU has a small library on the subject. It really gets their goat. We didn't win those cases, by the way; they're tough to prove . . . " He paused to sip his fizz, his eyes sparkling and dilated. Kessler was annoyed by Bascomb's treating his case like a conversation piece.

"Let's get back to what happened to me."

"Okay, uh—so they made a request to the biological computer we call a brain, right? They asked it what it knew about whatever it was they wanted to take from you, and your brain automatically begins to think about it and sends signals to the cortex of the temporal lobes or to the hippocampus; they 'ride' the electrochemical signals back to the place where the information is stored. They use tracer molecules that attach themselves to the chemical signals. When they reach the hippocampus or the temporal lobes, the tracer molecules act as enzymes to command the brain to simply unravel that particular chemical code. They break it down on the molecular level. They extract some things connected to it, and the chain of ideas that led to it, but they don't take so much they make you an idiot because they probably want your wife to cooperate and to stay with Worldtalk. You might not be close but she doesn't need the guilt. Anyway, the brain chemistry is such that you can ask the brain a question with neurohumoral transmitter molecules, but you can't imprint on the memory, in an orderly way. You can feed in experiences, things which seem to be happening now—you can even implant them ready-made so they crop up at a given stimulus—but you can't feed in *ready-made memories*. Probably that's 'cause memories are holographic, involving complexes of cell groups. Like you can pull a thread to unravel a coat fairly easily but you can't ravel it back up so easily... Look at that exquisite creature over there, she's lovely, isn't she? Like to do some imprinting on her. I wonder if she's real. Uh, anyway... You can't put it back in. They take out, selectively, any memory of anything that might make you suspect they tampered with you, but lots of people begin to suspect anyway, because when they free associate over familiar pathways of the brain and then come to a gap—well, it's jarring. But they can't prove anything."

"Okay, so maybe it can't be put back by direct feed-in to the memory. But it could be relearned through ordinary induction. Reading."

"Yeah. I guess it would be better than nothing. But you still have to find out who took it. Even if it turns up as someone else's project—proves nothing. They could have come up with it the same way you did. And you should ask yourself this: Why did they take it? Was it simply for profit or was it for another reason? The bigger corporations have a network of agents. Their sole job is to search out people with development ideas that could be dangerous to the status quo. They try to extract the ideas from the guys before they are copyrighted or patented or published in papers or discussed in public. They take the idea from you, maybe plant some mental inhibitors to keep you from working your way back to it again. If you came up with an idea that was *really* dangerous to the status quo, Jimmy, they might go farther than a simple erasing next time. Because they play hardball. If you keep pushing to get it back, they just might arrange for you to turn up dead. Accidents happen."

◆

But riding the elevator up to his apartment, trying to come to terms with it, Kessler realized it wasn't death that scared him. What chilled him was thinking about his wife.

Julie had waited till he'd slept. Had, perhaps, watched the clock on the bedside table. Had gotten out of bed at the appointed hour and padded to the door and ever-so-quietly opened it for the man carrying the black box...

And she had done it simply because Worldtalk had asked her to. Worldtalk was her husband, her children, her parents. Perhaps most of all her dreadful parents.

And maybe in the long run what had happened to him, Kessler thought—as the elevator reached his floor—was that the Dissolve Depression had done its work on him. For decades the social structures that created nuclear families, that kept families whole and together, had eroded, had finally broken down completely. Broken homes made broken homes made broken homes. The big corporations, meanwhile, consumed the little ones, and, becoming then unmanageably big, looked for ways to stabilize themselves. They chose the proven success of the Japanese system: the corporation as an extension of the family. You inculcate your workers with a fanatic sense of loyalty and belonging. You personalize everything. And they go along with that—or lose their jobs. So maybe it started with the Dissolve Depression. Jobs were more precious than ever. Jobs were life. So you embraced the new corporation as home and family system. The breakdown of the traditional family structures reinforced the process. And you put your employer above your true family. You let its agents in to destroy your husband's new career...

And here we are, he thought, as he walked into the apartment.

There she is, making us both a drink, so we can once more become cordial strangers sharing a convenient apartment and a convenient sex life.

◆

"Aren't you coming to bed?" she called from the bedroom.

He sat on the couch, holding his glass up beside his ear, shaking it just enough so he could listen to the tinkle of the ice cubes. The sound made him feel good and he wondered why. It made him visualize wind chimes of frosted glass... his mother's wind chimes.

His mother standing on the front porch, smiling absently, watching him play, and now and then she would reach up and tinkle the wind chimes with her finger . . . He swallowed another tot of vodka to smear over the chalky scratch of loneliness.

"You really ought to get some sleep, Jimmy." There was just a faint note of strain in her voice.

He was scared to go in there.

This is stupid, he thought. I don't know for sure it was her. She hadn't *exactly* admitted it. "That was just a hypothetical," she'd said later.

He forced himself to put the glass down, to stand, to walk to the bedroom, to do it all as if he weren't forcing himself through the membranes of his mistrust.

He stood in the doorway and looked at her for a moment. She was wearing her silk lingerie. She was lying with her back to him. He could see her face reflected in the window across from her. Her eyes were open wide. In them he saw determination and self-disgust, and then he knew she had contacted them, told them that he knew. And the strangers were going to do it to him again. They would come and take out more this time—his conversation with her about the money, his talk with Bascomb, his misgivings. They would take away the hush money they had paid him since he had shown he was unwilling to accept it without pushing to get back what he had lost . . .

Go along with it, he told himself.

That would be the intelligent solution. Let them do it. Sweet nepenthe. The pain and the fear and the anger would go with the memories. And he would have his relationship with his wife back. Such as it was.

He thought about it for a moment. She turned to look at him.

"No," he said finally. "No, we don't have enough between us to make it worthwhile. No. Tell them I said next they'll have to try and kill me."

She stared at him. Then she lay back and looked at the ceiling.

He closed the bedroom door softly behind him and went to the closet for his coat.

They hadn't taken the money yet. It was still there in his account. He had gone to an all-night credit kiosk, sealed himself in, and now he looked at the figure, $NB 760,000, and felt a kind of glow. He punched his fone and called Charlie Chesterton.

The screen asked him, "You want visual?"

"No," he told it, "not yet."

"Sap?" came Charlie's voice. "Huzatun wushant?"

Wake Charlie out of a sound sleep, and he'd talk technicki. *What's happenin'? Who's that and what do you want?*

"Talk standard with me, Charlie. It's—"

"Hey, my neggo! Kessler, what's happening, man! Hey, how come no visual?"

"I didn't know what you were doing. I'm ever discreet." He punched for visual and a small TV image of Charlie appeared below the fone's keyboard. Charlie wore a triple-Mohawk, each fin a different color, each color significant; red in the middle for Technicki Radical Unionist; blue on the right for his profession, video tech; green on the left for his neighborhood, New Brooklyn—an artificial island. He grinned, showing front teeth imprinted with his initials in gold, another tacky technicki fad. And Charlie wore a picture T-shirt that showed a movie: Fritz Lang's *Metropolis*, now moving through the flood scene.

"You went to sleep wearing your movie T-shirt, you oughta turn it off, wear out the batteries."

"Recharges from sunlight," Charlie said. "You call me to talk about my sleeping habits?"

"Need your help. Right now, I need the contact numbers for the Shanghai bank that takes transferals under anonymity..."

"I told you, man, that's like, the border of legality, and maybe over it. You understand that first, right?"

Kessler nodded.

"Okay, neggo. Fuck it. Set your screen to record... But for the record this is on you, *I* ain't doing any such transferral..."

◆

Bascomb's office was too warm; Bascomb had a problem with his circulation. The walls were a milky yellow that seemed to quicken the heat somehow. Bascomb sat behind the blond-wood desk, wearing a stenciled-on three-piece suit, smiling a smile of polite bafflement. Kessler sat across from him, feeling he was on some kind of treadmill, because Bascomb just kept saying, "I really am quite sure no such meeting took place between you and me, Kessler." He chuckled. "I know the club very well, and I'm sure I'd remember if I'd been there that night. Haven't been there for a month."

"You weren't enthusiastic about it, but you told me you'd take the case." But the words were ashes in Kessler's mouth. He knew what had happened, because there was not even the faintest trace of duplicity or nervousness on Bascomb's face. Bascomb really didn't remember. "So you won't represent me on this?" Kessler went on.

"We really have no experience with brain tampering—"

"That's funny, your saying that. Considering you obviously just had firsthand experience, pal."

Naturally, Bascomb gave him that oh-no-don't-tell-me-you're-into-that-conspiracy-shit look.

Kessler went on: "And I could get the files that prove you have dealt with the issue in court. But they'd only . . . " He shook his head. Despair was something he could smell and taste and feel, like acid rain. "They'd tamper with you again. Just to make their point."

He walked out of the office, hurrying, thinking, *They'll have the place under surveillance.* But no one stopped him outside.

◆

Charlie was off on one of his amateur analyses, and there was nothing Kessler could do, he had to listen, because Charlie was covering for him.

" . . . I mean," Charlie was saying, "now your average technicki speaks Standard English like an infant, am I right, and can't read except command codes, and learned it all from vidteaching, and he's trained to do this and that and to fix this and that, but he's like, socially inhibited from rising in the ranks because the economic elite speaks standard real good and reads standard alphabet—"

"If they really want to, they can learn what they need to, like you did," Kessler said irritably. He was standing at the window, looking out at the empty, glossy ceramic streets. The artificial island was a boro-annex of Brooklyn anchored in the harbor. It looked almost deserted at this hour. Everyone had either gone into the city, or home to TV, or to a tavern. The floating boros were notoriously dull. The compact flo-boro housing, squat and rounded off at the corners like a row of molars, stood in silence, a few windows glowing like computer monitors against the night.

But they could be watching me, Kessler thought. *A hundred ways they could be watching me and I'd see nothing.*

He turned, stepped away from the window. Charlie was pacing, arms clasped behind him, head bent, playing the part of the young, boldly theorizing radical. "I mean, I've got some contacts on the space Colony, up on FirStep, and they're getting into some radical shit there—and what is FirStep, man, it's a microcosm of society's class issues..."

The apartment was crowded with irregular shelves of books and boxes of ancient compact disks; Charlie had hung a forest of silk scarves in the Three Colors, obscuring the details like multi-color smoke. "And in Europe—that shit's getting *serious*—"

"Yeah, wars are serious, Charlie."

"I don't mean the fucking war, neggo. I mean the side effect. *Chegdou*, you know what's happening in Europe, man? The SA is taking over! And it's all being manufactured over here. Fascism, a fait accompli."

Kessler groaned. "Fascism! Don't give me that leftist catch-all cliché. It's bullshit."

"How can you say that after what's happened to you?"

"What's happened to me is business as usual. It's not really political."

"Business as usual is the very definition of politics in a world where corporate identity is more global every second. And anyway—you didn't used to be so negative about this shit. Maybe they cut some of your political ideas, neggo. I mean: How do you know? You don't remember—" He grinned. "Remember?"

Kessler shrugged. He felt like throwing in the towel, giving Worldtalk the fight. Maybe Julie was right.

"If you'd just talk to this guy I want you to talk to, man."

"I don't need any lectures from any more knee-jerk leftist theorists who'd probably give their right eye to be the rich and corrupt men they whine about."

"You're doing a devil's-advocate thing now, Jimmy. You trying to talk yourself into giving up?"

Kessler shrugged.

Charlie looked at him, then went back to pacing, talking, pacing. "This guy I want you to meet—he's not like that. He's only in town a week. He's not an armchair theorist. He's not really a... what... I don't think he's a *leftist* exactly. I mean, he came here to get some financial support for the European resistance, and he had to run the blockade to do it, almost got his ass blown out of the water. His name's Steinfeld, or that's what he goes by, he used to be—what's the matter?"

A warning chill; and Kessler had turned, abruptly looked out the window. Three stories down she was a powder-blue keyhole-shape against the faint petroleum filminess of the street. She paused, looking at the numbers.

She might have guessed where he was, he told himself. She had met Charlie; heard him talk about Charlie. She might have looked Charlie's address up. She went to the front door. The apartment's bell chimed and he went to the screen. "It's your wife." he said. "You want me to tell her you went overseas? Japan?"

"Let her in."

"Are you kidding, man? You *are*, right? She was the one who—"

"Just let her in." There was a poisoned cocktail of emotions fizzing in him: a relief at seeing her, shaken in with something that buzzed like a smoke alarm, and it wasn't till she was at the door that he realized the sensation was terror. And then she was standing in the doorway, against the light of the hallway. She looked beautiful.

The light behind her abruptly cut—sensing that no one was now in the hall—and suddenly she stood framed in darkness. The buzzing fizzed up and overwhelmed the relief. His mouth was dry.

Looking disgustedly at Kessler, Charlie shut the door.

Kessler stared at her. Her eyes flickered, her mouth opened, and shut, and she shook her head. She looked drained.

And Kessler knew.

"They sent you. They told you where to find me," he said.

"They—want the money back," she said. "They want you to come with me."

He shook his head. "I put the money where they can't get it—only because it's part of my proof. Don't you get sick of being puppeted?"

She looked out the window. Her face was blank. "You don't understand."

"Do you know why they do it, why they train you with that Americanized Japanese job-conditioning? To save themselves money. For one thing, it eliminates unions. You don't insist on much in the way of benefits. Stuff like that."

"They have their reasons, sure. Mostly efficiency."

"What's the slogan? *Efficiency is friendship.*"

She looked embarrassed. "That's not—" She shrugged. "A corporate family is just as valid as any other. It's something you couldn't understand. I—I'll lose my job, Jimmy. If you don't come." She said *lose my job* the way Kessler would have said *lose my life*.

Kessler said, "I'll think about going with you if you tell me what it was . . . what it was they took."

"They—took it from me, too."

"I don't believe that. I never believed it. I think they left it intact in you, so you could watch to see if I stumbled on it again. I think you really loved them trusting you. Worldtalk is Mommy and Daddy, and Mommy and Daddy trusted you . . . "

Her mouth twisted with resentment. "You prick." She shook her head. "I can't tell you . . . "

"Yeah, you *can*. You *have to*. Otherwise Charlie and me are going out the back way and we're going to cause endless trouble for

Worldtalk. And I know you, Julie. I'd know if you were making it up. So tell me what it was—what it really was."

She sighed. "I only know what you told me. You pointed out that PR companies manipulate the media for their clients without the public knowing it most of the time. They use their connections and channels to plant information or disinformation in newssheet articles, on newsvid, in movies, in political speeches. So..." She paused and took a shaky breath, then went on wearily. "So they're manipulating people, and the public gets a distorted view of what's going on because of the special interests. You worked up a computer video-editing system that sensed probable examples of, uh, I think the phrases you used were, like, 'implanted information' or 'special-interest distortions.' So they could be weeded out. You called it the Media Alarm System." She let out a long breath. "I didn't know they'd go so far—I thought they'd buy out your system. In a way they did. I *had* to mention it at Worldtalk. If I didn't I would've been . . . disloyal." She said *disloyal* wincing, knowing what he would think.

But it was Charlie who said it: "What about loyalty to Jim Kessler?"

Her hand fluttered a dismissal. "It doesn't matter at this point whether it was wrong or right. It's too late. They *know* ... Jimmy, are you coming with me?"

Kessler was thinking about the Media Alarm System. It didn't sound familiar—but it sounded *right*. He said, slowly, "No. You can help me. If you testify, we can beat them."

"Jimmy, if I thought they—No, no. I—" She broke off, staring at his waist. "Don't be stupid. That's not—" She took a step back and put her hand in her purse.

Kessler and Charlie looked at each other, traded puzzlement. When Kessler looked back at Julie, she had a gun in her hand. It was a small blue-metal pistol, its barrel tiny as a pencil, and that tiny barrel meant it fired explosive bullets. *They* had given it to her.

"Do you know what that gun will do, girl?" Charlie was saying. "Those little explosive bullets will splash him all over the wall." His voice shook. He took a step toward her.

She pressed back against the door and said, "Charlie, if you come any closer to me, I'll shoot him." Charlie stopped. The room seemed to keen ultrasonically with imminence. She went on, the words coming out in a rush: "Why don't you ask him what that thing in his hand would do to me, Charlie. Shall we? Ask him that. Jimmy has the same kind of gun. With the same goddamn bullets." Her voice was too high; she was breathing fast, her knuckles white on the gun.

Kessler looked down at himself. His arms were hanging at his sides, his hands empty.

"Lower the gun, Julie, and we can talk," Charlie said gently.

"I'll lower mine when he lowers his," she said hoarsely.

"He isn't holding a gun," Charlie said, blinking.

She was staring at a space about three feet in front of Kessler's chest. She was seeing the gun there. He wanted to say, *Julie, they tampered with you.* He could only croak, "Julie . . . "

She shouted, "Don't!" and raised the gun. And then everything was moving: Kessler threw himself down. Charlie jumped at her, and the wall behind Kessler jumped outward toward the street.

Two hot metal hands clapped Kessler's head between them, and he shouted with pain and thought he was dead. But it was only a noise, the noise of the wall exploding outward. Chips of wall pattered down; smoke sucked out through the four-foot hole in the wall into the winter night.

Kessler got up, shaky, his ears ringing. He looked around and saw Charlie straddling Julie. He had the gun in his hand and she was face-down, sobbing.

"*Gogido*," Charlie said, lapsing into technicki, his face white.

"Get off her," Kessler said. Charlie moved off her, stood up beside her. "Julie, look at me," Kessler said softly. She tilted her head back, an expression of dignified defiance trembling precariously on her face. Then her eyes widened, and she looked at his hips. She was seeing him holding a gun there. "I don't have a gun, Julie. They put that into you. Now I'm going to *get* a gun . . . Give me the gun, Charlie." Without taking his eyes off her, he put his hand out. Charlie hesitated, then laid the gun in Kessler's open palm. She blinked, then narrowed her eyes.

"So now you've got two guns." She shrugged.

He shook his head. "Get up." Mechanically, she stood up. "Now go over there to Charlie's bed. He's got black bed sheets. You see them? Take one off. Just pull it off and bring it over here." She started to say something, anger lines punctuating her mouth, and he said quickly, "Don't talk yet. Do it!" She went to the bed, pulled the black satin sheet off, jerking it petulantly, and dragged it over to him. Charlie gaped and muttered about cops, but Kessler had a kind of furious calm on him then, and he knew what he was going to do; and if it didn't work, then he'd let the acid rain bleach his bones white as a warning to other travelers come to this poisoned well—this woman. He said, "Now tear up the bedsheet—sorry, man, I'll replace it—and make a blindfold. Good. Right. Now tie it over my eyes. Use the tape on the table to make the blindfold light-proof."

Moving in slow motion, she blindfolded him. Darkness whispered down around him: She taped it thoroughly in place. "Now am I still pointing two guns at you?"

"Yes." But there was uncertainty in her voice.

"Now take a step to one side. No, take several steps, very softly, move around a lot." The soft sounds of her movement. Her gasp. "Is the gun following you around the room?"

"Yes. Yes. One of them."

"But how is that possible? *I can't see you!* And why is only the one gun moving—the one you saw first? And why did I let you blindfold me if I'm ready and willing to shoot you?"

"You look weird like that," Charlie said. "Ridiculous and scary."

"Shut up, Charlie, will you? Answer me, Julie! I can't see you! How can I follow you with two guns?"

"I don't know!"

"Take the guns from my hands! Shoot me! Do it!" She made a short hissing sound and took the gun from his hand, and he braced to die. But she pulled the blindfold from him and looked at him.

Looked into his eyes.

She let the gun drop to the floor. Kessler said, softly, "You see now? *They* did it to you. You, one of the 'family.' The corporate 'family' means just exactly nothing to them."

She looked at his hands. "No gun." Dreamily. "Gun's gone. Everything's different."

Siren warblings. Coming closer.

She sank to her knees. "Just exactly nothing to them," she said. "Just exactly nothing." Her face crumpled. She looked as if she'd fallen into herself; as if some inner scaffolding had been kicked out of place.

Sirens and lights whirled together outside. A chrome fluttering in the smoky gap where the wall had been blown outward: a police surveillance bird. It looked like a bird, hovering in place with its oversized aluminum hummingbird's wings; but instead of a head it had a small camera lens. A transmitted voice droned from the grid on its silvery belly: *"This is the police. You are now being observed and recorded. Do not attempt to leave. The front door has been breached. Police officers will arrive in seconds to take your statements. Repeat—"*

"Oh, I heard you," Julie said in a hollow voice. "I'll make a statement all right. I've got a lot to tell you. Oh, yeah." She laughed sadly. "I'll make a statement."

Kessler bent down and touched her arm. "Hey...I..."

She drew back from him. "Don't touch me. Just don't! You love to be right! I'm going to tell them what you want me to. Just don't touch me."

But he stayed with her. He and Charlie stood looking at the blue smoke drifting out of the ragged hole in the wall, at the mechanical, camera-eyed bird looking back at them.

He stayed with her, as he always would, and they listened for the footsteps outside the door.

◆

"Why should we leave when we don't know who it was who bailed us out?" Julie asked.

She sat hunched over, hollow-eyed. She seemed to be holding on, in some way.

Kessler nodded. "It could be Worldtalk's people, Charlie."

Charlie shook his head. "I saw the guy in the outer office. He's one of ours."

"Yours, Charlie," Kessler said. "Not mine."

They were in Detective Bixby's office, sitting wearily in the plastic chairs across from Bixby's gray metal desk. The overhead light buzzed, maybe holding a conversation with the console screen on the right of the desk, which hummed faintly to itself. The screen was turned to face away from them. On the walls, shelves were piled high with software, cassettes, sheaves of printouts, photos. The walls were the grimed, dull green such places usually are. Bixby had left them to confer with the detectives in the new Cerebro-kidnapping Department—the department that handled illegal extractions. The door was locked, and they were alone.

"At least here we're protected," Julie said, digging her nails into her palms.

Charlie shook his head again. "I called Seventeen, he said Worldtalk could still get at us in here."

"Who the hell is Seventeen?" Kessler snapped. He was tired and irritable.

"My NR contact—"

He broke off, staring at the desk. The console was rotating on a turntable built into the desk top, its screen turning to face them. Bixby's round, florid face nearly filled the screen.

"'S'okay," Bixby said. "CK's taking your case. Your video statements are filed, and your bail is paid. That'll be refunded soon as we get the owner of the building to drop the charges on the blown-out wall. Should be no problem. If you want protective custody—maybe not a bad idea—talk to the desk sergeant. Door's unlocked." As he said it they heard a click, and the door swung inward a few inches. They were free to go. "Good luck," Bixby said. His face vanished from the screen.

"Come on," Charlie said. "Let's do this fast before the fucking *door* changes its mind."

◆

The basement room was dim and damp, and old, cracking apart. A man was waiting for them there. The man was sitting on a cracked, three-legged wooden chair, just under the single light bulb; he sat with the chair reversed, resting his arms on the back, one leg extended to compensate for the missing chair leg. He smiled and nodded at them.

Kessler looked at Charlie, and Charlie shook his head.

"Is he from Worldtalk?" Kessler asked.

Julie's voice was hollow. "I don't know him. I don't know. Maybe they hired him."

The man said, "I work with Worldtalk. I work with the SA. And I work with Steinfeld," he said. "Not in that order." He was a big, soft bodied man, and he was too smug. He had an executive's neutral blue-gray hair tint, with just a streak of white, indicating he'd "risen in the ranks." Maybe he'd started as an accountant, or a typing-pool supervisor; he was entitled to wash the tint out, but some executives kept their early rank marks as a kind of warning: *I fought my way up, and I'm still willing to fight, so don't fuck with me* . . . He wore a dove gray suit, a real one, and the choker that had replaced ties in the upper classes.

"Man, you look out of place here," Charlie said.

The man in the gray suit chuckled.

The basement was empty on one end, the other dominated by a pile of detritus, accumulated junk from the old tenement above, including a lot of torn up carpeting gone mildewy gray, looking like The Thing That Lived in the Cellar.

"I'm Purchase," the man in the gold choker said.

He extended his hand and they shook all around. But no one else gave a name. Purchase's hand was warm and moist.

Charlie shrugged. "This must be the guy."

Purchase looked at his watch. "You were expecting a guy who looked like John Reed, maybe?"

Kessler looked at Charlie. "Isn't there a password or code phrase or something?"

Purchase answered for him. "The meeting place is the password. Who else would be down here?"

Kessler stared at Purchase. "I don't like anything ambiguous. You say Worldtalk, you say SA, you say Steinfeld. I mean, for all I know, I'm not really seeing you. Maybe they came in last night, maybe they treated me and Charlie and Julie so we share the same hallucination. Maybe they're trying to propagandize—that revolutionaries are really a lot of fat cats. Like the IRA and PLO chiefs who used to make fortunes off the black market. Maybe you're not here and I'm talking to an empty chair."

Purchase nodded. "That's not *impossible*, but it's pretty unlikely. You stood watches, last night, I presume. Anyway—I'm not a revolutionary. Never said I was. I'm an employee. I work for Steinfeld, while pretending to work for the SA, while pretending to work for Worldtalk. SA thinks I'm their man in Worldtalk; but I'm Steinfeld's man in the SA. Only, I'm not a radical. Not unless it's radical to want the United States to stay the United States. I'm a patriot—and I'm a mole, planted in Worldtalk. And I'm placed to keep an eye on the people who want to make the United States the Fascist States of America. Is that explicit enough? Two days ago I got the Worldtalk memo about Mr. Kessler's program. I happen to know that Steinfeld is working up something similar. He wants you with us. By *God* this is stupid. It's cold in this dump. Do we have to go into this here? There's a van upstairs, big and comfortable, right across the street. We'll talk on the way."

Kessler hesitated. Maybe he should still go to the ACLU.

But Charlie and Julie had insisted they had to go into hiding. "This Steinfeld will help me get my work back? My life?"

"He'll help you. If you help him."

Kessler took a deep breath, and nodded.

They went upstairs.

Part Three
SWENSON

11

ELLEN MAE CRANDALL stood at the head of the table, in Conference Room B, seventieth floor of the Worldtalk Building. It was an oblong table in an oblong room, a room with the usual imitation-wood-paneled walls and thick umber rug. There was just a trace of the shabbiness—a smutching of the transparent table, a fade in the color of walls and carpet—that such new places acquire after a remarkably short usage.

Sitting to her right, watching her without staring at her, John Swenson was thinking that Ellen Mae Crandall resembled her brother to an unfortunate degree. What were pleasingly masculine features on her brother were coarse on Ellen Mae. She had the heavy eyebrows; the deep, intense brown-black eyes; the wide, flashing grin showing a piano-keyboard spread of teeth, perfect and spotless, all the black keys missing . . .

Swenson smiled at the thought. There were no black keys in the Second Alliance. But some of the piano's hammers were black. They used whoever they had to use.

Ellen Mae wore a black shirt-suit with a lacy white collar. She looked pale, and her eyes were sunken even deeper than usual.

Swenson, conscious of his youth and good looks and trying to de-emphasize them—the last thing he needed to contend with was envy-seeded suspicion—sat across from Colonel Watson.

The Colonel was one of those ageless outdoorsmen who might be as young as forty-five and as old as seventy—he was closer to the latter. His florid face, weathered by the tropical sun during a hundred campaigns to suppress black independence, was British resolute, and British classic. His smoky-blue eyes flickered up and down the table, filing reactions, attitudes, levels of competence. Swenson considered him the number two power in the SA.

Sitting beside Watson was corpulent, nervous Sackville-West, head of Internal Security, breathing noisily through his mouth, scribbling notes which he screened with one cupped, doughy hand, like a priggish schoolboy who suspected his neighbor of cheating on exams.

The rest of the table was taken up by Spengle, Gluckman, and Katzikis and their secretaries—since the transcribing computer built into the table provided copies of all that was said, none of the secretaries were needed; they were there for reasons of pomp and Swenson ignored them. His mind was on Ellen Mae.

But Swenson was going to move carefully, softly, delicately. He had been investigated once, after the attempted assassination, and he had weathered it, had in fact come out of it in a position of strength. But two investigations would be one too many.

And Sackville-West trusted no one except for Crandall.

Ellen Mae called the meeting to order. She smiled and said, "The first order of business is to tell you that Rick is off the critical list, and his condition is now listed as serious. But Dr. Wellington informs me that Rick is pulling through with flying colors and is expected to be on his feet in two weeks—"

There was the expected murmur of relieved pleasantries around the table, Swenson carefully adding his own sigh of happiness.

"Now normally—" Just a touch of mischief in her voice, a mama with a Christmas surprise. "—I'd lead the opening prayer myself. But today, Rick is going to do it."

Heads snapped up. A few of the lower-echelon people muttered concern. Swenson waited, expressionless, guessing what was up.

Ellen Mae tapped out a brief order on the keyboard built into the table in front of her. A wafer-thin video screen hummed down from a slot in the ceiling behind her. She stood to one side. The room darkened; the screen lit up.

Rick Crandall faded in, in slightly drained colors; the picture was a little fuzzy around the edges. Crandall looked pale, but better than Swenson had expected. Makeup? Probably. Crandall was propped up a little in a hospital bed. An IV tube led from a wall panel to his arm. Crandall smiled.

There was a stirring around the room in response. That smile was short of a grin, but it was strong, and certain, and it sent a thrill of reassurance through every one of them.

"G'mornin', friends," Crandall said in his soft Southern accent—so soft it was almost missing. "I want to thank you all for standing by me in this time, and for holdin' the fort for me. I have a report here . . . " He gestured toward something off-camera. " . . . that informs me you have been faithfully manning the watchtowers. I'm feeling a whole heckuva lot better and looking forward to being back at Our Work in two or three weeks—that is, unless the doctor's maybe a Democrat or a Jew! And I guess if he's one, he's the other."

A ripple of laughter around the room. That Rick.

"Now if I could . . . "

Swenson said it in his mind along with Crandall, he'd heard it so often, *Now if I could just have your attention for the most important business in the world, we'll say a prayer.*

" . . . business in the world," Crandall was saying, "we'll say a prayer."

He closed his eyes and tilted his head down a little. Everyone in the conference room did the same thing.

" . . . Lord, we beseech you to let us learn from our mistakes; to care for one another so deeply we will not allow our brethren to stray for a moment from Our Work, which is *Your* Work; to give us the strength to persevere in this moment of vulnerability; to know the Devil when he stands among us. Lord, you sent the Devil among us, to teach us a strong lesson. You struck the stigmata of the Christian Warrior into me, to humble me and to illuminate the gravity of Our Work; Lord, we beseech you . . . "

The prayer came rhythmically, in something near a monotone, but it never droned. It conveyed urgency, but it was never hysterical.

Crandall was wounded, and sick, and this was probably taking a lot out of him, but you had to hand it to the guy, Swenson thought, he had the art down and he could lay it out from a hospital bed and still make you shiver way down in your bones.

He explained things in the prayer, simply and with finality: the would-be assassin had been the Devil's man, just that simple. In order to prevent such a thing from happening again, to prevent another diabolic incursion, we must search ourselves, and those around us: we must increase security and we must watch one another like hawks, in God's name. There are traitors afoot.

And Crandall had rung in stigmata. Without saying it directly—that would be sacrilegious—he had managed to imply that in being shot he was martyred, that in some sense he was a stand-in for Christ Himself.

And they would buy it, Swenson knew. The word *stigmata* would start a train of associations in their minds, as Crandall knew it would, and sooner or later they would proclaim him Messiah.

And Swenson thought, *Oh shit, Devereaux.*

Devereaux's mission was totally misbegotten. *I told them, use a bomb. The mission had to be a suicide. I told them a bomb.*

But then, a bomb hadn't worked when they'd tried to kill Hitler.

As the prayer ended and the lights came up, Swenson caught Sackville-West looking hard at him. The old man seemed an incompetent dodderer and more than once Swenson had wondered if he deliberately played that up to make his enemies underestimate him. And just now he was watching Swenson.

Making Swenson think: *I let myself slip out of character.*

And you can't even do that in your thoughts. Steinfeld had warned him. *You're an idealist, John, and you're too well motivated for deep penetration; they'll sense you, they'll smell you out, because you can't bury it deep enough.*

But Swenson had been the one, because Ellen Mae wanted him close to her, so there was nothing else for it.

Swenson forced himself into the role. He put a hand to his eyes and thought about Crandall and saw him as his Uncle Harry, whom he'd loved; Uncle Harry, who'd died of cancer; the method acting pushed his buttons, and the tears came. Reverential tears.

He cut it off quickly. Don't overdo it.

Ellen Mae smiled down at him. She stood close beside him, her bony hip pressed against his arm; she reached down and squeezed his shoulder reassuringly. Her own eyes glistened with tears.

"He'll be back. He'll be back soon," she said softly.

"I know," Swenson said, smiling bravely.

◆

In one of the notebooks in which Rickenharp wrote ideas and lyrics, the last thing he'd written was: *Synchronicity laughs when we see it and laughs when we don't.*

At the precise instant Swenson was replying to Ellen, a long way away, Rickenharp was saying, "Yeah, I know." Because Carmen had just said, "What did you expect? It's not easy and it's not fun and it's not romantic."

"I *mean*," she went on, "did you expect there would be a kind of TV fadeout on our shaking hands, agreeing to take you with us, and then maybe a quick cut to the action, some street fight in which you blow away the enemy, and then cut to the scene where you get your medals?"

"*No*, I didn't fucking expect that," Rickenharp growled. "But this is fucking ridiculous. I didn't know heaps like this still existed anywhere."

Yukio shrugged. "It's a typical Maltese fishing trawler."

Yukio, Willow, Rickenharp, and Carmen were huddled miserably in the hold of a fishing boat. A lantern swung pendulously with the wallowing of the creaking boat. An engine rattled and coughed somewhere behind them. The hold stank of rotting fish blood, and Rickenharp kept waiting to get used to it and he never did. Every breath was a fight with gagging. He was cold. The hold was clammy. The inner bulkhead behind drank heat from him. But if he sat anywhere else, or in the middle, he got seasick. He'd already thrown up twice, in the far corner, and he didn't want the dry heaves. The swinging lantern made him sick, but he didn't want the darkness either.

He'd sat hunched like this for hours. Somewhere between five and twelve hours—probably closer to five—and it seemed like days. He coughed, and he felt faintly feverish.

I'm getting a fucking cold, he thought.

But he'd complained once, and he wasn't going to let himself complain anymore, because Carmen's tone told him she was one step from contempt for him.

And the worst of it, the deep muddy trench of it was, *the drugs were gone.*

Here he was, slogging along in a boat Frankie's source used for smuggling drugs, among other things, but the hold was empty now, and they'd gone through Carmen's supply and Rickenharp's three grams—one gram ruined by a slopover wave when they'd boarded from the rowboat... They'd done them all, and now he felt burnt and enervated, and he was on a tightrope over the pits of the various pits of his personal hells, pits he knew like a man six months in solitary knows his tiny cell.

How much longer? he wanted to ask.

Is it much farther to Denver, Mom?

Your father's fed up with hearing that. You kids play with your holo-boy or something...

The fever rose, and warmed him, and he slipped into a pleasant delirium; driving with his parents across the country, he could almost feel the vinyl of the car's seats against his cheek...

We'll never get there, the little boy whined, in the delirium.

"We'll get there." Carmen's voice, from somewhere. "Or we'll drown and it won't matter."

◆

"Nationalism is the key to any nation," Watson was saying. He smiled urbanely. "Seems obvious, doesn't it? The very impulse that normally serves to exclude foreign control can insure the *success* of foreign control—if the key is turned from within the target country."

Watson was standing at the mini-terminal where Ellen Mae had stood; across from him Swenson took notes at his mini-terminal.

"We have NATO's leave," Watson went on, glancing at his notes, "to establish behind-combat policing bodies in Belgium, France, Norway, Spain, Greece, Italy, and, very soon, Holland. England for the foreseeable future will continue to be administered by the National Front, but—" he smiled "—the distinction is superfluous." Chuckles around the table. "They're all doing Our Work..."

Swenson smiled companionably. *Doing Our Work.*

"Our Work" meant full control over the countries in which the SA was established. It meant a takeover. It meant the Eclipse project.

"... establishing Our Work in these countries is simply a matter of utilizing each target nation's nationalist sentiment, a sentiment that is, everywhere, stronger than ever. The scenario is as follows, and I give it to you in a brief, general way with the understanding that the details that will come later are most important:

"Each target country is already in desperate need of order. Like Lebanon in the last century, the targets are unable to police themselves and have requested outside assistance. The SAISC being the only 'independent' security force large enough, being multinational, and being essentially a business without political loyalties—"

Here he paused to smile and they were allowed to chuckle again.

"—was awarded the policing contract for the target countries without significant dissent from the United Nations. The majority of our troops were in place as of last Friday midnight. Paris remains an exception; the war has severely damaged logistic channels into France. The troops will be airlifted in as soon as the neutrality agreement is finalized with Moscow. Once we're in place, the Russians will find out just exactly how 'neutral' we are..." Watson paused for another round of polite chuckling. With Crandall there was never a need for the polite response; the group responded to him naturally, liturgically, sincerely. But, of course, Watson was a typical high-military British bore. "... Each target nation has assigned a native liaison to coordinate policing efforts between the SA and the target's government or provisional government. In every single case, I'm proud to announce, our liaison was placed by the SA's Advance Services Bureau. The liaison is one of us. In each case it is a man with a public reputation for nationalistic sentiments. The man in France is Le Pen, great grandson of the last century's famous Front National organizer. The popular sentiment for nationalism has grown in France as in the other nations as a result of the incursion of immigrants, who take jobs away from nationals, and who transform their neighborhoods into something alien; and the Third World War itself, which, of course, has not made the common people pleased with foreigners. Steeped in this sentiment, young Le Pen is one step from the presidency.

"Our procedure in France will be roughly as follows: First, our troops will arrive and restore order. The food rioters, the looters, the bands of thieves, and the various terrorist and radical factions will be arrested, shot, and generally discouraged. Second, we will arrange it so that Le Pen will take credit for the restoration of order. Third, an information campaign will convince the public that Le Pen is in complete control of the SA troops, and that the presence of the troops is equivalent to the triumph of French nationalism. The problem, of course, is that most of the SA troops will be foreigners—the contradiction will be ironed out by inducting increasing numbers of sympathetic French nationalists into SA forces, and by creating the illusion that the SA is the tool of the French people, and completely in their control. Fourth, French troops thoroughly indoctrinated into the SA way of thinking will by degrees completely replace the rank-and-file of street-visible SA troops. But their superiors will ultimately be SA proper. Now . . . " He paused dramatically, looked up and down the table, and made eye contact. "Now, if we follow this simple formula, and follow through on its one thousand and one necessary details, we will, in less than five years, control every West European country of any significance. To put it bluntly, Europe will be ours. And we will begin to clean it up. The Zionist/neo-Stalinist conspiracy that controls half of the continent, and the Muslim conspiracy that controls the rest, will be eliminated, and eliminated with finality. *The solution is at hand."*

◆

Hard-Eyes and Jenkins sat side by side in twentieth-century steel-and-wood classroom desks. Jenkins looked fairly miserable. He was too big for the desk. Hard-Eyes felt all right. He was full; they'd just come from lunch. They ate well here, as Steinfeld had promised, and the room was warm, heated by an oil furnace in the basement of the old Paris school, an *école supérieure*; the vents gave out slow-rolling waves of warm air and a faint petroleum scent, a kind of industrial perfume which Hard-Eyes somehow found comforting. He was warm and well-fed. On an age-darkened bulletin board to one side were posters from twenty years before, extolling in French the virtues of democracy for some Parisian civics class. But listening to Steinfeld drone about guerrilla cell organization, Hard-Eyes was alternately mangling his own favorite victim of persecution, his right-hand thumbnail, and with his other hand nervously tracing the scorings of initials carved into the blond wood of the desk top. He felt himself careening, tottering on the edge of the abyss that was his future.

Steinfeld was saying, "Internal cadres organize into cells of three persons, only one of the three interfacing with command or other cells. A cell of three persons is the standard cell formation used in a classic guerrilla movement." As he spoke he drew a diagram on the blackboard.

And Hard-Eyes kept up an internal dialog with himself.

They are liars, he thought. All intelligence services employ liars, or, make liars of their employees; they have to, it's a necessary job skill. So Steinfeld might be working for anyone, including the fucking Russians. Who am I really working for?

What difference does it make? You know why you're doing it. For food and shelter and in the hopes you'll make contacts that'll get you back to the States.

Sure, okay, but the Second Alliance could be funding and directing this whole thing, could be behind the resistance to the Second Alliance! Some kind of disinformation system, say; or maybe creating a semblance of a resistance in some way gives them authority to use greater force, which would consolidate their power in the region.

Wha-at? Bullshit! Paranoia! I mean, come on.

Yeah? You can't *be* too paranoid anymore.

Yes, you can. Paranoia is a skill, neggo.

And then he forced himself to listen to Steinfeld, who was talking about propaganda teams, armed and unarmed. Winning hearts and minds...

◆

A week after that, and they were on a roof, looking down through a sheer, misting rain, at Place Clichy. There were no cars in the *place* that late afternoon. Preparing for the demonstration, the police had rerouted the automotive traffic around the square; the traffic didn't amount to much anyway, with the gas shortage, and because a quarter of the city's streets were impassable with rubble from the Russian shellings.

But the square was filled, was overflowing with people. Every age, every profession—but mostly people who had been middle class, and lower middle class, Steinfeld said. All of them white.

Steinfeld was there beside Hard-Eyes and Jenkins and little Jean-Pierre and Hassan . . . Hassan the faintly smiling, who had come from Damascus to join the New Resistance. Sometimes Hassan said that the Muslim Holy Alliance would send troops to help Steinfeld, because the SA had already begun registering Parisian Muslims, and because the Front National wanted to expel all Muslims from France . . . But the Islamic troops never came. Hard-Eyes supposed that they could not bring themselves to take orders from a Jew.

They were crouching in a small space between an ornamental balcony railing—wrought iron, the paint flaked off it, rust burning through—and a dormer window, looking down past the slick, runneling tiles at the demonstration forming up in Place Clichy. There was a statue in the middle of the square, but it was hidden behind bunting and placards and banners and French flags. Hundreds of people in the crowd waved smaller flags; the surface of the crowd had a plumage in the colors of France, as if the collective entity that was the demonstration was a kind of bird showing its tail feathers to declare itself to others of its kind.

In the foreground was a temporary wooden stage, about ten yards wide and two high, erected that morning. The NR operatives were seeing it from behind. Over it was a white awning and it was backed in a sheet of the same white material, so that they couldn't see the speaker on the stage. But they could hear him; his turgid intonations boomed from the stage PA and echoed off the buildings around the square. And they could see his shadow. Stage lights threw his shadow on the white stage backdrop, outlining him as if for a Japanese shadow play. And the shadow he cast was larger than life, a shadow Goliath waving his arms and gesticulating, pointing a trembling finger at the sky. It was the gigantic shadow of Le Pen, the Front National candidate, great-grandson of Le Pen, who had also been the Front National candidate. When the war situation shifted sufficiently to permit an election, this Le Pen would stand a good chance of being elected. So Steinfeld told them . . .

Steinfeld translated the speech for Hard-Eyes and Jenkins as it went into its dramatic climax. "He's saying, 'And now the diadem of Europe has been crushed; the gem of France lies in its wreckage. Who is to be blamed? Clearly, the Russians are responsible. They began the war, they invaded Allied territory, and they have tried to take Paris! But who is it who has sabotaged the metros, blown up the power stations, burned the Civil Defense headquarters? Those who are the servants of the Russians, the slaves of the new KGB! Where do they come from? The third world, and the Middle East, where the Russians wield control! The foreigners who we welcomed into our nation, and who repaid us with their cultural pollution, with espionage, and sabotage! All *to prepare the ground for the Russian Union's destruction of our city!* The Muslims, the Jews, the Algerian Communists, the Portuguese Communists—*the poison! The Poison!*'"

The crowd's response was thunderous.

"They really believe that?" Jenkins asked incredulously. "Things break down, so they blame immigrants?"

"You have penetrated the heart of their argument," Steinfeld said dryly.

For a moment Hard-Eyes wondered if Steinfeld was translating accurately. Maybe he was distorting...

But Hard-Eyes could see genuine rage in the crowd's fist-shaking, in the excessively energetic way the flags were waved, in their voices, and most of all in the posturing of that enormous shadow... That strangely familiar silhouette with its rhythmically gesturing arms...

And he could see the advance SAISC men around the edges of the crowd, and behind the stage, arms crossed over their uniformed chests...

And he knew the truth again, when he saw the Second Alliance reaction to the counter-demonstration arriving from the side street. The counter-demonstration consisted of half a hundred spectacled students and dark-faced Algerians chanting, *"Fascisme? Non! Fascisme? Non!"*

"Brave and stupid," Steinfeld muttered.

... as the SA ran to intercept the counter-demonstration, the security bulls wielding nightsticks, drawing guns. Twenty SA bulls in wedge formation rammed into the counter-demonstration, sticks swinging. The Front National crowd turned to follow them. The candidate shouted something inaudible in the roar of the crowd... The regular police, briefed for this, were holding their positions at the street corners...

"If you looked sharply," Steinfeld said, "you might have seen two members of the counter-demonstration backing out through their own demonstration just before the SA moved in. Provocateurs, setting up the real counter-demonstrators. They're either SA or Le Pen's agents. Or both..." He went on with the cool objectivity of a TV commentator talking about the decline and fall of Rome. *And on that same day the barbarians massed outside the gates of Rome*... "What you are seeing is part of the 'strategy of tension.'"

"That was a strategy the old school terrorists used," Jenkins muttered. He had turned away from the riot in the street below and lit a cigarette. Hard-Eyes continued to watch the riot, fascinated.

"The extremist right-wing propagandists coined the term to speak about the left, yes. But it is the right who most efficiently use terror. Terror and disruption of services creates an atmosphere of tension which sets the stage for a rightist takeover. Provides a rationale for liquidating a leftist threat. *Agents provocateurs* infiltrate the leftists, media for terrorists, bombings, plant evidence, incriminate detainees with their 'confessions' . . . There were other, earlier European extremist right-wing terrorist groups. One of them, founded by Stefano Delle Chiaie in the last century, has grown very large, and simply merged itself with the Second Alliance. It wasn't very well organized in the twentieth century. It didn't have a centrally coordinated body or even a headquarters. It was loosely structured, a circle of friends, really, neofascists and old-guard Nazis. Sometimes it was assisted by the CIA, because it was so fervently anticommunist. American intelligence recruited and sheltered Nazis after World War Two, you know. Those who were valuable to it. Those Nazis survived and went on to become part of the loose rightist organization. It factionalized, and that kept it from being efficient—until Crandall came along. He has a talent for finding some kind of ideological common denominator. He brought them all together under his umbrella. And now they're here. Their work is as you see it. Here before you . . . "

Staring down at the riot, the flags and the bloodied clubs upraised, hearing the dull thud of gunshots now, Hard-Eyes had a revelation; personal, internal revelation. It had been percolating in his mind for days. He'd been asking himself why he did it, why he stayed with Steinfeld. There were rumors of a route to Freezone, and from Freezone it was possible to work your way back to the States. It was risky, but not as risky as staying in Paris. So why did he stay?

Because he had spent his youth fighting a sense of unreality; a feeling of insignificance and transience. Partly it was the Grid, the outgrowth of the Internet, the spawn of the mating of television and the Web. It shaped the prevailing iconography, the backdrop Hard-Eyes had grown up in, middle-class urban America. As it shaped London, Paris before the war, Tokyo, New Delhi, Capetown, Rio de

Janeiro, Hong Kong . . . As it had been tincturing Russia, yes, even the People's Republic of China for decades. Steinfeld thought that the Grid was, perhaps on some collective unconscious level, the real reason the Neo-Communists in Russia had begun their post-Glasnost aggression. After the fall of capitalist post-Putin Russia, and the shambles of the new global recession, Russia had descended into near anarchy, giving the new authoritarian state the mandate to re-establish Communism. The new Soviet needed to pirate resources by conquest to stabilize its power. But it feared the Grid: The satellite transmissions blanketing the Earth with every frequency of the Grid. They tried to impose a Soviet-like censorship but Russia was pervaded with illegal satsend receivers; the black market in them boomed uncontrollably.

Hard-Eyes understood their fear of the Grid very well.

The minimono star Callais becomes hot. Overnight his image is everywhere. Endorsing in videos, holos; dancing, singing with charming minimono lugubriousness on animated T-shirts, and in playback glasses and on holo-posters and on screens in cars and buses and trains and planes and singing out of the radio . . . Or someone pushes a new style of clothing computer-designed for a computer-evaluated subtype: Westerclothes for the Distinctively Rough-Edged Man. *He's a Westerclothes Man!* . . . Political candidates packaged like a candy bar, like a line of clothing or a cigarette, while the politician's actual political reality is almost entirely undefinable . . .

Worldtalk with its glassine fingers in the news broadcasts, the printouts. Shaping, shading the data: Illusionists in the pay of special interests. There was, once, an American Underground—but one was never sure who the real enemy was. Who, finally, was responsible for the Dissolve Depression and the rooftop shacktowns it created; the increasing blasé acceptance of the USA as a nation under siege from within, manning the barricades with the growing legions of hired cops, gypsy cops, rent-a-cops, uniformed thugs insulating the rich from the poor?

The Grid shaded it all beyond clear seeing. War-support propaganda. Styles of talking popularized by characters from

TV shows. Catchy expressions deliberately created by TV-show packagers. Media-propagated intellectual fads, health fads, and art fads. Fads on fads within fads—gushed out from the great cornucopia of the Grid. The latest celebrity scandal—and sometimes the celebrity didn't exist as a physical person. Some were, all along, purely digital creations.

All of it transient, the day-by-day changing shape of the national self-image. Each man reduced to the status of a single pixel in a wifi transmission.

And now, in that split-instant, in a flash insight into his personal mental cosmos, Hard-Eyes knew why he was going to stay and why he would fight beside Steinfeld.

Because this...

...the SA cops in their beetle-wing helmets using their clubs, the confrontation with the true predator; with a clearly distinguishable evil...

...this was *real.*

◆

Bonham was standing in line, staring at the plastic-sheathed metal wall. The pilots called the Colony's walls "bulkheads," and the irritated Colonists had called the pilots "bulkhead blockheads"; now with the blockade they were "blockade bulkhead blockheads." To Bonham, it was a wall, and when he'd worked on the spaceships' shuttles the ship's "bulkheads" were walls, to him. He didn't like NASA jargon, he didn't like working for NASA, and he made up his mind he wasn't going to work out-Colony anymore. They didn't pay him for those kinds of risks. The Russians might take the next step, go from blockading to shooting ships out of space, and no way Bonham was going to put his ass on the line for a handful of newbux once a month.

One part of Bonham's mind was tracking angry free association; the next level down was watching the line of people waiting to get into the main shop and thinking, *There'll be nothing but crap left by the time I get in there. There has to be a way to get in sooner.*

He looked over his shoulder, spotted Caradine and Kalafi in the line down the hall behind him. He made the hand sign that said, *I'm going to initiate a resistance action, are you with me?*

Caradine and Kalafi signaled support. They were acknowledging his leadership and that felt good.

So Bonham took a deep breath, stepped out of line, and walked to the turnstile, ignoring the frowning clerk. He turned and looked down the line and shouted, "You want to know the truth about what's going on here, people? They're using the blockade as an excuse to hoard supplies! Admin gets all the supplies they need! The only way we're going to get what we need is *to take what we want!*"

They looked back at him with fear and uncertainty. But the cooling system was only intermittently functioning again and they'd been waiting there an hour and a half and the line was moving like a dying centipede and all they wanted was goddamn toilet paper and their protein-base ration and their rabbit meat ration and maybe some frozen orange juice...

So when Kalafi and Caradine joined him—and the three of them broke the line, pushed past the clerk at the turnstile, began the looting—the whole damn line followed their example. Bonham felt a surge of adrenaline-fueled pleasure in being at the cutting edge of the riot.

The rioters were whooping and cackling and feverishly scooping and grabbing, sweeping armfuls of groceries into their carts and bags, running out past the checker when they had all they could carry, kicking tables of cans over just for the hell of seeing them fly and clatter, terrifying the regular security guard—an old man in a uniform.

But some part of Bonham's mind wondered where Molt was, and listened for the amplified voices of Security bulls.

So he left the shop as soon as his cart was full, just as the good stuff was beginning to run out and the crowd was losing its mischievous-kid holiday mood and beginning to get genuinely surly. Bonham shoved the choicest of his groceries in a box, picked it up, and ran for it, not thirty seconds before Security got there. The cameras swiveled to watch him go.

♦

"It's sad that you never knew Paris," Besson was saying.

They were sitting beside the window in a café in the Eighteenth Arrondissement, Hard-Eyes and Jenkins and Besson. Besson made Hard-Eyes think of Baudelaire; he had the bulbous head, that forgotten hairline; the hurt, accusing eyes; the bitter mouth; and the threadbare dandyism. He wore an old-fashioned vested sharkskin suit and a bow tie; a gold-plated watch chain looped over his thin middle. Besson had sold the watch itself, a year before, when the Russians had the city sealed off and the first famines came. His shoes were taped three times, all the way round, and he'd put blacking on the tape to try and make it took like part of the shoe. His vest was missing three buttons, and he was unshaven. His nails showed negative quarter-moons of black. But he was elegant; still, he was elegant.

He smoked the wretched C-rations cigarette down till it burned his yellowed fingers. He sighed, crimped it carefully out, and put the eighth-inch butt in a Prince Albert tin he kept in a jacket pocket. "The bastard Yankee soldiers gave me one cigarette. Not even a chocolate bar. I'm not pretty enough, eh?" He gave a mirthless laugh. As if on cue, a truckful of American soldiers trundled noisily down the street. The truck ran on compressed hydrate crystals; the septic smell of methane trailed the truck as it swung, grinding as it changed gears, around the corner.

"Most of the Americans will be gone tomorrow," Besson said, and there was no regret in his voice.

Jenkins and Hard-Eyes looked at one another. Hard-Eyes shrugged.

Jenkins had tried to talk Hard-Eyes into surrendering to the American soldiers, pretending they were just lost American expatriates. More than once they'd thought about it, in Amsterdam. But the Americans didn't send you home, word had it. They pressganged you into civilian work crews. Or, worse, the COs had the power to draft you on the spot.

"You have never seen Paris," Besson said mournfully. He gestured contemptuously at the tired, wounded city around him. The café faced a narrow, brick-paved street below the Sacré Coeur. The onion dome of the ancient cathedral was just visible above the red tile rooftops; the overcast sky was breaking up in the late-afternoon breeze. Propaganda leaflets whipped down the gutter. The tall, stately buildings, narrow houses crowded together in gray stone and red tile, windows shattered out of them, were gap-eyed, lifeless. Most of the chimneys were mute, spoke no smoke; the sidewalks were scabbed with trash, a neglect unknown to Paris before the war. The café itself was almost empty. There were no supplies—it sold no beer, no liquor, only weak tea and a few exorbitant bad wines. The big copper espresso pumps were empty; Parisians were complaining as much from the loss of their daily caffeine as from the famine. The café owner kept the establishment open mostly out of habit. There were two old digital pinball machines against the wall, dead, cold as tombstones; there was no power. But the newly arrived SA technicians had gotten the natural-gas pumps working. There was gas, to heat the tea Hard-Eyes and Jenkins and Besson sipped beside their fly-specked window.

"This café, now, at this hour, should be overflowing with people," Besson said. "In the next room, they would fill their salad plates and eat, and the waitress would come to tell them the daily carte... They would have wine, and café after, a fine black café. Les Halles! I lived in Les Halles, I had a bookstore. I knew your Steinfeld very well in those days. He would come in, and we would argue..." There was a flash of genuine pleasure in Besson's eyes for a moment. "How I loved to argue with him! Wonderful arguments! We both enjoyed! And Les Halles—the tourists were the life of the place, and there were musicians and jugglers to take money from the tourists. The French musicians would try to sing American songs, the Americans stranded in Paris would try to sing French songs. Or Paris on a rainy night—you walk on the streets almost empty, and then you are filled with the romance of your misery. Just when you are cursing the rain, you see the glow of a *brasserie*, the light laughing out of it. There was a bread seller, Prochaine. He was said to make a wonderful bread, and the reputation of this bread was such that people would stand in line two hours to buy it, to buy one loaf, sold only in his shop. It was a heavy bread, not dark and not light, a little sour but also sweet, and it was moist . . . crystalline. *Comprends?* A very simple bread, and profound, *mes amis.* You could taste one bite for an hour. This *pain-Prochaine*, it was Paris. Just five years ago, my friends . . . Prochaine is dead now, and his son is dead, and when the Russians held the city, the Allies bombed a big gun in Les Halles, antiaircraft gun, and now the neighborhood is . . . " He shrugged and sipped his tea.

"And now the SA is here," Jenkins said.

Across the street, a man was putting up a poster. He peeled the backing-paper off and pressed it onto the big gray stone wall, beside the wide stone stairs terracing up to the cathedral.

The posterer was a knobby teenage boy in a ratty sweatshirt. His hair was twisted up into a flare topknot over his head, in imitation of last year's American fashions; but the tint was six months overdue for renewal; and he'd had to hold the shape with rubber bands.

Besson sighed. "Why do you Americans send us your stupid hairstyles?"

Hard-Eyes was laboriously translating the poster. It came out as something like:

THE *FRONT NATIONAL* HAS COME TO THE RESCUE OF THE FRENCH PEOPLE!! WATCH FOR THE SOLDIERS OF THE *STRATEGIE ACTUEL* AND STRUGGLE BESIDE THEM TO REBUILD PARIS!! THE *STRATEGIE ACTUEL* HAS RESTORED THE GAS!! FIGHT THE CONSPIRACY OF FOREIGNERS!!!!!!!!!!!!

The boy continued down the block, peeling the backing off the posters, sticking them up, leaving the slick brown backing to curl like oversized pencil shavings on the cracked sidewalk. He put up three more posters, each one different, and yet each one the same as the last.

The second said: "WHY HAVE WE ALLOWED THE ZIONISTS TO RAPE PARIS?"—and nothing more.

The third said: "PARIS IS A JAIL AND THE FOREIGNERS ARE THE JAILERS . . . BUT FRANCE HOLDS THE KEY!!"

A fourth said: "FOOD AND FREEDOM IS ON THE WAY! DON'T LET MUSLIMS, JEWS, OR LIARS TAKE IT FROM YOU!" Each poster was printed on a different color paper, with different styles of lettering. They were not of uniform size. They might almost have been put up by different organizations.

"When the electricity comes on, they'll start the radio propaganda," Jenkins said.

Besson snorted. "How? The Russians blew up the power plants."

Jenkins said, "Saw something out at Rond Point Victor Hugo. They had a receiver on a truck. A microwave power receiver. Maybe SA owns one of the power gathering satellites. Maybe they'll beam it down here. Not enough for a whole city—but enough for, say, a fifth of the town, two days a week. The people'll be glad for what they get. They'll know who to thank . . . "

"And the SA can cut it off when they want. When it suits their purposes," Hard-Eyes said.

"This talk disgust me!" Besson declared, flapping his hand dismissively. "You disappoint me. You are talking politics. I thought you were men of refinement. Do you think it was politics that made our situation? No, my friends. It was aggression. Politics is only the snorting of the bull before the charge. But—I can see that Steinfeld has chosen you well."

Hard-Eyes looked sharply at him.

Besson laughed. "I said the right thing, no? This bastard Steinfeld, he chooses men he knows will catch the disease of politics! The secret idealist, eh? Someone—Jean François—said to me, 'Why should I work with Steinfeld? He is a foreigner pretending to fight for France. There are Yanks and Brits in his troops. Maybe they are CIA, maybe British secret service . . . Why should they fight for us?' But I told him to remember the German resistance to the Nazis in World War Two. Not so much resistance, but it was there! The resistance against the Nazis was every kind of man, in Germany. There were Communists and conservatives and everything between. There were foreigners and there were fanatic German nationalists who simply hated Hitler."

"But why not you, Besson?" Jenkins asked. "Is the SA really much better than Hitler?"

"Why not me, because I am not one to march in parades—even clandestine parades! I watch them from my window. When my wife... died... she..." He stared out the window, tried to swallow the sorrow. "That part of Paris is poisoned now. We will not use the big bombs, they agreed, eh? So they use the *leetle* nuclear bombs. What do they call them?"

"Tactical," Hard-Eyes said.

"Yes. They only burn up a square kilometer, eh? Three square kilometers on the edge of Paris, one inside. Poisoned with radiation! So—it is okay to poison us only a *petite* amount, bit by bit? That is like choosing to torture a man to death instead of killing him cleanly..." He stood up abruptly, upsetting his chair, and walked stiffly out into the misting rain, without so much as an *au revoir*.

Hard-Eyes hugged himself, feeling cold.

"It's crazy, staying in this town," Jenkins said. But he said it musingly. There was no implication in it.

Hard-Eyes nodded, wondering, Why *are* we doing it? And the answer came: So that the world means something.

The boy came into the café and asked the shopkeeper if he could put a poster in the window. The shopkeeper shook his head, once, and hooked a thumb at the door. The boy made a great show of writing down the address of the shop.

Hard-Eyes thought, Surely it hasn't come to that, surely not so soon...

But when they came to the café the next day, hoping to find Besson there, the café keeper was sorrowfully boarding up the windows. Someone had smashed out the glass, and on the wall beside the broken café window was spray-painted, in French, HE COLLABORATES WITH THE ENEMIES OF FRANCE!

So they walked back to the hostel Steinfeld's people had put them in and said nothing on the way. They passed a supermarket, gutted and burned out in the lootings, and the posters were everywhere.

12

In Manhattan, and in the "A" building of the Second Alliance International Security Corporation, across the street from the Worldtalk Building, John Swenson typed up a coded communication to a man named Purchase. He told his terminal to send the communication to Purchase's terminal, across the street and up forty floors. The communication was a message within a message within a message. To a man who was an agent within an agent, within an agency. Message *one* told Worldtalk that SAISC's security preplanning for the Eighth International Congress of Orbital Manufacturers was complete. Message *two*, hidden within the signals for the first, was from the SA's Second Circle, the ruling committee, to Purchase the SA agent. So far as the SAISC knew, Purchase was one of eighteen Worldtalk executives with greater and lesser degrees of loyalty to the Second Alliance. Message *three*, secreted within the second, was from Swenson the NR agent to Purchase the NR agent. Warning him that SAISC was making plans to implement a full corporate takeover of Worldtalk—the world's biggest public relations firm and potentially the most powerful tool for propaganda known to modern man . . .

Swenson sighed and wondered if he had done well to send it through an SAISC terminal. How closely was Sackville-West monitoring everything that went out? There was no such thing as an unbreakable code. He looked at his watch. Ellen Mae ought to be alone in her office about now. He picked up a sheet of computer printouts and walked down the hall. Her door was open. He knocked on the frame and went in.

"What have we got here?" Ellen Mae Crandall asked, in her most musical voice, as Swenson laid the printout on her desk. "You could have *sent* it," she added, nodding toward her desk terminal. She smiled. She'd said it to give him his opening.

Swenson said smiling softly, "Maybe it's because any excuse to see you personally..." He shrugged. Ellen Mae blushed, really blushed, by God, and he wondered if he'd gone too far.

She looked hastily at the report. "Oh, the FirStep Colony. Is this from Praeger?" She frowned. "Why didn't he send it to me directly?"

"He sent it to Colony Intelligence Director—which as of this morning is yours truly."

"Oh, I forgot! There's so much, without Rick, to keep track of..." She sighed. Playing helpless female now.

He put his hand on her arm, telling himself to ignore the arm's slight excess of black hairs, and said, "He's going to be back with us soon."

She swallowed, flustered, but gave no sign she wanted him to take his hand away.

Purchase was right about her, Swenson thought.

She glanced over the report. "What's, um, the gist of this?"

He straightened, and put his hands in his jacket pocket. "There isn't a lot to it. They can't get anything but short transmissions out, and fewer of those lately, with the Russians sending out their scrambling signal. Rimpler is possibly cracking under pressure. He's unstable anyway. He's got a lot of popular support but among the technickis there are two other men Praeger thinks he can put in to replace Rimpler. On the technicki level, of course. Rimpler's daughter is a problem..."

She wasn't listening, she was staring straight ahead with a patently artificial look of having remembered something important. "Oh, my gosh."

Oh, my gosh? Swenson thought. Aloud he said, "Something wrong?"

"I've just realized I've got to get a full report on this to Rick, tomorrow. I've told him he shouldn't work, but he—well, you know how he is. You can't keep him away from it. If he were in a hospital maybe we could, you know, encourage him to take it easy, the doctors have some kind of authority there. But he's out at Cloudy Peak Farm, and he's just like Daddy was—once he gets on the farm, he's the Farmer and no one can say a word to him!"

Swenson chuckled, and thought, maybe the polite chuckling all the time is the hardest part of all.

She went on, "I promised him I'd get this to him—you know, my own analysis. But I don't think I can do it alone, and with everything else..." She turned to him as if she'd just thought of it. "John, do you think you could come out to the farm tonight? We could work late, so I could have it in the morning..."

"I'd be honored," he said, and in a way it was true.

And this time he was careful not to put his hand on her arm. It was all still a question of timing.

"Security will pick us up at six, at the front door," she said briskly, turning all studiedly businesslike.

"I'll be there with bells on," he said, knowing she liked old-fashioned expressions. He smiled at her and went back to his office. And couldn't suppress a stab of pity for her...

◆

AS THE helicopter settled down over Cloudy Peak Farm, Swenson hung on to the straps and closed his eyes. He didn't mind flying—it was coming down or going up to begin the flying that scared him. It wasn't the sky, it was the ground. The ground could be hostile to flying things. It smashed them, if they weren't careful.

And he'd already seen the Crandall's farm on the helicopter's first circling approach... A river cut a purple trail through the moonlit trees. The moonlight showed a great swatch of lawn, the glistening snail tracks of two steel fences, and the cluster of trees around the main house. Smaller servants' houses huddled to one side. Behind the house a barn, according to rumor, sheltered a few cows, a couple of sheep, horses—but it wasn't really an actual farm anymore. It was "a combination of pastoral religious retreat and Second Alliance planning center," to use Purchase's phrase.

He felt a sudden queasy hollowness in the pit of his stomach that told him the helicopter was dipping, spiraling down. In his mind's eye he saw it crash; saw himself burning alive in the wreckage.

He felt a cold sweat break out on his forehead and told himself fervently, "This is stupid," and then realized he'd said it aloud. But the thudding chop of the blades had blotted it out.

If they asked me now, he thought, right now, right this second, who I am, what my business is, I might blurt out the truth. *My real name is John Stisky and I'm working undercover for the NR, the New Resistance, an organization that wants to destroy you, all of you . . . Now, what do you think of that?* Because the fear made him mad, made him want to blurt everything. Tell them more than they asked. Tell them and tell them—

Thud. A disappointed whine as the engine cut. He opened his eyes—and drew back, startled by a man with eyes like a falcon, a beak of a nose, and a slash for a mouth, looking right at him, staring. Swenson almost said, *My real name is John Stisky and—*

And then falcon-face said, "You all right, sir?"

Swenson looked at the man's flat-black Security uniform, and panic passed. Just an SA Security guard. "I'm fine. I'm not so good at flying. A little dizzy for a moment—problem with the balance in the inner ear. Only happens when the altitude drops too quickly. No problem."

He brushed the man's hands away from his safety belt, unbuckled it himself, and stood. His knees wobbled and then found their strength. He took a deep breath and stepped out and down, needlessly ducking his head under the slowly spinning blades. He stood in wet ankle-deep grass and felt the relief rush over him, and once more he was John Swenson, deep in character, when Ellen Mae put her hand on his arm and led him to the house. "Are you all right, John?"

"Sure." He smiled sheepishly. "I'm not much for chopper flights."

"Maybe a glass of wine and some dinner. We can work after dinner."

"Now you're talking."

She squeezed his arm, pleased at his familiarity, and he thought, *I'm doing it right.*

◆

Memo from Frank Purchase to Quincy Witcher—High Encryption Protocol.
Subject: John Stisky
... was a priest of the Holy Roman Church assigned to the Diocese of Managua, Nicaragua. Within three weeks of arriving in Managua he came into conflict with his immediate superior, Father Gostello (see attached transcript of recorded fone interviews), when he requested leave to participate in a demonstration at the American Embassy protesting the occupying American army's refusal to consider a timetable for electing a new Nicaraguan governing body; Stisky defied Gostello and attended the demonstration. He was arrested in the course of a riot, and in jail met Father Encendez. Fr. Encendez had been four times censured by the Church for unauthorized political activity in the wake of Pope Peter's encyclicals denouncing Church involvement in progressive political causes. Encendez was later dismissed from the priesthood (as a move of conciliation to the occupying American Forces), when he published an article in an American news printout alleging that General Lonington, Director of the Nicaraguan Occupation, was "connected with anti-Semitic and anti-Catholic organizations and had in his boyhood several times attended meetings of the Ku Klux Klan–related Council of Conservative Citizens . . . may have been instrumental, as a young lieutenant, in helping Nazi war criminals escape an Interpol investigating team." Encendez continued his organizing after leaving the priesthood and in April was found shot to death in a muddy ditch ten miles south of Managua. Stisky pressed for an investigation and charged that Lonington had business connections with the Second Alliance Corporation. Crandall's church had already begun recruiting in Managua, and was the only American church organization allowed free rein there; Stisky pointed out that Lonington was a member of that church, and he demanded Lonington's removal. Stisky was subsequently defrocked . . . No conclusive evidence indicating a homosexual relationship between Stisky and Encendez, but Stisky's college records show that for several months he was a member of the New York University League

of Bisexuals . . . He left the university to enter the seminary in 1994 . . . Stisky's father was Jewish, his mother half-Jewish, but both his parents were atheists, and conceptual artists. His swing toward the Church might be considered an intellectual rebellion against both his parents' philosophy and their chaotic lifestyle . . . His relationships with women typically are abbreviated and stormy . . . He received psychiatric treatment for a nervous breakdown in July, spending two months in Fairweather Rehabilitation Center . . . his instability is a double-edge sword. It is connected with his extreme motivation—his hostile feelings for the SA are as heartfelt as any I've encountered—and his tendency to slip into quasi-pathological sub-characters. The latter tendency, when trained, is clearly useful in an undercover operative but adds to his unpredictability. Stisky is essentially a gifted amateur. Nevertheless, in the course of his chance meeting with Ellen Mae Crandall, last August sixth, she showed a marked interest in him . . .

◆

"I think we could break it down in three steps," Claire told her father. They were sitting in the living room of Professor Rimpler's apartment. Rimpler sat across from her, slumped over the dialed-up hump of the floor he used as a coffee table. There was a tray of liquors in crystal decanters on the table hump; the walls were dialed to light green, the light was adjusted to resemble the indirect shafting of sun through forest boughs. Claire sat on a confoam chair, her hands clasping her knees, watching her father with growing distress, thinking, *He's coming apart.* "The first step," she went on, trying desperately to engage his attention, "is to talk to this man Molt. He was one of their chief organizers. We can convince him that we're on his side. Second, we release him and he goes to the technickis and speaks for us. Third, to show our good will, we make some concessions. We release the looters from detention, we do double-checks on the field strength around technicki quarters to make sure they aren't getting extra radiation—I mean, why not? The whole thing'll defuse."

"What makes you think we're on their side?" her father asked, casually.

She looked at him in shock. "What?"

"You heard me. Yes, the technickis are in fact being discriminated against, to some degree. I'll tell you something else, Claire my dear—Praeger and his people have seen to it that blacks, Jews, and Muslims are no longer being advanced in Admin! Oh, yes! I know for a fact that he plans to weed them out under one pretense or another, when the blockade is lifted. There's discrimination for you. But we don't *dare* point it out—if Praeger falls, we fall. Things are at that kind of boiling point." His voice dropped from brisk to weary, cynical, marking his shift in mood. He poured himself a tequila, mixed in lime juice and grenadine, then drank off half of it and stared dully into space. "The Ozymandias principle," he said, mostly to himself. "The bigger the enterprise, the more ridiculous you look when you see it was all for nothing, when entropy makes a joke of it."

Claire stood, and moved to sit beside her father; but he only hunched even more. He wore white shorts beginning to yellow; a button-up shirt opened to show the steel-wool hair of his chest; on his feet were decaying thongs. He smelled sour. His eyes focused only on his drink. He held the glass up to the light; the beaded crystal was transfixed by a beam of emerald.

She put an arm over his shoulders; they felt thin and bony. He shrank from her touch, and she dropped her arm. She spoke in a parody of a teacher's recitation: "Dad—if a small meteor impacts the Colony's outer skin, the break is sealed up with the Rimpler alloy. All through the hull is a layer of Rimper Alloy. If the alloy is kept at ninety-two degrees, it's liquid; if the cold of space breaks in, it freezes instantly, fills the hole, restores airtight integrity . . . I make that little speech to the kids when I take them out to the hull observation station. Professor Rimpler made that alloy, I tell them, and he designed this home in space, and he's always trying to make it better for them. There's no alloy that reseals things if we break up in a civil war, Dad. We have to seal the civil breach. And it's you people expect to do it. You have to go on viddy and talk to them. You have to patch up the holes for them."

He pressed the cold glass to his forehead. Tonelessly he said, "If you can get Molt to help us, then maybe. But don't count on any help from him. They went down to interrogate him an hour ago . . ."

Claire stood and backed away from him. She looked at him hard, trying to recognize him. "Dad—how do you know these things? Praeger's 'racial weeding' . . . their plans for Molt . . . ?"

He gestured vaguely toward his console. "When I designed the comm system I . . . built a few safeguards into it. I can monitor Praeger's instructions. I get them all routed to me automatically; I have his code, too." He shrugged. "If you get Molt, I'll talk to the technickis. But just for you. Not because I care about them. They're a lot of *E. coli* in the belly of the beast."

She stared at him. And thought: *Let it go.* If that was his attitude about them, it was something that she couldn't change. Not now.

Claire turned and spoke to the door panel; it slid aside and she walked down the hall to her apartment, where she changed into her Admin Governing Committee jumpsuit, thinking: *E. Coli in the belly of the beast?* There was something pathological about putting it that way.

She pinned her Security pass to her collar, needing the semblance of authority. She took her father's private lift three levels toward Admin. Security level was the entire floor below Admin—like a moat around a castle. As the lift stopped, a panel over the door lit up red with the words SECURITY—PASSES ONLY.

Her palms were damp. She wiped them on her hips and told herself, "You are in charge."

The door opened and Claire stepped into the hallway. A camera looked at her. She held up her pass for the camera to see. Nothing stopped her as she walked down the hall.

She hesitated at the glass doors. Someone had stenciled *Happy Holidays* and a cluster of holly leaves on the glass, and she remembered that it was near Christmas. They would put the big artificial tree up in the Open soon. But no, not with all the vandalism that had been happening. The technicki vandals would make a wreck of it.

She went through the door. A young man smiled up at her from behind the glassy desk. Four small TV monitors to his right showed all four access corridors to Security. There was no need for him to watch them, really; the computers did it quite efficiently alone. But where possible her father had arranged for a human being to oversee cybernetic functions; the other engineers had hinted that the human backup arrangement was irrational, even eccentric.

The young man in the flat-black SAISC uniform kept smiling as he said, "How can I help you, Ms. Rimpler?" His face was pretty, almost angelic, but his hand lay on the desk within reach of the summons button. She and her father had been in Denver for a UNIC meeting when Praeger had revamped Security. They'd come back and found Second Alliance International Security Corporation men setting up new surveillance gear and sentry teams strategically throughout the Colony; the grim, gray-black uniforms could be glimpsed wherever the corridors made a nexus...

The SAISC struck her as altogether too secretive an outfit, almost cultish. There was, after all, its connection to Crandall, who was close to being a cult leader.

"I need four men to escort a prisoner from lockup," she said, trying to sound assertive. "Samson Molt."

The receptionist's smile froze right where it was.

"Let me see what I can do—" He turned to the terminal, tapped a fone number; a face appeared on the screen. She couldn't see it clearly from this angle, but she thought it was Scanlon's. The receptionist was going to the top, which seemed out of sequence. "Ms. Rimpler is here, asking permission to see a prisoner, Samson Molt..."

"To escort him out of there," Claire broke in. "I want to take responsibility for him. He is to be remanded to my custody. I need a few men to help me—"

Scanlon's voice, like his digitally compressed face, was too flat, too oblique.

"The situation is dangerously unstable, Claire. Molt's release would contradict the public information we've already given out; we've had to say repeatedly that we don't know where he is."

"No one believes that anyway."

"I'm sorry, Claire, but if you'd like to put in a formal request for his transfer, we will process it and try to give you an answer within two or three weeks."

"This is ridiculous, Scanlon. I want to talk to you face to face." But the screen went blank. "I'm sorry," the receptionist said blandly, the smile now completely gone. "He's out doing fieldwork. If you'd like to make an..."

Claire turned and walked out; it was as if she were swept along by something, washed into the elevators, and not until she'd gone down to Central Telecast and found Judy in the commissary did she really take note of her surroundings.

Claire looked around the commissary, blinking, and then sighed and sank into the cracked blue plastic seat across from Judy Avickian. Judy was small, eyes nearly black, waist-length curly black hair braided for work, looped over one shoulder to dangle in front of her white and gold skin-suit. Judy liked things white and gold; her earrings were ivory on gold wires. There was a suggestion of a mustache just above the corners of her pale lips, but it wasn't much more than a shadow, and she was an attractive woman; attractive and strong. She and Claire had had a brief fling, and then Claire had shrugged and said, "I guess I'm just heterosexual." Now they were friends, but when certain subjects floated by on the conversational stream, Judy's tone became acrid.

The room was too well lit, as cafeterias have always been; the vending machines built into the walls hummed, but behind the glass, the shrink-wrapped, vitamin-injected food in the little slots looked, in that harsh light, like wax imitations.

"You look pissed off," Judy observed.

"You know it." Claire told her what had happened at Security Central. "Two years ago it would've been unheard of. Those people worked for my father—for the Colony. Now they've..."

Judy nodded slowly, her eyes gazing at something inward. "The SAISC are invited in where there's a power vacuum. Where somebody in collaboration with them plans to fill the vacuum." She looked at Claire. "I was talking to a woman, the mother of a kid they arrested. She hasn't seen the kid in a month. They won't grant her visitor's privileges. She thinks something's wrong. She thinks they hurt him. Maybe he's dead. They hit him three times with an RR stick. He was thirteen years old."

"What's an RR stick?"

"Recoil reversal. The recoil you'd normally feel when you hit something, the kinetic energy, is rerouted back into the point of impact a split-second later—it's like the stick hits you twice when they hit you with it only once. The guy using it can't judge how much force he's used . . . "

"Jesus. When did you see her?"

"Two days ago. We've been gathering material for a story on it, but I'm not sure they'll give us permission—" She shrugged. "The bottom line, Claire, is that UNIC is taking it all away from your father."

Claire blinked and said, "I don't think it's quite that, uh . . . "

Judy shrugged and shook her head at the same time. "You want to get in to see Molt?"

Claire nodded.

"And you want my help?"

Claire nodded again, watching Judy. The bitterness was there. Judy's tone said, *I tried to warn you about this before. You should have trusted me, listened to me. Stayed with me.*

Judy stood up. "Then let's go get my class."

◆

There were four of them, Judy, Angie, Belle, and Kris. Belle and Kris were sisters, both of them tall and black. Angie was Swedish, blond and blue-eyed, her expression always fierce; she was a bulky, high-breasted, big-boned woman, and she wouldn't have looked out of place in one of the last century's National Socialist paintings of Aryan peasants. But Angie, Judy's instructor, was fervently Neo-Marxist.

They were Admin, and educated in standard English. But they were strongly sympathetic to the technicki cause.

They wore black exercise leotards, fencing masks, corrugated chest protectors. They looked like umpires for a woman's baseball team, Claire thought. Only, Angie and Judy carried nunchuks.

Angie had always looked at Claire with a kind of your-time-will-come disdain; she took off her mask just to let Claire see that expression now as Claire took charge.

"I'm going in first," Claire said. "I'll leave the door unlocked. When you hear me shout, come running."

Judy shook her head vehemently. "I think we'd better go in with you now."

"I don't want to provoke them. It'll be better if I can get Molt on sheer authority. If I can't, you'll hear from me." She tapped the comm button on her collar.

Feeling a little dizzy, she turned to the door.

This is rarefied air for me, she thought. Goddammit, Dad, if you were here...

She took the codekey from her pocket, looked at the coordination indicator: Level 03, Corridor C13. She was near the outer shell. She could feel it—the gravity was faintly greater near the outside of the Colony.

The codekey looked like a small handgun with a crystal muzzle; she turned the two dials at the back of the key to read 03 and C13; then she pressed the codekey to the lock panel and the door opened.

She expected to see a guard on the other side, but there was no one. A sheet of transparent plastic wall blocked her way, forty feet farther on. But she knew what it was, one of her father's security precautions, and she'd come prepared.

She dialed the codekey, and pressed it to the bulkhead. A small red arrow lit up on the bottom dial, pointing upward. She kept the key pressed to the wall, and moved the key upward; it chimed. The codekey communicated with the regulator on the other side of the bulkhead, and the plastic wall slid up.

She walked on, heart pounding, feeling like a burglar.

A door was open on the right. From inside it came a single drawn-out note, and after a moment she recognized it as sound made by a human throat: a high, fluting note, curling from fear to despair—and abruptly cutting off.

And then a voice, someone else's voice: "The simple thing would have been to get a neurohumoral extractor up here, take it all right out."

"Scanlon had a requisition in for one, Doc." Another voice.

"But you can't get anything through the blockade, and they're hard to get anyway. Illegal as hell. Problem with customs."

"Is it illegal now? I've been up here too long—I didn't know."

Claire made herself walk up to the open door and look in.

There were three of them who were *like that*. Faceless in helmets. And the horror of their faceless heads was tripled: one would have unsettled her, but three splintered her will. The helmets they wore, blanking out their faces with opaque blue-green visors, looked like things made of beetle wings. They were NA "security bulls." And she thought, security *bulls* is wrong: they're like insects, insects big as men.

They were bent over the man strapped to the bed. *Molt*. She saw what they'd done to him. She bit her lip. To one side, a white haired, white-coated doctor looked faintly querulous as he glanced up at her from his instruments. Like something startled from feeding.

Claire stepped back, turned, pressed herself against the corridor wall, beside the door, and stopped thinking. She shouted into her comm button. She heard footsteps inside the cell, and a helmet-muted voice saying, "I don't know but we're sure as hell gonna find out who she is."

Claire was remembering a time as a little girl when she'd walked in on her parents and her dad had been all tied up in thin white ropes and her mother was standing over him with a whip and Daddy's face was all welted and, not understanding the sexual game, she'd thought, *If Mommy could do that to Daddy, she could hurt me, too.* It had turned her world view upside down. And she felt the same way now.

The Colony was something maternal to her, and now, beyond all reason, the Colony was hurting its children.

A sudden, cruel pain in Claire's right shoulder and she looked around to see the blank beetle-wing face distorting her reflection.

The pain was his hand clamped on her. She pictured an insect claw clamping her shoulder, and she bit off a scream; and then the helmeted head tilted up to look past her, and magically, the carapace cracked down the middle.

Angie had come.

Angie followed up with a karate kick. The man staggered back, letting go of Claire's arm. The other women closed in as the second and third of the helmeted guards stepped out the door, electric stun batons swinging.

Judy pushed Claire out of the way; Claire fell back, and as she fell she saw something strange: Judy and Kris slapping the back of the beetle helmets. It seemed strangely like the sort of helpless-female gesture they abhorred, that slapping motion—and then Claire fell onto the floor. She lay still for a moment, trying to get her breath, then sat up and stared: the bulls were slapping at themselves, were screaming, writhing on their hands and knees, trying to claw their helmets off. Judy and Kris had—with what resembled ladylike slaps—attached high-frequency warblers to the helmets. Pain-inducing sound waves reverberated inside the helmets.

Then Judy and Angie and Kris stood around the fallen men and worked them over with nunchuks, whipping the chained clubs to strike in the unprotected places between the armored segments built into their flat-black uniforms. In their fencing masks and chest protectors, pounding mechanically with the nunchuks, the women looked as inhuman as the Security bulls...

Claire yelled, "Stop it stop it stop it!"

Then Angie was looking down at her, through the fly's-eye grid of the fencing mask. "What was it you said about using your 'sheer authority'?" she said.

Judy said, "Shut up, Angie." She helped Claire to her feet, and Claire made herself go in to help them take Molt off the bed. She didn't look at the unconscious men on the floor.

When they stepped into the room, Molt saw them and screamed, clawing at his straps, trying to get away from them.

13

It would be a real mistake to underestimate Ellen Mae Crandall, Swenson told himself, as he watched her talking to the Los Angeles SA recruiting staff on satvid. She likes to play shrinking violet, take-me-in-your-strong-hands, but for her it just might be a game, almost as vicarious as reading a romance novel. Or maybe that's wrong. Maybe when she changes, when she gets soft and pliable, she means it.

Maybe she's both people.

"Just make absolutely completely sure there's a clear division of intel awareness between the first two levels and the third. Need-to-know is the axis of the organization," she told the man on the screen.

Swenson, sitting hunched over the report spread out on the long wooden table, looked up again at the stainless-steel cross on the antique cabinet across the room. His eyes were drawn to it, again and again, and he knew that was dangerous.

It'll suck me right out of character, he thought. I could become Father Stisky.

He'd half expected to find swastikas on the walls at Cloudy Peak Farm. Portraits of Hitler. Something. But there was only the small German "iron cross" insignia, hardly noticeable, engraved into the intersection of the three-foot Christian Cross on its maplewood stand.

The long, narrow, book-lined room was log-cabin styled; halflogs on the inside and outside concealed the wall's electrical and electronic guts. There were tinted-glass Tiffany lampshades over the imitation gaslamps curving from the walls. An enormous flagstone fireplace hulked at one end. Swenson had looked twice to be sure the logs burning in the fireplace were real. In the acid-rain states it was illegal to cut trees for firewood. There just weren't enough trees left for that luxury.

The house wore its wood the way status-conscious socialites had once worn their minks. It had been "made out of the wood of the trees they found growing right here on the land, the way my brother wanted it," Ellen Mae had told him. "He likes things natural and simple, the way God likes them. God gave us dominion over all things of this world."

That's his problem, Swenson thought. He confuses what he likes with what God likes, all the way down the line.

And then he chided himself for falling out of character. *Don't even think things like that.*

She was standing over him now, and he looked up into her face—a face that looked craggier than ever in the uneven light, and he felt a purl of despair. *I not only have to make love to this woman, I have to do it well. I have to make her want more.*

"How's it look?" she said.

He stammered a moment, then realized she meant the report. "Um—I think it's just about ready."

Ellen Mae placed a hand on the table close to his left elbow and bent over him to look at the report, her arm around him like a schoolteacher looking at the work of a favorite child; his skin crackled with the slight furriness of her cheek. He felt a wave of revulsion—followed quickly by arousal, and he wondered where *that* was coming from.

"It looks fine," she said, scanning, flipping through it. Probably not really looking at all. Her breath smelled like iron.

She straightened and put her hands on his shoulders. "Let's visit Rick and we can give him this."

Oh, shit, he thought.

But aloud he said: "Great!" Sprightly as he could make it. He shuffled the papers together, put them in a folder, and added, "But maybe he'll want to see this as a readout. I could put the corrections on a datastick—"

"He wants it tonight if he can get it," she said. She sighed. "He shouldn't be working at night—he shouldn't be working at all—but just try to keep him from it."

Ellen Mae said it reverently.

◆

It was like finding a secret passage that led from a home into a hospital.

They turned a corner, and the wooden hallways ended. Abruptly, they were in a long white hall: white tile floors, white walls; shiny pieces of medical apparatus on steel tables equipped with rollers, looking malevolently arcane, waited to be wheeled in to Crandall's room if the doctors needed it. There were three doctors here, specialists who were staying on at Cloudy Peak while Crandall was convalescing.

Were the doctors in the SA? Swenson wondered. They must be, for security reasons. Swenson reflected on the surprising number of educated men in the SA. Even intellectuals. But then, the driving force of the neofascist French New Right were its intellectuals. It was an old paradox: a powerful mind was no proof against stupidity. Ideas rooted in brutality had an emotional origin. Emotion could make any notion seem reasonable. *Stay in character, even in your mind.*

There was an SAISC guard standing in the doorway, his face hidden in a dark green-blue helmet. He stood with his legs braced apart, one gloved hand clasped over his wrist. He was like a living gun.

But he stepped aside, seeing Ellen Mae. She didn't even glance at him; it was as if he were a wall fixture.

And then Swenson followed her through, and there was Crandall, in bed, smiling up at them.

Swenson smiled back. But he couldn't look Crandall in the eye. So he looked around the room. On the tables beside the bed were framed pictures, some of Ellen Mae alone, one of Ellen Mae and her parents, who were said to be living on a ranch somewhere in

New Mexico. In the picture Ellen Mae and her parents were sitting together on the bench of a picnic table. Ellen Mae looked like her father.

And she looked like Crandall. And Crandall had a lean, wolfish face that might have belonged to a backwoods imbecile—except for the personality shining through it, transforming it in some subtle way. The personality, the benevolence on a foundation of sheer self-certainty, made that inbred country face something magnetic.

Crandall had never been married. He said he was married to his mission. But in total there were four pictures of Ellen Mae, and Swenson wondered if there was some kind of repressed undercurrent of incest between Ellen Mae and Smiling Rick Crandall.

A bank of instruments clicked and peeped on the wall behind Crandall. From one of them a tube had extruded to sink its single silvery fang into a vein in Crandall's left forearm.

The room was decorated in soft white; the cabinets across from the bed were topped by pots holding a small forest of cream colored flowers. Swenson pictured the SA bomb detection team going through each vase and afterward meticulously putting the flowers back the way they'd been, and he almost laughed aloud.

He became aware of the tension knotting his chest then; he could see his own impending hysteria like the foreshortened horizon of a cliff's edge in the distance.

He fought it by sinking roots into the character, into Swenson.

Here's the trick, Purchase had told him. You have to be like a perfectly camouflaged bug in a fone. If it's made right, the antibugging team could take the fone apart and not find the bug. You've got to operate like a fone, buzz like a fone, do everything that a fone does, just exactly, and not transmit until it's time to transmit and then do it without breaching the illusion you're just a fone. You've got to think you're an ordinary "fone" until that moment.

But still, he thought, I could grab the guard's gun, I could kill them both right here. Sacrifice myself. Get it over with.

Only that wouldn't stop the SA. There was still Watson, and the others.

So he looked at Crandall and told himself, *This man's a hero. This man's a martyr. This man is here on a Holy Mission for God. This man is here to purify the world.*

And looking at Crandall, you could believe it. Even when he sat up, and they could see the bandages swathing his bony chest, and he muttered as he fumbled with the TV control unit to make the thin, filmy screen unreel from the ceiling.

"Something coming on TV, I want ya'll to see it," he said.

The viddy membrane dominated its part of the room. It held a perfect 3D image of a submarine surfacing, the water parting for the vessel like lace-edged stage-curtains.

"... As the art of making the ocean 'transparent' has improved," the commentator said, "techniques for making Russian submarines quieter improved almost simultaneously. This Russian 'bottom-crawler,' when in its cruising mode and not using its treads to crawl on the bottom, is outfitted with a new sound-damping device which absorbs the noise of its nuclear reactor's noisy cooling equipment, making it virtually impossible to detect with the sound surveillance system of hydrophones the Navy has planted along North America's continental shelf. Russian teams of saboteurs comb the shelves in bottomcrawlers, destroying fiberoptic sensor cables where they find them, further reducing our ability to detect enemy subs. The NSA has reported that the Russian ability to detect our submarines is enhanced by a new system of ocean-bed-implanted computers which monitor seabed vibrations and search for turbulence-vibrations typical of submarines. These developments threaten the delicate balance of deterrence that prevents the use of strategic nuclear weapons in the Russian-NATO war. If the Russians can detect American submarines carrying nuclear weapons, they could eliminate them, making a Russian first strike more practical."

Crandall switched off the sound. Images of deep-sea military juggernauts hunched silently across the screen. "Now, of course," Crandall drawled, "Mrs. Anna Bester might just be angling for more military funding, releasing this stuff. I had my misgivings about a woman president, but by gosh, the woman is no weak bleeding heart . . . But if this new threat to American subs is on the level, the SAISC might just have what they used to call a 'window of opportunity.' Our clandestine surveillance department has come up with something new we just might be able to trade to the Department of Defense for a little unbending on Our Work in Europe. If they gave us better logistical support, we'd have the European situation sewn up."

My God, Swenson thought. It hit Swenson like a blow to the stomach. *They're moving into everything.*

"The DoD has shown some interest in the new thing from Armaments," Ellen Mae said. "They'd like to see the Jægernaut field-tested . . ."

Crandall glanced at Swenson—and Swenson felt a chill.

"I think it's best we hold off on talking about that, Ellen Mae honey," Crandall said.

Because I haven't got a top-level SA Security clearance, Swenson thought.

Or is it more? Do they suspect me?

Purchase's people had gone to elaborate lengths to build up an identity for John Swenson: Birth certificate and baby pictures planted in a small Midwestern town; elaborate schemes to obtain letters of recommendation from SA members and supporters who were led to believe they knew Swenson when they didn't: Purchase had access to Worldtalk's memory-tampering systems. He fed false experiences into the men who were to give the recommendations; they seemed to remember Swenson's assistance, Swenson's right-wing politics, Swenson's sacrifices and invaluable advice.

Sackville-West had had six hours of video interviews with SA sympathizers who "remembered" Swenson. And all the documentation was there.

But maybe Crandall smelled a ringer.

There'd been just the faintest flare of suspicion in Crandall's eyes, somehow not at all incongruous with the smile, when he'd shaken Swenson's hand.

Was it suspicion . . . Or jealousy? Swenson wondered. Crandall would know that Swenson and Ellen Mae were on the verge of becoming an item.

Suddenly Swenson was uncomfortably aware of the armed guard standing behind them, quiet as a piece of furniture, lethal as a bullet.

Crandall changed the subject, and Swenson forced himself to listen to Crandall's diatribe on a threatened liberalization of the ironically-named Antiviolence Laws of 2025.

" . . . The principle is very simple, as I see it, John," Crandall was saying. "And since it was voted into law, violent crime has been reduced in the country. I don't know the precise statistics . . . " He looked at Swenson.

Swenson knew he was being tested. The John Swenson created by Purchase was supposed to be an expert on the Antiviolence Laws. They'd steeped him in them. He knew the statistics, all right.

Swenson nodded and said, "Violent crime was reduced by twenty percent in the first five years, then by thirty-eight percent in the second five years, and now we're down forty-one percent. As I understand it, the program as it stands calls for the death penalty for the second homicidal violent crime—the first in cases involving sadism or torture—and for the third occasion of non-homicidal but nevertheless violent crime. Constitutional rights to appeal are suspended after the second conviction. The convict is to be executed within twenty-four hours of conviction, as inexpensively as possible. Senator Chung and Senator Judy Sanchez are leading the fight calling for the law's repeal . . . " Swenson paused, wondering if he was reciting *too* well. But Ellen Mae was beaming, nodding encouragingly, so he went on. "They are, I believe, uh, pointing up statistics showing that more people are executed who are later shown to have been innocent . . . But, of course—" He shrugged expansively, as if he couldn't understand how they could so stupidly miss seeing the obvious. "—the program's architects knew perfectly well that more innocent people would be convicted, by accident, because of the hastening of the judicial process . . . But because the program reduces violent crime by creating a stronger deterrent, and by taking killer-types not only off the street but out of the world, there are also fewer *victims* of violent crime. Which compensates for the rise in the number of innocent convictees. Victims of crimes are innocent, too."

Swenson cleared his throat apologetically, as if to say, Sorry about running off at the mouth that way. He looked modestly at Crandall and waited for the verdict.

Crandall grinned and said, "My Good *Lord* but he's got the gift, don't he!" He turned to Ellen Mae. "I wonder if Mr. John Swenson here could be convinced to do a little testifying for the CSO when they give their testimony in *support* of the Antiviolence Laws next month . . . ?"

"Well, don't look at me!" she said, laughing. "Why don't you ask him? He's standing right there."

Crandall lowered his voice to a stage whisper. He pretended to talk to her behind his hand. "You think ah dare tuh?" His accent deepening for the sake of humor.

Ellen Mae giggled.

Swenson thought, The CSO: Commission for Social Order. Controlled by the SA. Funded by the SA's friends. Advocates of a more "broad-minded" interpretation of the Constitution . . . Advocates of the imposition of martial law in high-crime areas. Most of the country's military manpower, including the majority of the Reserves and the National Guard, were either fighting the Russians overseas or massed along the USA's coasts. The implementation of martial law would require that some paramilitary, mercenary, or private police force be hired to supplement the urban police. And the biggest such organization was the SAISC.

Swenson marveled at the scale of Crandall's ambitions. But was it Crandall—or was it Watson? Or was there someone else, someone less public?

"Well, now, John boy, I was just wonderin' . . . " Crandall began, drawling it out slowly to give him his cue.

Swenson chuckled and said, "By some chance I happened to overhear. I'd be honored to testify for the CSO."

And he'd do it with conviction. He'd been a Jesuit for a few years—and he'd never believed in God. He could be an intellectualized fascist, too. He was good at playing parts, at being anyone but a man named Stisky.

◆

Ellen Mae Crandall came to him just five minutes after midnight, wearing an oversized, remarkably non-erotic bathrobe.

She was playing the lost, weak woman now. Her eyes were large and shiny in the dialed-down light of the hallway. She was carrying what he thought was a glass of warm milk, and her voice was slightly slurred. He smelled brandy on her.

"Hi... Could I talk to you about something? I'm sorry if you were asleep. I just—"

"I couldn't sleep, in fact," he said, moving back from the door to invite her in.

Swenson was wearing a bathrobe over pajamas. He felt strange in pajamas—he never wore them normally, but they seemed appropriate in this house. There wasn't even a computer console in his room.

Ellen Mae looked to see that the hall was empty. Then she padded into the room. He closed the door behind her. There was a moment of awkward silence. She held the glass up between them. "You—you really have to try this. It's my mother's recipe..." He smiled and took it gratefully, glad he wouldn't have to do the job without having a drink in him. He sipped and almost spat it out in his surprise. It was eggnog, with brandy in it. Thick, creamy, almost without sweetening. He thought of semen. He said, "Whoa. It's good."

"A little libation lengthens the life, my grandmother used to say."

Quoting her goddamned grandmother, he thought. And then he warned himself: *Get into the role!*

She rubbed her eyes. "My eyes are so tired. Looking at a screen all day..."

Swenson knew what that meant. He turned and dialed the light lower. "How's that?"

"Better."

"Come and sit down, and tell me about it."

In the dimness, he almost liked the way she looked. Or maybe it was the brandy.

She sat down beside him; the bed didn't creak—they never did anymore.

He took one of her hands between his, smiled, and said, "Tell me about it."

It was all in his voice. He felt her squirm a little with pleasure.

"Well, you know, I love Rick. I really believe in my heart he's been chosen by God for a special mission. I'd never say this in front of him because he won't have anyone putting on airs for him, but I truly believe he's the most important man in the world today. Not because of what he is—but because of what he'll be. But . . . I have to have some life of my own, outside of Rick. You know—a little more life than Our Work." She made a soft sound of guilt and indecision. "I don't know—maybe I'm wrong to want it—"

Again, he knew his cue. "Not at all."

"But—Gramma always said, 'Follow your heart.'"

He listened to her in wonder. She could talk blithely and with expertise—about demographic surveys, clandestine cellular organization, and security enforcement techniques. And out of the same mouth she spouted this incredible *corn*.

"Does—does Rick disapprove when you have a private life?"

"Well—he disapproves of, you know, anything *intimate* that happens outside of marriage. And I have to be very careful about getting married because it's a media event."

"Of course. But if you are discreet . . . "

He could almost feel her blush. "Yes, but . . . it's a sin."

Uh-huh, he thought.

He didn't believe for a moment that she or Crandall gave a damn, as it were, about sin. Except for the cameras. Not in any real way.

"I understand," he said gently, pressing her hand. "But—surely God understands your special predicament. And in any event, Jesus said even the worst sinners are forgiven if they genuinely ask. You'll be forgiven."

"Oh . . . " Just melting now. He'd said it right.

She bent and rested her head on his shoulder, tilted up just enough.

He let go of her hand, slid his right arm around her waist, and bent to press her wiry lips with a kiss.

He had been afraid he'd be unable to get it up for her. But his imagination performed the miracle for him. In fact, her angular body was not so different from that copper-skinned boy's, the boy later found in a ditch with so many holes punched into him, like Saint Sebastian transfixed by arrows . . . It was the image of Saint Sebastian writhing in martyrdom, the arrows so stiff and masculine in his wounds, that made Swenson stiff and masculine, made it possible to transfix her, to pretend, to pretend within the pretense.

How our special pathologies do serve us, he thought, as he pressed her back onto the bed.

◆

When Rickenharp came out of it he sat up—and almost fell over with the weakness.

"Too soon," Carmen said, pressing him back. He lay back and felt better. He was still weak, but the gnawing soul-horror was gone. All he felt now, besides weak, was hungry.

The world shook around him, like it was laughing, a growling sort of laugh, and then he put it together. He was in the back of a truck. They were on the flatbed. The light came from the space between the tailgate and the canvas cover over the rusty slats.

It was bluish light, and he thought it might be dawn. The air on his face was cold, but warmth seeped up from the engine, and a faint scent of methane.

"I'm hungry as a bastard," he said. His throat was dry, he realized as he tried to talk. It came out a rasp.

But she understood. "We haven't got any food. Maybe next stop, if we're lucky. Anyway, your fever seems to be gone."

"Where are we?"

"Northern Italy. North of Naples. You've been out for days. Willow . . . " She paused and he saw the flash of her teeth. "Willow wanted to dump you, more than once. I was inclined to agree with him. Keeping you isn't practical. But Yukio says you're some kind of samurai. He wants you along." She shrugged.

Italy? Fucking crazy. He closed his eyes and visualized sausage tied up in strings and platters of steaming pasta.

He could smell the sea in the breeze now, as they took a curve, and a fresh wind hit them.

What was it she'd said?

Willow wanted to dump you. I was inclined to agree with him.

They'd almost thrown him overboard into the Mediterranean. No doubt for the "greater good."

"My fans," he muttered.

"What?"

But he didn't have anything to say to her.

To hell with her.

◆

Ellen Mae was gone when Swenson woke. There was a silk rose lying on the pillow beside him. The brandy-eggnog glass was gone. He had, literally, a bad taste in his mouth.

Swenson sat up and his head throbbed. Wan sunlight filtered through the yellow-curtained windows to either side of the bed.

A discreet tap came from the other side of the door. He groaned inwardly, thinking, *Not her again so soon!*

But he put on his robe and said, "Come in."

It was a uniformed houseboy, an old man with age-blurred eyes, silent except for his labored breathing as he wheeled in the breakfast tray and poured the coffee. Somehow, Swenson was surprised that the old man wasn't black. But he thought, Of course not, they wouldn't trust black servants, they could be infiltrators.

The old man shuffled out and Swenson lifted the old silver cover off the plate. Bacon and eggs and biscuits. None of it looked synthetic. It would be interesting to see what they tasted like.

But he almost gagged on the bacon. You could really taste *the animal* in it.

There was a note in an envelope on the tray.

He assumed it was from her, but it wasn't.

> Welcome, John! Meet me out at the front gate at 0900.
> —Watson

So Watson was here. Swenson glanced at his watch. Almost eight.

He got up and dressed, muttering, "Oh-eight-hundred. Shit." But he almost ran to get there on time.

Outside, he found a sky the color of granite, the sun a blur of brass behind the overcast. And the massive posts of the original front gate were granite, old granite torn three centuries before from the ancient New England hills, much of it painted bright yellow and red by lichen. The old stone fence to either side of the gates had fallen down in places. But it didn't matter; a few feet in from the stone fence the steel-mesh barricades loomed, two of them, crested with concertina wire.

A pair of German shepherds paced restlessly between the steel fences—seeing Swenson they threw themselves against the links, making the fence ring like chain mail as he approached the first checkpoint. He expected the dogs to bark, but they didn't. They snarled, furrowing their muzzles, fixing their yellow glares on him. He remembered the strong taste of the bacon, and his stomach lurched.

His shoes crunched in the agate cinders of the drive. A helmetless SAISC guard looked at him with a dilution of the same look the dogs gave him. The guard stepped out of a small wooden shack on the other side of the hurricane-fence gate and said, "Name, please?"

Stisky.

He almost said it. And what frightened him was this: it hadn't been an accident. He badly wanted to say it.

The guard was blond and blue-eyed. The blue eyes were narrowed now. Because Swenson had hesitated.

"John Swenson."

The guard nodded, his eyes still narrowed. "The colonel's gone on already. Said you could catch up with him at the chapel."

The flat blue eyes regarded him steadily, the glare gone, only unflinching appraisal now. The eyes were lined with white-blond lashes, long and soft as a small boy's.

"Where's the chapel?"

The guard pointed. It was off to the northeast, half-hidden in the oak trees that fringed the grounds. Looking at it, Swenson felt a spike of ice through his belly.

The chapel was beautiful. And he was afraid of it. Moving like a wooden soldier, he began to walk toward it.

It was a simple chapel of white wood, with stained-glass windows. He couldn't make out from here what the figures in the stained glass represented.

The chapel stood almost demurely in a stand of oak trees shaggy with moss and mistletoe. Swenson crossed a lawn to reach it, his shoes getting soaked by the dew in the fragrant grass. He shivered. It was a chill, clammy morning. There were wraiths of fog, yet, under the oak trees. Fallen leaves whispered beneath his feet as he walked up to the chapel's front steps. The chapel was bigger than he'd thought. Room for two hundred.

The oaks creaked faintly in a puff of breeze.

Oaks, he thought. *Druidic.*

He opened the green-painted chapel door.

There were two Nazis, in full uniform, kneeling before the altar, pig-shaven heads bowed in prayer.

To one side stood Colonel Watson, in a neat gray suit and trenchcoat, his face florid with the chill. On the other was Sackville-West, sitting in a pew, head bowed, hat in hands.

Over the altar was a twelve-by-eight-foot oil-painting, professionally but cornily rendered, showing Jesus sitting on his throne, his face uncharacteristically creased in a scowl of judgment. On his head was a circlet of oak-leaves. Sitting at his feet were Rick and Ellen Crandall, painted with just a little flattery, both in white robes. There was a steel cross on a blond-wood stand under the painting, and imprinted at the intersection of its bars, no bigger than a silver dollar, was an "iron cross." To either side of the dais area were furled flags—an Old Glory, a Confederate flag, and one he didn't recognize, its insignia folded away. White tulips stood in a silver vase on the altar, a floral benediction.

The room blushed with rosy light from the stained glass. He looked at the stained-glass figures and didn't recognize them.

There were paintings along the walls to either side of the pews. He couldn't make them out from here, except that they were neurotically intricate and allegorical, with figures suspended in the heavens in hallucinogenic clusters.

Swenson couldn't move. He was transfixed there at the entrance. He told himself, *Don't be stupid. Don't be a child.*

But he stayed where he was until Watson looked over and beckoned.

He walked down the aisle past the empty pews toward the black-coated backs of two Nazis in full, mid-twentieth century SS uniforms, kneeling at the altar in silent prayer.

Watson stepped out of the chancel, and with the exaggerated quiet of a man wary of a sacred moment, walked down the outside aisle, then gestured for Swenson to join him three pews back.

The two men sat down side by side on the hard wooden pews.

"Sackville-West wants you along," Watson said, more a mutter than a whisper.

"Along on what?"

Watson snorted and nodded toward the two Nazis, figures from a propaganda painting. "We're going to 'initiate' those two nitwits..." He shrugged, and the briskness of the motion told Swenson that the colonel was irritated; irritated just short of fury. "A man named Strawling from Idaho—he attended one of our conventions out in Orange County. By some administrative mistake, this man Strawling was allowed into the SA-Initiates meetings, attended Special Services, the whole bit. Got himself all excited. Turns out he belongs to the National Socialist White People's Party! We'd had no idea, of course.

We don't need unsubtle dunderheads among the Initiates... But somehow he slipped through the screenings... He told his pal, the one kneeling there beside him, and they came out here... Just drove up to the goddamn gate at dawn, told the guards they wanted to see Rick Crandall. They heard about the assassination attempt—wanted to be his bodyguards!" His voice dripped with contempt. "They were all got up like that! At the gates of Cloudy Peak Farm, dressed like *that*! Like old school twentieth century Nazis! Christ, if some reporter was hanging around..." He shook his head. "Naturally we didn't let them in to see Rick. The guards rang Sackville-West and old Sacks rang me out of a sound sleep and we went to see Rick. He said they should make their peace with God, so here they are. I don't know why Sacks wanted you along—" Swenson felt Watson look at him. "But I think it's a kind of initiation for you, too. Not the kind those two are getting, of course..."

Swenson nodded. He sat like something carved into the wood of the pew, remembering the Second Circle, and the Services, the pageantry of it, and how he'd almost lost himself...

◆

Excerpt from a memo
From: Frank Purchase to Quincy Witcher

Thought you would be interested in the following letter from Stisky to Encendez. Father Encendez was in prison at the time of the letter's composition. The letter was never mailed. We found it when we went through Stisky's effects.
 ... the truth is, I never believed. When I entered the Church, I "suspended my disbelief" like you do when you're reading a novel. You believe in the novel's subjective world while you're reading it, but of course you know it's all made up. But you prefer to believe, while you're reading, because you love the intricacy, the marvel of it, the sublime distraction of it. I feel the same way about The Church. The Church is a she, and I once fell in love with a woman, and knew that, despite all she said, she didn't love me back, not really. The love I fantasized was unreal, and I knew it, but I made myself believe in it because it was a

delicious reassurance. The Church has a thousand volumes of love letters it has written to itself, in the form of the Apologias and so forth, in all their manifestations. The Church is a beautiful lie. I saw no harm in the necessary casuistry. And it gave me a base to work from, to help the poor. I wanted to get in among the people who needed me, and it put me there. I wonder about my own underlying motives, though. The pageantry of the Church, the patina of glamour on the rituals; the pleasantly musty homeliness of a Jesuitical library; the asceticism so weighty with our self-congratulation. But most of all the pageantry, like the tarted-up garishness of a Parisian whore, the rituals, the accoutrements, all of it seduces me . . .

As you can see, our "Swenson" has a profound psychological need for ritual. The more dramatic the ritual, the better. Again, his predilections are a double-edged sword. I worry that when he undergoes the SA's Second Circle training program, and sees the neofascist splendor of their Services, he may fall under their spell. He denied his faith, in private, and he was rebellious, but ultimately his actions bespoke a strong loyalty to the Church, until he was defrocked. If he develops the same neurotic attachments to the rituals of the SA's inner circle, we may lose his loyalty entirely . . .

◆

They were walking through the slowly dissipating mists, under the oak trees. An SAISC guard in full mask walked ahead, carrying a rifle, like a platoon patrol's point man; then came Swenson with Watson and the two Nazis walking to Watson's left. Behind them were two more faceless SA guardsmen.

They strolled along a trail, under a tracework of damp black twigs having the look of old electrical cords. Winter-withered ferns arced dripping to either side; there was a smell of rotting wood and mushrooms. A single blackbird trilled and warbled and trilled yet again. Swenson was cold. He zipped up his jacket and balled his hands in his pockets.

He thought he could feel the guards looking at his back.

The Nazis were wearing their shiny billed caps now. There was a young one with beetling brows and a weak chin, and an older one with a face like a knot of old tree wood. They both had Western accents; they'd come from northern Idaho. "The panhandle," they said. They both owned businesses out that way, but they'd decided coming here was more important. A man had to choose between profit and duty sometimes, the young one had said. No matter what they said, Watson acted as if he saw the perfect rightness of it. He nodded and said, "Mm-hmm, oh, I agree," now and then. Their dress uniforms were knife-creased, neat as a pin, complete with swastika armbands; their boots spit-polished. Swenson saw Watson wince when he looked at the armbands.

The two men didn't seem to understand what was happening. Except that, now and then, the older one glanced nervously over his shoulder at the guards.

They came to another steel-mesh fence; the sentry let the German Shepherds tug him along between the inner and outer fences.

The trail veered left, hooking back toward the chapel, and they turned to follow it. They walked along silently for another hundred feet and stopped when they came to a small clearing. The brush had grown up thickly around the clearing. To one side was a wooden bench cut from a log. Watson smiled wearily at the Nazis and said, "Sit down, boys." They looked dubiously at the log; the dampness would stain their uniforms. But they sat.

Suddenly the older one, licking his lips, looked up and said, "Maybe we shouldn'ta come here like this. Guess we shoulda called. But we got the runaround when I tried to write. I figured I had to go right to Reverend Crandall. But if you say we leave, well, I guess we'll sure leave."

"Nobody said anything about your having to leave," Watson said neutrally. He took a neatly folded handkerchief from his coat pocket and blew his nose on it. "You see," he went on, "we have us a problem." His shift into rustic speech mannerisms was more friendly than mocking. "Now, it's like this. You had access to things you weren't supposed to have access to. Just a mix-up. Ours really. But people at your level of activity aren't supposed to be seen in association with

Reverend Crandall. It's not good public relations. You're not even supposed to know how to find him. I just hope and pray no one was watching when you folks drove up dressed like that: Now, we can't take the chance that you'll leave here and tell some more of your people where to find Rick. And then again, you represent a security risk in other ways. We don't want people running around who might feel rejected, and become disgruntled with the Reverend. Especially not people with a bombing record." He looked at the young man, who went pale. "You see, young man, we know all about you already. We know where your friends and family are . . . How many others did you tell?"

"Nobody else!" the older Nazi said indignantly. "I knowed it was top secret."

Watson smiled. He glanced at Sackville-West. The old man shrugged.

"I believe you," Watson said. "But . . . we'll have to look into that."

It had taken the younger one a while to get the upshot, but he burst out, "You saying we oughta be ashamed to come here dressed like this? This uniform symbolizes our martyrdom to the Aryan cause! We're pariahs and we know it and we do it 'cause it's right! All over the world people are interbreedin' with animals! White women and men having congress with black animals and stinking up their blood with the blood of monkeys!"

"Very colorful way to put it," Watson said, dabbing daintily at his nose with the handkerchief. "You know, in a way I almost agree with you."

"Almost!" The young Nazi looked at the impassive faces around him, at the faceless helmets, and let his exasperation carry his voice into shrillness. "Hey now, I got to get this straight. Do you folks believe in the Triumph of the White Race or *not*?"

Watson looked musingly into his handkerchief. "I suppose you deserve an answer at least . . . My boy, the answer is yes and no. I believe in it, but not the way you believe in it. You see, I happen to believe that Negroes are in fact an inferior race, in a certain sense. For example, some claim they don't pan out on the genetic scale for intelligence quotients. But you know that conclusion could be disputed, and I'd be willing to listen to evidence that maybe they're as intelligent as we are, after all. Maybe they are. Maybe they're not a *bit* inferior. I don't know. Rick Crandall doesn't know. And what's more, we don't care. We happen to think, first of all, that miscegenation—interbreeding—is a bad thing, leading to genetic impurity, but not because the other races are low but because it creates too many uncontrollable variables in the genetic process."

"Genetic process! You people believe in *evolution*?" the younger one sputtered.

The older one had put his elbows on his knees and his head in his hands. He groaned and shook his head. "Best not get us in any deeper, Elwood."

"Well now, we believe that genetics is God's Tool," Watson said. He chuckled at some private joke and went on, "Now, in the beginning, could be that God created the world in seven days. Like it says in the Book. But after that, after he sent Adam and Eve out of Eden, he used genetics to do some of his work here . . . " He cleared his throat, and Swenson, watching him, felt sure that Watson didn't actually believe in Creationism of any sort. Swenson felt light-headed. He almost laughed aloud.

"We in fact believe," Watson went on, warming to his subject, "that racism, as it's called, ought to be an instrument of administrative policy in the coming world government. And we know precisely how to use the social phenomenon that historians call 'fascism' to further that ambition. But you gentlemen have made the fatal error of mistaking the means for the end. And the . . . *trappings* you've chosen are no longer appropriate. They are socially poisoned by the awkward people who wore them before."

"Awkward?" the young man was shocked. "You talking about *Adolf Hitler*?"

His outrage was palpable.

The older Nazi groaned, "Dammit, Elwood, shut up. Shut the hell up."

"Hitler?" Watson shrugged. "Hitler was a madman. Worse, he

was unsubtle and inefficient—Well, you could argue that he very efficiently got rid of the six million Jews, and, of course, he did us all a favor—those people are too smart for their own good, or ours. But otherwise—"

The young man sprang up with tears in his eyes. "I ain't gonna listen to any more of this!"

"You won't have to," Watson said gently. He stepped back.

Sackville-West stepped back, well out of the way. Swenson mechanically followed suit.

Not you, Swenson, you're going where they're going.

Swenson froze.

And then he realized he'd heard it in his mind. No one had spoken to him. The voice was a product of his suppressed terror, the twisting fear that he had been brought out here to be executed—

The two Nazis jumped to their feet and turned to run. The guards pointed their guns and opened up, and the terrible thing was, there was almost no sound.

The automatic weapons were fitted with suppressors. They made only soft, stammering hisses as the two Nazis exploded with blood under the impact of scores of rounds, as if magic made them open up with little faucets of red, made them dance and spin ... in the quiet morning...

Then they'd fallen, slumped over the log side by side.

Swenson thought, *I should be happy.* Two more Nazis dead. Killed by their own kind. Steinfeld didn't even have to waste bullets on them.

But he felt only a kind of gnawing numbness.

He seemed to see the body of a beautiful, copper-skinned young man dead in a ditch, riddled with bullets.

And then he visualized the painting of Saint Sebastian, skewered with arrows...

Oh, no, he thought. *Oh, God, no. I've got an erection.*

And the sickness passed.

A fourth guard strolled up, carrying two body bags. "Where will he take them?" Swenson heard himself ask dazedly.

"We have a crackerjack incinerator here," Watson said. "Just the best."

"Waste of time, all that speechmaking," Sackville-West said. He was notorious for his taciturnity.

Watson smiled and said, "Where's your feelings, Sacks? They had their hearts in the right place, after all. Anyway, I thought our friend Mr. Swenson here could use some clarity on where we stand."

No one spoke for a few moments. Swenson peered up through the interlacing branches, trying to see the sun. The sky beyond the naked twigs was uniformly steel gray. The woods were silent, except for the strikingly unnatural sound of the body bags being zipped up.

14

"Hey—how about leaving me a gun?" Rickenharp said. "What the hell. I mean, if I have to stay in this fucking truck alone—this fucking truck I've been in all fucking day long. Not to complain or anything."

Carmen paused, straddling the truck's closed tailgate, and looked back at him. She'd just said, *Stay here, don't move, if anybody speaks to you play dumb. We're going to see if the pass is open.*

Now she was a silhouette, spiky black against the deep indigo of the late evening sky. Even her cold-plumed breath showed in silhouette.

And Rickenharp was sitting with his back to the cold steel, his muscles cramping with the chill of it.

Carmen made a hissing sound of impatience and swung back into the rear of the truck. She crouched by her pack, and he heard the crisp sound of nylon rustling. She took a wedge of darkness from the pack and, moving crabwise, came to hunch beside him.

He felt something cold and heavy pressed into his hands. She was a figure of darkness giving him the means to kill. "It's a machine pistol," she said.

Her hands were still on the pistol, and the pistol was in his hands. It was an assassin's benediction. She was touching him via the pistol.

There was a faint, neat-edged click in the darkness.

The gun glowed in his hands; it shone from within.

The pistol was transparent and electrically lit up. It was framed with stainless steel; the inner sections of the gun were made of glass-clear hyper-compressed plastic. He could see into the magazine, could see the bullets in the clip like a row of robot larvae. A tiny light in the pistol's butt and another under the breech gave the gun an eerie blue glow.

She ticked a black-painted fingernail against a stud just above the trigger guard. "That's the safety. *Up* is safety off. After that all you have to do is aim and squeeze the trigger. Those are .22 rounds. Not big, but very precise. The small rounds give you a clip of forty... "

Willow hissed from the tailgate. "Put out that bloody light in there! And come *on!*"

She showed Rickenharp the light switch on the back of the butt and flicked it off. "Light shows up your position—it's only in case you have to check the gun when you're under cover. Don't shoot unless you're sure someone's shooting at you, or about to. You might shoot a friend by accident. These plastic guns look like children's toys. They're not." She moved away and slipped out of the truck.

He wanted to ask her, *What made you so sure I didn't know anything about guns?* But he realized it was a stupid question.

Carefully, holding the gun up so he could see it against the screen of night sky above the tailgate, he took the grip in his hand and slipped his finger into the trigger guard.

He looked at it for a moment; in the darkness it was like an outgrowth of his arm. And a door opened inside him, and something slithered out of the door, leaving a trail of thrill behind it.

Rickenharp drew the gun close to his chest, between both hands, and looked out into the night.

Now and then he had to shrug down farther into his coat, to shake the shivering off. He took deep breaths, trying to stoke oxygen fires in himself, and thought, *Christ! Maybe I'm drugged-out delirious. Maybe I'm still back in Freezone, hallucinating in my shit-hole hotel room. Or maybe I really am somewhere in the Alps with a machine pistol in my hands.*

He thought of Ponce and the band. *That scene ain't real, you Grid-nipplers. THIS is real! Gridfriend help me, this is real.*

He wiped his nose on his sleeve and listened.

No sound, except the the snap-sound of the wind whipping the canvas. The minutes passed—or maybe they didn't. He wasn't sure how long it was before he heard the voices.

Guttural voices. Foreign language.

He thought, *Russians*.

Willow had talked about it, blasé as a trucker talking about the highway patrol. "Some of the Alps are Russian and some parts aren't, and the bloody borders keep shifting. NATO territory today is Russian tomorrow and vice versa, like," he'd said.

... Crunch of footsteps...

I'd have heard gunfire if it was the Russians, he told himself.

But not necessarily. Yukio, Willow, and Carmen might have walked right into a trap—been forced to surrender without firing a shot. Maybe a mile down the road they're tied up, lying gagged in the back of another truck. Russian truck. Or SAISC—worse. And the SA could be anywhere.

The talking had stopped. *Crunch*. Footsteps again. Closer.

He brought the gun around and rested his elbow on his right knee. He trained the gun on the rear of the truck.

And the Russians torture everybody for intelligence nowadays, Willow had said. Even sheep farmers.

He reached across the top of the gun and flicked off the safety.

The guttural voice again. He tried to be sure of the language. Couldn't hear it clearly enough.

A creak as someone stepped onto the rear bumper, two shapes blurred together in the rear, the guttural voice again, and then the rear of the truck lit up—

It lit up with strobe flashes, four of them, going off like flashbulbs, making the scene at the rear of the truck into a choppy motion-picture sequence: Carmen, hand lifted over her eyes, mouth opened to shout, a strange man beside her in a watch cap, his eyes wide; Carmen with two red holes in her chest; Carmen with arm flung up; Carmen falling back.

The back of the truck echoed, a metallic lisp for each gunshot.

And Rickenharp realized he'd squeezed the trigger.

He thought, Willow said something yesterday about meeting some Swiss friends.

And then: I shot Carmen.

◆

"The truth is," Molt was saying, "there are two factions in administration. One faction is basically in favor of martial law in the Colony. Their attitude is something like, the danger to the station's life-support system is too great if they let things go on."

Bonham sat in the After, listening to Molt talk on an old twelve-inch TV sunk flush with the wall, thinking, *Molt sounds tired, mechanical. Barely maintaining.*

And the TV in Prego's After was tired itself, barely maintaining, the talking-head image of Molt warping into the outline of a peanut shell, making Molt look even more tired.

Bonham nestled back in the easy chair. The chair took up half the room. Like everything else in the small room, the chair was frayed, ripping out at the seams, and grimy. The walls were papered with fading printout porn; marker graffiti overlapped unreadably on the walls between the printout girls. There was a mattress behind the easy chair stained with a revolting potpourri of effluvia. This end of the Colony had some kind of heat-convection problem and Prego had been issued a space heater to compensate; the heat rose and its waves lifted the papery girls by the corners of their pages; the heat had activated the decay factor built into the paper, so that the underprinting was showing through: TIME TO RECYCLE ME. There was a heap of Prego's laundry beside the TV set; its sourness dominated the room.

There were three rooms in Prego's After; the other two malodorous, trashed-up rooms were bigger, crowded with people drinking Prego's foul home brew; *fermented garbage,* Molt called it. Bonham had the door closed and the TV turned up as loud as it would go, to beat the sounds coming from the other rooms: laughter, minimono blaring; he had to strain to hear as Molt, on TV, went on, " . . . The other faction is . . . I believe . . . sincerely interested in negotiating a compromise with strikers. The blockade state of emergency is a time when we should all be working together to survive . . . " He paused to glance at his notes. Bonham saw that Molt's hands were shaking and he blinked too often.

Molt was replaced by Asheem Spengle; the technicki commentator's triple-Mohawk was comically warped by the distortion in the upper half of the screen so that he looked like a tropical bird. He said something in technicki, which was translated at the bottom of the screen in subtitles. ". . . And that was our excerpt from Radleader Molt's media conference, which he gave yesterday after his release from Colony Detention . . . We noticed that more than once Radleader Molt referred to a written text in giving his statement. We cannot help but wonder who wrote that text. Was it indeed Radleader Molt? Or was it written for him by Colony Admin? Molt's statement was followed by an endorsement from the Colony's own founder, Professor Rimpler, and his daughter Claire . . . Clearly Molt's involvement with these two high administration figures sheds doubt on the sincerity of his—"

Bonham changed the channel, muttering, "Bullshit."

Another news show, this one in Standard English delicately articulated by an anchorwoman who looked like she was from the Middle East: " . . . have renewed their demands on a document teletyped to Admin officials today; the council of radleaders demanded a timetable for technicki integration into Admin housing projects in the Open, technicki representation in all Admin governing committees, guarantees of improved living conditions, and removal of SAISC 'conflict prevention guards' from technicki gathering places and hallways . . . " Bonham leaned forward, seeing himself on the screen, a slightly wobbly image, a burst of static fuzzing the anchorwoman's words. He caught, " . . . Bonham, chairman of the Radleader council, speaking today . . . "

Then he heard his own voice and hated the sound of it over TV. It sounded bloodless, too high-pitched. And Prego's damn screen was warping his image, making his head quiver like a soap bubble. He heard himself say, " . . . amazed they think we can be manipulated with double-talk out of George Orwell like 'conflict prevention guards.' Storm troopers are storm troopers."

Bonham shrugged. It was okay. Sometimes they used a slice that made you sound a fool. But that one went right to the point.

The anchorwoman was going on to something not directly related to Bonham, and Bonham began to lose interest. " . . . Full power was restored to the top four sublevels today by Admin technicians, despite technicki striker efforts to sabotage the conduits to—"

" 'Con-dew-its,' " Bonham said. "Nobody uses that word anymore. But I like the shape your lips make when you use it."

He kicked the switch with the toe of his rubber cowboy boot and sadly watched the lovely brown-eyed face compact and vanish into itself.

He looked at his watch, and thought, *I'm late, just about the right amount.*

Bonham got up, stretched, and picked his way through the room, through the door to the next, larger room crowded with partiers, thudding with minimono; he moved deftly through the tangle of legs, avoiding the ones who deliberately tried to trip him; he blinked against the thick smoke, thinking the smoke seemed to be moving to the music (but that couldn't be possible, could it?), and found the door.

The After was illegal, and Admin was beginning to crack down on places like it, correctly figuring them to be hotbeds of radical fermentation. So he paused at the monitor screens, checked the hall for bulls, swiveling Prego's camouflaged TV camera both ways. All clear.

Bonham opened the door, stepped through, closed it quickly behind him. Rubbing his eyes, he hurried down the corridor to the nearest crossover.

He passed a gaggle of technickids graffiting the corridor wall; they froze when he turned the corner, looking over their shoulders at him. He smiled and shrugged, and they grinned, relaxing. There were four of them, all about eleven years old, and they were in four colors: Hispanic derivation, black, Caucasian, and one that was maybe southeast Asian. Their jumpsuits were tricked out with buttons and patches—their parents' tech rating patches, next to minimono wiredancers looking dolefully out from glossy buttons, as unreal as the buttons showing cartoon characters.

The corridor here was riotous with graffiti, almost black with it in places; the sloganeering that had begun it was clotted over with obscenities and identities and gang symbols. There was more gang graffiti lately, and he wondered if it was time to take the techni-kid gangs seriously as a threat.

The door into the crossover for the Open had been vandalized off its hinges. Halfway down the crossover, an SAISC guard blocked the way. Maybe the guard was that far back from the door because the ones who stood right in the doorways were just begging for a lob. Bonham had once lobbed a Molotov himself, and then thought, *Am I crazy? If this place burns down there's nowhere to run to.*

Could the Colony burn? Some said yes, some said no, some said portions of it could, and there might be flammable insulation in the walls, and if flammable wire burned back to that flammable insulation, the place could fill with smoke, and even though there were theoretically enough gas masks and shelter-suits to go around, word was about a third of them had been vandalized or decayed past use . . . Bonham occupied his mind that way, trying to throw off the jitters and only making it worse as he walked up to the armoured guard.

He couldn't look up into that blue-green curved-mirror face, he just couldn't make that, so he looked at the middle of the gray-black chest and said, "Bonham, security pass 4555." The bull tapped his wrist console. "Repeat."

Bonham repeated it for the voice analyzer; the analyzer transmitted to Security Central's computer, which compared the registered sound waves with Bonham's own, checked the code number, and flashed a picture of Bonham to the tiny screen on the inside right of the guard's mask.

"Go ahead, sir, and have a nice walk," the bull said, stepping aside.

Bonham walked past, and looked at his watch. He picked up his pace . . .

... She was where she said she'd be, and she had only one bodyguard with her.

Judith Van Kips stood in the very center of the construction site. The fiberplas frame of the unfinished condo rose around her like a cage. It was a gilded cage, because the Open's light had been filtered and tinted red-gold to make a sunset; in another hour it would be dark. The corridors, too, would dim, normally, in order to produce regular circadian rhythms. But they were well-lit full-time since the strikes, the riots...

The light from the sunward glass made black bars of shadow across the red-dirt site, across Judith Van Kips' long, straight flaxen hair and the black uniform of the masked guard behind her.

Heart pounding, Bonham stepped through the frame of the door, thinking, If I change my mind and back out now, the bull's going to grab me, and they won't let anybody bust me out like Molt.

"That's close enough," she said.

Bonham stopped ten feet from her. "I don't like the bull listening."

"He's my Personal. We can trust him. Hold still now."

He waited it out, rigid and sweating, as the SAISC guard ran a weapon detector over him, then patted him down.

The bull put the instrument back in his belt pack and drew his gun. Judith Van Kips smiled when she saw the fear on Bonham's face.

"It's just in case," she said.

Bonham shrugged, just as if he hadn't been a fraction of a reflex away from rushing that gun. "You and Praeger bought that bozo Spengle."

She didn't say anything to that.

He went on, "I'm going to cost more than Spengle." He smiled. "Some journalists are more expensive than others."

She waited.

The breeze, the carefully engineered breeze, played with the precisely cut ends of her flaxen hair, drifting them across her carefully engineered face, a face too perfect to be natural.

"I want the money, and I want out. Home. Earth. Maybe—" He shrugged. "Trinidad might be nice. Or Freezone."

"The blockade." Her voice was almost inflectionless.

"Don't bullshit me. I know about the treaty. They're going to allow limited shipping to go through. For food, basic supplies. Bare minimum, no import, no export, freeze on all transport. But ships coming in will have to go back. Some of your people will be going back on them. I want to go, too."

"Where did you hear about the treaty?"

"One of my boys—maybe I'll call him my *Personal*—he, uh—he has got the touch, and Gridfriend's always at his elbow. He sucked your commlines. He and I are the only ones who know. Unless—" He shrugged. "Unless he blows it. But I don't think he will."

"His name."

Bonham shook his head.

She looked at the bull, as if thinking of having the name squeezed out of Bonham. But she thought better of it. Praeger had plans for Bonham.

Finally, she shrugged. "Keep an eye on your friend. And be careful no one learns about the treaty. We've gone to great lengths to keep it out of the media."

"Is it you, jamming transmissions from Earth?"

"Some frequencies yes, some frequencies no. As for moving you to Earth, it might be possible. I'll speak to Praeger. If he authorizes it, you'll be told by coded comm, same code as previously."

"I want the money in a sealed credit-cassette. A tamper-proof credette. Twenty-five thousand newbux."

"That's five thousand more than we agreed on."

"I'm doing more than risking my life. I'm betraying my people. And I got to live with that. In a way I'm throwing away a lifetime."

"You're not betraying anything you really believed in, or you wouldn't be capable of doing it at all. I personally will authorize the additional five thousand. But there will be no more."

"Okay. So what do you want me to do—precisely?"

"First, reinforce Spengle's intimation that Molt might be under someone else's control. Second, and most important, militate against any compromising with Admin. Insist it must be all or nothing."

Bonham's stomach flip-flopped with sheer disgust. Disgust with them—and disgust with himself, because he knew he'd go through with it. If he pushed the technicki radleaders into an 'all or nothing' posture, Admin would be "forced" into complete martial law, multiple arrests, sweeps of technicki quarters.

And executions.

Legally, Admin had the power to declare martial law. Once martial law was declared, Admin was authorized to execute anyone it regarded as threatening to the airtight integrity and general life-support-profile of the Colony. The accused had the right to *one* hearing. After the hearing, execution could take place, at the council's discretion.

It was spelled out in the fine print of every Colony resident's contract. And it was there because, despite all the engineering and fail-safing, the Colony was fragile. It wouldn't survive a full-scale uprising. Some of the technickis knew that—others considered it Admin propaganda designed to keep the proletariat down.

"All right," Bonham said at last. "But I want you to know why I'm going to do it."

She snorted softly. "You do? Then you're a weak man. But go ahead."

You're a weak man. He wanted to tell her to fuck herself. But he had to go on with his rationalization. The urge was overpowering. He knew it was pathetic, but he couldn't keep it from coming out.

"I'm going to do it because the Colony is a dead loss. Because the Colony is not going to make it. Within a year, it will be a dead shell. Everyone in it will be dead. So it doesn't matter."

She looked at him steadily. "You know something we don't? Has someone built a large bomb, for example?"

He shook his head. "Nothing like that. I think the risk you're taking is going to get out of hand. I think you underestimate how angry these people are, how irrational they are, and how far they're willing to go. They have to be stopped—or everyone will die."

"You underestimate Praeger." Something discreetly worshipful in her voice when she said *Praeger*. "He's planned for all of that. I have been authorized to inform you that Praeger thinks highly of your ability to manipulate crowds. You have talent. On Earth or in the Colony, we will have other uses for you. You can take that as a guarantee that you will be paid as promised."

She turned and walked away.

The security bull stayed where he was, between Bonham and Van Kips. Watching. Ready.

Bonham turned away and walked on leaden legs out of the site, through the long grass, and into the gathering shadows of the Open's parkland. An SA Security patrol trundled by in a small vehicle like a golf cart, shining hand-spots into the dark places.

Shine them into my gut, Bonham thought.

The patrol flashed a light over him and drove on, probably already informed of his authorization. They all knew just where he was.

They were going to have other uses for him, she'd said. *Oh, shit. Oh, God.*

He walked through the gate into the crossover, and down the transparent-plastic corridor leading to the Technicki Quarters level.

There was the guard, halfway across...

No. He was closer to the door now, bent forward a little. Listening.

A shout echoed down the corridor, from the far door beyond the guard. The guard started toward the door. Bonham fought an urge to warn him.

The guard reached the door, drew his club, looked out.

A flutter of red light trailing through the air...

A lob, Bonham thought, as a Molotov cocktail exploded in the center of the guard's chest; a second burst on his helmet.

His scream was amplified by his helmet mike.

The armored guard staggered backward, flailing, already a human torch, a man of fire like something from the vision of an Apostle. He clawed at the extinguisher on his belt, but the second lob had dripped its gel over his faceplate and he couldn't see to use it. The guard suits were supposed to be fireproof, but the underground's technicians had worked up a new burning agent that ate right through the nonflammable synthetics making up the guards' armor.

The fire reached the burst-charges of the teargas grenades in the guard's pouch, and they blew and sent shrapnel into him . . .

The guard fell, flailing, and a third lob hit him. Bonham backed away, feeling the heat on his face, smelling petroleum base, burning plastics. The sound of sizzling plastic was overlaid by screams.

A bit tardily, the Colony's bulkhead sensors detected the fire and activated sirens, mechanical screams augmenting the burning man's own cries. The sprinkler system came on—but only sporadically, here and there down the hall. It had been vandalized. The fire-suppressive liquids didn't reach the burning guard. The guard's mask was melting onto his face.

Bonham thought, Someone's been cutting corners on their armor. It's not supposed to burn *that* easily.

Portions of the helmet were burned away; part of the face was exposed. Bonham thought, Did my people do it? Or was it Praeger's agents, setting the stage for martial law? Did this guy's armor burn so easily because he was issued a suit intended to burn?

And as Bonham turned to run, he thought, When it burns, you can see it: there's a man inside that suit. A man.

Behind him, the man stopped his thrashing. SAISC guards arrived in patrol jitneys. The smoke rose black as anger.

15

THE LOVEMAKING happened in stages. In the first stage Swenson was going through the motions, playing images in his head so he could maintain tumescence, feeling as if he were in a gym, working out on a press bench; in the second stage he found pleasing familiarity in her angles and planes, and he descended into the mindless enjoyment of yeasty genital communion; in the third stage he began to hallucinate.

He saw things, as he did things to her—to her and to the copper-skinned young priest he was unable to disentangle from Ellen Mae.

He saw—

She was a hard-bodied woman, tensile and angular, and Swenson saw himself rearing above her—and then he saw a hammer pounding a nail into a board.

And now a hammer pounding a nail through a man's palm.

Pull back from that riven palm, to show the man's arm on the raw wood of the cross, the sag of his body against the upright piece. Back up, flashback now: he saw the First Sorrowful Mystery. Swenson, as Father Stisky, had taught Nicaraguan children how to say the Rosary. He'd had to explain how the recitation of each "decade" was accompanied by meditation on the fifteen events of the Mysteries. The Joyful Mysteries, the Sorrowful Mysteries, the Glorious Mysteries. Sometimes the children were frightened when he taught the Sorrowful Mysteries. Perhaps frightened by something in the good father's eyes. The Sorrowful Mysteries told of the agony of Jesus . . . The First Sorrowful Mystery was Jesus in the garden of Gethsemane, a copper-skinned, Hispanic Jesus praying for the sins of the world. On to the Second Sorrowful Mystery, in which Jesus is scourged by the guards and the spiteful Jews who condemned him to Crucifixion. On to the Third Sorrowful Mystery, and Swenson saw Jesus carrying the cross up the hill to Calvary. On to the Sorrowful Mystery of the Crucifixion, Jesus nailed to the cross, the nails going into His palms, into the wood, the hammer driving the nails, driving His blood into the flesh of a tree, driving the nails into the wood, driving the nails, pounding in, in, until the blood—

He screamed as he came, a scream of anguish.

He saw the two Nazis, kneeling in the chapel, saw the bullet holes appear in their backs like stigmata. They're dying for their cause, though they know it not, he thought.

And then it faded as Ellen Mae, beneath him, gasping, asked, "Are you all right?"

"Yes. It's taken care of."

"What? What's taken care of?"

"I—I don't know. I'm not thinking straight." He smiled, tried to make out she was making him muddled with desire. "You devastate me."

What *had* he meant by *It's taken care of?* He'd been repeating something.

Something Watson had said. They'd been in the kitchen, coming in through the back door. Ellen Mae was up making bread from scratch. It was something she did in the mornings. She said it was her "meditation time." She hadn't looked at Swenson at all. She was kneading dough, and she glanced up at Watson and said, abstractedly, "Did you take care of those awful men?"

Watson nodded. "It's taken care of."

"Oh, good. I don't like those sort of little backwoods Hitlers around, they upset Rick. Would you like some coffee?"

Listening, Swenson had been sure she hadn't meant, *Did you send them away?* She had meant, *Did you kill them?* Casually as a farmer's wife asking if he'd slaughtered a pig for supper's pork chops.

Why was he bothered by the execution of the NeoNazis? Vile men, after all, by any measure. The world was better off without them...

That morning, he and Watson had sat in the kitchen breakfast nook, just the two of them, drinking coffee, eating sweet rolls.

Now, more and more, he felt as if he were watching himself on a screen. Stisky watching Swenson, and Swenson wasn't Stisky anymore, and Stisky wasn't sure he could control Swenson...

"I've had my eye on you for a while, John," Watson had said, smiling his most avuncular smile.

Swenson searched Watson's face for double-meaning, saw nothing but the smile.

"We monitored you at the Service. When Rick was preaching on the video, there and, ah... well, Old Sacks did it, really. Via wires in your robe. Test your response. Everyone to be admitted to the circle was monitored. Of everyone there—you showed the most positive response. Your pleasure centers were working overtime. Your pulse was up where it was supposed to be and... I won't go into all the details. Suffice it to say, we feel you're rated to be a deacon in the Second Circle." He had the look of a father who's just told his teenage son he's getting a new Mercedes for his birthday.

Swenson looked appropriately gratified.

And now, lying beside Ellen Mae, he thought, *They don't know who I am. They think I'm Swenson. I'm Stisky. And yet they know who I am better than Steinfield does. They know me.*

God help me.

Agnus Dei, qui tollis peccata mundi, miserere nobis.

◆

James and Julie Kessler sat on the sofa together, watching television. This hotel room had a holocube above the screen, for the holo channels, but Kessler had turned the holo function off. He didn't like seeing miniature 3D people caper through deodorant commercials on the other side of the coffee table. With the ordinary TV, you could maintain your distance more easily; when they were three dimensional, they were more intimidating, and you almost felt compelled to buy whatever it was they were selling—or to shout at them to leave you alone. And of course they couldn't hear you.

So they were watching the low-income transmissions. "What time is it?" Julie asked.

Kessler felt a twinge of irritation. "What difference does it make? We're here at least till tomorrow night. Nothing changes. We aren't expecting anyone and we can't go out."

"I just like to know," she said gently, touching his arm.

He put his hand over hers and sighed. "Sitting around and relaxing is making me tense."

"At the risk of annoying you again—*exactly* what did Purchase say last night?"

He shrugged. "Basically, we wait. They'll protect us in the meantime. They'll contact us."

"I don't mean basically."

"Well—he said the hotel is owned by his people. He said Worldtalk's people are looking for us. Worldtalk has been taken over by the SAISC. The SA has its own intelligence service. The New Resistance people are setting up a kind of 'underground railway'— only it'll be by Lear jet—to some island in the Caribbean."

"I understand that much but—*what* island? And what'll it be like there? I mean—it could be a prison for all we know."

"I don't think so. Steinfeld was . . . I just believe him. We'll have a cottage and be protected. I'll work with his people to develop my screening program. Purchase has gotten his hands on some of the program through Worldtalk. They can use it to counteract the SA's propaganda—that's something valuable to him. They wouldn't brutalize us when they need my cooperation. That wouldn't make sense . . . But they won't tell us where the place is precisely, because if the SA finds us before we're moved, then, uh . . . " He shrugged.

She squirmed against the cushions, her hand tightening on his arm. "Maybe we should . . . I don't know . . . go off on our own somewhere. Like Canada. Maybe we're taking risks with these people that—well, what do we know about them?"

"I was impressed with Steinfeld. The feelings we have about people *have* to matter. Anyway, I've known Charlie for years—he's part of it, and he's going with us."

"It couldn't be," Julie said, "that you like the fact Steinfeld is taken with your program? An ego decision?"

He opened his mouth to deny it, and then thought better of it and said, "Maybe that too. So what? What difference does it make where we go? Running is running, hiding is hiding."

She didn't say anything for a while.

He tried to take an interest in television.

Channel 90 was occupied with the televising of a National Spirit Rally. Five hundred grade-school children in red, white, and blue marched across a football field in formation, creating an eagleshape with the flags they carried. A hundred more in the stands above lifted composite cards to make up a picture of the maternally beneficent—kind but firm—face of Mrs. Anna Bester, president of the United States of America. The children sang the hit pop tune "We're Gonna Kick That Russian Butt!" until a large holo of Mrs. Bester appeared on the stage, smiling and waving—

Kessler changed the channel.

Channel 95 showed the young country-pop singer, Billy Twilly, winding up a song with a grave endorsement of "Anna's new program." As his band played softly behind him, he strolled across the stage with his head down, one hand in his pocket, like a humble man a little embarrassed by the great responsibility that has been thrust upon him. He stopped, looked up into the lights and said, "Anna's new program is more than just a new ID system. It's safety—safety from the threat of terrorism for every American. Last year a thousand people were killed by terrorist bombs around the country. The only way we can be sure that the bombing is stopped is by identifying everyone, clearly and without any mistake. Some call it submitting to authority—I call it friendship—and faith. Faith in Anna Bester, and in the United States. Now, I'd like to sing—"

Kessler changed the channel, muttering, "I'm not sure anyone *needs* my program—some of this stuff is so..."

"It's not always so obvious," Julie said.

Channel 98 was a technicki channel...

"... *Soisezim, whudduhfiugyuhmina* ... " the comedian said, running a hand nervously along his quadruple-Mohawk. "*Neesud, hey—*"

Kessler changed the channel.

It was a CGI cartoon. Grommet the Gremlin, grinning toothily, his sine-wave eyes sparking, flew in loop-the-loops around a tight formation of Russian skatebombers, nipping in to effortlessly pluck rivets from their wings.

The wings fell off, and the planes hung for a moment in the air, as if unable to decide to crash. The Russian pilots looked in consternation at one another, and one of them said, "I told you, comrades, we should've got planes built in America!" And then the cartoon plane spiraled down and exploded into flames, the pilot's head and arms flying bloodily off to bounce into the air, Grommet the Gremlin using a pilot's severed bloody-stumped arm like a baseball bat to whack a severed head into—

Julie changed the channel.

On Channel 100 a man wearing a headset whispered confidentially, "I never miss *anything* on the Grid! A Gridfriend brand portable satlink puts me in touch with—"

Kessler changed the channel. Commercial. A young woman in a bikini strolled across her sundeck. The man beside her looked nervously around and said, "You sure it's safe to sunbathe? I mean—"

"Sure, silly! We've got Second Alliance Security here! It covers the whole development! There hasn't been a sniper here since the SAISC came around!"

A trustworthy male voice intoned, voiceover, "Second Alliance International Security Corporation—The Only Real Security is Full Security!"

Kessler turned the TV off.

They sat for a moment staring at the blank screen.

"You're depressed," she said.

He shrugged. He squeezed her hand. "Don't worry about it."

"I have to tell you something. The reason I'm worried about where we're going ... "

He looked at her. He knew. He felt a wave of joy, a wave of sheer dread, a wave of anxiety, a wave of joy...

As she said, "I think I'm going to have a baby."

◆

Hard-Eyes and Jenkins were awash in fog. They were walking across a bridge over the Seine; the morning fog was thickest here, rising from the river to hide most of the city from them. The sun was a hot pearl in the east.

"Trouble with these black-market assholes," Jenkins said, "is you can't find the bastards in the same place twice in a row. Where he is yesterday, he isn't today. But with any luck..."

"Can he get coffee?"

"Claims he can," Jenkins said, shrugging. "Claims he can get genetic pharms, too. Morph-trance, epinephrine, norepinephrine, neurotransmitters..."

"How's he get this stuff?" Hard-Eyes asked, looking around—not seeing much but billowing fog.

"Certain brigades, American army spikes the food with combos of that stuff to make the men more combat-ready. Lots of adrenocorticotrophic hormone... Some of the experimental troops are outfitted with injectors. Little box strapped on near the kidney, shoots 'em up with what they call chemcourage. Some real berserker shit. They're experimenting, trying to get a combination that makes them careful but not paranoid, aggressive but not likely to attack their COs—"

"Sick shit to do to a soldier."

"Yeah. Anyway, this guy works in the Yanks' camp."

"You calling them Yanks, too? You're a fucking Yank yourself, Jenkins, me neggo."

"Yeah. But—you see enough of this shit, you don't wanna be a Yank. I mean—Yank or Russian either. They can *all* kiss my ass."

They paused, listening. Distant, hollow thuds. A long shivery metallic shriek. A quick succession of booms. Silence.

"How close does that sound to you?" Jenkins asked nervously.

"A few miles away. Hard to tell in the fog, but it sounded like it was coming from north of the city."

"Fuck. Fighting moving back to the city. Just fucking great."

"Hell with this coffee dealer. Let's see if Steinfeld's back. They said last night he'd be back."

"They said he'd be back every night for a week."

"Let's look in . . . Shit, here comes a patrol truck." They saw the black silhouette of an SA patrol truck, just a squarish bulk in the fog, coming onto the bridge.

Jenkins was over the bridge rail first, Hard-Eyes a half-second later. They hung from the rail, heads below the stone edge, the column of a bridge lamp hiding them, the toes of their boots on a two-inch ledge taking some of their weight.

The truck moaned slowly nearer . . . and nearer. The river susurrated below them. Hard-Eyes could feel its cold breath on his back. The river's splashing seemed amplified by the overarching bridge. A spotlight came on, atop the truck's cab, as it drew close; the truck slowed, and the small spotlight beam slashed like a saber through the fog and flashed over them, and Hard-Eyes thought, *They're going to see us.* There was a second of uncertainty. In that second, he realized two things: first, that he and Jenkins must not be taken. The SA was dragnetting anyone who couldn't be definitely identified as French, US Army, or a soldier of the NATO forces. And even the French were suspect if they were not registered with the Front National, or if they were Jewish, Muslim, or Communist. Those taken vanished into the SA's Center of Preventive Detention. The SA was said to be using an extractor for some, torture for others. There were rumors of exterminations, but there was no proof. And there were no investigative journalists looking into it. Invoking their NATO-granted power of martial law, the SA had simply closed down the local Internet news sites, and the few remaining print publications. The TV transmitters had been destroyed by the Russians. If Hard-Eyes and Jenkins were taken, the SA would soon know whatever they knew about the New Resistance. There was no way of keeping anything back from an extractor.

So, in that second, Hard-Eyes knew that if they were seen, he and Jenkins would have to jump into the river.

His second realization was, they would probably not survive the river. At this time of year it was high and cold. Exposure would kill them or would drag them down till they drowned.

And that's why he was NR.

Because this...

... the truck passing, slowing, searching for them with its spotlight, the confrontation with the predator, the imminence of a mortal choice...

... this was real.

The truck came to a stop. The spotlight beam kept moving.

The light passed over the stone railings, swept past Hard-Eyes and Jenkins, lifted to hold for a moment on the black metal statuary, sweating with fog, mounted on columns along the rail. As if these figures from mythology were objects of suspicion.

And then the truck rolled on.

They waited, fingers freezing to the stone balustrade, till the truck's red taillights were completely swallowed by the mist. Then they climbed stiffly over the rail and, thrusting numb fingers into coat pockets, they walked on, side by side, saying nothing.

But inside himself, under the layer of silence, Hard-Eyes had a buzz on.

◆

By the time Jenkins and Hard-Eyes reached the safe-house, they were both hoping Levassier had gotten some food in. Their meals had been cut to once a day, and the once had not come for the past two days. They found Levassier on the third floor of the safe-house, which had become an infirmary.

The old pile had been built in the mid-nineteenth century and hadn't been renovated since the mid-twentieth. You passed through two old cast-iron doors, brass knobs in the center of each, and into a courtyard, conscious you were being watched as you approached, and watched as you entered, though you saw no one watching at all;

no cameras, no one at windows. The white-painted wooden shutters on the windows were kept open. The curtains were not drawn. Lights showed, even on the dormer windows of the red tile roofs. Every care was taken to make the house look as if it kept no secrets. The SA used roving cameras, the bird-drones; if a camera should flutter up to the window, hover like an oversized aluminum hummingbird to peer electronically through, it would see kerosene lamps, or the few electric lights if it was during an accredited electricity ration period for the area. The remote-control operator looking through the bird's camera-eye, gazing in rapt boredom into a TV screen back at the SA center, would see a banal, shabby room, containing, perhaps, a wan child listening to the propaganda broadcast on the radio, or two old women commiserating. Levassier, Steinfeld's adjutant, fretted that some alert inspector might notice that the rooms seemed too small for the volume and style of the house. He might realize there were other rooms he wasn't seeing.

Having passed inspection twice, Hard-Eyes and Jenkins stepped through a closet, through a hidden door, and into the infirmary, where Levassier was said to be with his patients.

Levassier was a doctor, and an old-fashioned radical—yes, a *Marxist*—but Steinfeld had said, "I forgive his politics in gratitude for his morality."

The strange truth was, politics were irrelevant in this particular political battle. And this was another reason Hard-Eyes remained in Paris.

The infirmary was a long, windowless room, fuggy with continuous human occupation and bad ventilation. Three walls wore faded lily-patterned wallpaper, water-stained at the upper corners; the fourth wall, built by NR personnel to cut the original room in half, was an ugly thing of cinder blocks and drippy mortar. There was barely room to pass between the end of the second-hand hospital beds and the papered wall. The room was lit by two dim bulbs in the cobwebbed ceiling, at either end of the room. As Hard-Eyes and Jenkins entered Levassier was cursing the lack of adequate light. He was bending over a man wearing a chest cast in the middle of the three occupied beds.

Levassier was an intense, birdlike man, big-nosed and pale, his eyes magnified in thick rimless glasses. He sniffed continuously from a cold he'd had all the time Hard-Eyes had known him. He had the pinched lips of a zealot, and little sense of humor. He wore a white doctor's coat now, probably for its psychological value to the patients.

"*C'est la merde*," he muttered, "*C'est la merde.*"

Hard-Eyes found a lighter in his pocket. It was nearly empty, there wouldn't be another, so he hoped Levassier appreciated it: he crossed to the middle bed, bent over the patient, and flicked the flame alive, throwing a small pool of yellow light.

Levassier said, "Eh?" and looked up, annoyed at the distraction.

"Light for your work," Hard-Eyes said.

"You will eat soon enough; do not cuzzle up to me," Levassier said.

"That's *cuddle* or *cozen*," Hard-Eyes said, grinning.

"*Arrete!* You frighten zuh bird! It makes droppings when it is afraid! Disgusting to have it here, but he won't let us take it away ... "

Hard-Eyes saw the bird then, a big black crow perched on the gray tube-steel frame at the foot of the bed. It cocked its head and caught the reflection of his lighter flame in its eyes. It cawed, showing a snippet of pink tongue. Hard-Eyes switched off the small flame and put the lighter away. He looked at the man in the hospital bed more closely now.

"Smoke?"

Smoke nodded, smiling very faintly. "It's good to see you're still with us, Hard-Eyes. I've only been here three days from Brussels. Waiting for Steinfeld. No one's told me a thing."

"You don't look the same," Jenkins said. "I mean, you don't look like you."

"I've put on weight. They cleaned me up. Cut my hair." Hard-Eyes stared at Smoke, thinking he had a striking face, now that the grime and beard was gone. A little pinched, the eyes deep-set, but aristocratic; something illuminated about it. The word *saintly* came into his mind, and in sheer embarrassment Hard-Eyes tried to banish it, but it wouldn't go. Saintly.

Hard-Eyes looked away. "Who else have we got here?"

A girl, asleep or comatose, was lying on her back, her chest bandaged, her mouth open, looking parched. Her hair was spiky.

"That's Carmen," Smoke said. "Accidental gunshot."

The third patient looked over, hearing that. He was gaunt, big-eyed, his face mobile, too elastic. On the verge of madness, Hard-Eyes thought. He was sitting on the edge of a bed. Perhaps he wasn't a patient at all. He was wearing a leather jacket. His hair was short, streaked, but it had lost its shape, whatever it had been. He looked vaguely familiar. From the earring, jacket, the hunched attitude on the edge of a bed, Hard-Eyes judged him to be a retro-rocker of some kind. He had the habitual sullen posture of a rocker missing his stage, and missing the activity of his scene.

"That's Rickenharp," Smoke said. "He hasn't said anything in three days. Since he came in with her. He shot her himself. Accidentally. Apparently he wasn't sure who it was, but he hadn't intended to shoot, and his finger twitched on the trigger." Smoke shrugged with his eyebrows. "Amateur with a gun. He's making a great thing of not forgiving himself. He's tried to maintain a vigil. Tried not to sleep. Gave in last night, poor fellow. He's very . . . dramatic. But then, Rickenharp's a stage person."

Smoke was speaking so that Rickenharp would hear him. Maybe trying to jolt him out of his funk.

"Rickenharp . . . " Hard-Eyes repeated. "The guitar player?"

Rickenharp looked up at him, unable to conceal his gratitude, and a friendship was born.

◆

"What you have to understand, dear Claire," Rimpler was saying, "is that we are all trapped into what we are by what we thought we were."

"Dad . . . " But she didn't know quite how to say what she needed to say.

They were in her father's apartment, in the Admin quarters of FirStep, the Colony, and they had just finished watching InterColony evening news. A report on the shortage of air filters due to the blockade, causing worsening air quality. Small protest fires set here and there about the Colony were exacerbating the condition. (Claire thought, The *air* here is fine. Admin has a different ventilation system. The best filters go to Admin.) Reports of more rioting. Arrests. Three rioters hospitalized. The man Bonham was everywhere, throwing fuel on the fire, somehow the police never touching him, though they had arrested most of the other leaders.

Rimpler had turned the newscast off halfway through. And he'd made himself a drink. He wore the same shorts, the same grimy bathrobe. He hadn't shaved.

He sat on the rug beside the sofa, making another drink, humming to himself. She watched as he dropped a pill into the drink. It fizzled.

"Dad—what are you putting in your drinks?"

"A little something to give them more punch. Making them into Punchy Punch." He sipped, and shuddered. Then his eyes became languid, the lids drooped, and he began to talk. "When you're a young man, or woman, Claire, you try to build things. Businesses or homes or books or space stations or . . . schools of ideas. You have a wide freedom of choice as a young person. Relatively speaking. As you grow, you build on to what you've built, and on to that, and onto that, and you attach yourself to it, and you create a sort of web of . . . of conceptions and misconceptions of the world. Wrong or right, these ideas solidify around you, and hem you in. And you do things in accordance with the ideas, and, then . . . why then you must justify what you do, if you are to live with yourself. So your choices diminish *until you are no longer making them*, you are simply building a pattern on a pattern. It's like a man who's built a skyscraper with his own two hands—I saw a Popeye thing like this as a boy on TVLand—the skyscraper got to be up in the clouds, and he was up there, atop it, but he hadn't built stairs and there was no way down or off, so he had to keep building, up, up . . . Where he gets the materials I don't know, and there the analogy breaks down . . ."

He's completely maundering, Claire thought. Who's Popeye?

"Dad—we've got to make up our minds where we stand on this thing . . ."

"But that's what I've been trying to tell you. I've built myself into the Admin and I must support Admin. Right or wrong. I've gone as far as I can with you."

"You know there's no 'right or wrong.' The way things are now, Admin is just plain wrong."

"Yes." Dreamily. "I believe we are."

"But you don't care."

"I can't do anything about it."

"Even if you can't take a stand, you can help me in other ways. I'm barred from council sessions now. You're not."

"I'll tell you what I learn . . . if they let me go," he said, nodding.

"How can you accept it all so passively!"

"Please don't shout."

She felt near weeping. "You weren't like this before."

"No. But since then I've seen them. I've seen *into* them. And this man Molt must go. His being here risks the peace of my retreat . . ." He gestured at the room around him with his drink. "My . . . hermitage, my dear, dear child. You fail to understand how serious our Praeger is. Because you don't know *who* he is. Praeger is one of the chiefs of the Second Alliance. They wish to make the Colony their world headquarters—when the blockade is lifted. Crandall wants to come here. He feels safer here. Ironic, as things are now. But if they could perfect their control, they could turn the place into a perfect police state. It would 'hum with harmony,' to use Praeger's charming phrase. It would be safer for Crandall."

"How did you get all this?" Her voice came out a croak. "About the SA's plans for the colony and . . . ?"

"You always seem surprised by my keeping tabs on the thing I built myself. Why, my dear child, I tapped their comms . . . they had run tether satellites out to transmit past the blockade . . . to Crandall's farm. To a man named Swenson. And a certain Watson. Even their names sound alike to me. Swenson and Watson. Praeger and Jaeger. These people are the vectors for the new conformity, and maybe they'll all change their names to sound alike, Watson, Wilson, Winston; Crandall, Kendall, Randall, Rendell—"

"Dad—you're saying that the Security Section is now a political organization?"

"It's run by one. The new fascists, dear girl."

The door opened.

Claire looked up at the door in shock. No one was supposed to be able to open it from the outside with a key, except...

Except Security.

Two Security bulls stood in the door, one with a face, the other faceless. But the one with a face might just as well have worn a helmet, for all his expression told them. It was friendly, with a faint regret. He was a Security administrator whose name she couldn't remember. He was here for the sake of decorum. Professor Rimpler was not some technicki bumpkin.

"Professor Rimpler," the administrator said politely. "Claire Rimpler. I have executive orders to bring you with me, for questioning and detention, in connection with a detention-cell breakout and the maiming of three guards."

"May I finish my drink?" Rimpler asked. Casually, just as if he didn't know full well that these men had come to take him to prison; as if he didn't know that it was a prison he would never come away from.

"Certainly, sir," the administrator said, smiling.

"Took them a while to make up their minds they could politically get away with arresting us," Rimpler mused, rattling the ice in his glass. "Or maybe they simply needed time to arrange the appropriate political background."

"As to that, I couldn't say, sir," the administrator said, glancing at his watch.

Claire looked around. The moment, the arrest, made everything look different. How little we normally notice, she thought.

Now the whole room seemed to spring into relief. The walls were adjusted to a soft, dimpled texture, making her think of a padded cell. The two men standing in the arch of the doorway were remarkably detailed; she saw every fiber in their armored suits, every stud on their belts, every pouch and fastener and wrinkle. She noted the play of light across the faceplate of the one on her left. She heard a faint squeak and rustle of synthetic material as he shifted his weight. She could hear him breathe, very faintly, through his helmet amplifier, even dialed to low output.

She was listening for something else. *Molt.*

Molt was in the next room, sleeping. He slept whenever they would let him, taking tranks cut with antidream. The administrator hadn't said anything about him; hadn't looked at the bedroom. Maybe they didn't know he was here.

She'd taken pains to make them think Molt was hiding somewhere behind the Corridor D barricades, with the other radicals, technickis and the Admin progressives like Judy and Angie and Belle and Kris who were sympathetic to the tecknickis. She looked at the guard's RR stick, on his belt. His right hand was resting on its pommel. Not threateningly. A little behind the stick was the gun in its locked holster.

Claire listened...

Molt sometimes moaned in his sleep.

Professor Rimpler finished his drink, sighing, setting it down with a *clack.*

He stood and said, "Well, shall we go, Claire?" The Security administrator smiled approvingly.

The bedroom door opened. The administrator looked at it, his smile fading. The bull drew his RR.

There was a faint hiss.

A small hole, a centimeter across, appeared in the center of the guard's chest. He shouted some meaningless monosyllable.

The administrator threw himself down.

There was a *whumpf* and the guard's suit expanded like a balloon, in a split-second puffing the chest to four times its normal size. Blood jetted from the tiny hole, squirting out in a neat arc. The bull's arms snapped up and down, once, and he fell over backward. He hit the corridor's floor with a wet sound, blood fountaining in a thin stream from the single hole. His suit began to deflate. Slowly.

Molt stepped through the open bedroom door and pointed the thing in his hands at the administrator on the floor. The man was getting to his feet and now truth showed in his face: it was contorted with naked fear.

Claire shouted, "Don't!"

But the thing in Molt's hands—it looked to her like a little bicycle tire pump she'd had as a girl—hissed again and a hole appeared in the man's back as he turned to run; the suit expanded; blood splashed out from the collar. The man tried to scream, but all that came out was a gurgle. And the blood kept coming.

She thought, *It's so red. There's so much of it and it's all so red.* She looked away. The man scraped at something on the floor, moving spasmodically... wet sounds.

Then the room was quiet.

Molt's heavy face was dead. His eyes were lifeless. He slurred as he spoke. "It worksh like you shed, Rimpler. Right through the shuit."

Rimpler nodded, his head tilted to one side. "The only one in the Colony. Far's I know. But maybe not: Praeger requisitioned explosive bullets. Not that all explosive bullets are necessarily fired from—"

"How can you talk that way! Like hunters over deer!" Claire burst out. Her stomach churned. She was shouting to keep from throwing up.

"It's a way of adjusting," Rimpler said, bending to make himself a drink.

A flash of heat went through her. She knocked his hand down, and his glass broke against the table. He stared numbly at the fragments.

"Dad, we have to go! *Now!*"

"Oh, no. You and Molt go. I'll report that this was done by rioters."

"They won't believe that. They'll arrest you. They don't *extract*, Dad. They *torture*."

He sighed. "I suppose... they won't leave me alone."

Molt was dragging the bodies inside. "They have a transmitter in the suit," Molt was saying, pronouncing his words more carefully. "If it'sh cut off, it shets up an alarm, and they send someone to inveshtigate."

Claire looked at the leaking suits, the bodies, then at her father. "So let's go *now*, dammit!" She wanted more than anything to get away from there.

As they went down the hall—her father in his absurd shorts and sandals and bathrobe, Molt in a grimy technicki jumpsuit, she in her Admin jumpsuit—Claire knew that she wanted to go farther than simply away from this end of the Colony.

She wanted off, and down. To Earth.

16

THE MESSAGE encoder worked like this: Swenson sent a e-message from the SAISC administration to Purchase at Worldtalk.

It was a non-classified message re the acquisition of Worldtalk by the SA Corporation. The message was relayed in groups of signals, each group of signals representing a group of letters. The interval between the transmission of a group of letters was supposed to be uniform. But certain groups of letters arrived fractions of a microsecond later than they should have; a half-microsecond late corresponded with a certain word; one-tenth of a microsecond later corresponded with a certain letter; one-eleventh with another letter, and so forth. Purchase—having reception software equipped to listen for the encoded delays—received first the ostensible message; then—after securing his comm line—he told his console to listen for the delays, make the letter and word correspondences, and print out the decoded message. The message from the SA Second Circle to SA-initiate Purchase read:

> Joseph Bonham, political liaison apprentice, arriving on treatied Russian exchange ship from Colony, transfer to SA shuttle orbit, L2, 2-10/0800 EST, arrival New Brooklyn seaport 01100 EST. Meet with double Security, supervise transfer of Bonham to Detention Unit Three for extraction and implantation.

There was a third message hidden within the second. After the second message was decoded, it was transmitted from the computer to the printout mechanism; another decoding unit in the printout mechanism—a unit known only to the NR—heard another set of fractional delays in the transmission of the group of signals, a kind of meaningful computer stuttering, and translated them into the third message, which it printed out after the second.

In the message from Swenson, the SA Second Circle operative to Purchase, the SA Second Circle operative, was a message from Stisky/Swenson, the New Resistance agent, to Purchase, the New Resistance agent.

The message read:

> They are prepping me to give Senate testimony against reform of the Antiviolence Laws. Have asked me to stay on at Cloudy Peak. I cannot manage it much longer. Psychological pressure too great. Give me orders or get me out. They are trying to obtain memory extraction experts. They also plan to provide DoD with new submarine silencing techniques in exchange for covert federal backing of SA projects. Tell me what to do, let me do it, and get me out, repeat, get me out. They are going to hold a Service soon.

Purchase read the printout twice. On the outside, he looked like a businessman who was annoyed by a sudden burden of extra work. Inside Purchase, bridges were buckling, guy wires snapping, ceilings falling in.

He glanced abstractedly at his office door, as if simply letting his eyes wander. But looking to see if anyone was in the hall.

No one.

He got up and closed the door. He transferred the message to a high-priority garbled transmission unit, rerouted it through a coded modem—which he had to take from its hiding place in his closet and interface with his system—and relayed the message to Steinfeld, via Joseph Bensimon, the NR contact at the Israeli Embassy. Bensimon would relay the message to the Israeli Secret Service, the Mossad, who, if they could get through the various static blocks, would send it via satellite to Steinfeld.

There was another *if*: if Steinfeld was still in the Mossad's good graces. The Israelis had had a generation of peace, after the Arab Spring and the Cairo 13 Treaty; Jordan, Kuwait, Egypt, Lebanon, the Saudis, Iran, and the State of Palestine signed the treaty, after Israel signed a pledge to accept a Palestinian state and after it ceased building new settlements. (Iran had come into the fold when the regime of the Ayatollahs had fallen to reformists.) Israel was neutral in the US/Russian confrontation, even when the war moved into the Middle East, as the Russians tried to capture oil fields in the few Arab nations aligned with the West. So far, the Russians had left Israel out of it. Israel's frontiers were massively defended. The Knesset had gone from pugnacity to moderation, and Steinfeld was regarded by some Israelis as a firebrand, a fanatic who saw Nazis under every bed.

But Purchase sent the message, after which he detached the special external modem unit and packed it into a Styrofoam-and-cardboard container in his closet, so it looked like an ordinary extra kept in case of a breakdown.

Then he sat at his desk, drinking cold coffee from a plastic cup. There was a hairline crack in the cup; coffee leaked through in beads to run down onto his hand. He stared at it, thinking, *By the time we get advice from Steinfeld it'll be too late.*

He sighed. Stisky had been his project. His enthusiasm. Witcher had said, "The guy's almost too good to be true." And Witcher had been right. Stisky/Swenson had sat in on the last planning session with Steinfeld, before they'd placed him in the SA's Second Circle. That had been a mistake.

Stisky knew some things. He knew too many names.

And they had a memory extraction man now. They would do a routine extraction on everyone, and if they asked Stisky/Swenson's memory center the right questions, they'd know about Purchase, and they'd know where Steinfeld was.

Swenson was your idea, he thought. *Take responsibility.*

He turned to the console and told the computer he wanted to send a message to Cloudy Peak Farm.

◆

Rickenharp was trying to understand. Some of the talk at the conference table was in French, some in English, some in Dutch. He'd made out that the French resented meetings carried on in English, but Jenkins had pointed out that at least half the "active" members of the Paris NR—active meaning those prepared to take up arms at any time—were English speaking, and they translated everything. Then the French guy—actually an Algerian immigrant—had complained that this Steinfeld was recruiting all the wrong people and perhaps they should replace Steinfeld with a Frenchman.

But when Steinfeld came in, sitting in the empty chair at the head of the table, the French guy shut up, just like that.

Everyone shut up. They were like children fighting till the teacher came back into the room.

And it was a schoolroom, the teacher's conference room of the old *école*, with its cracked plaster walls and the oily warmth from its furnace. The school was receiving its electricity ration today and they had electric light, for now; old, humming, tubular fluorescent lights. The room—half its original size—was without windows; the windows had been covered by a false wall, to deceive the spy birds. Two guards stood at the two doors at either end of the room. Each with an old Uzi slung over his shoulder. The actives at the table were armed only with whatever they could carry without showing it. It was considered cloddish to display your guns, except in an actual firefight. But the bigger guns were nearby, under the coatrack, in a case, and loaded.

There were fourteen people around the long, gray-painted metal table, sitting in rickety plastic chairs, daydreaming about coffee. Four women, ten men.

So this is the Paris resistance. Kind of pitiful, really. Does that make it more heroic?

Song lyric in there somewhere . . .

Smoke sat on Steinfeld's right, Yukio on his left. Hard-Eyes sat beside Rickenharp, Jenkins on the far side, both of them silent and bored. Yukio and Willow sat across the table from Rickenharp.

Carmen was there, sitting beside the doctor at the corner. She had insisted. Rickenharp stole glances at her. Her complexion was gray, but there was no droop in her posture. She'd changed her look, Rickenharp thought. And then he realized that what she was wearing wasn't a "look." She was wearing fatigues and a flak jacket because she meant to fight, and she wanted everyone to know it. She hadn't said anything to Rickenharp since she'd regained consciousness. He'd tried to apologize, of course. (Thinking: How do you *apologize* to someone for putting bullet holes in their chest?) She'd acted as if she hadn't heard. There was no angry chill about it. It was as if she'd made up her mind that he didn't exist.

I'm an embarrassment to her, Rickenharp thought.

Somewhere in Italy—somewhere inside him—he'd made up his mind to get the hell back to the States or Freezone at the first opportunity. He'd played at being one of the guerrillas, almost believed it, especially when he'd pictured telling the band about it. But he'd had no real intention of going *through* with it. Not after that ride in the boat.

And then the gun. The feeling it was an instrument he wanted to learn to play. And then—

He squeezed his eyes shut, but the image came. Carmen falling back, those little neat round holes punched into her...

But now it was different. Now he *wanted* to be NR. It was as if he'd been slapped awake. Sitting there with his eyes shut, he thought: *Until I shot her, I was asleep, sleepwalking through ego games.*

The rest of the world had been unreal, except in the way it reacted to him; the way women reacted, or an audience. But now it was as if he'd been slapped—

"And who's this? Is he asleep?" Steinfeld's voice, and suddenly Rickenharp knew Steinfeld was talking about him.

Rickenharp opened his eyes and looked down the table. Everyone was looking back at him, except Carmen.

"I'm not asleep," Rickenharp said.

"This building is no longer a school, in the traditional sense. So don't sleep in it," Steinfeld said. His voice was mordant. Some of them laughed, and Rickenharp realized it was a joke.

Steinfeld, though, was not laughing. He was waiting.

"I'm Richard Rickenharp," he said. It felt clumsy in his mouth.

"I'm sponsoring him," Hard-Eyes said.

Carmen looked at Hard-Eyes, annoyed, and Rickenharp had to smile.

"Me too," Jenkins said. "I'm, uh, sponsoring him too."

Steinfeld tugged at his own beard, hard, as if wondering if it was a fake. "But isn't this the young man who—?" He looked at Carmen.

Oh, God, Rickenharp thought.

But Rickenharp cleared his throat (Thinking, *For God's sake, don't let your voice quaver!*) and said, "I'm the guy who shot her. I take responsibility. I shouldn't have insisted on having a gun when I didn't know how to use it . . . "

"I'm not at all sure it's your responsibility," Steinfeld said, surprising only Rickenharp.

Carmen was looking at her hands folded on the table. She nodded. "It was my fault. I should never have given it to him. I knew he didn't know how to use it. And it wasn't an emergency."

Steinfeld nodded. "Still—if he's to be an active . . . " He shrugged.

"We've put in ten days target practice in the catacombs," Hard-Eyes said. "Rickenharp's working hard. He won't make the same mistake."

The catacombs. Rickenharp seemed almost to hear the echoes of the gunshots ringing off the curved stone walls. *Smelling the wet mineral smell of the place, the underscent of sewage, then the smell of gunpowder. Seeing the cold gray stone reach of the subterranean target-practice room, with its woebegone, ravaged wooden silhouettes. Feeling the gun cold in his stiff hands, then feeling it grow warm with its compressed internal explosions. Hearing the hail-clatter of spent shells hitting the floor. Visualizing a guitar but holding the machine gun and fighting the urge to—*

"He's learned fast. He can take the weapons apart and put them back together. He's accurate. He's careful. We work on hand-to-hand; Jenkins teaches him field communications. He works hard."

—the urge to laugh.

"Mr. Rickenharp is a . . . performer, right?" Steinfeld said. "And we are not performing here."

"I know that," Rickenharp began. "I—"

"Are you trying to make up for shooting Carmen by working hard to be one of us?"

Rickenharp sensed that Steinfeld considered that kind of motivation insufficient. But he also sensed Steinfeld would know it if he lied. "Partly. But—" He reached for words and couldn't find them, but plunged into trying to explain anyway. "It's *more*. Everything's different when you—well . . . it's like you're . . . like that Poe story where the guy is tied to a table and there are rats all around him. But in my version, it's like the guy was asleep, and there was someone there trying to untie him and save him from the rats, and a rat bites the guy who's tied up, so . . . uh, when he wakes from the pain, he strikes out and accidentally hurts the guy trying to untie him and then he realizes what he's done so he wants to kill the rats but it's also because it made him realize, you know, something he never realized before: *the rats are all around him*—"

"Oh, for God's sake, stop babbling!" Carmen said, very definitely looking at him now—looking two round neat bullet holes into him.

But Steinfeld was shaking, silently shaking, and after a confused moment Rickenharp realized he was laughing.

"Well—" Steinfeld tried to speak but the laughter made it impossible. He had to wheeze for a moment. Then he tugged on his beard and, with an effort, stopped laughing, and shook his head, his face red. "Well, that's a wonderfully, uh, baroque explanation, my friend; and the frightening thing is I know just what you mean!"

Some of the others were laughing now, the English-speaking ones. The French speakers looked confused.

Carmen permitted a smile to lift a corner of her mouth, for just a moment.

Rickenharp saw her as she'd been at the club, bare-breasted and spike-crowned. He wanted her, and he knew that, now, he'd never make the move. Having made a small *faux pas*. Having *shot* her.

Steinfeld raised a hand, and the laughter died down.

Rickenharp felt a strange combination of mortification and deep relief.

"Does anyone else sponsor our young singing poet here?" Steinfeld asked.

"Yes. I do," Yukio said.

"Yeah," Carmen said, with a sigh. "What the hell. Me too. I mean, if Yukio does." Shrugging.

Rickenharp was limp with relief at that.

"The sponsors will be responsible for this man's further indoctrination, briefing, and training," Steinfeld said, all business now. "Just see to it he isn't prone to being a dilettante, or being a, what's the word, a grandstander. In fact—I wonder if he's aware . . . " He looked at Rickenharp. "That if he tried to go to the States and tell the media all about his heroic 'journey' with the resistance, and write songs about it, and draw attention to us. We'd kill him."

Rickenharp looked back at Steinfeld, and swallowed. The guy was not kidding.

Steinfeld kept looking at him, eyebrows raised. "Well?"

"I do understand that," Rickenharp said. "I wouldn't do that anyway. I understand why you think I would."

The NR leader looked at Rickenharp for another long, assessing moment, then nodded. Steinfeld took out a handkerchief and mopped his brow. "It's hot in here. Now, first the good news—I did bring a little coffee and a few other items back for the actives."

There was a general murmur of pleasure at that.

Steinfeld gestured to the doctor, who translated for those whose English was shaky. "*Il fait chaud ici . . .* " Levassier began.

"Just the important stuff, Claude," Steinfeld said.

The doctor nodded curtly and translated the part about the coffee. More murmurs of pleasure. He waited, as Steinfeld went on.

"But as for our steady supplies . . . "

Steinfeld told them that the food ration would be reduced by one-third, but it would be twice a day. They were running out of furnace oil. There would be measures taken to conserve all supplies . . .

And he told them that the Russian/NATO front was holding steady forty miles north of Paris. Both sides were showing great restraint in the use of tactical nuclear weapons, which meant that fallout dangers were minimal just now.

The seat of France's right-of-center government had been moved to Orleans, about one hundred fifteen miles south of Paris. The government currently had very little influence on affairs in France outside Orleans and the provinces of Guyenne and Provence. Of the other provinces, those not controlled by the Russians had fallen under the authority of local petty demagogues whose power was in actuality reliant on their working relationship with the Second Alliance. The badly decimated, desertion-plagued French military was chiefly occupied in maintaining logistics for the NATO forces at the Front, or in protecting the government at Orleans. The few French soldiers remaining in Paris were attachés to the police department and were effectively absorbed into the Second Alliance, since the SA had been given authority over the police. As a sop to the hard-line nationalists, Le Pen had been appointed Minister of the Interior, his principal responsibility now the administration of the police.

The police and SAISC troops were largely occupied in rounding up anyone the SA's intelligence branch designated as a "criminal or disruptive element," i.e.: Communists, dark-skinned immigrants (for whom suitable crimes were invented), left-of-center Jews, and dissidents of any kind. And, as an afterthought, looters and conventional outlaws.

Steinfeld went on, "The line will hold steady in France for a while, I should think, unless the Russians manage to take out Milstar 2."

Milstar 2, the USA's orbital military warning/communications/observation system, was protected by a series of orbital battle stations and watched over by a "fence" of tethered satellites. The Russian disadvantage in space technology had so far kept Milstar 2 safely insulated.

"Our source in the Pentagon informs us," Steinfeld said, "that the Russians are about to launch new anti-sat weapons, specifically to take out Milstar. If they're successful, NATO will find it more difficult to watch its back: and as we found out at the beginning of the war, its back is space. The Russians could shuttle troops in behind NATO lines..." He paused for the translator. Then: "The city would once more become a battleground. More accurately, it would quickly become rubble. If that happens, the SA will dig in behind NATO lines. We will follow the SA, wherever they go, to disrupt them in any way we can. In the meantime, we—"

"*C'est suffit!*" the Algerian said. "I am need to know this: What have we been waiting for? We do nothing but print posters... *C'est merde.* Why do we not fight? We do not use the explosives, the guns, we keep them like a greedy child hiding his toys! Only a little, we use, here and there. Nothing. Why are we wait? Eh? Why we wait for big push?"

"It's very simple," Steinfeld said with a wintry smile. "You've been waiting for me. The waiting is over. I'm here. And now, we go on the offensive."

◆

Corridor D was choked with debris, with bad smells and the atmospheric tension of relentless jeopardy. Belle had told Claire, "We call it Alphabet Town. After a neighborhood in old New York, where the avenues were named A, B, C, D..."

Claire sat with her back to the wall, behind the barricade, supposedly on duty. There were four others on duty. Two technicki men, up above on ladders, looked through the notches atop the barricades. Angie and Kris below, in the truck cabs, were looking down the empty corridor in front of the barricades. And Claire knew Angie was quietly, urgently hoping to see someone coming. Someone to shoot at.

Claire was supposed to act as a messenger and gofer for the barricade guards. Mostly, she brought coffee. The corridor here was a litter of trash, trampled beyond recognition; the news sheets were still soaked from the riot hoses the SA bulls had used before the barricade had gone up; empty emergency ration canisters clattered underfoot whenever she went back to the corridor rest station to try and find a toilet that wasn't stopped up. And the air filtration was working at one-quarter efficiency. It smelled like a maggot's belch.

At the back of her throat, the odor was met by the smoke from the empty, rusting lubricant drums fulminating under the vent behind the barricade. Technicki rebel bravos stood around the barrel warming their hands, spitting into the flame to watch it hiss, laughing and bullshitting. The air vent sucked at the black smoke but much of it slithered away and coiled near the ceiling, increasing her sense of choking submergence...

"Wonderful," Claire said, now, tasting her own bitterness as she stood up, looked through a crack between boxes, down the corridor at the sacked shopping mall: the shop doors slack-jawed on their hinges, department store mannequins with heads twisted to look over their backs tangled in torn-down, charred drapes. Shards of plate-glass windows on the floor were a fallen, frozen mockery of the stars outside. She muttered, "The only thing they haven't done is take shit from their diapers to draw pictures on the walls."

Goddammit, she'd grown up in the Colony. True, she wanted to leave it—she realized now she'd always wanted to leave it—but in some way it was part of her. It had been her home for years. It was a frontier outpost for mankind. It shouldn't be treated like this.

D was one of the main corridors. It was twenty-five feet from the floor to the glowing strip along the ceiling's center, and fifty feet wide. Before the barricade, D had been busy with jitney traffic or small electric trucks towing a train of supplies; with bicycles and tribikes, and electric mopeds. There were two trucks here now, nose-to-nose across the corridor, part of the front-side barricade. The barricade was reinforced by ore crates filled with crushed asteroid rock hijacked from the storage bins at the south end's smelting works, moved into place with forklifts and stacked to within a foot of the ceiling. The truck cabs doubled as lookout stations. The armed lookout would open the driver's side door and climb in, lean on the window frame of the passenger's side door, to watch the corridor through the door window. A rear barricade blocked off access from the corridor's end, sixty yards behind them.

There had been a Security station by the mall. The 9th Precinct, Belle called it. It was burned out and abandoned after the first riots, and a panicky Security bull had deserted his post without clearing out the station's small armory. The rebels had found four 30.06 rifles—semiautomatic, gas operated with computerized sighting scopes—and a crate of shells; they'd found one .22 pistol with a magazine of thirty explosive bullets. They'd found a launcher for teargas canisters and four guns that fired only rubber bullets.

"Most of the Colony bulls don't like to use their guns because of the danger of ricochet damage to the ship's life support," Bonham had said at the bonfire meeting at the edge of the Open. "But the walls are heavily reinforced. The bulls are too careful. We don't have to be. Most areas there's no real danger to life-support systems from bullets, or even explosives. The station was built to weather a variety of internal disruptions."

Thinking about that statement now, Claire wondered if she should try to convince them that the Colony was more fragile than they knew. But she was Admin; she was barely tolerated. She and her father were constantly watched, and Claire didn't feel safe unless Angie was with her. So Claire thought, *I wish you luck*. And she said nothing.

She buttoned up the collar of her coat and thrust her hands quickly back into its pockets.

The cold that seeped in from space, when colony maintenance decayed, had a whole different quality from cold on earth. It gave you a sensation in the bones that seemed to resonate with thoughts of death, absolute death, final death.

The fucking bulls, she thought, sitting down on the crate. The fucking SA bulls had shut down the general heat conduits. There were local heat generators drawing on sunlight collector stations. But it wasn't enough. It was supposed to be for emergencies.

Now and then a friendly lady-voice, an Admin Voice, asked them in technicki to remove the barricades and come back to work, so that Admin could turn full heat back on and begin work restoring air quality...

And what was her father doing? Chuckling. Rimpler strolled up to Claire, hands shoved in his coat pockets, collar turned up. Looking around and chuckling. "It's all been an experiment," he explained. He spoke mostly in non sequiturs now. "It's a great experimental organism, the Colony. When it goes wrong you learn something from its death, and you say, 'Aha. Why didn't I see this before?' This—" He pointed at the barricade. "This is arteriosclerosis. You want to know why I'm not angry about what they're doing to the thing I made—because *we* did it, *we* grew it, *we* crossed the orange tree with the parasitic vine . . . I've *been* angry. Praeger used to make me angry. Remember?" Chuckling. "Sometimes I still feel it. But it's not just anyone's anger. If I'm anything, I'm a refined man." She saw he'd put on his greasy bathrobe over the overalls they'd given him. His hair was matted, his chin a cactus, his teeth yellow and going green. "There is something exquisite in the delicious, intricate rage of a refined man. The rage that soars! The rage that writes Damn All Children on every balloon released from the Venusian Palace in Disney City! Maybe I should have made this place into a sort of big amusement park, my dear . . . Yes, the next one shall be a . . . " And he wandered off, as if his feet were following the train of his free association.

Claire stared after him. She wanted to find a place to cry, just to get it out. *My father's gone insane, and I don't think he's ever getting better.*

Someone was striding over to her.

She looked up. It was Bonham.

She looked down.

"We've got the microwave working in the cafeteria," Bonham said. "There's hot food. You can go if you want. Your father's there."

"Thanks," she said woodenly, then stood and turned to go.

He held her with his tone when he said, "You look pretty unhappy. Things could be worse. The technickis wanted to ransom you."

"Admin wouldn't give up a toothpick for us."

"That's what Molt told them."

Claire glanced at Molt, who was sitting on a torn mattress near the fire, holding the pistol he'd used on the guards. He was looking at the wall graffiti like an archaeologist trying to puzzle out an obscure hieroglyph.

She snorted. "I'm surprised he spoke up."

"We had to ask him what he thought. He's changed. He used to be... boisterous. I heard him speak twice since coming here. *Twice.* Both times to answer questions." Bonham shook his head. "It shows what torture does."

She said nothing. She waited for him to let her go. He was in charge here.

"You want out," he said suddenly. Sudden and soft, a whisper.

She looked at him.

He answered her unspoken question. "Yeah, out of the Colony. Off. Down. *Earth.*"

She kept looking at him, waiting. He leaned toward her. He was too lean, too hungry, and his breath smelled of canned stew.

"Claire—I can get you out. I'm going myself." He started to glance over his shoulder, then realized it looked craven, and stopped the motion.

"The blockade," she said.

"There's a way past. It's arranged. If I take someone—it'd be dangerous, but I have a pass to get to the docking bays. There's a way."

"Why? Why risk it to take me?"

"I watched you for a long time." He hesitated, looking for a way out of the awkwardness of his desire. There was no way out, so he said it bluntly, "I wanted you. I want you now."

Her heart was thudding. Her stomach coiled and uncoiled and coiled.

Out. Off. *Down!*

That was the thudding.

But with him. That was the coiling sensation. Revulsion.

He'd sold them out. She knew that and had nearly told the others. Now she was glad she hadn't. Because she wanted out.

Out.

"I can't go the way they want me to." Bonham was saying. "I had a warning from someone on their side—The SA's going to take me if I go back their way, for brainwashing. Hardcore extraction and conditioning. If we go back my way, we can use the NR for an escape route."

"What's the NR?"

"New Resistance. Antifascists."

She snorted. "Do they know who you sold out to?"

His face went blotchy red. "I—it was because the place is doomed. It's going to die. You and I know it. So I do what I have to, to get off."

Off.

"Is there... a bargain we have to make?"

"An understanding."

"Okay," she said, hating herself for the first time in her life. Down. After a moment she added, softly, "I do want to go."

To Earth.

17

THE MESSAGE was for Watson, but Ellen Mae was the only one in the room when it came in at Cloudy Peak Farm. The main console was in the living room, its screens looking alien in their glossiness against all that wood under the deer antlers and the badger pelt. She was walking through on her way to the kitchen to make the bread, her mind sorting details for the upcoming Service, and the console lit up just as if her passing by had wakened it.

She glanced over the message, saw it was coded. No one else here so she used the password. The console scanned her retina, then gave her the message. It was for Watson, and she almost lost interest and then her eye caught a name—*Swenson*.

She read it all carefully then.

It was from Purchase. Requesting the presence of John Swenson at the Worldtalk Building in New York. Some executive there had met Swenson, had taken a liking to him, wanted to make him permanent liaison between the SAISC and Worldtalk, this meeting very important to facilitate smooth acquisition of Worldtalk, urgent that Swenson come to New York immediately...

Nonsense, she thought. Worldtalk was already as good as acquired. Purchase was kowtowing to his Worldtalk boss, that was all. Forgetting who he answered to, really answered to.

Ellen Mae deleted the message. The hair rose on the back of her neck as she did it. This was against procedure. Rick wouldn't approve. Watson wouldn't approve. Sackville-West would positively glower.

But she didn't hesitate. She sent Purchase a message: *John Swenson has more important work to do, right here. Don't contact us again unless it's really urgent.*

And she signed it *Crandall.*

Well after all, she was a Crandall, wasn't she?

Feeling deliciously mischievous, she went to make bread dough, smiling as she thought, *I did that just like the lady spies in the old movies.*

◆

Swenson was sitting alone in the chapel. Outside, the snow fell in bleached-white flurries. The snowfall rippled the light, making the stained-glass figures seem to quiver as if they were about to move.

It was chilly in there; he had his hands tucked in his armpits. He was looking at the figures in stained glass. After looking a long time, he'd decided that one of them was definitely Charles Darwin. Another was Gregor Johann Mendel. How did Crandall square this with Christian Fundamentalism? With creationism? He didn't try. The "Christianity" Crandall showed the public was not the strange faith he practiced in private.

The pseudo-Christianity of the Second Circle was almost crypto-druidic. Its imagery was pastoral. Its interpretation of genetics was almost fertility worship. Its intellectual content owed something to the Sociobiologists, even more to Nietzsche and Bergson and Heisenberg. It had its own mythology. Its own vision of the future.

The Second Circle's vision of the future came into the chapel, with Watson.

It was a boy.

Watson was wearing a heavy wool overcoat. There were snowflakes melting on his shoulders. The boy wore a gray-black SA uniform, charmingly miniaturized, down to the overcoat and the black gloves. A black watch cap was half tucked into Watson's coat pocket. The boy held his own black-billed cap in his hands. They stood at the beginning of the aisle, between the first set of pews, a few yards to Swenson's right. They looked around, Watson looking at the chapel as if he'd never seen it before. He stood behind the boy, one weather-reddened hand on the boy's shoulder.

In college, John Stisky had written a paper on Fascist Ideology. Looking at the boy with Watson now, he remembered a line from the English fascist James Barnes: *The present* Weltanschauung *of fascism may be summed up in one word—youth.*

He was a little surprised to see the boy had brown hair. He'd expected blond. But then, Crandall's vision of the earth-born purity of American fascism was rooted in the American countryside, especially the West. Crandall collected Frederic Remington originals. Cowboys were most often depicted as having brown hair.

But blue eyes, oh, yes, and his features were from another of Crandall's collections: His Norman Rockwells. The painting of a bright, tolerant, curious young WASP boy scout.

"That's Darwin, isn't it?" the boy asked, looking at the stained glass.

Watson smiled. "Very good."

But Watson's smile was replaced with a mild frown of concern as he turned to look at Swenson.

"You're not feeling well this morning, John?"

"I'm all right, thanks. Just thoughtful. Distracted. There's . . . so much to do."

"I know how you feel," said Watson and went on, perfectly serious: "It staggers the mind, the job we have ahead of us. The shaping of a world!"

Swenson realized that Watson was talking portentously for the boy's sake. "I assume our friend here is . . . ?"

"This is the lad," Watson said proudly. "Jebediah Andrew Jackson Smith."

The boy looked humbly down.

"Our new junior deacon!" Swenson said, kindly. "Welcome."

And as he said it he thought, *Maybe this is the one I should kill.*

Jebediah Smith was Crandall's great experiment. "The proof of the pudding," Crandall had said. "And the cream of the crop."

Jebediah was one of a group of ten-year-old boys and girls raised in Colton City, the SAISC's "ideal town." Swenson had never been there. He'd only recently acquired the security clearance that made it possible. He'd seen pictures. It looked like the Hometown USA section of Disney City. Except, in the background, you could see the guard towers. Colton City was in a "low-fallout probability" area, in northwestern California. It was highly protected, insular, and permitted no tourist traffic. Its town motto was "Colton City: Beautiful, Comfortable, Safe, and Christian." Jeb and twelve others had been raised in the town's Christian Fellowship Center. Jebediah was supposed to be "deeply and resolutely imbued with our principles."

"I feel a Power in this place," the boy said, with complete assurance. He walked up the aisle, alone, unafraid, and stepped up to stand beside the altar. He put a hand on the altar and looked around. "I feel a Power here," he repeated. "I feel this place is chosen as the place for a new beginning. A new creation."

Holy shit, Swenson, the former priest, thought to himself.

Because there was nothing like a false note in the kid's voice, nothing histrionic or rehearsed. The boy was speaking out of his depths.

God help him, Swenson thought. What had they done to him?

Watson said, "You just look around to your heart's content, son." There was a touch of awe in Watson's voice now. He looked shaken.

He sat down beside Swenson, said softly, "The boy still amazes me."

Swenson nodded.

Watson looked at him. "Want to tell me about it, John? I mean—what's troubling you?"

Swenson wanted to. He wanted to tell him what was really bothering him: Sackville-West was going to put some of them under extractors, and John Swenson would be one of those extracted, and they would ask him about himself, and find out his history was false, and ask him about his real one, and they'd hear all about the NR, and Steinfeld, and Purchase. And there would be a bloodbath along with his own execution. *And so you see, Watson,* Swenson would say, *I was just sitting here wondering if I should try to borrow a car, maybe make up a reason to drive into town, get past the gates, run and hide.*

Only, Watson, I have a feeling they won't let me leave till after the information extraction.

But that was not the worst of it. Not for Swenson. The worst part was, he was beginning to feel like he belonged here, in this chapel. Like he *should* tell them everything.

He watched the boy Jebediah, who was staring up at the oil painting of Crandall sitting with Jesus, the boy maybe wondering where he would fit into the painting. A boy with a sense of destiny...

"You don't want to talk about it, John?" Watson went on. There was no suspicion in his voice.

But Swenson knew he had to respond, and quickly. Watson sensed he was gnawed at by something. They all knew about him and Ellen Mae, of course. All the more reason he must be monitored very closely. He had to give Watson something...

Swenson sighed. "Perhaps I *do* need to talk to someone about it . . . I guess I worry that we might be betraying young Jebediah here, and all the other young ones. We might be moving into this thing too fast. Biting off more than we can chew. It's *the war* that worries me. We're deploying thousands of troops in a war zone and the risk that the war trend will change, that the front will move back to include, for example, Paris. That our outposts will be overrun by the Russians . . . " He shook his head. "It seems like an awful risk. A gamble. We're biting off too much too soon and we're risking the overall Program . . . "

Watson nodded appreciatively. "You're a wise young man. We are risking a great deal—but not everything. Unless the Russians win the war, we will prevail, John. At the moment, they're losing. You see, the war works in our favor simply by being there. It acts as a kind of . . . a kind of *eclipse* that blocks out basic values, conventional morality, leaves people open to extremes they wouldn't consider any other time. Take World War One, for example. After the Treaty of Versailles, Europe was at a loss. It was a junkyard. Everyone was looking for someone to blame for their plight. In Germany, national pride was nearly shattered. People were desperate for direction, identity. National Socialism offered them someone to blame. They could blame the Jews and their friends the bankers. It offered them pride: in national identity. It offered them a way out of the Depression and want: the Nation would take responsibility for rebuilding, for providing work and food. But for that, they told the people, we'll need control. Socialist control. 'Only, don't get the idea we're Marxists! We're *National* Socialists . . . ' " Watson shrugged. "The same situation exists now. There are millions of homeless since the advent of the war. The refugee camps are swelling—our recruiters are finding them very fertile ground indeed. Do you know what a refugee camp is? It's a microcosm. The camps automatically divide up by race. That's instinct. The wogs on one side, the Africans over there, and the European natives over here. But the Red Cross and the other people who run the camps give out the food evenly. And there isn't really enough. So the hungry native Europeans see the immigrants, the various shades of darkies, getting a good deal of the food. And they resent it . . . and they listen to us when we talk." Watson was becoming excited now, relishing his old pseudo-intellectual fashioned racism. He ground the palms of his hands together like a man trying to crack a walnut.

Jebediah had come to listen, standing by gravely, nodding as if he understood as an adult would. And who knew how much they'd tinkered with the boy's brain? Perhaps they'd robbed him of his childhood, Swenson thought. Perhaps he did understand Watson's twisted logic.

Watson was saying, "I'll tell you what these people in the camps are—they're base clay! They're malleable!"

"What shape will we make them into?" the boy asked, surprising them both again.

"The shape of salvation!" Watson said. "Salvation for the very clay we're shaping. We're teaching them strength and a taste for purity! Our people—yes, white people, Western civilization's people—will better survive and prosper if they expel foreign impurities. Impurities of blood, religion, culture, and economic philosophy: the decadence we've all been living in is like the . . . the excretion, the bodily pollution of those foreign influences . . . "

Swenson nodded and patted Watson on the shoulder, just admiringly enough so it was believable. "You could be a preacher yourself. A good one."

Watson chuckled and said, "Oh, Rick's preacher enough. But of course I do write... uh, *help* him write his sermons."

Watson mused silently for a moment. Swenson shifted on the hard pew, aware his legs were going to sleep, his feet numb from the cold. He wanted to go back to the house, but this seemed a holy moment for Watson, and he sensed he'd best let it round itself out.

"The ironic thing," Watson said, "is that it doesn't matter if we're better than they are, or *not*. It was what I was telling the two bumpkins from Idaho. It doesn't matter if we're better than the Jews or wogs. We're *different*, and..." He gestured toward the stained-glass figure of Darwin. "And we must struggle with them, win out over them. We must show who is the fittest! Not superior, fittest."

Swenson said, "Yes, I think I..."

Watson turned sharply to him. "*Do* you see? Really? The Russians may overrun some of our positions—but in the meantime our men are planting the seeds of the new shape among the common people, the common clay. We make contacts, we develop relationships. We attach strings. And when the new shape arises... Ironic, again, to think of the Jewish legend of the golem, the man-thing made from clay... When our golem arises, it will answer only to us."

Jebediah's eyes shone with an understanding that should have been beyond a ten-year-old boy.

If Steinfeld saw this boy, Swenson thought, he would be afraid. He would want to kill him.

But Swenson knew he couldn't do it.

Watson was looking at the boy with a kind of quiet wonder. And perhaps a trace of fear. He had forgotten about Swenson's misgivings. He stood, and stretched, and said expansively, "Well! Let's go back to the house where it's nice and warm and have some cocoa, shall we?" He turned to Swenson. "Coming, John? A little hot cocoa, eh?"

Swenson smiled, falling back into character, letting the character drive for a while. "Just what the doctor ordered."

He stood and stamped some feeling into his feet, then followed them out the door, hearing Watson say, "You see, Jeb? We're all family here."

◆

Swenson had seen them arriving at Crandall's compound all day. By sunset, there were forty of them. Twelve of them were children, grave and soft-voiced and much doted on.

At a few minutes after eight that evening, they all set out for the chapel again, this time as part of a candle-light procession. Swenson, like the others, wore the gray-black hooded robe, and held a red candle in a black wooden holder. The night was almost windless; the flames guttered only slightly as they trudged across the snowy meadow between the house and the chapel.

Swenson walked along, looking at the ground as if afraid of stumbling. And he was: afraid he'd fall if he looked up at the chapel. But Ellen Mae moved up beside him, whispered in that Hallmark Card tone of hers, "Look at the chapel! Isn't it beautiful!"

So he had to look. It glowed against the backdrop of the woods. Light from the windows made a broken, mixed rainbow across the virgin expanse of snow—and the snow was iridescent, crystalline, immaculate.

"The snow around the chapel looks like a clean soul," she said, and it should have made him recoil inside with contempt. That saccharine drippiness. The show window of a religious souvenirs store.

But it was a measure of his mood, his susceptibility, that he looked at the snow and thought, *Yes, like a clean soul.* "We walk our footprints across it like sins," he said, saying things himself that would have made him chuckle back in the seminary. "And by morning the Lord wills another snowfall to cover it all. His redemption falls from heaven."

She reached out and briefly squeezed his arm. He felt a surge of emotion. Real emotion, real feeling for her; for the chapel, the procession. At the same time thinking, *Someone get me out of this.*

The chapel's light glowed out the door and windows. A floodlight illuminated the steel cross up top. *A thing of steel,* he thought. In his mind's eye he saw Jesus—no, it was Rick Crandall—waist deep in hordes of unclean Muslims and Jews, dwarfish things only coming up to his waist, clawing at him, and Crandall had the steel cross in his hands, was using it like a battle-axe to sweep them from his path, smashing with it, blood flying...

He shook himself, to make the image go. A little hot wax dripped on his hand from the candle he carried, and he cherished its burning reproach.

The snow squeaking under his feet. The chant beginning when they were halfway to the chapel. Crandall and Watson, at the head of the procession, leading the litany.

> THE INVOCATION: Who is our Lord?
> THE RESPONSE: Jesus is our Lord.
> What is His will?
> His will is purity.
> What does He purify?
> The world He purifies.
> What is His sword?
> Our Nation is His sword.
> Who is our Lord?
> Jesus is our Lord.

And on. Crandall and Watson chanting the invocation, all the others responding, Swenson too—feeling emotion tremble in his voice, and thinking he heard distant thunder. No, he had heard a single snowflake fall in the forest. Thus the Lord hears all.

Someone get me out.

The children chanting the response: *Our Nation is His sword.*

And then Swenson saw the copper boy.

Swenson stared and stopped walking for a moment, so that someone behind him made a tsk of irritation, and Ellen Mae took his arm, whispered, "Are you all right?"

Swenson moved on mechanically but stared at the copper boy, who moved to keep pace with the procession but didn't walk; his feet didn't quite touch the snow. Didn't change his pose. The boy was standing nude, arms down at his side, giving Swenson a puzzled smile. The smile seemed to ask, *Why are you with them?*

Ellen Mae looked in the direction Swenson was looking. "What is it?"

She doesn't see him, he thought.

He shook his head and kept trudging, staring at the boy, waiting for the mirage to vanish.

It wasn't really a boy—the youth was on the cusp between boy and man. He'd been precocious, graduating from a high school in Managua at sixteen, going right into the Jesuit college... Found in a ditch, the mud mingling with his blood, plants to grow in his decayed flesh...

... Swenson/Stisky ... saw Saint Sebastian lying in the snow, near the procession, the saint breathing hard in a kind of ecstasy of mortification, and with every breath the arrows would sink themselves into him more deeply...

But it wasn't Saint Sebastian, it was the copper boy, bleeding with the red arrows, the arrows whose fletches were candle flame, the boy saying, *"John, you wrote me a letter once, about the Church... you said, It's the rituals that matter. Nothing else matters. The historical vindication of Jesus doesn't matter. The Christian philosophy doesn't matter. Faith doesn't matter. For me, the rituals, the compression of symbols, the march of our apotheosized yearning for security... the sense of family, of belonging... and the glamour of the Church's sweetly absurd artifacts... This is what matters to me, what holds me. It's a kind of fetishism, you said, John, remember? A terrible compulsion that works on me quite apart from my political considerations... I hate the Church the way a junkie can hate his dealer. Get away before it's too late... Remember?"*

"A ritual is a ritual," Swenson said.

"What?" Ellen Mae whispered.

He shook his head. He looked at the chapel. They were almost there. He felt the chapel door pulling him. He visualized a fish in a stream reaching a dam, sucked into the spillway. Plunge through into a shining lake where all is enclosed by bank and you never have to wander again...

"No," the copper boy said. *"Fight the pull! It's your sickness."* Swenson looked and now the boy was dressed as a priest at mass. The black, the gold. *"Don't go in there, or you will lose me,"* the boy said. But now his face changed, becoming more mature—now he was Father Encendez. *"These people murdered me, John."*

What does He purify?

The world He purifies.

Through the open door he could see the holographic projection floating above the altar: a shining molecule of deoxyribonucleic acid, DNA, the double-helix model, turning, shining like a sort of Christmas tree bauble, the images of Jesus and Rick Crandall behind it.

He thought, *If I go in, I'm lost.*

But the current was ineluctable: it came from inside him, and a man cannot bite his own teeth. The current swept him along.

The procession took him into the chapel, and the ritual began.

◆

The occupation army had blocked off the roads leading out of the immigrant ghettos in the Twentieth Arrondissement: Algerian ghettos, Congolese, Pakistani, the others. There were SA observation posts in the corner apartments of the buildings overlooking the intersection. Inside the ghetto, the SA proceeded with its registration of all foreign-born residents, or those whose parents were foreign-born. Immigrants were allowed outside the ghettos only if they had SA work permits and photo ID. Once a week, police examiners entered the ghetto bearing lists provided by collaborators; "proved and potential" insurgents were rounded up and taken in two trucks out past the roadblocks, past the checkpoints and the observation stations, into moonlit streets under the cold glitter of the winter sky.

On such a night, at 8:30 p.m. the gray-and-olive four-ton SA trucks with their load of prisoners drove down rue Hermel to rue Ordener, turning at the church across from the *mairie* of the Eighteenth Arrondissement; the ancient mayorage had once housed a police station, now it was a bombed-out shell. Most of the neighborhood, the streets below the hill of the Montmartre, had become architectural crusts, the outlines of the stone row-houses filled with rubble. In the faces of the deserted buildings their windows shadowed deep blue, their cornices and figured-stone ledges picked out all sickly in the chilled aluminum moonlight. One lane of rue Ordener had been cleared of rubble. The trucks turned past the former metro station . . .

And Steinfeld, in the ruins of the *mairie*, threw a switch. The street blew up ten feet in front of the lead truck, the driver suddenly faced with a fountain of burning asphalt. The truck fishtailed to a stop at the edge of the crater, flame licking up at its grille. It tried to back up, but the second truck, just coming to a stop, was still in the way.

Hard-Eyes was the first out of the eastern exit, Yukio out of the western, followed by Jean-Pierre, Rickenharp.

Behind Hard-Eyes came Jenkins and Willow and Hassan and Shimon.

Hard-Eyes was laughing to himself, all the bottled-up sense of urgency boiling out, a rifle fitted with an M-83 grenade launcher in his hands as he angled left. He stationed himself behind the streetlamp that stood in the rubble choking the sidewalk like the single tree surviving a forest fire. The armored windows of the stymied truck were opening for the driver's gun muzzle as Hard-Eyes propped the M-83 on a metal collar around the post and aimed.

He heard a crackle in his headset, then Steinfeld's voice telling the others, *Hold your fire unless you see them outside the truck, until Hard-Eyes—*

Hard-Eyes squeezed the trigger, and the rifle's muzzle jumped, the launcher hissed, there was a splendid Fourth-of-July BOOM, and the truck's right front tire flew into rubbery flinders, was replaced by a ball of flame; the truck chassis lifted up like a clumsy steer rearing back to stamp a hoof; the blast flame lit up a piece of street and the truck's underside for a full second—then the truck fell back down onto the flame, splashing it out, huffing a ring of smoke.

He could see the axle was bent, the engine twisted unnaturally out of its case, forcing the torn hood back; the oil-spattered engine looked like some primeval hatchling half out of its metal egg. Then smoke twisted up around the engine, small fires licking after it.

Hard-Eyes felt a bubble of elation expand and pop in him. He laughed again, and all his senses hummed; the cold night air crackled on his hands and face. The smell of burning, of cordite and nitro and blood, made his heart pound...

He was chambering another round, a grenade no bigger than two fingers together, when Yukio opened up on the SA in the second cab—or maybe the enemy fired first, it was hard to tell, the flame seemed to leap out simultaneously. Hard-Eyes was aiming, firing, without thinking, without having to, and the second truck's right front end blew out.

Just over his head, sparks flew from the old iron post. It took him a moment...

And then he knew they had made him, were firing at him, and his cover was scanty. His scalp contracted with fear. He heard Steinfeld shout, "Give Hard-Eyes covering fire!" He glimpsed Rickenharp up and running toward the truck, firing the Uzi-3, a double-barreled submachine gun, letting go from both its barrels, shouting something; the truck door swung open, a man flopped out... Hard-Eyes thought, *That guitarist's got balls.* He ducked back, hunkered behind a big fallen cornice on a pile of debris, almost immediately bullets skittered across rubble just by his head. Not a better spot, maybe worse. Raised his head a fraction to see a man getting out of the truck on the other side, firing through the smoke and flame rising from the twisted hood, returning Rickenharp's fire. Rickenharp running toward the back of the truck... 9-mm rounds kicking chips out of the street at Rickenharp's heels.

Steinfeld's voice in his headset shouted, *"Hard-Eyes, if you're clear, run back of the station, come round to the rear of the truck, supervise the liberation—"*

He wasn't clear but Hard-Eyes ran, thinking, *Any second now I'll know what it feels like to get a rifle slug in the side of the head.* Maybe it wouldn't feel like anything, if he was hit by an explosive round. His nervous system would be exploded with the rest of him before it could transmit the information. *Sure, keep telling yourself that.*

Then he was at the back of the truck and Yukio was there ahead of him, had cut the chains looping through the steel rings. (Where was Rickenharp? He heard the maniac rattling of the Uzi-3, realized the rocker had circled behind the truck's driver, was taking him out . . . heard Willow shout from the back of the second truck, yelling at the prisoners to get out, but where were the guys who'd guarded them? Watch it, watch your ass, those guys must be . . .) The prisoners—dark faces, leaping out, looking around, eyes wide—

Suddenly a man without a face, SA bull in full armor was there, tracking the pistol to Jean-Pierre. Little Jean-Pierre in his black cap, face blacked out, funny little guy, would scream like the devil if you beat him at checkers and beg you to play again. Standing between Hard-Eyes and the bull. Jean-Pierre's back to the bull. Yukio turning, trying to shoot past Jean-Pierre. The armored SA soldier pointing something, it was hard to see in the shadow of the truck—Hard-Eyes was trying to get a firing angle—the dark killing thing in the bull's hand spraying white fire. Jean-Pierre's head erupted, bits of it flying out to carry the cap off—

Yukio fired and the bull staggered. But he was armored, was still on his feet, tracking the gun toward Yukio. Hard-Eyes thought, *If I hit him at this range with a grenade, it'll kill Yukio, too.*

Then Rickenharp was running up behind the bull, shoving his gun against the back of the guy's neck, under the helmet—at that range no armor's going to help—

The helmeted head lit up with the fire behind it and tilted from the neck at a strange angle . . . the bull staggered and fell . . .

The prisoners were running helter-skelter for the subway station, Jenkins and Willow herding them. Sporadic fire racketing as the others exchanged rounds with two SA bulls crouching in the rubble across the street.

Hard-Eyes fixed on them, crouching behind an overturned stone bench, firing at someone he couldn't see. He raised the M-83, set up a grenade round and tracked till he felt that little interior bell ringing: *You're sighted in.*

He fired and the bench flew backwards, maybe five hundred pounds of stone leaping back and smashing the men. *Damn, it makes you feel bigger than human. And then sick.*

Steinfeld was shouting, "Retreat, trucks coming!"

Hard-Eyes ran through the veils of smoke, saw someone kneeling, trying to get up, blurred through the smoke but—*It's one of ours.* Hard-Eyes bent to help him up—*oh, it's Hassan*—bullet through his leg, looked like it had taken out the man's knee; he was going to need a brace... The two of them running like men in the three-legged race...

Down they went into the wrecked Metro station, flashlight beams whipping, all wavery with the running of those who carried them...

Someone else, Rickenharp, was helping him with Hassan, who in his pain was shouting for Allah. Then they'd reached the station, were onto the tracks, the pool of light around the lanterns. Sympathizers who'd waited there took Hassan onto a stretcher, the Arab trying not to weep with the pain and then giving in, and they hurried down the tunnel to the camouflaged entrance that led into the sewers, and the escape route, Hard-Eyes thinking, *My mouth is so dry. Lips chapped. Wish I had a beer.*

◆

In the Cloudy Peak farmhouse. Walking down the hall. The copper boy was gone. But some small, still voice tried to tell Swenson, Now's your chance, go and get into a car, smash through the gates, Stisky, run...

The guard was walking ahead of him, down the hall. Escorting him to the extraction. "Just a routine CC extraction, sir." Cerebro-Chemical extraction.

Just draw out a little of your brain juice, sir, through a straw, sir, won't hurt a bit, sir, won't damage you, won't erase anything, it'll just tell us exactly what you've been up to and that you're not who you're pretending to be and who all your associates are. Sir.

They'd tried to do them all before the Service. But Swenson had been last on the list, and they'd been running late, because one of the servants, it turned out, had been a member of the Communist Party, and had to be dealt with, though in all probability his membership had been a caprice of years ago, and chances were he was utterly loyal to Crandall...

It was nearly midnight. The guard had hidden a yawn behind his hand. Had shrugged apologetically when Swenson had asked, "Can't it wait till tomorrow?" The guard wasn't wearing his helmet, a sign that this was more or less a formality. He had his gun, the kind that fired explosive pellets, strapped to his thigh. Unlocked. He had his back to Stisky. Most of the house was asleep. Stisky... Swenson... could grab the gun, put the man down, run for the garage, get a car, and with a little luck get away.

So why didn't he do it?

It was as if he were still in the procession. He was floating along, still seeing the Service, the DNA icon slowly rotating there; what a marvelous thing when the boy Jebediah came to stand before the altar and the holo image of the molecule descended to enclose him, began to spin, and the chanting reached a climax, and the wooden bowl was passed, in it the oak leaf, and a little blood from each was taken so that the oak leaf was floating in blood when it reached Swenson... Stisky... Swenson...

"An end to wars," Rick Crandall told them, "when all bloods are of the same blood, when only one race remains. Will that race be divided against itself? It will not."

Run, Stisky.

The beauty of the children's voices lifted in hymn, singing, *Our Nation is the Sword.*

And they were all united in their unthinking, unquestioning belief in Rick Crandall. I was the fly in the ointment, Swenson/ Stisky thought. I was the muddying track in the white snow. A man divided against himself.

Run.

The guard was opening the door for him, and he stepped through, carried through by the current, and it was too late to stop. He didn't look at the technicians. He saw Ellen Mae at the foot of the bed, whispering urgently to Sackville-West, the old man scowling as he listened, shaking his head now.

She doesn't want him to do it to me, Swenson realized. *Because she's afraid they'll extract the details of my relationship with her, she's afraid they'll hear about all the things we did...*

Poor Ellen Mae.

Thinking of the boy dead in the ditch, Swenson took off his shirt and lay down on the bed. They opened their bags and black boxes, and they put a plastic breathing mask over his face, and he smelled what sleep smelled like.

... He couldn't remember a transition. The mask had come down, and he'd gone out and they'd done the extraction. Now he felt as if his head were a balloon half filled with air, flaccid, beginning to fill up, and as it filled, a sensation grew taut in his head. Pain. Another sensation in his chest.

Iron filings. That was the taste in his mouth as he woke, looking at the room through a layer of gelatin. Hearing a technician say, "He's coming out of it sooner than the others..." But they had it. He could see it in Ellen Mae's face, looking at him in horror, shaking her head, telling Sackville-West it must be a mistake.

He heard himself talking. "I betrayed you as much as I betrayed Steinfeld when I let them do it, do the extraction... And I *did* let them. Understand that. Tell Rick. I could have found a way out. I could have run! But it was my confessional." Aware of the guard standing close beside the bed, taking handcuffs from his belt. The man was left-handed. His gun was on his left hip.

"I cared about you, Ellen Mae," he heard himself say. "Come and say good-bye to me. I only did what I was trained to do. So come and say good-bye."

Sackville-West shrugged.

Ellen Mae moved around to the left side of the bed. The guard on Swenson's right opening the handcuffs. The blurriness was going from his eyes.

My arms don't work very well, he thought, as he lifted them to embrace Ellen Mae, felt her wet cheek against his. But they'd work well enough. They'd taught him about those guns. Purchase had sent him for weapons training. Poor Purchase, they'll get him now.

Sackville-West coming around to the left side of the bed to tug at Ellen Mae.

The sensation in his chest was a keening, a violin playing high C. The violin player stopped playing but the string continued to resonate as the player tightened it with the peg, tightened the string, made it tighter, the string about to break, so tight it's going to break, stretching . . . to . . .

He reached up and took the gun from the guard's holster and heard someone shout a warning as he pressed the gun between himself and Ellen Mae and pulled the trigger twice.

. . . stretching up to break. Snap.

As the pellets exploded he thought, *I should have shot Sackville—*

Didn't even have time to complete the thought before the thunder consumed him. The thunder of a single snowflake hitting the ground.

18

HAD SHE slept? Claire wasn't sure. Yes, she must have, because her father was gone from his sleeping bag, and if she'd been awake she'd have noticed his going.

Claire sat up and looked around at the stainless-steel and fiberplas panels of the cafeteria kitchen area. They'd policed the trash yesterday so the room was mostly clean, but the air was fuggier than ever. The lights were dialed low for sleeping. Angie and Judy were bedded down under the counter, sleeping in the same bag. So they were lovers now. So what.

Then she had a sinking sensation, followed by a rasp of annoyance, as she realized she had her period. She could feel it, sticky, a little wet. Great. There'd be blood spots in the sleeping bag, blood on her underwear, she didn't have another pair. And, goddamn it, she didn't have any tampons. There just weren't any left. She reached down to the bottom of her sleeping bag, where she'd stashed a roll of toilet paper. She used a swatch of it to clean blood from the inside of her thighs, then rolled some of the soft synthetic paper around two fingers, making a makeshift sanitary napkin, and positioned it. She sighed, and unrolled her jumpsuit which she'd used as a pillow—and climbed into it, then went to see if they'd turned off the water, so she could rinse out her underwear.

"Oh, thank you, Gridfriend," she muttered, when she saw the toilet was unstopped. Some technicki plumber had finally earned his rating. She used the toilet, then tried the suction flush. Working! The water in the tiny bathroom's tiny sink's tiny tap was running, too. But not much longer, she thought as she rinsed out her panties. The hot-air handdryer was running, so she used that to dry them. Mostly; they were still damp when she had to put them on because someone was banging on the door. She climbed into the jumpsuit, difficult in the constricted space, and went out. It was Angie. "Everything's working today."

"They turn off the water tomorrow, your father says." Angie pushed hurriedly past her into the bathroom.

"Does he know that for sure?" Claire asked through the closed door.

"You tell me. We woke him up, asked him to come to tell us what he thinks Admin will do, or how we get to supplies. But he's not much use. Talks crazy half the time. Everybody's getting mad at him, they think he's faking."

"They're stupid," Claire said.

What now? Find her father? But he made her mad, too...

She started to walk away and heard Angie shout, "You bastards!"

And then the Pleasant Lady spoke from the wall speakers. "Corridor D, your water has just been shut off. Your electric power will follow and finally airflow. The air you have is bad, but it's not as bad as having no air at all. It's time to come home now. Those of you who are sports fans might be interested to know that tomorrow is the playoff for the opening of the technicki teams Jai Alai champ series. Those who come out today will receive a full pardon and free passes to the games. Those who do not come out will be arrested, tried, and sentenced." Maternal regret in her voice; *hurts me more than it hurts you*. She repeated the message in technicki.

"Pricks," Claire muttered.

There was a banging behind her, and Angie burst out of the bathroom, her face red, her eyes blinking too often, the way they did when she was trying to hold her anger in check. "Your father is lying to us on purpose!" she shouted. "He said we would have water today."

"You said yourself he was only guessing."

Angie shouldered Claire aside, and Claire stared after her in the shock of sudden realization: *It won't be safe for me among these people much longer.*

When Claire returned to the place below the microwavers where her sleeping bags had been, she saw Bonham and her father coming down the aisle together. Were they drunk? The way they walked . . .

No, her father was hurt, and Bonham was helping him walk.

Not such a bad guy, Bonham, she thought. And then she wondered if she was only trying to prepare herself for having to be his whore.

Professor Rimpler was grinning at her, and that made his smashed lip, his swollen eye look worse. His feet were bare, and one of them looked swollen.

"Dad . . . " Feeling her voice cracking. "What did you do this time?"

She and Bonham helped the old man onto his sleeping bag. He immediately turned onto his side, away from her, sighing.

Bonham took her arm and led her a little ways away, looked around. They were alone. "I think he provoked them on purpose. They were already hostile but . . . he told them they were going to die, that the bulls hold all the cards . . . " He shrugged. "Then he started to babble. Something about a hermit crab, we're all hermit crabs fighting for a shell, we should give up and crawl away . . . Molt hit him. I tried to stop them but it was all too fast: someone hit him in the foot with a gun butt. Then your father started laughing, hysterical laughter. They moved away from him. You know what I mean? I think your father is exaggerating his . . . his mental problem. Was maybe having a nervous breakdown, but now he's playing it, real cagey about it. So they don't expect much of him."

She stared at him, thinking about it. Then, slowly: "Maybe you're right . . . Was Angie there when they hit him?"

"No. Why?"

"She used to be my friend. Judy and Angie. Lately . . . " She shrugged. "What now?"

He glanced around again, crossed his arms over his chest, leaned a little nearer. "We leave when the lights go out. They'll turn out the lights in a day or two. I'll have a flashlight. We'll go back to rear launch."

"It's closed down, guarded."

"The guards'll be expecting us. It's part of the deal."

Her stomach twisted. But she said, "Okay. They expect three of us?" Looking at him meaningfully, waiting to see if he'd say, *Your father can't go.*

"They expect only me. But they'll let us through if I insist. I have a priority pass and that means anyone I authorize." He hesitated.

"Yes? What else?"

"Molt. I'm worried about Molt. I think he suspects." He shrugged. "Nothing I can do about it..."

He broke off suddenly, stepped back from her. Angie was coming toward them.

Claire thought, *When the lights go out...*

◆

"You know what's funny?" Rickenharp said. "That you can get used to being shelled. Bombs exploding around and after a while it's like being used to traffic noises."

"I am no bloody *way* getting use to it," Willow muttered.

They were in the basement of the safe-house, tiny dirt-floored rooms once part of *les caves*, the wine cellars, when the building had been someone's house.

Rickenharp said, "I mean, anyway, it's just like I imagined it. Something hits, and the place shakes, a little dust comes down from the ceiling. You feel a vibration go through you. Only it sounds different than I thought it would. Sometimes. There's a kind of whining sound after the blast. I think it's metal breaking—"

"Rickenharp," Hard-Eyes said suddenly, "you proved yourself on three raids now. You did great. Everyone thinks so. You got balls. But Rickenharp, shut the fuck up."

Rickenharp shrugged and shut up.

Hard-Eyes was far from used to the shelling. It scared him more than a firefight, though he was probably less likely to get killed here. It scared him because he was helpless. The whole shebang could come down on his head, and it was no use trying to shoot back at it.

There was no strategy except run to a hole and hide in it. You just sat and waited to see if your number was up. It sucked.

The Front had moved back. The US Army had been backed into Paris, and now the Russians were shelling it. Rubbling all that history.

The town was down to a fourth of its population, maybe less; more streaming south every day, running from the shelling. Thousands were clogging refugee camps, trading one kind of suffering for another. But maybe it was better than being stuck in the ghettos, hammered helplessly by shells.

He looked at the others in the light from the lantern, trying to get his mind off it. Rickenharp, Willow, Yukio, the doctor, Jenkins, Carmen. The others in other cellars. Everyone here looking sullen, or looking as if they were trying to keep from looking scared, except goddamn Rickenharp, that brain-damaged asshole, expression on his face like a kid watching fireworks. *Ceiling falls in and we'll see if you're having fun, pal.*

There was a little room left near the door. He was surprised Smoke wasn't there. Smoke usually hung out with Yukio.

"Where's Smoke and the—" He broke off as they heard the thud, felt the vibration pass through the room, chattering teeth as it rippled through them. Dirt sifted down from the ceiling.

"Smoke's gone to the States," Carmen said. "You were out on a hit, you weren't in on that. Steinfeld set up—"

Another thud, another nasty vibration, feeling closer now.

She went on, her voice straining for normalcy. Rickenharp was looking at her, not smiling now. Thinking what Hard-Eyes was thinking: Carmen's scared, wants someone to hold her, but her pride won't allow it.

She said, "Steinfeld set up a route, everything. Smoke's going to do some kind of lobbying in the States to get backing for us."

Jenkins said, "That old burn-out?"

Carmen said, "Steinfeld says Smoke's not a burn-out. He used to be some kind of traveling reformist. Philosopher, writer. Then something bad happened and I guess he gave up, lost touch . . . He's like, changing, Steinfeld says. Says he used to talk to himself all the time.

Now he talks to the crow or to people and that's all. He writes stuff in notebooks... Steinfeld says he's got some kind of special talent..."

Hard-Eyes thought of the scarecrow Smoke had been when they'd met. He nodded. "Yeah, he changed."

They were silent for a while. So were the cannons.

The Algerian came to the door, a lantern in his hand. *"Okay ici? Bon. Steinfeld dis, C'est fini."*

"What's 'e fooking know about it?" Willow said irritably.

Yukio said, "His listening station in the north. He picked up their radio commands. We have the code."

Hard-Eyes felt something unwind in him. He was going to live another day.

He found himself looking at Carmen. Thinking, Funny how, after you almost get snuffed, you want to fuck.

But she was looking at Willow.

Hard-Eyes shrugged. No accounting for taste.

◆

Kessler's first impression of the island was of a strange, almost featureless flatness, and a blaze of light.

Julie put down her hand-luggage, and fished in her purse for her sunglasses. "This light's *great* for my headache," she muttered, slipping the dark glasses on.

"It was a long flight," Kessler said. "You'll feel better after you get some rest."

"I just can't sleep on airplanes. I'm afraid they'll crash while I'm asleep."

"That's the best time for it if—oh, there they are." Charlie was coming toward the Lear jet in a three-wheeled jitney; the jitney's driver was an islander, skin so dark he was almost purple. The pilot and the steward came down the metal steps behind Kessler. The pilot pointed a plastic matchbox at the plane and pressed a button; the steps retracted, whining, and the door sealed itself.

The jitney pulled up, Charlie jumped out, grinning under his mirrorshades, and pumped Kessler's hand. "'Sap, man!"

"Hi, Charlie... This is all our luggage, just carry-on."

"Shit, I came here with less than that. Come on."

They rode the jitney across sticky black asphalt smelling of hot tar, through the heat-shimmer to the little glass-fronted airport building. There was no customs at all. "This island is *ours*, Jimmy," Charlie said. "No one comes here but NR. If they do, they're arrested, and put under an extractor..."

Kessler grimaced. Charlie said, "Yeah, I know. I don't like the fucking things either. This one's the only one we got. Anyway, anybody comes to the island by accident, they take 'em into custody—but they let 'em go later if they extract out legit."

"This island got a name?"

"Merino. No government except a little police force, and Witcher acts as a kind of local judiciary, when he's here. He's here a lot now. He's getting paranoid. Officially, Merino's a territory belonging to—um, I'm not supposed to tell anybody what it belongs to, because if you got extracted they'd know what area to search through... I found out by asking the locals. And then got a big lecture about it. When it comes to extractor proofing, ignorance is safety. Anyway, Witcher's got a deal with the country that the island belongs to. He owns it—shit, it's only about thirty-five square miles."

Kessler shrugged. He was enervated and logy as they got into a limo. It felt cold after the heat outside.

"Oh, God, air conditioning," Julie said gratefully. They rode along a white crushed-shell road, between rows of palm trees, parallel to a glittering white-sand beach. The sea was a vast blue gem.

They drove through two checkpoints, past electric fences crested with barbed wire; under the unwavering gaze of CCTV cameras that rotated smoothly to watch them. Past guards with rifles.

Julie looked at him, and he squeezed her hand. He knew what she was thinking. That this might turn out to be a kind of prison for them.

Kessler said, "Charlie—they let us come and go from the compound as we please?"

"Absolutely. But they give you a list of things you can talk to the locals about. They speak a dialect sort of half Spanish, half English. They understand you, though."

They were driving through landscaped estate grounds now, cacti and exotic plants he'd never seen, flowering on both sides. A fountain. A tennis court. But at intervals: concrete bunkers, showing the snouts of heavy machine guns and small cannons.

They passed through a gate, and into a kind of small village. Cottages, two cafés, two bars. They pulled up in front of a whitewashed cottage with red shutters and solar panels on the roof.

"This is your place," Charlie said proudly. "Bigger'n your apartment in New York. Witcher really set it up nice for us here."

They went into the cottage. Inside it was shady, cool, comfortable. Wicker furniture, an old-fashioned wooden four-poster bed. Julie lay back on the bed, took off her sunglasses, and threw an arm over her eyes. But Kessler knew she was listening as he and Charlie talked.

"Witcher's okay," Charlie was saying. "A little straight. A capitalist—but then so are you. He's . . . You know—gets his money from a private cop company, in competition with the SA, and from patents on surveillance devices. His people developed camera birds. So sure, he's straight. But he's a good guy."

"Why's he do it? Why's he fund the NR?"

"Not even Steinfeld's sure. Witcher says he hates racists and anyway the SA's his biggest business competition. But I don't know. Thing is, you can trust him. You can feel it."

"Steinfeld here?"

"No. He's stuck in Europe. Maybe in deep shit . . . You'll get the whole briefing later. There's a guy coming, Jack Brendan Smoke."

"Yeah. I read him. He was way ahead of everyone else—"

"He's going to be working with you, to counter Worldtalk's subliminals and the PR for . . . You'll get it all after dinner."

"Okay. But—" Kessler hesitated, not sure what it was he wanted to say. What was bothering him was, he supposed, simple disorientation. And worry. Could he really trust these people?

"Hey, Jim—" Charlie put his hands on Kessler's shoulders. "You won't have to stay in this place forever, but you got to understand: *this is home!* These people have been through it all—with Worldtalk or the SA or the fucking CIA. There's a woman here who was extracted by Worldtalk—you can talk to her. I'm tellin' you. The fences are to keep the enemy out, not to keep us in. You're home, man. You're home . . ."

◆

Purchase was sitting in one of Worldtalk's video conference rooms, thinking he needed to go to the enzymologist and have his stomach acid turned down again, when Fremont on Screen One said, "Look, let's boil the problem down to its basics. We have journalists, congressmen, you-name-it—not too many, but then, any amount is too many—accusing the SAISC of anti-Semitism, of creating racial pogroms in the war zone, of misusing NATO funding, of—hell, everything."

Chancelrik, on Screen Three, said, "Basically they're hinting the SA chiefs are actual *fascists*, for Christ's sake. Well in fact—I don't know if you fellas saw this report—that there's a group that calls itself the New Resistance responsible for—" He paused to read off a printout. "—thirty-five military attacks on SAISC stations and personnel in six European capitals, and according to this source they're spreading propaganda calling the SA 'Nazis' outright."

"Okay," Fremont said, "that's the upshot. But you note that ninety percent of the accusations have to do with things happening in the war zone. We can point up that things in the war zone come to us garbled because of the difficulty of getting clear information through the Russian blockade, all the antisat scrambling, you-name-it. Any thoughts on that, Purchase, my boy? Heard scarcely a peep from you."

"Uh-huh. What I think is . . . " Purchase contemplated the faces on the screen—Fremont transmitted from LA, Chancelrik from Chicago, Barley from Miami. " . . . I think you're on the right track, Sammy, and uh—" He thought desperately, managed, "I think we should suggest through our news-sheet editorializing channels that there's a kind of prejudicial attitude here, behind these accusations, because, uh, our lady prez has come out as a supporter of the warzone policing program so, uh, basically what we have is the Democrats seizing on an issue, spouting a lot of hearsay and, uh . . . "

Something about the way Barley was clearing his throat a little too loudly into his headset made Purchase realize he was blowing it. Barley said, "I think—correct me if I'm wrong—I already brought up that point, remarkably close wording—"

In his humorous drawl, kidding him about it.

Purchase said, "Of course, sorry—I'm out of it today, little personal problem. Uh, in fact I've got to make a call about that, do you guys think—"

"Hey, you take as long as you want, Purchase, my boy!" Fremont said.

"Sure! Go ahead!" the other two chimed in.

"Thanks." But he knew as soon as he was out of the room they'd say: *Isn't it a shame about Purchase, guy isn't keeping it together anymore.*

He stood up and put his screen on hold, then went down the hall to his office, thinking that maybe it was stupid to wait it out.

He'd been waiting for word from Swenson—or about Stisky. Confirmation that Stisky's cover was blown. But maybe it was a mistake to wait. Maybe he should run—*now*.

He'd told himself he had work to do here. It was a crucial time. If he could find a way to sabotage the SA's Worldtalk propaganda campaign . . .

No. He made up his mind. The risk was too great. He'd leave here, join the others in Merino. He was holding back out of sheer inertia, really. Habit. He'd come to the office every weekday barring holidays for eight years, and old habits—

The thought broke apart and spiraled into irony: *Die hard.*

Because when he stepped into the office he saw the two SA bulls in full armor standing to either side of the door. He saw them reflected in the window beyond his desk.

"Mr. Purchase," one of them said. Wearing the helmet they wear when they come to take people away.

"Okay," Purchase said. "I understand."

Thinking, *Try to call the cops?* These guys had no real legal authority to do more than detain him, as long as he didn't resist. But they'd never let him call the cops. They planned to take him somewhere quiet, and interrogate him, and eventually kill him.

He turned to face them, smiled, and said, "Let's go." He started to go out the door between them—then stopped and snapped his fingers as if just remembering something. "Uh—you mind if I get my wife's picture from my desk?"

One of the guards turned his opaque faceplate toward the desk. "There's no picture on the desk, sir."

"It's in the drawer," he said, turning to the desk casually as he could manage, his heart pounding, sweat starting out on his forehead. "I don't like to have her on the desk there staring at me accusingly all day, so I keep her in the drawer—" Little chummy laugh there. "But I'd like to have the picture"—opening the desk drawer—"to look at now and then." Reaching in.

"Mr. Purchase, I'm getting a rising heartbeat rate and a respiration signal on you that's a little worrisome. I think you'd better hold it right there—"

As Purchase turned with the gun in his hand.

But the one on the right had taken a step closer and had his RR stick out. The stick was already whistling down at his head, and Purchase didn't even get the pistol's safety off. He felt the crunch and the explosion of pain, and nothing else.

The bull had hit him a little too hard—maybe because of the gun—and Purchase was still comatose in an SA-owned hospital six months later when, after the fourth extraction try proved futile, the euthanasia judge signed the papers and Worldtalk pulled the plug.

And then Purchase finished dying.

◆

The Radic technickis controlled only a relatively small part of the Colony. The back section of Corridor D and, for a while, about half the technicki dorms. On the twenty-seventh day of the occupation, a little over two months after the Russians had blockaded the Colony, Security stormed the barricaded dorms and retook them. About twenty percent of the Radics were taken prisoner. And Security found the body of Guy Wilson, ripe from decay, in Wilson's sealed dorm room. Wilson had been beaten to death, "probably with the butt of a rifle." The Admin—not citing its evidence—officially charged Samson Molt with Wilson's murder, *in absentia*. It warned the technickis, over InterColony and intercom, that Molt was "still at large."

In fact, Molt and the Radics' hard-core had been driven back, into Corridor D. They sealed off the corridor behind them and now occupied the burnt-out corridor mall, the cafeteria and its kitchens, and the corridor's main passageway. But they were in touch, via hastily rigged wifi transmitters, with technicki sympathizers on the outside of the barricaded area. And it was this source that got word to Bonham and Molt that the bulls were coming in force now from every main access, were massing around the bend in the corridor and in the transverse passage that led into the corridor area from the dorms. They were carrying flashlights and rifles.

Minutes after this report came through, the lights went out in Corridor D.

Immediately there were panicky shouts insisting that no one panic, no one panic, and flashlight beams stabbed at the ceiling, the walls, as if trying to see through them, to see the unseen enemy...

Bonham had known the exact time the power cut would come. He and Claire had rendezvoused at the intersection of Corridor D and Transverse 67. Forty yards back from the front barricade. The front barricade, on the Admin side, was the most heavily guarded.

The rear barricade had only three men on it, because the sympathizers on the outside had not reported significant Security activity in the end of the corridor. The Radics' sabotage had wrecked transverse access to the rear barricade area. The bulls couldn't get through that way without clearing away great mounds of debris.

The only other way they could come from behind would be from the rear launch levels. The Security bulls could, conceivably, take pods or repair shuttles from the Admin area through space to the rear launch and get at the back barricade that way. But the rear launch levels were far smaller than the Admin launch levels. They could accommodate only two small vehicles at once . . . And only about five men could come through the small airlock at any one time. The process of bringing in men that way would be time-consuming and could be monitored by the Radics' crudely rigged TV surveillance system. But the power cut had turned off the Radics' surveillance gear as well as the lights. The rear was blinded. The three men on the back barricade argued about what to do—the Radic-occupied territory was clearly being attacked from the front, one of them argued, so they should go and help support the front barricades. The others argued for staying where they were.

◆

Bonham and Claire waited in a dark doorway to one side, listening to the argument.

Claire whispered, "What if they stay on the barricades?"

"They'll let me through. They're used to seeing me as a leader." But there was no certainty in his voice.

The pitch-black corridor area was shot through with lances of light. Pools of illumination danced over walls and ceiling, quivering with an urgency that corresponded with the shouted directions, and arguments, and more cries of "Don't panic!" And thirty feet to Claire's left, the senior of the three guards was shouting, "All right, fuck it, we'll stay, but if Molt . . . " The rest was garbled by interruptions from the others.

Claire huddled against the cold metal wall, chewing a knuckle, searching through the fragmented darkness for a glimpse of her father in the patches of light. "Goddammit, where's Dad? . . . Damn him! I told him, I wrote it down for him where we'd be—"

"You should have brought him with you."

"Molt had me on barricade duty. It wasn't safe for Dad to be out there with me where everyone could see him, he'd start ranting and they'd—you know—"

She shrugged. He didn't see her shrug in the dark, but he understood her.

◆

The old man was crouched under the big mixing table in the cafeteria kitchen, smiling absently in the darkness. The darkness was almost complete. Now and then a light splashed the wall across from him as someone carrying a flashlight ran past. His world was dark but splashed with light; it was cold, and yet he felt feverish, and that was like space itself: black but shattered with light, cold but charged with radioactive heat. Maybe, he thought, this is an old-fashioned omen. A taste of what's to come—when the Colony's turned inside out and we're all dissipated into the void.

Rimpler's back ached. Without thinking, he shifted his position to ease the ache. That turned him enough so he could see the luminous dial of the pocket watch Claire had scrounged for him. Automatically, he registered the hour, and saw it was past time for him to meet Claire.

The time demanded a decision. And a decision came, one that had been struggling to get out of him for days. He'd sat there in the darkness for an hour, not thinking about any one thing in particular—but all the time some part of his mind had been thinking, and by degrees coming to one starkly unavoidable conclusion. He'd had a towering responsibility, had willfully taken it on himself. And just as willfully had thrown it aside. Jettisoned it. And now he was going to have to try to find it again. And never mind that it was impossible, and that it was too late. He was going to have to try and take it back.

He wondered if he should try to explain to her, make her understand what he had to do. How would he put it? *Claire—I made it possible for thousands of people to move into another world, to start over, and they turned against me and I handled it badly. And I lost the world I made...* He could imagine her response.

"You telling me that Jehovah has been disenfranchised?" She had more of her mother in her than she liked to admit.

I've been asleep, Claire. I put part of myself to sleep because of what happened to Terry—and because the thing I spent my life building fell apart around me. Now I'm going to take charge again, and make it right.

What would she say to that? She'd say it was a childish fantasy. That it wouldn't work. And he knew it probably wouldn't work.

He remembered telling Claire about the tower a man built himself into over the years, the tower of convictions and habits and ineradicable decisions. He visualized his own personal tower of Babel, and in the vision he saw it tottering, beginning to shiver apart...

And the trouble was—he wasn't in that tower alone. He had every man, woman, and child in the Colony up there with him.

Feeling his way along the wall, he crept out of the kitchen and into the cafeteria, straightening up to look around. Ahead was the door into Corridor D. The lights and shouting danced together there. He walked into them.

And out into the chillier open spaces of the corridor.

Someone loomed over him: a big, angry man with a gun in one hand and a flashlight in the other. Molt himself.

"Where are they going to come from, Rimpler? Where will the bulls come from? From the dorm crossovers? From the rear? The front?"

"Probably from the front," Rimpler replied distractedly. "I intend to meet them, to tell them that I'm taking over again, so there's no need to worry about it. We'll negotiate a settlement with you people. It will include an amnesty."

Molt stared at him, open-mouthed. Rimpler had forgotten that he was a beaten-up old man, grimy, hair matted, chin stubbled. That he'd been behaving half-cracked for days. It was as if a Bowery bum wandered into the mayor's office and announced he was taking over. "You pathetic old has-been!" Molt burst out. "You've really lost it this time."

Rimpler snorted. "So I'm crazy? You're locked in here, surrounded by hostile professional warriors far better armed. You have almost no light and you'll soon have no air. You're wanted for murder! And *I'm* irrational? You got yourself into this, Molt. You're a glory-hounding leech who's dragged a lot of discouraged people into the shitpit which is your natural home. Now go and tell them that I'm—"

But Molt had stopped listening. He was looking around, his face—lit from beneath by the flashlight in his hand—was grim with suspicion. "Where's Bonham?" He demanded suddenly. He grabbed Rimpler by the neck and shook him, threw him to the floor. "Where the hell's Bonham? The lights are out, the bulls are coming—and Bonham disappears!"

Rimpler sat there on the floor, stunned. Molt reached down and pulled him to his feet, shook him again. Rimpler felt as if everything that had gone wrong, all the forces that had gone wild around him, were incarnate in Molt; were wrenching Rimpler's shoulder, shaking him, screaming at him. "*Where's Bonham?*" Molt shouted.

"He's gone!" The reply coming from deep inside him somewhere. "Gone! He and Claire went out the back way—by now they're gone! You can forget him!"

"*What?* You old *pig!* Why didn't you—?" He couldn't articulate his outrage, after that. Molt shouted in wordless fury, and brought the flashlight down, overhand, hard onto Rimpler's head.

Rimpler saw it coming, and time seemed to slow so he could appreciate the sight...

The shining electric comet arcing down to him, a light roaring to hit him right between the eyes. Rimpler shouted: "Terry!" He heard a crunch, and then a crash resounding like the fall of the Tower of Babel.

◆

Claire saw the luminous dial of Bonham's watch as he raised it to check the time.

"Right about now," he said.

Five breathless seconds passed. And then they heard the rattle of semi-auto rifle fire from the front barricade. The rifle fire was instantly followed by the big, sloppy *HUH-UMP* of an explosion as the bulls fired a concussion shell into one of the barricade's trucks; a rumble as part of the barricade collapsed. More rattling gunfire, flicker of flames growing from the front of the corridor. A rackety mechanical noise followed by a SCREEEE as Security used a bulldozer of some kind to push the ore crates out of the way. More gunfire, strobe flashes, another explosion she could feel vibrating in the metal of the wall. Her nails dug into her palms, her eyes hurt from the strain as she tried to see her father in the confusion of running men, flashing lights, fencing flashlight beams. Instinctively she started toward the front, calling, "Dad!"

Someone grabbed her arms, pulled her back. After a moment she knew it was Bonham, whispering urgently in her ear. "You can't do it! You'll get shot if you go up there! Look—they're gone from the rear!"

The eruption at the front had drawn the guards off the rear barricade. He dragged her to one of the jitneys used as barricade support.

She stopped resisting Bonham when she looked over her shoulder and saw Molt jogging clumsily after them.

Molt shouting, "Bonham! You ain't goin' nowhere, man!" Still twenty yards away, Molt stopped and raised the rifle . . .

The light was all patchwork around Molt. For a moment he stood there with his back to the conflagration at the barrier, like a man in a cave standing silhouetted against a campfire. He was outlined in flickering light, his face in darkness.

Then the muzzle flash lit his face as he fired at Bonham—three rounds, all three missing, pocking bullet dimples into the metal of the jitney's cab. Bonham let go of her and turned, climbed into the jitney, and through it to the other side of the barrier.

Claire stood snake-fascinated, staring at Molt, who was moving toward her again, centering the rifle on her chest . . .

Screams echoed from the front barricade. The bulls had broken through. Claire saw seven, maybe eight Security bulls in full armor, opaque faces catching the uneven light, as they ran up behind Molt, shouting with amplification, "SAMSON MOLT, DROP YOUR WEAPON, YOU ARE UNDER ARREST—"

Molt spun, pointed his rifle at the nearest bull, and fired. The man staggered but kept coming, raising his own weapon and a flashlight. Molt threw the rifle aside and drew a pistol.

She heard Bonham shout, behind her, "*Claire!* Come on! They're waiting for us out here!"

Molt fired the pistol, a pistol using explosive armor penetrating ammo—a guard fell, his armor ballooning. His amplified scream echoed with ear-ripping shrillness off the steel walls...

Molt ran shouting at the guards... flashlight beams whipping around him...

Claire squinted, trying to see her father...

Bonham shouted at her from behind...

And then Molt stopped as one of the guards shot him. Molt seemed surprised that the bullet hadn't hurt him much. Then he laughed and moved toward them again.

And, running at them with his gun upraised, howling with laughter—he exploded. The small explosive bullet buried in him detonated and the red of the explosion's flash was complemented by the red of blood-splash.

We forget we're made mostly of red liquid, Claire thought. But now she could see it was so—as Molt became a fountain of red liquid. She felt a few hot red drops spatter her forehead.

She saw the bulls move toward her, booming. "CLAIRE RIMPLER, YOU'RE UNDER ARREST—"

Dad's gone, she thought. It's hopeless.

She turned and climbed frantically through the jitney built into the barricade, trying to worm out the window on the other side, all the time expecting to feel an armored hand clamping her ankle to pull her back. But Bonham's hands, instead, pulled her through the jitney's window and past the barricade. She was in semidarkness, on her knees. Amplified shouts from behind her: "CLAIRE RIMPLER—"

"Why are they trying to arrest me?" she gasped at Bonham. "You said you arranged it."

"The arrangement had to be secret. Only a few of them know. Come on!" Bonham helped her up, and they ran around a corner, down a transverse passage, up a ringing metal stairway, following the blob of Bonham's flashlight jiggling on the wall—coming out on the access to the launch deck.

It was lit up, here, and there were uniformed men standing around, looking bored, waiting for them.

Claire screamed with frustration.

Bonham said, "It's all right—they work for Van Kips. It's part of the deal."

One of the men demanded, "You got the transport authorization?"

"Yeah, yeah... uh... here it is..." Bonham handed the man a paper.

"Okay. Come on."

And Claire burst into tears.

Her father was gone. She had abandoned him.

◆

URGENT: WITCHER TO STEINFELD
Decoded:
They extracted Stisky. He is reported dead. Ellen Mae Crandall reported dead. They have Purchase. You are compromised: they know your location. Repeat, they have made Paris as the location of NR field leadership; you in particular. Message intercepted relaying orders from Watson, Paris to be sealed off, the city to be "taken apart if necessary." New weapons deployed. Leave Paris, repeat, leave Paris...

◆

URGENT: BENSIMON, ISRAELI EMBASSY, TO WITCHER
Decoded:
Your message transmitted on to Steinfeld. However, Russian damage to allied sats and other factors make Steinfeld copying message unlikely. Computer report: probability only seven percent that Steinfeld received message. Strategic good news: high-level decision in Tel Aviv resulting from new intelligence confirms extreme anti-Semitic activity SA prompting Mossad to take active part against SA. Will do what we can to get Steinfeld and cadre out.

Part Four
HARD-EYES AND HARPIE

19

Hard-Eyes and Rickenharp were picking their way through the ruins of Paris, en route to checking out the landing pod Steinfeld claimed was coming down a kilometer northeast, when they saw Besson frying the last two fingers of his left hand.

They could see Besson—his image distorted but recognizable—through the fire-warped bubble of the burnt-out McDonald's plastic window. He was cooking something they couldn't see, at that point, using the grill's abandoned bottle of propane. True to form, Besson had camped out just two blocks from the Arc de Triomphe, on the Champs-Élysées. What was left of the Champs-Élysées . . . Besson was never far from the arch; his wife had been buried alive after a direct hit on their apartment building a few hundred yards from the monument.

And Besson returned to the shell of the building at night, to talk to his wife.

Rickenharp claimed he'd seen her himself; translucent and luminous, she drifted over the rubble, smiling enigmatically. So he said.

Maybe he *did* see her. Because two days after the front moved on north again, leaving Paris in the hands of the SA, the *Strategie Actuel*, and a few beleaguered cops, Rickenharp had made a deal with a black marketeer, traded an antique Chinese jade-and-silver bracelet ("First thing I bought when I got the royalties on my first hit. Everybody else bought a car") for half an ounce of blue mesc.

You do enough blue mesc, you see anything you want.

It was a damp, chill evening; gloomy but suffused with the pearly gray afterglow. There were shreds of fog gathering, knitting together in the blue shadows of the ruined walls.

They stood outside the wrecked MacDonald's, the steel of the Belgian assault rifle growing cold in Hard-Eyes' hands as the dusk wore into night. There was a .45 holstered on Hard-Eyes' right hip. Rickenharp carried something he'd scavenged from an SA ordnance dump: a Heckler and Koche Close Assault Weapon System (CAWS) automatic shotgun, model three. Gas operated with recoil assist, bullpup layout, internal operation floating system; 12-gauge. It was a thirty-four-inch gun, with the flash-hider, squarish, made of lightweight permaplast, carbon-fiber and plastic, stronger than steel. Twenty-round box. Rickenharp carried a pouch of seven readyloaded boxes, and he'd practiced slapping them into the magazine till he could do it faster than the eye could follow. The CAWS was lethal out to 150 yards.

Rickenharp said, "What you think, neggo? Let's go see how old Besson's getting on. We're, like, the only civilians left in Paris unless you want to count the cannibals in Pigalle."

Hard-Eyes shrugged. "Steinfeld won't like it. We gotta get to the thing before the fashes do, Harpie."

"Probably not a landing pod the spotters saw, man. How likely is that? Orbit drop pod? Sure. More likely helicopter. Talk about fashes, it was probably them." The fashes: the Fascists.

"Yukio saw the sensor profile and he knows spacegear. But fuck it, let's look in on Besson." He stepped into the MacDonald's as he spoke, "Five minutes tops and—oh, shit." That's when he saw what Besson was cooking. His fingers...

They'd gone into the refugee camp, recruiting, more than once, and they'd seen things there, that—well, this shouldn't have bothered Hard-Eyes as much as it did.

His gut contracted as he watched Besson stab a fork into his fingers and bring them to his mouth, start chewing, his eyes blank. He had a submachine gun, a Russian model cadged off some corpse, slung on a strap over his right shoulder.

"Hey, Besson, man, uh—" Rickenharp said softly. "Put down the gun and—everything. You come with us, we'll find you some rations, man. We didn't know you was so hard up." Stupid thing to say: everybody was hard up. Rickenharp's pale face had gone grim; his Adam's apple bobbed on his long neck as he swallowed to keep from gagging.

Besson looked at them—and growled.

Looking into Besson's small red eyes, at the sores on his emaciated face, his scalp and hair missing in patches, Hard-Eyes knew he was burnt. Gone, blown. He'd gone into the neurotoxin-dusted sectors, maybe without knowing it, scratching in the rubble for food, and the stuff was killing him slowly, making him mad first, as it was designed to do . . .

And now he was pointing the machine gun at them, holding it against his hip with his good hand. One of his charred fingers still clenched in his teeth. He growled again—a warning, like a dog with a bone.

He'd probably shoot at them if they moved, even if they backed away. A man got that way if he was yellow-dusted.

So Rickenharp pretended to faint.

He fell into a swoon, sighing, falling flat out on the shard-strewn floor. Besson gaped, confused. The charred finger fell from his mouth. Finally, his burnt brain decided: something moved, and even if it was only to fall, better shoot it.

So he lowered the gun to point it at Rickenharp on the floor.

Hard-Eyes drew his sidearm and did Besson a favor.

Besson fell with a neat round hole through the forehead, and Rickenharp, lying on the floor, started to sob.

Hard-Eyes felt empty. He reached down and pulled Rickenharp to his feet. "What you gonna do if we run into Carmen's patrol, she sees you like that," Hard-Eyes said, a catch in his voice. "Cut it the fuck out."

Rickenharp staggered out the door and took deep draughts of the cold night air. Hard-Eyes came to stand by him. "Later on," Rickenharp said, "we take his body to his old house, bury him with his wife."

"Okay . . . He's better off, Harpie."

"Yeah. I guess." He took an old, ornate snuff box from his pocket, opened it, scooped a strong hit of blue mesc with a thumbnail grown extra long for just that purpose. He snorted it up, and, still sniffing it back into his sinuses, said, "Yeah—" Sniff. "Probably better off now—" Sniff. "Than he has been for years." Sniff.

Hard-Eyes watched dolefully. "Hodey, I shouldn't be trusting you with a gun anywhere near me when you're on that shit. I'll be glad when you run out."

"Hey, it just makes me a better shot."

"Sure, if you're shooting at gray aliens and fairies."

"Hey, I'm the head producer, the programmer of my hallucinations, neggo."

"Just fucking come on." Hard-Eyes led the way off through a narrow side street, the buildings on the other side mostly intact, heading northeast again.

"You believe in life after death, Hard-Eyes?"

"I don't know." He didn't believe in it at all, but he didn't want to say that to Rickenharp just now.

"I do." Sniff.

"What a surprise."

"I mean, something's up with this life. It's weird we're alive. So it'd be weird if we're . . . " Sniff. " . . . just alive for this little blip of time, man." Sniff.

"Will you stop sniffing that crap? Dammit, you're gonna make some mistake . . . Seriously, you oughta give that mesc crap up."

"Tell it, Hard-Eyes: it's brain rot. Stay real, stay real, neggo! Brain *dam*-aaaage!" He grinned. His features were lean and smudged and hollowed and wiry, and when he grinned, it pulled his face into something that would have given chills to a horror-flick makeup artist.

But when Hard-Eyes didn't respond to the grin, it faded, and Rickenharp shrugged and said, "Yeah, well—I gave up the stuff twice before; last time it was for a long time. But here I figure it doesn't matter if I fuck up my health, because how long am I gonna have my health here? We're likely to get popped before we get outta here, I don't know if anybody clued you in on that classified secret."

"Hey, you know something? Steinfeld says we don't talk unless necessary when we're out, because the fashes got listening posts everywhere, and not just radio, they use boom mikes, too. Okay? If you think you can shut up on that crap you're packing in your sinuses."

"You pissed off at me?"

"No."

"I mean, we never follow that rule—"

"Rickenharp—"

"I know. Shut the fuck up. Right?"

Hard-Eyes smiled. They pushed on, passing through a region of flattened buildings, seeing the cat-sized gray rats ooze through the broken ends and endless jumble, and Hard-Eyes couldn't keep from thinking that Besson's death was a bad omen. That the ax was falling, and he'd just heard the whistle of its coming.

They turned a corner, and there was the blackened wasteland of the Parc des Buttes Chaumont. "There's the park," he whispered. He pressed himself to the corner of a building and peered across the Avenue Simon Bolivar at the park. A layer of black smoke hung over the pitted earth. The street was cluttered with cars, some burnt-out, some overturned, all covered with a layer of ash. Nothing moved. As they looked, the darkness seemed to settle in, running the shadows together.

"Okay," Rickenharp said. They moved across the sidewalk, picking their way through rubble from a looted storefront, brick chips and glass crunching under their feet (too loud, dammit!). They felt vulnerable out in the avenue as they hurried on, crouching between the cars, jogging for the park.

Hard-Eyes thinking, *We're moving like the fucking rats. Becoming like them.*

Then they were in the park, trudging between the craters, through the rubble, smelling the char. Seeing a group of disjointed skeletons, gray-white in a blackened, wheel-less US Army jeep.

"Shit," Rickenharp said, "there's no goddamn landing pod."

But there was. They found it at the far end of the park, beyond a copse of trees burnt like used wooden matches, shriveled and black; beyond hummocks thrown up by shell blasts; beyond hulks of exploded armor and a bone-dry pit once a duck pond. In the one relatively level field remaining in the park, a squat, six-legged landing pod, like some myth-sized mechanical spider, sat steaming in a crater rim kicked up by its own retros. A little ways away, deflated, was an anomalous swatch of woven silvery fabric; the shriveled bag of the parachute-balloon that had slowed the pod's descent. The pod was just a silhouette against the skull-colored ruins at the edge of the park; its slatted ports giving out downslanting beams of red light near the thick, charred heat shield.

They could smell its fuel, its hot metal—and they saw shadowy figures moving near its jointed legs.

The shadow-people moved out from under the pod. Three people, walking toward them on what was left of the asphalt path.

Hard-Eyes moved off the path; Rickenharp moved where Hard-Eyes moved, following his lead. It had been that way as long as they'd known one another.

They squatted behind a hump of crater edge, watching the strangers and looking around. Why hadn't the SA Fashes come to check out the pod? Maybe they were busy. The Parisian NR's ranks had grown; about half of every group of prisoners they liberated joined them. The city looked dead, but a great deal went on in it. Steinfeld gave the Fashes a lot to do.

The three strangers walked nearer. The one in the lead carried a flashlight, its beam of blue-white swiveling over the scarred earth like a blind man's cane. Hard-Eyes checked his rifle, switched it to auto, raised it, at the same time squinting through the dark, trying to see what uniforms the strangers wore.

Rickenharp whispered, "Yo, Hard-Eyes, what if there's Jægernauts out at the edge of the city like Steinfeld said? If they're active, they'll pick up the heat register from the landing pod. They'll come."

"Ease your ass, hodey. You're all paranoid. It's the blue . . . *Shh.*" The strangers on the path had come parallel, were walking past.

Hard-Eyes stood, raised the assault rifle, and barked, "Freeze! Drop your weapons!"

The strangers froze. Two sidearms fell to the gravel.

Hard-Eyes moved in closer and around in front of them, keeping the rifle leveled at a woman and two men. He saw in the glow of the flashlight the young woman had short-clipped, soft-looking auburn hair; a pixyish face; strangely doll-like lips; and big, intelligent-looking, dark eyes. She was short and slender, wearing a gray Colony staff one-piece jumpsuit. She looked familiar, too.

"We're neutral," said the thick man beside her. He had a thick nose, small eyes, and an ash-colored crew cut. He wore a pilot's jumpsuit, and a heavy pack on his back. "Refugees from FirStep. The Colony."

"Who, uh, are you with?" the second man asked. Thin guy, brown-haired, sad eyes.

Rickenharp for once was struck dumb. He was staring at the girl.

"Train that light at the ground," Hard-Eyes said.

She tilted the light downward. He moved in to retrieve their guns. Two small pistols. One of them for explosive pellets.

"Let's have the pellets, too," Hard-Eyes said.

The skinny one glanced at the others, then handed over a canvas packet the size of a deck of cards. Hard-Eyes stowed the weapons in his belt. The skinny guy took a step toward him—

Rickenharp popped the CAWS butt into the hollow of his shoulder, took a bead on the lanky one's chest, and rasped, "Don't you move that neutral ass again, friend."

The man became a statue. But a talking statue. "Ah, right. I'm Frank Bonham. This is Brett Kurland—our pilot. And this is Claire Rimpler. She's the daughter of Dr. Benjamin Rimpler."

Hard-Eyes clicked. "I thought I'd . . . Yeah, okay." He lowered his rifle. " 'S'okay, Harpie," he told Rickenharp.

Rickenharp kept his gun level. "Say what?"

"Said put away your piece. I recognize her." He was embarrassed to say it. "I did a paper on the Colony-administration system for a sociology class. I watched an interview with Rimpler and his daughter. That's her. She was a kid then. They're Colony. Neutral."

"Neutral is bullshit." But Rickenharp lowered the shotgun. He went on, "Neutrality doesn't mean shit if they meet the SA. The fashes don't care if you're Russian or American or Australian or a dog. In Paris, anyway, if you're not fash, you're the fashes' enemy."

"Fashes?" the girl asked.

"Tell you all about it on the way," Hard-Eyes said, looking at the sky. He'd heard something...

"On the way where?" Bonham asked.

"Our bunker." Hard-Eyes was scanning the rooftops.

"Hey," Rickenharp said, sounding like a kid at his aunt's picnic basket, "you got any goodies in that pod? Like coffee? Freeze-drieds? Fresh water?"

"It's all here in my pack," Kurland said brightly. Trying to sound helpful.

"Put out the light," Hard-Eyes said suddenly.

Claire switched the flashlight off. They looked to see what he was staring at.

Lights were approaching over the ravaged skyline. "Jumpjet," Rickenharp said. "The trucks'll be right behind." He turned to Hard-Eyes. "Let's make for the metro—"

Hard-Eyes hissed, "Run! The bastard's moving in!"

The wedge shape of the jumpjet was approaching with jerky movements; like a dragonfly, darting ahead, pausing, darting ahead. Now and then it stopped in midair to shine its spots on the ground, moving on slowly now, tacking the light along the path—stopping to hover over the pod.

Hard-Eyes and Rickenharp, Claire and Bonham and Kurland ran through the shadows. They ran down a six-foot-deep erosion ravine toward the rue Botzaris. Across Botzaris, hot with exertion now, they made their way gasping through a maze of abandoned, rotting furniture spilled from the back of a deserted, wheel-less furniture truck, then down the rue de la Villette toward the metro station.

Hard-Eyes heard Claire cursing between gasps. This was probably not what she expected to find on Earth.

When they got to the metro entrance, Claire switched on the flashlight, and they ran down the steps. They paused in the rubble at the bottom to catch their breath. It was an eerie, oppressive place in the glow of the flashlight. "We'll have to crawl to get past the rubble here," Rickenharp said. "But after a few feet it opens up, we can walk..."

Claire dropped the flashlight, and sobbed out of the darkness. Bonham picked up the light, and touched her face to comfort her. Hard-Eyes felt strange, seeing that. He didn't like Bonham touching her.

Neither did she. She slapped his hand away. Her voice was cracked as she said, "I'm... it's stupid to cry now."

"Good a time as any," Hard-Eyes said. "We can sit down for a few minutes, we're under cover now." He tugged her wrist, and she hunkered down to sit on a slab of broken concrete, atop the rubble heap.

The flashlight was pointed downward; he could just make out her shoulders shaking as she sobbed. "I don't know..." she muttered. "But God... I wanted to come back so bad... But it's so strange here, it's like... it's heavy and cold and exposed... and it's worse than the Colony..."

"Not worse," Rickenharp said. "We got a sky here. And there's parts of the planet—big parts—the war hasn't touched. You hang in there, you can go see 'em."

Hard-Eyes said nothing. Let her believe it. But the chances were, none of them would get out of Paris alive. After a while, she said, "Okay. Let's go." Her voice was steady now. Hard-Eyes took the flashlight, and they went on.

◆

Walking down the tunnel. Flashlight beam flaring the red eyes of rats, spotlighting fist-sized mutant roaches.

Rickenharp sighed, world-weary, when Claire fell in beside Hard-Eyes.

"What's at your... headquarters?" Claire asked.

Hard-Eyes snorted. "Headquarters consists of a hundred raggedy guys and a few women sitting in the basement of a bombed-out apartment building. Cleaning guns, arguing politics, reading. Playing cards with a deck that's wearing see-through. Guys from every nationality... Most of them speak English. It's not cozy there, but we got some chemheaters, ersatz coffee, small store of canned food. Now and then we find somebody's hoard in the ruins... We got to turn down this tunnel, we can't go on that way 'cause the tunnel's collapsed..."

"Your friend said something about the SA."

"Fashes. Neofascists."

"The Second Alliance."

He looked at her. "That's right."

She laughed bitterly. "We have that particular species of cockroach on the Colony, too. They took over. A coup, really. They're calling it an emergency police action. When we left they'd overrun everything. They're in complete control there now. Martial law. Praeger's little dictatorship. My father..."

"I was going to ask you if he was still... how he was."

"I think he's dead. He..." She shook her head, her eyes closed. After a moment she opened her eyes and said, "Bonham had a pass on to an outgoing ship, but we had to hijack the pod when we got to Station One. They had us scheduled to go down in the States, and I'm pretty sure the SA would have arrested me there. And Bonham thinks they wanted to brainwash him. So we had to steal an unscheduled pod, and we happened to be over Europe, and Bonham heard the NR was in Paris..." She shook her head. Her voice was dry, so dry it cracked. "We didn't know it was like this."

"It wasn't this bad till they sealed off the town. No one goes in or out, unless they crawl the whole way maybe. Lot of people are starving. They got wind that Steinfeld is here..."

Rickenharp said sharply, "You're talking a lot, man. If they got extracted..." He licked his lips, twitching from blue mesc.

"Fuck off," Hard-Eyes growled. "SA already knows everything I've said."

"Steinfeld is your leader?"

Hard-Eyes nodded. "They're flattening the city looking for him. Methodically trying to dig him out . . . There's no fuel left in that pod?"

She shook her head.

He shrugged. The fashes had it now anyway.

She said, "I can't believe what they've done to Paris."

"Most of it was done by the Russians and the Americans. Rickenharp there, and me, we were Americans. We fucking swore it off."

"What kind of people are in the Second Alliance army? Around here I mean."

"They're a mix. A lot of them are Hispanic and Italian, but none of the Latins rise far in the ranks. Around here, mostly British, Afrikaner whites, Lebanese Phalangists."

"So—what are you people going to do?"

He shook his head grimly. "You picked a bad LZ. You put your foot in a bear trap. We're just hanging on, hoping some of our allies get through. They tried to run a chopper in for Steinfeld once—it was shot down. They'll try again. Well, there's something else . . . "

Rickenharp looked at him. "Hard-Eyes, man, she could be captured."

Hard-Eyes nodded. "But I'm going to tell her anyway. Coming down in this shit, the woman's got a right to know. We get captured, you think we could keep anything back, the equipment they got? They'd get it from us, too, Harpie."

"Go on, blow it then. Shit," Rickenharp muttered.

Hard-Eyes hesitated. Maybe Rickenharp was right. But he was tired. And it seemed important that she know. He glanced at Claire—and found it impossible not to trust her. "Our people are moving in from the other capitals, planning to drive through to get to Steinfeld. If it weren't for the rest of us trapped in here, I think Steinfeld would tell 'em to forget it, write him off. Because it probably won't work. The SA lines around the city are tight and well entrenched. And they got the Jægernauts."

"What's that?"

"A—killing machine. *Big.* Hard to describe. Anyway, we've changed our base op three times in three weeks. They're crowding us in. Maybe we'll just take our stand around the arch and let 'em know we're there. Get it over with, take a few of them out with us. Free the rest of the NR to go on. We'd be martyrs. Good political strategy—if anyone ever hears of it."

"You mean—take a stand and let them kill you?"

"Uh-huh."

"Like the three hundred Spartans. Romantic."

Rickenharp cawed at that. His voice trembled a bit, his eyes blinking too much, as he chortled, "Romantic. Yeah. Mostly it sucks."

"Why—why take your stand around the arch? You mean the Arc de Triomphe, right?"

"Uh-huh." He shrugged. "Maybe it's foolish. Corny political symbolism. Trying to rally the French behind us. The arch is one of the few places of old Paris left standing mostly intact. So it's the symbol of the NR. It's on the NR flag. We had a prisoner tell us the fashes are planning to use Jægernauts to level the arch. 'To try to crush what can't be crushed,' Steinfeld says. Meaning our spirit, I guess. Sometimes he talks that way. Makes speeches about dying meaningfully and . . . all that. We make fun of the way he talks but—" He broke off, embarrassed.

He never had to explain Jægernauts to her. Except to say, later, "They were built by a Second Alliance armor subsidiary, a German firm run by a guy named Jæger." He didn't have to explain because when they came up out of the metro station at Clichy, they heard the world-filling roar of a Jægernaut. Saw it a few minutes later when they were jogging along the sidewalk, a few blocks from the new safe-house.

Rickenharp and Hard-Eyes looked at one another. And started to run.

But it seemed to Claire that they ran the wrong way:

They ran into the cloud of dust that surrounded the Jægernaut, Hard-Eyes shouting for her and her companions to wait where they were.

◆

The ground shook and the air itself shook, with the noise of the killing machine, the THUNK-rumble-THUNK-rumble. The crashes, the squeal of snapping metal, crystallized steel grinding stones into dust... They saw it up ahead, lit up along its axis; yellow and red lights that made the dust cloud glow...

The Jægernaut loomed above them, a five-story double swastika of plasteel, wearing the dust cloud like its cloak of power.

Hard-Eyes squinted up at it, his eyes burning, lungs wracked with the smoke billowing from the rubbled gap where the building had been: the building that had housed their headquarters.

The Jægernaut finished it work. It hadn't spotted Hard-Eyes and his companions. Plowing through massive buildings as a tank would plow through a fiberboard house, it crashed away from them; bricks rained to either side of it like spray at the prow of a boat. It used tight microwave beams to soften up the stone and iron as it shouldered through...

The whole machine was a giant wheel without a rim. Like two rimless wagon wheels with eight-jointed spokes on each side. Hydroplas "muscles" kept it churning, digging, gouging, plowing through, looking to some like a Rototiller—but fifty yards high. At the axis, between the two sets of gouging spokes, was the nuclear power source, and you'd be sorry if you blew that part up. Each spoke was four yards thick. The power source remained stationary; the axis turned around it. The Jægernaut was terrifying to behold, even before it began to move. It was the ideal instrument of state terrorism. A half-dozen could level a city in under a month. And they were a bitch to bring down.

Rickenharp and Hard-Eyes forced themselves to clamber over the remaining crust of wall, coughing through the smoke and dust. They felt the thrum of the departing Jægernaut, heard its monumental clanking, the shudderings so heavy in the air it was like moving through another medium, a kind of shock-wave liquid...

Then they climbed down into the smoking socket where the New Resistance HQ had been.

A small fire burned in someone's leather jacket, where a chemheater had been smashed. The fire-flutter was the only motion—the smoke rising in wisps like the departing wraiths of the dead. Here and there were hanks of skin, hair, shredded fatigues. A bloodied yet bloodless hand thrust like a claw from one of the mounds of rubble. Bloodied black bandannas now mingled indistinguishably with the flesh and brains of the wearer.

The Jægernaut had gone over the place more than once.

Hard-Eyes felt a jolt as he found what was left of Jenkins. His heart turned to slag inside him.

"They're all dead," Rickenharp said shakily, sounding like a lost child.

Hard-Eyes shook his head. "No—they . . . maybe some got away . . ." It was a dream. He tried to imagine how it had been real. "The sentries . . . the fashes send commandos to kill the sentries. Then they bring the Jægernaut in on quiet trucks. Auto-assemble the parts maybe a block away. Activate it, it unfolds itself—it's pretty compact when it's folded up . . . And it comes down on them before they know what's happening . . ."

Rickenharp said, in a voice kept carefully flat, "It makes a lot of noise coming. Even if it was close—must have been some of them got out of the building. *Must* have been."

They looked around a little more. Found nothing alive; found pieces of their friends.

The sound of the Jægernaut was receding now. It was like an iron foundry walking away.

Another sound came. A humming, grinding of gears. Jeeps. Trucks.

"Fashes coming to check it out, man, Harpie," Hard-Eyes said.

Rickenharp just stared around him, mouth slack, eyes smoldering with growing rage—a hair-trigger rage. Very carefully, Hard-Eyes laid a hand on Rickenharp's arm. Rickenharp whirled and pointed the shotgun at him, squeezed the trigger, snarling.

The safety was on. Hard-Eyes swallowed to force his heart down out of his throat and said, "It's me, Harpie. Jesus fuck."

"Sorry. I . . . "

"You *gotta* get off that blue mesc shit."

"It's not that . . . " Rickenharp's eyes overflowed. Tears streaked the grime on his cheeks. "They're . . . "

"I know. I'm telling you man, *had* to be some of 'em got away. Hey, the fashes are coming. We can kill some of 'em if we—if we get to high ground. Okay?" Rickenharp let Hard-Eyes take his arm and steer him out of the ruins. The noise of trucks got louder. Hard-Eyes saw a light stab through the smoke, seeking. "Shit, where's—"

Then Claire and Bonham and Kurland ran up, coughing in the smoke. "There's soldiers," Bonham said, gasping. "Are they—"

"They're SA," Hard-Eyes said. "Come on." He led them down the street, away from the sound of the approaching men. Out of the thick of the cloud, down one of the twisting, twenty-foot-wide side streets.

They paused here to catch their breath. "Shit, I'm exhausted." Claire said.

Hard-Eyes looked down the alley, saw a man silhouetted at the other end. Carrying a gun. Hard-Eyes raised his assault rifle. But the man waved and spread his arms, gun out to the side, offering his chest as a target. Surrendering. Walking nearer.

Then Rickenharp said, "All *ri-ight!*"

It was Yukio, in khakis and black bandanna. Over his shoulder was a rifle fitted with an M83.

He walked up, his face blank, lowering his arms. Hard-Eyes put a hand on Yukio's shoulder. The Japanese was rigid with grief. "There are two others who made it," he said hoarsely. "But the rest in the HQ are dead. This is the second family I've lost to them."

"Who made it?" Rickenharp asked.

"Willow and Carmen. They went out to find . . . privacy. We were having a party. This is why—we drank too much. Or we would have heard it coming. Steinfeld gave us the last case of wine." He smiled weakly. "You missed the party."

"Party?" Rickenharp's tone was pure incredulity. "What the fuck?"

"For Steinfeld. Ten minutes after you go out, a call comes through: the Israelis captured an SA jumpjet. Room for two passengers. They sent it through for Steinfeld and Dr. Levassier. Steinfeld goes to direct the assault to get us out. It will fail." He shrugged. "Steinfeld is out, though. He is safe, for now. He can go on. It hurt him to go. I saw it. But he knows where his work is. He went."

"Steinfeld is out!" Rickenharp said. His mood did another wild swing. He danced around, pretending to play the shotgun like it was a guitar. "*Fuck* these fascist pricks!"

"Keep your voice down, Harpie," Hard-Eyes said.

Yukio was staring at the newcomers. "From the pod? Colony people?"

Hard-Eyes nodded. "Let's move out."

"Where to?" Claire asked, slumping against a wall.

"Shelter, for now," Hard-Eyes said. "Till we can regroup with another cell."

"Gimme shelter, the man says." Rickenharp chuckled. "Gimme, gimme, gimme. I know a place. Wait'll you see, Hard-Eyes. Come on. One block."

◆

Hard-Eyes sat with his back to a wall, his assault rifle across his knees. It was an old gun, from late in the last century, repaired twice in the NR machine shop. They were camped out in the wreckage of what had once been a music-supplies store. Yukio, Hard-Eyes, and the refugees from the Colony, hunkered behind the sales counter. There was a smashed-open cred-scanner lying on its side like the skull of a beheaded robot, and there were sheets of music printout scattered yellowing on the floor and nothing else except the faint glow of a Coleman and the flicker of the chemheater in the back of the hall.

Turned out Rickenharp had stashed the lamp and the heater here. This is where he'd come, those times he'd disappeared.

Down the hall, the Rimpler girl was lying on a bed of sheet music, near the chemheater, snoring softly. Bonham and Kurland sat near her, whispering. Across from Hard-Eyes, Yukio sat with his head on his arms, arms propped on knees, knees tucked against his chest, muttering Japanese in his sleep.

Hard-Eyes whispered, "Rickenharp?"

Rickenharp's voice from the other side of the counter. "I'm still on, man. Still wired. Get some sleep. I'm watching."

Hard-Eyes put his head on his arms, imitating Yukio, and drifted into a fitful sleep, waking now and then at little sounds. He heard Rickenharp sniffing something up—probably synmorph this time, to take the edge off the blue, and to keep from thinking too much about the friends who'd been butchered, pulped, during their only celebration in six months. Drifting...

Next thing he heard was Bonham and Kurland arguing; hearing Kurland's accent more clearly now. "But we can't know that these 'fash' people are, ah, you know, the way they are advertised to be by their—" Kurland lowered his voice. "—by their *opposition*. I mean, the opposition always describes the other side as bad news and bloody tyrants... Now, if we explain to these Second Alliance people we're not subversives, we're neutral, surely they—well, I think we should go to them, and—"

Bonham said, "Oh, don't be stupid. They'd ID me; they know I skipped out on them. They'd ship me to one of their rehab camps. You they'd read as a possible accomplice—you took a bribe from us, so you'd worked in someone else's employ against them. Claire worked against them, so they want her in their clutches. Forget it."

"But, I say—"

"I said *forget it*." A lot of authority in the weedy little guy's tone when he wanted it.

So Bonham had collaborated. Hard-Eyes filed it away, and went back to sleep.

◆

"Dammit, Hard-Eyes, wake up!"

Hard-Eyes sat up straight, wincing. His back ached from the cold concrete wall. "Whuh you want, man. I go on watch?"

"No, Yukio's standing sentry... C'mere."

Hard-Eyes stood, stretched, and, carrying the assault rifle, followed Rickenharp down the hall, past the Colony refugees sleeping around the metal shell of the chemheater. Hard-Eyes glanced at Claire. Her face in sleep like something from a Pre-Raphaelite painting. He felt a pleasant tug, looking at her. He smiled, seeing she was sleeping with the machine pistol Yukio had given her; it was clutched to her chest the way a little girl sleeps with a doll... They walked past, down to the left. Down the stairs into a musty basement storeroom. Rickenharp switched on a flashlight.

"I was poking around here once... I saw these boards looked recently nailed on, like somebody was hiding something back here..." He laid the flashlight on the top of a stack of cardboard boxes, so the beam faced the wall, spotlighting a door. The door was boarded over. He pulled at the planks and they came away easily. He'd pried them away before and then put them back; loosely reinserted the nails.

He tossed the boards aside with a crash that made Hard-Eyes flinch, shined the flashlight through the low doorway.

"Check it out!"

Hard-Eyes bent and went in, Rickenharp following with the flashlight.

It was a small room, twenty by five feet, just a long closet, filled with musical instruments. Mostly guitars, amplifiers, speakers, microphones, and PA equipment.

Hard-Eyes shuddered with intuition and a sense of displacement, staring at the hoard. To Rickenharp, it was the Treasure of Tutankhamen.

"Eyes, my man, this is Kismet." His voice thick with conviction. "Destiny. I was intended to find this stuff. I feel like Ali Baba... I guess these were like demonstration models the music store hid down here when the Russians started shelling. There's even a tuba over there. Can you believe it? I tried twenty music stores, man, before I could find anything that wasn't busted. But I knew it was there waiting for me in one of 'em..."

"Too bad you can't use it. Got no power. And the fashes would hear."

A grin lit up his corner of the room like an electrical arc. "Oh, yeah? Look-a-that!" He stuck out his hand. A chromium cube glittered in his palm. "You know what that is? That's a Firestormer, made by Marshall Amps. Intense battery power for the biggest amp concentrated in that little thing. Costly sucker. Good for five days of top-volume playing. And scan this: Earphones. Two sets. They plug into the amp. Built-in volume controls. I can play and the fashes won't hear a note. You wanna hear something? I already got the guitar tuned..."

Feeling like he was denying food to a starving man, Hard-Eyes said, "Uh, not just now, man. I'm pretty tired, got a headache."

"Headache? Great. Just put the headphones on. I'll clear your headache up. There won't be room for an ache in your head! I got me an old Telecaster here, 'bout fifty years old, works fine... I crank this sucker like so, jack in here, insert the battery here..." The amplifier's lights winked hot red in the semidarkness. Rickenharp had left the flashlight on the floor. He bent near it to snort a long line of blue mesc from the back of his hand. A bluish light bled up from the flashlight to accent his face eerily, as if he were glowing from the drug.

Hard-Eyes sighed, put on the earphones, and turned the volume low, prepared to listen to a twenty-minute self-indulgence, electric ego-swell tedium, maybe some interminable variation of one of Rickenharp's favorite twentieth-century tunes.

Rickenharp strapped on the guitar, put on the earphones so he could hear himself...

A hummm in the earphones...

The first chord rang like a church bell. Long and slow and full. The second quivered bluesy like a woman wailing at a New Orleans funeral in the churchyard where the bell rang. Rickenharp was playing a funeral dirge for their friends, dead under the crystallized-steel jackboot... And then he played a theme that resonated anger, vengeance, renewal of purpose; picking up the tempo, doublepicking for a rhythm section, and he was off and running, rocking for real.

The notes pealed and tripped, dashed into speed-rapper's digressions, dashed on, paused like a comedian timing an irony, and then seemed to carry on a monologue that had a rhythm to it like Rickenharp's style of talking. They segued back into the thematic riff and—okay, Hard-Eyes was impressed.

Finally, Rickenharp was finished. Hard-Eyes took off the earphones. His ears rang.

"Rickenharp, man, I had no idea."

"This is my instrument. Could have been custom-made for me."

"You want a hit of this blue, Eyes?"

"No, hodey, come on, you know me better than that. But play another tune. I'm not quite deaf yet." He put the earphones back on.

◆

Rickenharp and Hard-Eyes were smiling when they came out of the back room.

There was no one in the hall. Hard-Eyes frowned and flicked the HK's safety off. He led the way up the hall, thinking, *All that noise in the earphones, anything could've happened out here, we'd never know it.*

They went up to the counter. Heard a rustle, an urgent whisper, couldn't make out what was said. Hunched over, they moved around the counter, looked out into the main room . . . Room strewn with fiberplas crates, the guts of a smashed piano, broken glass. A little light bleeding across the room from the busted-in windows on the left. Movement to the right, behind the crates. Rickenharp turned that way, stepping out from the cover of the counter.

Then Hard-Eyes saw the men in the doorway to the left. "Harp—" he began.

But Rickenharp stepped into the open, and the darkness was splintered by muzzle flashes; the walls echoed with thudding automatic weapons. Rickenharp went spinning, falling. Two stray rounds slammed into the broken piano, making plaintive, discordant notes . . .

Hard-Eyes bellowed and jumped out to fire at the door with the HK; it leaped in his hand, funneling his anger; the room lit up with strobe flashes from the muzzle. One of the men yelled hoarsely and fell. Hard-Eyes instinctively moved back to the cover of the counter.

In the strobe from the gun he'd seen Bonham and Kurland lying facedown on the floor, hands behind their heads. The men had come in, seen them in the main room maybe. They'd surrendered... Where was Claire?

"Rickenharp? Yo, Harpie!" Hard-Eyes hissed.

"I'm... okay, man."

"Don't move."

Hard-Eyes peered over the top of the counter at the door. Saw no one.

He bent and moved on into the middle of the room, groped till he found Rickenharp. "Where you hit?"

"Leg. Hip."

"I gotcha." He slung the assault rifle over his back, bent to help Rickenharp.

But before he could pick Rickenharp up, light stabbed from the doorway. A man barked, "Hold it, drop your weapons!"

Hard-Eyes looked, blinking in the light. Above the glare he made out three men coming in, weapons raised. SA Regulars. No heavy body armor on them. But they had the drop on him.

"Harpie..."

"I say fuck 'em," Rickenharp said.

Rickenharp had his CAWS across his chest. Grimacing with pain, he sat up, fired across his body at the men in the door. The autoshotgun roared like a small cannon, booming and leaping in his hands, and the man in the lead was torn apart by four 12-gauge rounds at a range of thirty feet, his left arm separating from his shoulder; his body, seeming to liquefy, splashed back on the others. Then the booming stopped and Rickenharp hissed, "Fucker's jammed!"

Hard-Eyes was trying to bring his HK into firing position, but it was too late, the other SAs were firing; Rickenharp grunted and fell back; 9-mm rounds were whistling so close by Hard-Eyes' head he could feel the friction, and any split-second now one would—

Claire popped up from behind a crate like a jack-in-the-box, the machine pistol blazing, rattling in her hands. She sprayed wildly at the door—both men went down.

The flashlight was lying in the doorway, still shining, making a reflecting pool of puddling blood.

Hard-Eyes was shaking, his heart hammering in his chest.

He told himself, *Get calm, get calm.* Rickenharp was alive, his head bleeding, trying to get up. "Lay still, ya damn fool," Hard-Eyes told him. He walked on wobbly legs to the door, picked up the flashlight, wiped warm slick wetness from it on a SA uniform. He straightened—and the flashlight beam fell over Yukio. He seemed to be embracing someone.

He was lying facedown atop an SA regular, his right hand still on a knife stuck in the dead man's throat. His side was bloody. His left arm was shot through, a welter of blood and protruding bone splinters. But he was breathing.

Claire walked up from behind. She said, "Kurland went to look out the window. Yukio told him to go back inside. They argued, and then the SA men came. Yukio shot one of them. Another one shot Yukio, and Yukio dropped his gun and fell down. But when the guy came to check him, Yukio jumped up, stabbed him, and they fell down together . . . And then some more SA came and Kurland surrendered . . . And then you came . . . " She shrugged.

Her voice was dead; her face was expressionless.

Hard-Eyes looked at Rickenharp. Kurland was there, spraying a dressing on Rickenharp's wounds from the first-aid kit in his backpack. Claire took another medikit from a belt pouch and bent down to see what she could do for Yukio.

Hard-Eyes went to the door, looked down the streets. "They were probably just a patrol. Maybe we're okay here."

He went back inside. Kurland and Bonham were carrying Rickenharp into the back room. They laid him down by the chemheater. He was unconscious, bleeding from the right temple.

"Lad took a ricochet, maybe just a fragment, from the size of the entry wound," Kurland said. "That second salvo, after he shot at them . . . maybe not too bad, though . . . Might be just badly stunned."

Hard-Eyes and Claire—she was stone-faced, efficient—dragged the dead SA patrol to the back of the main room, hid them behind the flattened piano.

They laid Yukio beside Rickenharp. Yukio stared at the ceiling, ground teeth against the pain but making no other sound. Hard-Eyes injected him with synthmorph from the medical kit, and he gave out a long, soft sigh, and went almost immediately to sleep. Hard-Eyes used a field cast-kit to set Yukio's broken arm in a temporary plaster brace. The wound in Yukio's side was superficial.

◆

It was about four a.m. when Rickenharp woke and asked Hard-Eyes to shine the flashlight in his eyes. His voice was raspy. Hard-Eyes shrugged, got up, and shone the light in Rickenharp's eyes.

"Do it, Hard-Eyes. Shine the light on me . . ."

"I'm doin' it already, man."

And then they knew he'd gone blind.

"Bone splinter probably," Rickenharp said, trying to sound clinical. "Severed the ol' optical nerve. Or maybe a blood clot."

"Shit, man, we'll get you out; they'll operate . . ."

Rickenharp said, "Blind." Tasting the word. More amazed than horrified at first. "Blind. What a scene, man. An Anti-scene, really. *Blind.*"

The bullets Rickenharp had taken in the leg had made flesh wounds, and missed the arteries. But he was weakened and lay on his back near the chemheater, head pillowed on Hard-Eyes' rolled-up jacket, playing the Telecaster, listening to himself on the earphones. A little behind him stood the small amp, its red light glowing like a supernatural eye, as if Rickenharp's demon crouched protectively near.

After a while, he stopped playing but, smiling faintly, seemed still to be listening to something. "Hey, Hard-Eyes," he rasped.

Hard-Eyes went to crouch near him. "Yeah?"

"Take the earphones off me. Put 'em on. Listen." Hard-Eyes took the earphones and listened. He heard static and, very faintly, a voice.

Hard-Eyes burst out, "It's Willow! Willow's voice! . . . This thing picks up one of our frequencies!"

"Yeah, they do that sometimes. You hear what he said?"

"Yeah, he's repeating it over and over. All units meet at rendezvous twenty, oh-nine-hundred. Damn—What was R-twenty?"

"You're supposed to have it memorized, expert! It's the southbound platform at Metro Franklin Roosevelt. That's on the Champs-Élysées—not far from the arch. Oh-nine-hundred. Tomorrow morning. You know, things happen real symmetrically, Hard-Eyes. We get a little good luck, a little bad luck, a little good luck. Latest good luck, we snag this regroup message. Latest bad luck, we're on the wrong side of the fucking arch. Nazi shit-heads're camped all around it. We could get *to* the arch but not past it. On one side is the yellow-dust zone, on the other side they got their headquarters. The streets are blocked off unless we go right under the arch . . . So how do we get through to regroup at Frankie Roosevelt?"

"We'll figure something."

"Hey—that was a rhetorical question. 'Cause I got something figured, man. I want you to promise you won't fuck me up on this. Give this to me. My last gig, Hard-Eyes. Listen . . . "

◆

"This is bloody stupid." Kurland muttered.

It was an hour before dawn. They were trudging through the gouged streets, through blue-black shadows and silver-limned patches of fog, through rubble and char and the cold smell of ashes. And they were carrying sound equipment on their backs.

Hard-Eyes could hardly believe it himself. But when Kurland kept complaining, Hard-Eyes said, "There's no talking him out of it. We're gonna do it. So shut the fuck up."

Rickenharp, leaning on Claire, grinned at that. "Good to hear you say that to somebody else, Hard-Eyes."

"You shut the fuck up, too."

Claire was carrying a guitar and medical kit. Kurland had the PA horns. Yukio carried weapons—and a rhythm box. Bonham had cords and mikes, miscellaneous hardware, and Rickenharp's shotguns. Hard-Eyes had two portable amps strapped to his back and the assault rifle in his arms, the M-83 over one shoulder. They carried their gear through the twisted stub of a skyscraper, between fantastic shapes of melted glass and plastic; through the ribbed remains of a cathedral; through a field of ravaged mannequins where a department store had stood. All the time sweat was running icy under their clothes.

"Fucking absurd, I'm telling you," Kurland growled, as he shifted the weight of an amplifier.

Claire said, "The war is absurd. Racism is absurd. This—" She gestured at the wreckage of Paris. She didn't have to finish the sentence.

"I just hope I don't get rained out," Rickenharp said.

They hid from passing patrols twice, and then crept on, concealed by mist and the night and the megalomaniac overconfidence of the fashes.

◆

And then they'd reached the Étoile. The Star. The arch stood at the center of the twelve-pointed star where the avenues met. It had been decreed by Napoleon in 1808, begun by Chalgrin the same year, not completed until 1836. Made of massive stone blocks, the Arc de Triomphe was fifty yards high, forty-four across the front, twenty-two on the side. Its facades were intricately carved, its arch sheltering the flame of the unknown soldier. Long since gone out, overwhelmed by the wind of a thousand thousand unknown soldiers passing on...

On the face of the arc facing the Champs-Élysées was the high-relief group, a carving representing the departure of the war volunteers. The central figure was the Marseillaise with her wings spread, her out-thrust sword pointing the way, her mouth opened in an eternal shout, a shout carved in stone.

The Arc de Triomphe was bullet-scarred but still standing.

Nearly dawn. The night sky relented a little, admitting some blue. Most of the fashes were encamped on the far side of the arch. To rendezvous with the NR, Hard-Eyes had to get past them.

There were a few sentries on this side of the arch—but between Hard-Eyes and the sentries was the cover of overturned trucks, crashed hovercars, gouted tanks, rubble, and long shadows.

Aching under their burdens, they crossed the Étoile; crouching, darting through the twisted wreckage, Kurland and Bonham with their thoughts written on their faces: *This is irrational, this is insane.*

Just inside the door that led to the stairwell, in one of the arch's massive legs, two neofashes squatted by a sickly-yellow chem-fire.

Hunched down behind a truck, Hard-Eyes screwed the sound suppressor onto his assault rifle. He crept around the circular curbing surrounding the arch till he was out of the line of sight of the sentries, and then dashed back to the arch's support, pressed himself flat against the stone. He listened, heard soft, unconcerned voices from inside. A trapezoid of sulfur-colored light projected onto the concrete from the door to his left.

Don't let 'em get off a shot, he told himself. Quiet, got to be fast and quiet.

He edged up to the door.

"The bloody resistance is a bloody fucking joke," said someone inside. "Waste of time to be sitting out here for a bunch of ticked off frogs and wogs."

Hard-Eyes smiled. He pivoted, turning to step through the door, tracking to center his sights as the men looked up, gaping. The rifle's suppressor hushed the report of the bullets, as one man fell over backward, his chest opening up with faucets of blood, while the second was training a submachine gun at the intruder, at Hard-Eyes, who was thinking, *Right through the brain so he doesn't get a shot when he goes down.* Letting his trained fingers do the work, the HK spitting flame, hissing, licking away the top of the guy's head; the man spun, blood spiraling from his shattered skull, the gun clattering to the floor. That was the only sound the gun made.

And they had taken the Arc de Triomphe.

◆

They carried the equipment up piece by piece. Up the stairwell inside the arch; up to the observation deck at the crown. Claire and Hard-Eyes helped Rickenharp climb the stairs. They set up the equipment, jacked in Rickenharp's guitar. Rickenharp sat on the amp, to everyone's amazement meticulously tuning up the guitar in the earphones, the chill, damp wind whipping his hair. Charcoal-edged, silver-hearted clouds flowed behind him. Rickenharp smiled crookedly, as he tinkered with the guitar settings, looking weaker, paler than ever. Yukio sat beside him setting up the grenade launcher, the automatics.

Hard-Eyes made them up two shots apiece with the syringes from the medikit; each shot contained a solution of one part blue mesc, one part synthmorph, one part energizing vitamins. Just to see them through. He made it in a tin mess cup belonging to the dead sentries.

Kurland stared but said nothing.

"It's funny, the arch being the symbol of the NR," Rickenharp whispered. "I mean—seems like I remember it was all about Napoleon. A fucking tyrant."

"Became a symbol of the French Republic," Yukio said, finishing setting up the weapons. He sat back, resting, his voice distant, eyes closed. "Democracy. Anyway, we appropriated it. Gave it our own meaning. Fascism is anti-traditional. What's good in tradition is what makes people want to fight Nazis . . . Arc celebrates culture, tradition, for us. Not tyranny . . . for us it's not about tyranny . . . "

"Rickenharp," Hard-Eyes said, as he pulled back on the syringe plungers to suck the solution through the needle, "an operation might restore your eyesight. Or a transplant or a prosthetic."

"Come off it, man. That whole side of my body's going numb. I still got strength in my arms, my fingers. But it won't last long. Something's busted in my brain, Hard-Eyes. Always was—" He grinned. "But now it's fucked up for good. You guys won't get through unless Yukio and me create a diversion. And Yukio and me—we're screwed anyway. He ain't gonna leave his arch. Made up his mind when our compadres got flattened. These Japanese motherfuckers are crazy!" Said admiringly. "And Yukio feels bad, man, that he didn't get it, too. With all of his friends. And..." He gave a crooked smile.

"It's the band, though, really. Isn't that it, Rickenharp? You got it in your mind your career is dead. And that's your whole identity. So you think you got to die, too. Rickenharp, buddy, it's *dumb* to—"

"No, Hard-Eyes," Rickenharp broke in. "Don't tell me my big moment is dumb. No, you don't see. This *feels* right. It's like I been rehearsing my whole life for this gig..."

"Harpie..."

"No, I mean it. I ain't hopin' for nobody to talk me out of it. Now scan this, man..." His voice got some of its old excitement back in it. "The Jægernauts, they got cameras on 'em, at the stationary part of the axle, right? You can see 'em pop out of the slot when they want a good TV-shot to show the troops for the Triumph-of-the-Will scam. You know? They'll show us getting plowed under and they'll send it back—with sound, man! Back to that neofash hometown in California and show it to the kids and the young ones, and the kids'll see me, they hear the tunes, they might react differently than what the fashes expect, right?"

"Maybe so, Harpie." Not believing it for a moment. But let the guy have his fantasy.

"Anyway, I always wanted a live gig on TV. They made us lip-synch."

He grinned and there was blood on his teeth.

So Hard-Eyes gave the primed syringes to Yukio, embraced Yukio and Rickenharp, and went to the stairs without a word. When he looked back, just before going through the door, he saw Yukio taking a red ribbon from his jacket, winding it around his head, kneeling in preparation for a Shinto ceremony.

◆

Hard-Eyes and the refugees hid themselves in a tangle of cold, twisted black armor and waited for daylight. They were in the back of what had been an old half-track. Once, Bonham tried to hold Claire's hand. She jerked it away from him and shut her eyes. His expression went hard, but he said nothing. After a while he climbed off the back of the half-track and went around the front, where, in the cover of an overturned truck, he pissed against the half-track's engine.

Hard-Eyes could see only a bluish section of Claire's face, enough to see she was awake. "Suppose we get through," he said. "What will you do? If you could go anywhere, do anything? Dumb question, I guess: You'll try to get back to the States."

"No. Where's this thing headquartered? The Second Alliance I mean."

"The military headquarters? Main one is supposed to be in Sicily."

"So why don't you hit the island?"

"Not enough manpower—or seapower. NATO's guarding it. NATO thinks—or claims it thinks—that the SA is just a privately owned peacekeeping force like it pretends to be. Sort of high-quality mercenaries subcontracted by the UN and NATO. So we got to get past NATO too. And those guys aren't our enemies. But Steinfeld was working on a way to get in, before they found him."

"He'll try it, sooner or later."

"Uh-huh."

"I want Praeger," she said, her voice chillingly flat. "If we can get to the Second Alliance's command, we can bring Praeger to justice."

"Who's Praeger?"

"We get out of Paris alive I'll tell you about it." Daylight wasn't long in coming. Hot-metal blue edged the ragged, truncated skyline when they heard the first amplified note pealing over the square, that bizarre church bell again, declaring a new and electric morning.

They heard, from ten yards away, the captain of a passing neofash patrol burst out, "What the bloody 'ell is *that*?"

Claire almost wept with silent laughter. She whispered, "What kind of music's he going to play?"

"It's mostly retro-rock, twentieth-century stuff . . . but it's more than that," Hard-Eyes murmured.

Rickenharp began with a bash-out of the Blue Öyster Cult's "Cities on Flame with Rock 'n' Roll," slammed on to The Clash's "London's Burning," and then segued into Lou Reed's solo version of

"White Light/White Heat." Rickenharp had jacked a mike into one of the amps and he bellowed the lyrics in a voice that made Hard-Eyes sure Yukio had given them the shots. Rickenharp was coming on to his last high. The digital rhythm box started, thudding out a martial backbeat that shivered like controlled thunder from the faces of the wrecked buildings around the Étoile.

It was still dark enough for Hard-Eyes to lead the others through the shadows around the perimeter of the Étoile, in the ruins, and over the dead fountains, toward the Champs Élysées.

Now Rickenharp was segueing from a Sisters of Mercy cut to a Nine Inch Nails tune: "Head Like a Hole." He yowled, *"Head like a hole, black as your soul, I'd rather die than give you control!"* his voice echoing thinly up and down the Champs-Élysées. And then an updated "Street-Fighting Man." Each chord peacock-tailed out into beautiful distortion, echoing around the wide, breezy, broken space of the Étoile.

Hard-Eyes chuckled and hefted his assault rifle, muttered, "Christ. He's pulling it off!" They were crouched behind an overturned troop transport truck. He peered out between a bent-out fender and the grille at the entrance to the street. Dozens of SA entrenched there, staring up at the arch, mouths agape. Maybe Rickenharp had been wrong about how they'd react . . . If they didn't take the bait, Hard-Eyes and Claire were fucked . . .

Rickenharp banged through some mid-1980s tunes. The Clash, Dead Kennedys, The Fall, New Order, U2, The Call, and Killing Joke's "Requiem." Into the nineties with Panther Modern's "Sometimes It's Better to Die."

He paused, made a chord oscillate drunkenly, and yelled, *"Hey! You pathetic wimps frightened of a guitar?"* Bellowing it so loud his voice fuzzed in the amp. But they understood him. Louder now: "YOU! YOU LIMP-DICK INTESTINAL WORMS! YEAH, YOU, THE BRAIN-WASHED, PECKERWOOD BIGOTS! RIGHT: THE SHIT-EATING DUMB-FUCK RACIST PRODUCTS OF BACKWOODS COUSIN FUCKING! LET ME BE MORE EXPLICIT! I'M TALKING TO THE FAGGOT SA NAZIS SUCKING THEIR THUMBS OVER

BY THE METRO SIGN! *YOU PUSSIES SCARED OF A GUITAR? COME ON! COME ON, YOU COWARDS!"*

There was another minute of debate amongst the SA. Then the fash commander gave the order—and the SA charged the arch, spraying its crown with automatics. Dust and chips of stone flew from the top, where Rickenharp howled on at them. "COME ON, YOU PHILISTINE PECKERWOODS, *LET'S GO!*"

Yukio waited till the neofascists were halfway there before opening up on them. He'd set up two grenade launchers, already had them cranked for range.

Three explosions burst before the arch like giant flame-hands flashing open. Fragments of concrete and metal rained. Dust bloomed... and cleared.

As Rickenharp played the Stooges' "Search and Destroy"...

Twelve of the Second Alliance assault force were sprawled there, broken and unmoving.

Six more kept coming—Yukio stopped them with short, precise machine-gun bursts. Another wave of them came on, took cover in shell-holes, began returning fire. Yukio kept moving, kept low, kept firing. He had a better angle for shooting than they did. And all the time Rickenharp's guitar wailed and roared...

Yukio fired an M-83 round across the Étoile; it blew up in the commander's tent, setting it on fire. Another M-83, and another. The SA ran helter-skelter for cover, their lines in confusion.

Beyond the burning tent, forty yards beyond, Hard-Eyes could see the metro entrance he wanted.

"Come on!" he shouted. *"This is it! Run like a bastard!"*

He took Claire's elbow and—Bonham and Kurland close behind—they sprinted across the open side-street. They were almost there before the regrouping sentries spotted them.

"Down!" Hard-Eyes shouted. He and Claire flung themselves down behind an overturned lamppost.

Bonham threw himself flat just behind.

Kurland panicked, gaping around, shouting, "We gotta go back, we gotta..."

A burst of machine-gun fire caught him in the mouth, blew his upper teeth up, through his sinuses, through his brains and out the back of his head; and he fell like a puppet with its strings cut.

The machine gun was set up in what had been a magazine kiosk, its muzzle flaming over scraps of posters advertising *Le Opéra*. It was in a spot that would be hard for Yukio to hit.

"HEY, YOU IN THE MAGAZINE STAND!" Rickenharp's voice boomed. He paused to giggle into the mike. An amplified giggle heard through the popping of gunfire. "HEY, YOU WITH THE MACHINE GUN! COME ON! GIVE ME YOUR BEST SHOT, YA NAZI COCKSUCKER!"

Hard-Eyes smiled.

The machine gun fell silent for a moment. The muzzle swiveled to the arch. Some officer shouted, "Ignore that arsehole, you bloody fool! Cover the—"

But the officer was too late—Hard-Eyes gestured for Claire to stay where she was, then he jumped up, zigzagging, running, thinking, *Maybe this time I'll find out what it feels like to get it in the head. Maybe it's the biggest goddamn rush you can imagine.*

As 72-mm rounds whined up, ricocheting from the street near his ankles...

But he reached the kiosk, circled it, found a hole in the side, shoved the muzzle of his assault rifle through, and squeezed out his clip, raking back and forth over the kiosk. The muzzle of the machine gun tilted back, leaking a little smoke. He signaled Claire. She and Bonham jumped up, sprinted to him. Hard-Eyes slapped another clip into the assault rifle. Yukio was firing to give them cover as they ran for the metro entrance. Blurred glimpses of SA soldiers... the whine of rounds sizzling the air around them...

And then they were down the steps, under cover.

"Oh, shit," Bonham said, gasping. "The entrance's blocked."

"Looks like it but it's not, really," Hard-Eyes said. "We set 'em up that way... Dig there. The stone with the paint splash on it. Pull it out, start digging. It's just camouflage." Bonham and Claire began to dig.

Hard-Eyes turned and went back up the stairs, to look out over the metal-strewn battlefield to the arch, trying to see Rickenharp. There—a tiny figure on the crown of the arc, almost unseeable. But hearable. His voice and his guitar, kicked through those mean little Marshalls, were audible even over the gunfire. Some original tune now, Hard-Eyes suspected. He couldn't make out the lyrics, but he knew what it was about. He'd heard a thousand permutations of it, over the years. It was an anthem, and it was about being young. A song called *Youth*.

And then the Jægernauts rolled in from the east and west, two of them converging on the arch. They came on like the neofascist war machine itself; they came on like mortality. Killing machines as big as five-story buildings, they cast shadows that drank up whole blocks . . . From here they looked like five-story spoked wheels, the spokes digging into whatever was in the way. There were clouds of dust, showers of bricks. The neofashes scattered, cheering, pulling back. Yukio kept sniping at the fascists, and more than one fell.

The echoes of his gunshots rolled like bass lines for Rickenharp's electric wailing. Rickenharp had cranked the amps all the way up; he could still be heard over the squealing of the oncoming Jægernauts. The two sounds went well together.

It was monumental, that destruction. The two Jægernauts converged on the Arc d'Triomphe from opposite sides, began to grind gigantically away at it, spinning in place at first like the wheels of a mud-stuck Hummer, then biting into the corners, crunching down as the microwave beams took the fight out of the stone. Yukio's bullets whined off the blue-metal scythes, the Jægernaut's spokes. Metal bit down on stone with a screaming that was another kind of heavy-metal jamming against Rickenharp's final chords: fat blue sparks shot out from the machine's grinding spikes; cracks spread like negative lightning through the huge monument; the hundred-pound head of a Valkyrie snapped from her stone neck and tumbled, bounced from a shelf of stone to fall and shatter on the grave of the unknown soldier; the arch's great crown bent, buckled inward . . . and all the time, *the whole time*, Rickenharp played on, a solo fast as he could play it, keening and ascendant, Rickenharp standing on an up-jutting stone, the last upper corner of the arch; a tiny figure of pure defiance silhouetted against the sky; Rickenharp the performer playing this one for all it was worth . . . the cracks spread farther . . . the microphones picking up the sound of the monument's cracking, crunching, rending . . . a final furious and defiant guitar chord—one last thunderous guitar chord!—and a last burst of gunfire from the arch's top—

And then the arch fell into itself—and was replaced, for a moment, by a great pillar of dust and a monolithic silence. Silence. Silence. Silence. No guitar. Silence.

Hard-Eyes thought, My friends are dead.

On the outside, he showed no flicker of emotion. On the inside, a raincloud was bursting.

The Jægernauts walked over the rubble, stamping back and forth, grinding the remains of the monument into powder. Powder, and blood.

The Arc de Triomphe, the flag-ensign of the New Resistance, the symbol of the struggle against the neofascists—was crushed into gravel; was flattened. The Arch of Triumph was gone.

But Hard-Eyes knew who was triumphant. As he turned to go into the tunnel, he seemed to hear Rickenharp's final chord echoing on, and on.

Epilogue

The frightening thing about racism is that it can be made to sound rational.
—Jack Brendan Smoke, *Essays for the Year 2040*,
"Too Long Anno Domini" (Witcher Press)

"I've got good news for you, Smoke," Witcher said.

Witcher's private jet had been circling Manhattan for half an hour as it awaited landing clearance for JFK International, in Queens. The interior of the jet was clean, and brightly lit, and new-smelling. The only passengers, aside from the staff, were Witcher, Witcher's secretary—who was asleep in the bed compartment—and Jack Brendan Smoke. And Smoke's crow.

Smoke was wearing a light cotton suit the color of ashes. They had picked it out for him at Freezone. Complete with fashionable notched turtleneck—an alternative to the gold choker.

Smoke was still gaunt. But they'd had him on a rehab diet, and his eyes were bright. They'd even cleaned his teeth, implanted new ones to fill out the gaps. He would be able to walk the streets of New York and pass as an affluent citizen. But he felt displaced. Lost. It seemed he identified with the wreckage he'd left behind.

There was a lounge, with a wide observation window, and Smoke sat at the bar, looking out the window at the island of Manhattan gleaming austerely in the ascetic sunshine of a cloudless winter day.

Witcher was in his late sixties, but he had a good glandularist, good enzymists, good telemerase virologists—and he looked about forty. He'd allowed a little silver to streak his shoulder-length, neatly clipped brown hair and his short, equally neat beard. He wore a brown suit with leather shoulder insets. He'd kept his wide mouth and flattish nose and deep-set brown eyes. He could have afforded something glamorous.

"What's the good news?" Smoke asked, without looking away from the city.

"Have a look." Witcher slid a glossy printout across the brass bar to Smoke. He'd just brought it back from his office, in the rear of the jet. Smoke picked up the printout.

The plane tilted a little, and Smoke's glass of club soda slid away from him. He let it go. The bartender caught the glass before it fell.

Witcher glanced at the bartender, then said, "Go ahead on up to the bed compartment and have a rest, Jerry, if you would." When he was gone, Witcher said, "The hell of it is, Jerry's been with me twenty-two years. Loyal as they come. We should be able to say anything in front of him—but with extractors . . . " He made a dismissive gesture. "Loyalty means nothing."

Reading the printout, Smoke took a deep breath and let it slowly out. Then he smiled. "Steinfeld, Hard-Eyes, Carmen, Willow, Levassier, Hernandez . . . Who are these others?"

"Refugees from FirStep, apparently. The girl claims to be Professor Rimpler's daughter, Claire Rimpler. She's joined the NR. She says her father was murdered on the Colony. We've had no confirmation of that from Colony Admin. The other guy—this Bonham—has some kind of deal he's trying to make with us. I'm not sure what it is, yet . . . There's a story behind this Colony refugee thing. We can use it at the news conference."

Smoke turned to the crow in its cage on the floor. "You hear that? Steinfeld, Hard-Eyes, some of the others—they got through!" The crow tilted its head and seemed to shrug as it ruffled its feathers.

Smoke turned to Witcher. "How'd they do it?"

"What Steinfeld calls 'pincer coordination.'" The units trapped behind the lines hit the SA roadblocks at the same time Steinfeld's people hit them from the outside. Two-thirds of the NR trapped in

Paris got through and got away. They're camped somewhere in the French Alps now. There's a list of the confirmed casualties here."

Smoke nodded, but he didn't look at the list.

"How long will we be in New York?" Smoke asked.

"Four days. We can't stay long—the public exposure is a risk for you. You'll be heavily guarded, of course, but..."

Smoke nodded. "I know. Where do we go after New York?"

"The Antilles. A little island where... you'll see."

"This man Kessler is there?"

"He is, yes, with his wife. You and he'll be working closely together—at least, that's what Steinfeld's hoping."

"In some ways Steinfeld's very . . . practical. But he's also a wild-eyed idealist like a college kid of twenty. With his fantasy of restructuring the Grid itself. Giving the media back to the people. Raising consciousness in one global flash..." Smoke shook his head.

"You think it can't be done?"

"I think any real social restructuring is unlikely short of nuclear holocaust. But . . . " He smiled wanly. "But of course we'll try." He looked out the window, at New York City. "Why do you do it, Witcher? You can't be making a profit on this. You don't strike me as an, um..."

"As the humanitarian type? I'm not. I admire brave men, but... But mostly, it's business. Three times the SAISC has tried to take over Witcher Airlines, Witcher Computers—three times each. The SAISC is a corporate predator. They started it—I'm just fighting back."

Smoke shook his head. "That's not the reason." Was Witcher the twenty-first century's Oskar Schindler? Or was there something else, something hidden several layers down?

He tried to see what was at the very tip of the Worldtalk Building. The plane was tilted, circling the south end of the island, swinging in toward Queens, and he felt as if there were an invisible string connecting the tip of the building and the plane, the plane spinning on the string like a child's toy.

"Well, now," Witcher said, "you're a sharp man. Steinfeld said you were. You're right: it's not the real reason. Someday I'll tell you the reason, maybe. When it's safe."

A blank TV screen behind the bar flickered and then lit up with a fish-eye image of the cockpit. The copilot turned to look at them. "We have clearance, sir. We're making our final approach."

Witcher nodded at the screen. "It's about time. Double-check to see that our security meets us."

"Yes, sir." The screen went blank again.

Smoke said, "Of course, the good news from Paris is also bad news. Because it means the Second Alliance have Paris to themselves. Just so much more captured territory."

"They had it already—too many of the French were with them . . . " Witcher shrugged. "And the rest of Europe is falling in step."

"There are plenty of French who are not collaborating. And Steinfeld's still in France." Smoke murmured, "And Hard-Eyes. And the others. And they haven't given up."

The plane passed over the city, and Smoke had a glimpse of the traffic sweating through the avenues . . . The urban organism humming with life . . .

"This city is very much alive," Smoke said softly, to the crow. "But then, so was Amsterdam, not so long ago."

THE END OF BOOK ONE